HALF TRACE

HALF TRACE

Bryn Ellis

Acrux
2015

First Printing: 2015

Cover Art by Adrian Lockhart

Acrux Publishing
PO Box 489
Macksville NSW 2447
Australia

acrux.net.au

Dedication

Half Trace was begun in October 2001 and completed in June 2007 throughout which incubation it was cradled in the auspice of a blessing from Rhiannon — the other horse goddess.

It is dedicated to my mother, Shaaron, who raised me on raisins and raison d'être, and to all those who know the true revolution is in the heart.

This work also stands in tribute to Oasa and the disappearing isle.

Author's Note

My authenticity with regard aboriginal culture begs poetic licence. Neither the language, tribal names or dreaming stories are factual. With apologies to any aboriginals of the coastal Yarra basin or Kimberly areas. Further, the incidents at the gardens and subsequent expedition were only grazed by fact.

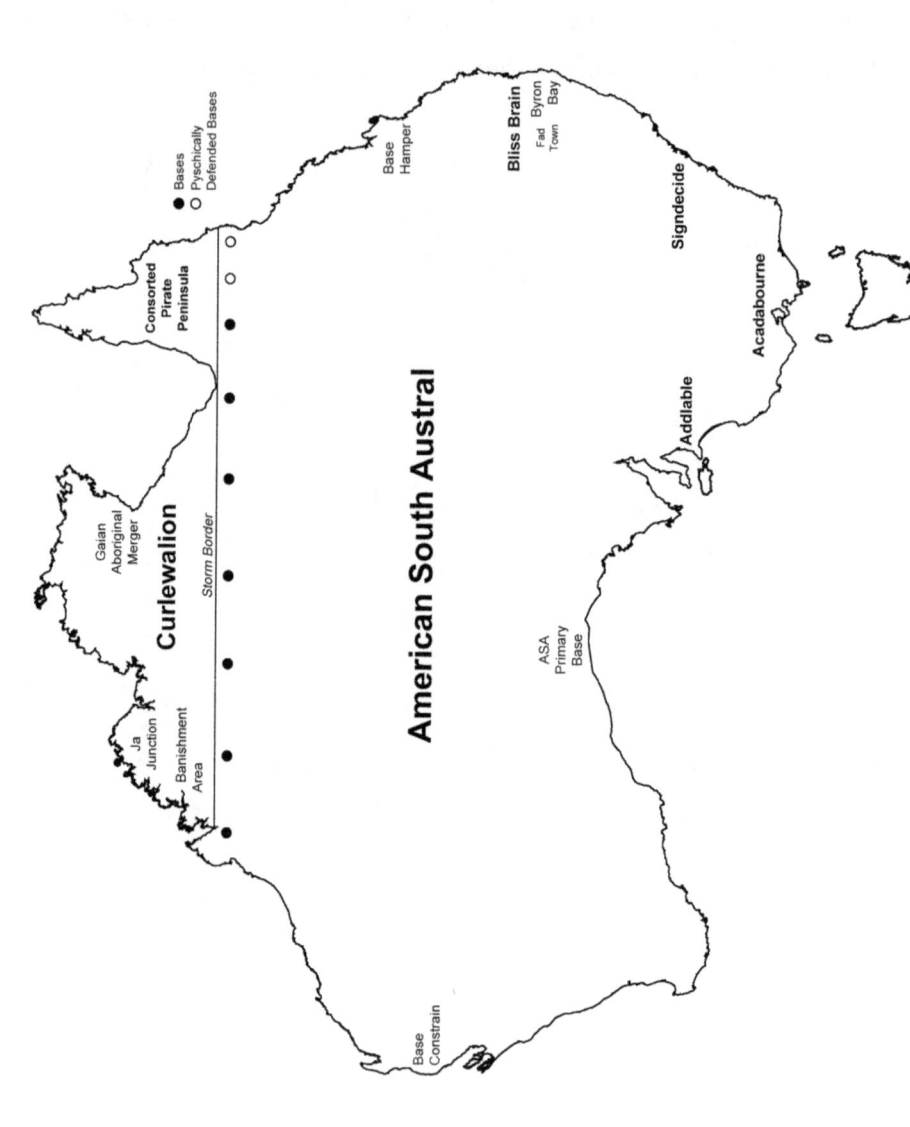

● Bases
○ Pyschically
   Defended Bases

Base
Hamper

Bliss Brain
Fad
Town
Byron
Bay

Signdecide

Addlable

Acadabourne

Consorted
Pirate
Peninsula

Gaian
Aboriginal
Merger

Curlewalion

Ja
Junction

Banishment
Area

Storm Border

American South Austral

ASA
Primary
Base

Base
Constrain

Foreword

The Year 2193

More than a hundred years after Curlewalion brought the World American Reform government to its knees that self-declared monochrome world authority has patiently entrenched its martial power, as well as its economic rulership, via an integrated psychic reward system for its stock and trade workers. Meanwhile the nation of millions of refugees and free thinkers, Curlewalion, annexed from the north of Australia, is flourishing and still safe from hover attack behind its mysterious storm border.

Over generations the libertarian land has adapted to now incorporate the Consorted Pirate Peninsula in its north-east and the deeply mystic Gaian Aboriginal Merger alongside its own Om Trine. The Curlew Alliance also has the moral support of two revolutionary nations formed in its wake, Anarchtica and the Horn of Drums. Using its spies, 'the Mist,' and psychics, Curlewalion has long monitored the W.A.R. government's nuclear capacity. It had forced the closure, thirteen decades prior, in 2063, of all world nuclear facilities and destruction of all warheads using the stolen Mouth satellite, equipped with devastating solar reflection weaponry as leverage, thus ensuring the nation's inception.

HALF TRACE

Humans are, on the whole, rope. Beginning as a nice soft bundle we unwind into a tangled sprawl. And if ever anyone could seamlessly re-join the length of us — all those isolate strands and knotted worlds — could we really dangle across mountains and ravines? Or would some scampish force of truth just use us to swing from in a joyous fooling of gravity?

Prologue and Prophecy

'In time the passage will pass from form'. Between malt-flecked, elongated fingers, Boabben considers the rough-carved semblance of a boat with its skim of wax-like cargo and reads the words burned into the curved wood of its side. He notes the green flush on a thumb tip that has layered erratically into the nail. It is rare that he gathers such corporeal trophies, but for a hammer he had possessed only a stone, and his haste has recently become exponential. Somewhere around here... The trees, a clasp of emerald eyes on lover's brown, immerse the striding man in a muted ocean, darkly reticent.

That sense of urgency, contrasted with the stillness all around, disorients him. It is not that the land is calm, but rather that it has slowed, slumped into itself to become a crushing monotony, as had the long mornings by the turf fire in his boyhood, awaiting the lifting of the fog and the freeing of the light. Certainly he can see the majesty of nature that endures upon this range, yet he has no emotional savouring of it; he no longer believes it might survive. Not in this form.

Boabben moves along the river edge through a drift of crinkly purple leaves that birth the querulous spires of cycads, stubborn in their ancient design. He fingers the blaze of a stolid leaf in passing...they are another good sign that, with the faint quartzite veins in the river bank, decides him. Three times he cups water for himself, and the coloured thumb bruise is like a tiny crayfish dipping into the clear flow. Sweet the breath of moss and wild water fills him — a happenstance his crafting will soon drive from all this country — but it is the only way. His stretched frame alit with concentration, he looks out from his heart cage at the monotone world to make quick final gauging. The red head on the strong Celtic neck is angled to conceive its targets, the sky and great plunge of land before him, as if a sunray broken by the canopy. He sees the skew-whiff hills beyond the far lip of the waterfall, amassed on the plains as though they had once been giant beasts, glutting on a vale of grasses in long prelude to the sowing of trees by father time. All now fallen to the indefatigable stealth of the rainforest, ensured defeat, he muses, by a multitude of belated spears in their backs — security towers and hover stacks.

He slips the little wooden thing toward its first cascade. And the fate of Earth's most irreplaceable substance, a tiny alloy of hybrid firefeather within, is cinched to the heaving breast of the river. A sudden wind howls up the high valley, unusually cold and whipping spray off the rapids into him. He shudders, the chill pulsing through his spine again, but this time it will not desist. He is sorry for the girl, for the thing she must face, the horror of which only he fully understands. They had found her yesterday, after a first brief sighting some days before, as his vision had stipulated.

Boabben steps beneath the canopy to assay the lizard smooth belly of a prototype passenger hover car as it skims the tree tops, the algalate ribbon of its rudder shimmering wildly to transmute the extra magnetic lode of this volcanic country. The magnetic field inducer of the cone-capped triangle had betrayed its presence, the civilian model underscored with a purring static, unlike Affiliate craft. But it is other than the sycophants trained to doggedness by the W.A.R. government that today concern the endlessly sad seeming man. Those of his ilk are close enough now to prick the ginger hairs of his arms into electric wariness. With birdlike precision, his wide face resolute and eyes of grey shifting as though with clouds, he meters his final journey from hilltop to vine thicket with the question and answer.

Will passage pass from form?'
In time.'

Chapter 1

'This is the seer leaving the thicket of the mind hive. Not a sentry or a worker but an aperture for the Earth to plug into. A frame carrying eagerly awaiting senses to a place where they can gain amplification.'

From early Curlewalion barding

In the rescindant, marmalade glare of what had been a hot summer afternoon the two women languorously hanging towels beneath the umbrella, steading wine flutes beside their chosen lounge, and lying to flick sunglasses from eye to fringe — imbibe a nervous beauty. The liquorice-haired one considers her surroundings.

Peering down through the six-storeyed maze of mesh balconies on the building flanking and mirroring their own, she sees vague shapes flit across the courtyard. What had been the faint hum of solarisation lights a week ago now records a steady drone, as neighbours prepare for the blanketing of sun that will occur with the completion of the still largely skeletal building hulking ever higher opposite.

Sway considers the one brittle blessing of the tower, its cogs and hammers fallen silent for the day. Were it not to soon prove the sundecks of these flats useless, they would still need fedora here, but two students could afford this year's lowered rent. Sway pushes aside the residual ache from her yearning dream since the sorrowing to live alone; it is redundant now and would never have been possible. In nearly all of Acadabourne — known previously as Melbourne — space was exhausted. Yet it was not solely its shortage that made living alone illegal. A security order a handful of years prior had deemed all citizens above ten must be within sight of a person in possession of up-to-date loyalty diplomas for at least five waking hours daily. These and other facts were recorded, signed and stamped once a week at Regulative Enforcement Domes.

She looks through chinks in the canyonways at the emerald filling between. Since the obsolescence of private ground traffic, Acadabourne had become greener. While the older gardens had been claimed as restricted botany research centres, all save a few roads had been ploughed in to become tree-packed thoroughfares. Car parks had been levelled, replaced with high-rises and hover-stacks — narrow devices, vertiginous spires constructed around a central elevator. Green were the avenues accommodating bikes and foot traffic in a constant stream of staff and students to the eleven universities. These avenues were mostly covered with reinforced silicon tunnels to guard lecturers and Master students from assassination attempts. The gullets of the World American Reform government had to be hard things to bring their harvest safe to the nest.

Sway interrupts her musings as Tiana fills her glass. The dead blue eyes in her flatmate's otherwise flawless face regard her with that you'll-never-guess-who-pinned-me-down-in-the-cafeteria-and-said-he-could-do-a-better-job-of-spreading-my-crumpets kind of look. Flirting was something the new regime did not reprise — in fact overt sexuality was encouraged.

Sway gives what appears her full attention to Tiana's well groomed monologue of lust. Her own thin lips curl in a lewd snarl as the blond tells of a recent satiation. She laughs as shrilly and discordantly and keeps her black eyes, peripherally struck with hazel, dull and confusedly shifting. After all, she was majoring in comparative physical discipline and had failed inherencies of human energetics. She was a dumb. Even Tiana could grasp more than sports, and she reigned with an imperious scorn over her black-haired flatmate.

Which is not the reason Sway slips a nightshade concentrate into Tiana's drink, as her head, thrown back in a bray of forced laughter from Sway's well-timed conversation cue, coincides with the dusk change for all cameras to infrared. In fact, Sway is sorry to lose the powder, a preparation of leaves laboriously picked from the Uni grounds, with toes stuck through a purposed hole in her shoe, in bunches small enough to secrete quickly in a low, hidden trouser pocket.

From the rubbish bin Sway surreptitiously removes an empty vodka bottle and places it next to the mostly full one before the sleeping girl. She will have to steal another empty bottle for the bin, on top of everything else tonight, to give her suggestive lie its glue on Tiana's groggy reawakening.

By the time the five minutes she has allowed herself to assemble and check her equipment has passed, Sway is feeling confident and invigorated. Something feels right in the air. From a multitude of covert thefts, smuggling and protagonism, she has developed a sixth sense for the possibility of hidden Agents. Sway is as tactilely gifted as any of the hundred Curlewalion Mist operating in this embodiment of nightmare had to be.

The twenty-four year old has never even seen Curlewalion, and unlike the bulk of the others trained there, she is self-taught and personally motivated. That had been different once. Being this deep in the hub, she is out of touch with all except the most rudimentary communications regarding the revolutionaries. Even given a narcissistic overreaching, she knows she has mastered the discipline of each formwork seeded by her parents' hands, and tended in the eleven years before their flight north and her statutory warding by the state. In three-hour sessions in the dark each night she has superseded their ability. The university gym had helped, especially as she had been all but sanctioned to weight training, deemed too klutzy for contact sports. Even then she knew the old ways for building internally, and when the muscles didn't show she was scripted extra time on the iron. Tonight the focus of all her power would culminate in the rescue, and her escape — if she could counterpoint the weight of resistance encircling her.

Sway shrugs off her boxing pants and tee-shirt, and begins to work into one of her most important stolen items — a body stocking of lacto-silk armour. The gauzy material clings to her sleekly muscled torso and firmly mounded breasts, and snugs her long thin neck. A balaclava and gloves of the same material will complete her protection. On one wrist she fastens an electronic sensing and demagnetising band, and on the other a tiny remote for a chloro-fluoride gas bomb. Three anti-gravity rings almost as broad as her torso she straps beneath her breasts, then slides around to her back. Four flight chrysalis units, already collared, she affixes to her calves. She steps into boots that are capable of firing eight poison darts each from a toe trigger.

With two minutes to spare, Sway sashes the adrenal needles to her chest, then garbs as before. She pulls at a skirting board and unties a neat hanging sack containing her grapple gear which has dropped from the ceiling. Tugging on the gloves, she steps out to the deck and drapes a blanket over Tiana. The food hover opposite is beginning its ascent to the managerial bivouac on the unfinished building. Acting as though lounging on the balcony rail, Sway fits the anchor for her grapple gun into a strong steel mesh join, and laments again that to use a hover-pack would attract the attention of every hover-sensing monitor in sight. The reassuring coo of the pigeons she has been feeding the month past comes to her from the ventilation housing just below. Surreptitiously, Sway brings the rocket out of the bag. She primes the half-foot of cylindrical steel, feeling by touch, and with its magnetic head dressed roughly as a pigeon, she cradles the rough steel as though a coddled bird she is about to set free. With her other hand Sway fiddles the electric frequency of a third story solarisation unit. It explodes with a great shuddering burst of whistles and sighs. The first of the pigeons spook, and Sway fires her fake pigeon through the flock at the food hover.

Almost instantly the magnet latches to the hover and a shape like a comatose pigeon falls away from the small clunk. With one hand either side of her retractable staff over the cable, Sway plunges into the dense mass of pigeons in front of her. The first hundred metres take two seconds to cover, but then the cord inclines, and she is slowed to a running pace as she comes up to the suspended hover. At the last she lets go, the staff remaining looped to one wrist — and sensitising her fingers, she grabs the hover's landing plate. So far there are no alarms, but this is the most dangerous moment for some hidden camera she had been unable to factor to snag a definitive image and give it to the computers. Sway opens the bonnet on the magnetic head, and a large sticky cloth unfurls like a miniature radar bowl. A safe distance away, dangling from the sill of the open rear window, she releases the magnetic lock on the grapple anchor. The cord already stretched to its limit, and aided by a spring in the head, zings across to be neatly caught in the bonnet. Sway slips in through the window and crouches under a microwave bench. She has only just stowed the grapple in behind her when the two caterers step back in.

As soon as the fat man presses floor fifteen, Sway mutineers their ship from under them by collapsing those pressure points in their necks which keep them upright. The two sprawl in a semiconscious position, in what she hopes is not too much pain, cramped, utterly immobile.

Sway contents herself with sprinkling a potent but slow-acting nerve toxin into the wardens' food. To kill them now would only bring a flood of Agents as the checks fail. There are nine wardens, three building security and two roving council guards. Their more elaborate meals are on one trolley. No enticing aromas arise from the thirty-three meals for the prison gangers on the second trolley.

Sway strips an apron from the woman, and an identity card over which she pours her staining syrup from a tiny vial. The woman is bundled into a cupboard and the man slid on his back under the microwave bench, his knees made to bend in the classic mechanic's pose. As she crosses the fifteenth floor, she puts on an aspect of disdainful cool.

"Right," she says, entering the caterers' doorway she has watched for the past month through focals from her deck. "Come and tuck in, loves. Not only am I covered in pissing chilli sauce, but Andre wants me to feed the mongoloids in the cell while he jacks the microwave."

In that atmosphere of weary boredom it would have been easy for the shock of seeing a new face to become suspicion. Curiosity creases the lines on the brown-suited commandant's face, where he sits before a paper and a wine bottle at the end of the bleached, spartan mess hall, but it seems a whingeing cater-maid, especially one with an angel's figure, just adds to the ambience of dinner.

A few officers come through a side door from the radio and surveillance alcoves as cigarettes are stubbed out, and staff settle back lazily to eat. The commandant gestures to the rostered guards at attention by the door. With an impatient, grumpy air, Sway follows them back over to the cater hover.

"You know the best way to get that chilli out of your blouse," says a particularly hairy blonde guard through his beard, "is to have me suck it off."

He has broken away from the other two and follows Sway into the hover. She sees him glance at the legs sticking out from under the microwave bank and bends down further than necessary to unlock the trolley wheels. She can feel the Viking's eyes divert from his study. *This one will be easy*, she thinks. As they re-join the main guard she says, "Mate, if you're that desperate to eat something, then it's best we hurry and get this done before your food takes cold."

It is minutes now until she will see him, but after six years her excitement can wait. It is the culmination of cold rage that drives her each step closer to Mendez. He had been one of hundreds of students to be press-ganged into construction following a riot in which security mandates were breached. For five years she had known his support and love, before he and two of their closer friends had been smashed into the road alongside her and dragged into these slave presses.

Thus had she spent three years in the Barbie stunt on a tip that gang seven would be in the construction detail. Still, she had despaired of getting them out until she remembered that all three could fly a chrysalis. Therefore, when the two doors distanced by three metres of camera-filled corridor slide open, and she sees the rows and rows of men packed along bunks like sardines, she hardens her heart to them all except Sean and the two Spaniards, one of whom is her lover. The Viking begins to slap trays on the table, and she sees the recognition on Mendez's scarred and bruised face.

"Way, boys, way, way, way, way down far below you boys is where decent people walk free." She repeats the nickname they gave her at Uni to give their tired souls time to gel. "But the only way you could get out of here would be with a flight pack." Glints of recognition shine their mercy from some few faces.

"Don't goad the mongrels," snaps Viking.

Bent over beside him getting trays, Sway looks up, then says, "Oh shit."

"What?"

"I dropped my ring in there somewhere." She very lightly puts one hand on his back and one on her heart.

"I'll have a look," he winks, getting half on the shelf of the trolley. The inside of her leg is the last thing he feels. Sway kills him with a boot dart in his femoral artery and bears the body's weight with her precision strength to a balanced position half-inside the trolley.

"Well, do hurry; I can't stand the smell in here any longer," she says over a shoulder, walking towards the two door guards. She smiles a tired smile and stretches a little between them, flicking her extended staff in a fierce slash that cracks one's throat and the other's temple.

"Now, compadres!" Sway yells as the alarms blare, jamming her staff in the outside door at knee height. It judders with bending pressure on each side of the reinforced rod. The fraction longer the inner door takes to shut allows the three men through before resealing the remaining inmates.

The building's ragged corner is a tracery of silver girders opening out from a concrete node, joining others in the gash of space below like an engineered knuckle and compassing upwards in resemblance of an impossibly massive and cleaned fish gill. She hurls the anti-gravity rings out to one side of the construction.

"Stay away from the windows, they could be ribboned; follow the Shark, Lizard, Fig," Sway says to Enrique and Sean, rapidly rubbing a hand along each spine to relax their diaphragms for the adrenaline just injected into their legs.

"Curlew, Curlew," the pair refrain in one impassioned voice, leaping lithely to grab the anti-gravity rings a few metres out-and-down from the building's edge. She presses her lips onto her reclaimed love's wrist before turning her eyes up to his own.

"See you in Lion," she says into those so long unexplored mahogany halls. Then she throws another disc and turns, sprinting along the edge of the scaffold.

Mendez sees her jump across a cable-house roof as he descends slowly beneath the ring that almost bears his weight in a sinking that begins to build momentum. The others stream beneath him, and as he prepares for that sudden lift the opening of the wings will give him, he notices the bracelet of seeds she has slipped onto his wrist.

Sway is moving fast to intercept the threat to her plan. Stumbling around the corner of the detention block, a guard clasps his stomach and tries to train his gun on her. Without thought, for she can let nothing disturb her concentration, Sway delivers a burst of Ki through her palm that accelerates his liver toxification and he collapses.

Then the robosillica tops the building's roof, as her dismayed senses of both feeling and hearing had told her it must, its hundred legs like snakes

10

constantly shifting to purchase on anything metal, while in each of the three metre-long arms thrust out above it is a person. The Affiliate has responded fast, and two Agents ride the steed normally reserved for surveyors wishing to exactify building levels from a distance while sedately armed with equilibrium sights — not the weapons that now spew yellow rays toward the gliders. The pair are intent on securing a better vantage from which to menace the fleeing men, and see her a second too late.

Sway lands from her three-metre drop on the upper spine of the Agent in the control arm. With the crack that is his complete paralysis, the furthest one, indistinguishable beneath the helmet, fires a laser burst at her and pilots the crab-like arm to its full stretch, three times her height. His shot is wild, and absorbed by a lactosilked shoulder. Sway latches beneath the metal arm to which the paralysed Agent is secured, seeking cover. Bursts of laser fire break around her. She can sense the Agent trying to manipulate an override for the robosillica's other arm, which is why she is able to slip out and spear a prised-off hydraulic pipe through his helmet, collapsing the locomotion of his brain with a blow to the nasal phalange. Without sparing a backward thought to purloin their lasers — Agents' hardware was tripped to explode for all but its recognised user — Sway pries off another pipe and hurries to greet the members of the Affiliate; the Agency for Furthering Interior Loyalty, Information and Technology.

Basically a military unit, its city branching was designed to deal with riot, disaster and surveillance maintenance, though this represents only their second real call to arms for months, and the last was actually Sway's training run. In that endeavour she had roughed up security in the corporate planning tower, managed to shut down their electricity supply, and melted into facelessness before returning home to watch her movie. What she had recorded with a camera left on the patio table were two Affiliate ships racing close by her flat and veering along the eastern side of the building she now stands on.

With this in mind, Sway sallies once again into space, a hand each side of a pipe along a metal cable which upholds tiny night lights and large speed advice boxes purposed to slow or direct legitimate daytime traffic during periods of dangerous building. Sway clamps down her thin disc of explosives about halfway out, then drops off and chrysalises around the building's corner. Angling back towards her apartment, she cuts up its near side, under fire now from a bustle of what must be — from the feel of the bullets striking off her armour — warders or building guards. A bullet rips her chrysalis, but thankfully not the main ribbing, and Sway easily controls the slight stagger to spiral and land on a rooftop with a view of the building site.

The humming domes beside her are highly combustive ionisation and filtration units, and due to their presence the figures at the construction site bring no fire against her. Gas ballistics, however, begin to streak through the night sky and Sway holds her breath and fingers the detonator eagerly. The ships finally skate into view, two double tiered patina-black triangles flying side by side. Sway lays her scythe of fate upon them, willing coldness, albeit her nerves feel crushed with the violence.

Some debris escaping the fireball falls around her, yet the grenades have all stopped. In fact, a slab of the rooftop is missing, and with the breach in the magnetic locks, she knows the prison gangers will be scrambling for freedom. She glides over the mass of running citizens and blare of sirens below, weaving a looping course through little lanes but gaining speed and distance with every turn. Sway soars away from the skyscraper banks along the river until she sights a mass of green branches to screen her landing. She alights silently in a dense cedar, doffs her chrysalis and breathes a sigh.

She is a shadow of avenged power praying to go unnoticed for the three kilometres to the greenway. Before her, the old botanic gardens and the sanctuary she had planned. She sees no pursuit at air or ground level. Moving fast, she fishes water and a jogging suit from a carefully prepared cache, giving her warmth as well as guise. As she patters along the road, the sublime feeling of having achieved her life's work drops from her like ashes. She is chin-to-the-wind fleeing, and though the sound of her heart drowns out the booted feet pursuing her, she glimpses movement on all sides through the trees; black-silked Agents and hovers of the Affiliate.

The Agency hovers, electrifier equipped, mean there is no chance she can lose them in the lake, where she could easily submerse for several minutes. Her only chance is to get beyond the research fence and lose them downtown. She breaks toward a thick patch of verdure in the direction of the city. Laser fire stings into her chest and she staggers once, then reaches the green, feeling the branches of the Lilly Pillys flow beneath her and snake her into the canopy as fast as her silence can allow.

From a tree's spreading top she leaps onto a slender eucalypt, and releases it to again swish straight, as it nods her into a palm tree. Lacking momentum, her next leap is amazing, over toward the neighbouring palm. She hits the fronds with her whole body tense, and rolls down and through their leaves, bringing herself into alignment as she lands. An Agent lies sprawled where Sway's mid-fall kicks have levelled him. She hurdles the body and rushes uphill toward a grove of mighty oaks. At the last second she sees the figure in the bushes' edge and throws herself back as a volley of flaming light passes over her. Suddenly, the Agent falls forward with a dart from Sway's boot in his eye.

Halfway across the leafy copse, a hot punch of laser fire strikes her from each side, though deflected by the silk. Ahead she can see a cordon of Agents bearing down the hill, and like a black leopard she bustles up into an oak and jumps across to another with an unclimbable trunk, the canopy shielding her from the hovers which have just arrived, although not the ground Agents' infrared.

Laser fire bursts near her head and she faints back against the trunk, gasping. Her vision clears in time to see an Agent training a short-range laser on her from the first tree she had climbed. She kills him with a dart. Three more fall from the trees before a laser strike discovers a weakened place in her suit, and with a squelch, Sway's shoulder catches fire. As she hugs her blistering arm to herself, its medial flesh already feeling molten, she thinks of the free land she has never seen and the lover she will not re-join. Still, when she thinks of their freedom and the knowledge they will take with them to Curlewalion, she feels poised for her death.

As if reading her thoughts, an assault hover only two metres long appears, needling through the forking trunk of a distant specimen yet to gain its spring leaf. In a final defiance, she nestles her pipe between the boughs, and drops to hang head first from it before the heavier lasers can fire, dangling with all save her toes shielded by the trunk of the tree. Sway doesn't see the Agents on the ground take careful aim or hear the persistent assault hover tracking around to the other side — she is looking up at the beauty of the trees that she has always loved.

Like three moths navigating a maze of spider webs, the gliders twist by walls of steel and concrete and only their intricate knowledge of the building format sees them clear the tangle. Without losing speed, they cut down one laneway, then another. As they pass the last building of the northern city mass and their goal becomes visible, a wave of screaming sound comes at them and they bank sharply from the skyscraper's electro-modified walls. Not all buildings are fitted with ribbons, but designed to eradicate nesting birds and pests, these razoring waves of electricity would have killed the escapees had they neglected Sway's warning and been a little closer.

They each drop into a spreading fig, flicking their chrysalis closed and snatching off even these light encumbrances. Fruit bats abandon their feeding and flap away with croaking screams. The massive tree stands central in an old garden, recently encompassed by a glasshouse over which the fig has been allowed to span. It must be this very fig they used as an icon during their student demonstration plans. Enrique and Sean discuss Sway's urgent, hushed directions, coded and reversed against chance of surveillance enhancement. Hurriedly, in whispers, Enrique explains to Mendez that they must get into the drains here, and follow them down to the river. They select a place that has lush vegetation beneath it, and simultaneously drop onto the glass roof, crashing down into a jolted and flayed mass on a bed of ferns and lilies.

Luckily, minus sprains or fractures, the three begin to search for the drain-hole and finally clamber down a wide bunker and into the storm-water system. All they have to do is follow the flow of thick effluvia, for the river cannot be more than a mile away. It is cold in the knee-high water, and what light shines through narrow culverts in the street seems only to accentuate the dark. But if they make it to the river, Sway's 'shark' will be waiting to take them to freedom; a Curlewalion submarine, Enrique thinks, that can run the radar gauntlet of American South Austral.

It is the Agents' triumphal sporting gloat that saves Sway's life, as they jockey for position to take the fatal shot at her unprotected eyes — these are wide open and staring spellbound at a creature moving purposefully through the canopy. It is two metres long, with a wide, short head like a badger's, its steely muscled form covered in close, russet hair. Without a sound, it springs some six metres at the Agents, and the attack coincides with a like assault by other creatures, leaping from nowhere to smother the Affiliates. She sees one turn its head in a ripping motion, then snake aside a paw to open an Agent's neck as he reaches for a laser.

A thick laser rope streaks into the side of one of the animals, and in a breath they all scatter, leaving the fallen beast in a twisted pile of Agents. The shot came from the diverted assault hover, but before it can close in, there are four explosions and the pairs of standard and assault hovers plunge in fiery execration. Two Agents run to the slaughter beneath the tree; one kicks at the shot creature when suddenly it is up and biting her neck, a paw flashing across to silence the other Agent. Then it topples, last strength spent.

As Sway pulls herself up, screams fill the night and she sees fountains of fire through the trees. A huge man appears before her wearing only a loin cover; the beast on which he sits measures two-and-a-half metres from nose to nub of tail. The whites of his eyes are stark in the aboriginal-like face, and as he focuses intently on her, the roiling pain in Sway's shoulder eases somewhat, perhaps from the sheer shock of his apparition. He points to the head of a curiously yellow-eyed creature that clambers up the tree trunk and lies sinuously between them. Then he points to Sway, and is riding his beast off through the branches and mounting smoke. Lacking alternative, Sway heeds the proffered help, deciding that she would rather be atop the animal anyway, than it her.

The creature purrs, as Sway struggles in agony up behind its shoulders, finding matted hair along its ruff to lock her feet into, and then with a curious, half-bounding gait, they are down from the tree tops and sprinting after the thickset, dark-haired man. Without pause, the animals leap the fences — the old wrought iron and new electric one — and then they are bearing down on a grotto of limestone, created in time past as a feature hill, and now completely covered with bristling cactus. Sway closes her eyes as the beasts sail over the first of the monstrous plants, their fleshy leaves spread to funnel rain, tilted at their ends into a syringing spike. Her body waits to register the ranks of needle tips that jut from the rocks below. They land on soft grass by a fire where a grouped dozen of the dark, daunting beings are sitting silently. Most of the remaining space is taken up by the creatures who fought for her, and before she slips from pain into unconsciousness, Sway notices a very young one sticking its head out from its mother's pouch.

Chapter 2

Mostly a stagnant measure of water are humans. Their cities dams. But rogue clouds are they who bring storms. Limber and wandering, without false measure or constraint, melded to the ease-mind of all beings.

From the Hobbogyrant.

It is of a sort of soul-attesting green, he decides at last, a viridescence, a hungry ghost sea that rises up to wait for a few more forgotten dewdrops, as it has since ever the first dawn. Over all it murks — the violetta trunks of red gums, the chalk scrub, the overripe dust. He cannot discern whether the aural taint on the land is a mere phantasm. If so, the silence pulses in awe of it.

Softly shining stars give a resolute light, the glimmer of mischief in the eyes of children. Their presence is reflected on the tips of leaves by the roadside, but truly, Larker walks in dark glutted all about him, and the sentient green he beholds is secreted by an enigmatic tracery of power that enwraps him in its own prescience, and guides the fifteen year old boy through the arid dark, compelling for its own requite.

'The owl leaves a clear note and a soft feather behind him; but what will my wise mind deed to the world? Perhaps a story that can take the reader to the burlap and treasure of his ancestors, or a drum that will return its own powerful rhythm to the player's beats?'

Larker looks on as his mind spins fluency between new shifting emotions and the hope underpinning his being, dispassionate as a clown reflecting its audience, trying to excise a recognition of the absurd from even sadness, a sense of the ridiculous from worry. As he attempts absorption of the chaotic strands, plying them into a votive truth, he marvels at how like a snake is the cavalcading quota of his being; forever turning on itself, with each clarity a proportionate twist towards mystery.

His snort of laughter hollows briefly into the black sea, and then shyly flees from the old star children. He had remembered the snake — a young taipan he had held before the skillet for its final fry in herbs and bean sauce. Then in a seethe of bewilderment, Brother Jacobin had appeared by his camp fire.

"That is generally considered by us to be Satan whom you will victual on," he had flustered.

"A small part of me believes it irresistibly delectable." Larker had rejoined. The head monk, huffing up towards busyness, had enquired which part. Larker had pulled up his tee-shirt to show a belly both taut and hairless on which sat a beautiful tattoo of a kookaburra.

"The laughing jackass part."

Larker listens to creatures stir in the wake of his erupted mirth. He has felt their presence, and over the last few nights has come to know their surreptitious animations. A large kangaroo swallows on a noisy belly, a possum reaches around a trunk to find a more comfortable view to support the hidden head peering just along the line of the bark. But this night it seems his flippantry has disturbed some new beasts. They skittle along, sounding like overgrown chickens, leaping logs and up and out of trees. He peers along the track — the vital green seems strengthened, but is still mantled in a comprehensive darkness.

The ad had read: 'The St Petersins Co-operative of Monastic Endeavour seeks saline psychic for one month initial period. Working knowledge of fibre transpiration keys will be useful. Terms: food and board to successful tender.'

Rumour of cash jobs on the government vegie-fuel estates had lost their allure when Larker had first spoken with Jacobin. Five kilometres out of Pomino! He had studied the country's maps since a child. Pomino was a mere day east of Exmouth and only nine weeks travel if he could find both a hitch with a hauler and an approachable boat with pirate sympathies to get him around the border impasse zone, and through to Curlewalion. Larker had seen pirates several times in coastal cities, their sheer violence and equipage of ready trade articles winning them leeway through the shadows. His father had said that such as they might smuggle a couple of wayfarers into the free lands.

It was to Curlewalion that he and his father had been heading, the man's vital work being ever more hampered by bureaucracy, when he had been apprehended and taken to a retirement home. It was a world his wanderlust-filled father could never survive — as evinced by a terse missive delivered some months later to his sister's home. After the grieving, Larker had felt compelled to the north, and by monastery cash that might vouch him a place in the hold of an illicit vessel, but a healthy, good-humoured youth with a quiet repose and tufts of short, russet-brown braids was never bound for a smooth transit among such a serious and stretched-looking bulk of passengers.

As soon as one of the Empowerment Cadets pretended to trip on Larker's curved hazel staff of dowsing wood that jutted slightly into the aisle, the rest of the two day trip on the desert subway became a little hell. After a series of furtive kidney punches in crowded aisles, the pack psychology mounted against Larker's inner reserve in constant abuse, large and small. He stayed in the observance area for the entire second day, though it was mandatory that single travellers only remain on the recordings for five hours. The teen shook with relief to be hitching out of Croperth.

Here his dowsing staff earned him lifts from more knowledgeable farmers, driving their slow but efficient hopovers — and information. Dire was the nomenclature with which most of those wry faces with the beseeching eyes told it, just like farmers everywhere. The threat facing still tractile land in the marginal wheat and emu belt in this part of Western Farm was uniformly occurring across all land away from the coast. Heat refraction from crystalline white sprawls and banks of surface salt was conflagrating in whirlwinds, not unknown to deposit humans along with thousands of tons of dust kilometres from the point of origin.

Scar waves still hit the land, and although properties tenured by pig-headed flood irrigators could expect a deepening of the scars, they struck anywhere with equal randomness. There were beliefs that it was the insurgents who caused the damage, though more explicable possibilities lay closer to home. Whoever was to blame for the seismic phenomena, the quakes were large. Clays were cut by sub-strata movements, or keystone slipped, and the result was land that could lower by six metres in hectare-long scars.

Ant armour these farmers wore. Plastic pants to their ribs where a silicone gel bonded them to their skin. The ants were the survivors, feasting on dead and dying soil-life. Worms were becoming very rare — where ants throve, crops grew better, for at least they oxygenated and buried plant material in their workings. One rumour Larker heard had him scratching at a feeling of something brooding. Trees assumed long dead, desert cypress, bull oaks with trunks skirted in salt crystal, were suckering uncountable trunklets. Unleafed, foliant only in a tight whorl of tip, as a razor to touch.

The musings on the surface of Larker's mind are interrupted by a deeper movement. Like the sound of residual magnetism between two notes of birdsong, he hears it. He leaves the road at an animal track where an iridescent glimmer in granite flags and rocks proves to be masses of tadpoles ensconced in every nook. With only a pause to ponder this oddity, Larker tilts his nose to feel the passing of bats on the hunt. A faint swirl of breeze alerts him to their general direction. On a cool night like this they would be sortieing from their home — probably the largest hollow red gum somewhere along the dry wash. Possibly, if his accumulated hunches are not sheer fancy, it will be the very tree he seeks.

Two swirls of stacked sandstone had marked St Petersin's entrance, its chapel and outbuildings hedged with hardy, impenetrable saw palms. The main monastery was styled as that engineering balm for hot places — the hacienda. Seamless, poetic stone form. A visionary, simple design for the Catholic Church — even of a cult so obscure as these Gregorian monks. Yet by far the most visionary of achievements, and dominating all else, were the hills and vales of olives in burgeoning Grecian abandon.

Early in the new millennium, St Petersin's profits from olives increased exponentially, but the pressing sheds that had extracted the most premium of golden oil for a century and a half were cannibalised. In place of crushers, washers, and separating lines came a cryogenic facility and bio-surgeons' workshops. Laser and zero gravity chambers honeycombed the cool innards of the large stone sheds. For olive bark — that is, strips of pulpy sap wood just inside the bark — it seemed could be made do a wondrous thing.

It could be impregnated with human genomes and harvested four years later, following re-carbonation and hydrogenation in the bio-shops, then placed on human skin and made to graft. It had a magnifying effect on oxygen production, killed anything from warts to cancer, and after a time destabilised, falling away to leave new and miracle skin behind. It could only undergo its alchemy if sourced from trees with consistently low moisture content.

St Petersin's orchard represented a quarter of the world's olivacea. The big winners were the bio-companies and the local aboriginals to whom the monks channelled most of the millions the pharmaceuts paid them. The olive trees were the losers. One tree could produce three square metres — or enough to bring salvation to sixty humans. Mortally taxed, the trees died within a decade, their thousand year longevity spread thinly among the years of reprieved humans.

The job afforded Larker came about as an irony of life-threatening proportion. The olives were all healthy, producing a mass of flower-set, and entirely too luxuriant growth. Irrigation regimes were halted. Some trees were no longer accepting the genomes. Tests on groundwater detected no extra moisture rise. The trees sung of growth and strength to the keen nerves in Larker's body as he ranged those first days through the sylvan acreage.

Very early on he dismissed ever obtaining the substantial cash bonus to which pharmaceut director Mr Soiler had alluded. Perhaps, the little careful monks tanned appropriately dark olive had suggested, the trees were aware of their fellows' fate. Did they somehow draw moisture from passing birds, or did dying trees transmit the water to their friends through some subtle process he might detect?

Perhaps, Larker had deferred — while neither nights nor days of query furnished answers. Studying Merriglade's O*lea species* in the candlelit library had him intoning the brief Latin passages of olive-crowned kings outstretching olive branches. It was more to enjoy the rhythmic sound in that hushed place than in any hope the words contained encrypted clues. Latin his father had taught him, and the root of many things.

Days he was hunched over his hazel staff above the fulcrum point of the three-hundred-acre grove. He had found this place easily. Below it was a magnetic mineral deposit. Powerful lode-rock formations included two double-pointed carnelian crystals as large as him, but dormant. The underground stream, or sedentary water table some thirty metres beneath the stones, affected small presence. Anchoring his essence in the larger crystal, another skill gifted from his father, he had looked with the carnelian's understanding at the soil structure.

Dry and limey, but the salt was stable. It could be exerting no adverse force on soil transpiration. In fact the whole property was inclined to comparably-slowed salt movement. Well cared for, never knowing surface stress from chemical or machine, even worms still lived here. Only at the fringes of the grove was the lifeless taint of salt beginning its characteristic increase and mounting pressure, like fire in a forest. No hollow soil with trapped water, no abnormal root stretching, there was nothing, and yet…the trees had a feeling of power to them. A secret force swelled their cells, fleeted through soil and air like a hover invisible above low cloud.

The bats comport him reliably to within sight of his goal. He tests the two lengths of strapping that he had thieved from storage. Strong enough to belt weak trees together, he is sure that he can shimmy up to the tree's crown, alternatively sliding the straps with his feet and arms, though it will require his most skilled climb. Half a mile along the dry course is the discernible hulk of the imponderably huge red gum. Radial arms of nonchalant growth pinion out from the lightning strike at thirty metres high, visible as a great gash in the primordial skyline. Upon reaching the giant, he finds it marooned in a snarl of mulga, devil's twines, and every type of hoary, desert-hardened plant. Experiments prove his assay correct; the tangle over huge fallen limbs, and the nursery they harbour, has made of the tree's periphery an unyielding wall, and he will still need energy to ascend the behemothic trunk and view the hollow.

Larker's croon of disappointment hangs on the thick brush. The features of his face relax in concentrated meditation on the problem. Long thin lips sag from their jostle of the plump cheeks, air flexes the slightly upturned nostrils in deep rhythm. Soft eyes, a fraternal pale blue, opaque and flecked with brown, assume a vaguer-than-usual expression. A fall of something raw and obdurant lands across them, and becomes enmeshed to the perpetually surprised-looking forehead that cannot register any further shock. Looking up, Larker is in no doubt of why it had chosen to purblind him, for the illuminated eye of the owl considering him in crystalline ferocity stretches paralytic awe through his every nerve. It props on the trunk of a desert ash half a metre above him, shoulders sloped forward to display the essence of its namesake — powerful.

'Catatonia and poison bring land the new man.'

Larker knows it is the owl, though the jewel-precise beak only snaps a few times as if to taste the electric excitement that permeates the air. The words appear illumined in the apex of the visual chamber in Larker's mind. There is no sound, the words expand and contract akin to the beats of his heart.

'Are you ready for remaking?'

Larker's world seems to narrow to this one blot in time. As he pulls the cowl of spider webs from his face, he allows himself utter inurement with any strangeness, regarding the dry forest from his wildest, intuitive self. There is no feeling of danger, and the moonlit steel that is the owl still seems worshipful. Memories and thoughts are joined in a happy flow too interlinked with this point of time to be the mere coincidence of his mind's leavetaking, or to mean the bird is the genetically created trump of someone's foolery. The squat, tawny youth enthuses in a low voice from the centre of himself the words that the million shamans of Earth have uttered at their initiation throughout history. His is to be the first direct initiation into such a world as this.

"I am ready."

A vacuum begins to form in his heart and his emotions are spent into the night until even the tang of sorrow is gone. His senses swell in proportion to the redundance of emotion. Suddenly his mind is a-whir in a pattern that is not quite sound or thought, but rhythm cloaking all else, encasing all else in its gradually faster spin. It foremost underpins his being, this tide of energy, though he can feel something similar emit from rocks and trees, while a power almost as strong as his own emanates from the owl.

That being, whose name appropriates to Hearkenwoad, dips off the log and tumbles with an easy flip into an economic flitter toward the highest branches of the tree. With acuity of foreknowledge, Larker knows how he will gain ascension to the tree hollow. He begins to grope with his raw power at the immediately obstructing vine tangle but then conceives of an easier idea. He broadcasts the pattern of yielding beneath a fallen limb onto the whole tangle ahead.

With a flail, a shocked gasp, the plants withdraw their water content into bulging roots and Larker walks forward. The mass has no more resistance than moulded paper and he projects that crashing overlay of future limb-fall until there is only the massive trunk before him. With the keenness of a whip, thousands of filaments uncoil into the night, and the plants snap back into place.

Larker considers the vast and hoary gum. *'Camulensis,'* he muses — to store. Unfortunately, though each is long dead, it has retained many branchlets on its trunk, too many for him to climb it with the belts. Dispassionately, he feels the movements of the many beings within it, and their replete strength, as he considers the puzzle of the climbing. The young shaman's gaze on the crown lies clear and steady as the Moon's on the Earth, and he feels himself just as far from reaching his goal of the orbit of his last weeks. A beckoning light pulses in the canopy, as it had when he first wandered the obscure side track in restless search for answers, though not to the questions he thought he had been asking. Then he had known himself witness to the supernatural, but watching in agitation, assumed some earthbound spirit pulsed its loneliness there; a grey light sucking to maroon, and an orange were-light that flared against the cradle of the sky, delineating the wispy leaves of the tree's crown.

He had since concluded what beings might be within the trunk, and now he feels them through the power graft they have given him. Hob Goblins. Users and manipulators of water and all that it touches, the shape of freneticism wrapped around a keen and opportunistic eye that glowed mostly birdlike. He had seen his father's sketches of them — one had been depicted as half-kangaroo. In mastery of any erratic nerves, Larker responds to their silent willing for him to ascend without the aid of props, and with dry hands, simply hoists himself up piecemeal. In the brittle tatters he selects to bear his weight — a twist of bark or an old leafless branch thirty metres from the ground — there plays the strength of the tree's sap, and to that living blueprint the frail-seeming supports are still snared.

When seated at the top on a kind of double burl, he is propped just above the source of the light emanations pulsing from a symbol of infinity styled by a rope of sap, with the uncanny result that his silhouette is cast gargantuan to sit its stoic vigil in the amphitheatre of the tree's venerable crown. Gradually the light dims, soon reborn as a dull glow deep in the hollow.

A babble of hale voices in a Latin dialect, occasionally punctuated by some beseechment, spills up from the dark and flows steady as a geyser. Larker finds, not without a swelling of his already acute wonder, that he can understand a deal of what is said.

"We have passed this through the vicissitudes of the shrub realms, Peyunk. Surely now we need only vent for Dalima's swift decisiveness."

"Amilluk is right. The logio of the eagle is needed and then we must supposit the firefeather before the brush of dawn."

"I shall synergise with Dalima and provide access for him to betoken his readiness."

Unobtrusively in Larker's mind, a word-reach forms.

"I am Fortusenay. Greetings, Larker warm-mind. You are family to us and the needs which your father guessed at, we betrust to your heart of hearts."

With the words, an image coheses of his father and mother transported by the beautiful bitter-sweet of lovemaking in a forest, and through the curtain of long, sweat-soaked hair swaying over his face, he follows his father's shining gaze to five beings watching him, shyly clinging to a stout blackwood.

"I am Amilluk, hope spinner of the Hobbogyre. Know you that we have founded our way together since ever your spirit coming into this world. You must provoke in your kind the memory of the unity of Earth, and the way of sacrifice. For this you will be given the fire to guide your spontaneity, to guard your wisdom. The laughter protect you."

Larker's head now fills with broadly connected information. The way human actions had impacted at last on these creatures' world, where always they had been able to sidestep humanity, the Earth-memory ground down by the horrors of human experience and destruction such that dryads were stirring, albeit that their wakening would come much too late. Yet other beings flexed the muscles of intervention and confrontation, where before they had remained cryptic. They were great, but so few. Somewhere, lost in a nether-world to time, were more of them. It seems his ultimate fate is to return them, somehow, to this dimension. He sees that if this task is not achieved, then all the futures of Earth point to lifelessness.

The light flares brilliantly in the stump, and the scene below resembles a broiling tea party of puppets, as hobs swarm over and around each other in a flow like water. Diagrams of intricate design, alternately flashing real scenery as though through a portal, appear in the middle of one group. A hob with a purple face stretches elasticine lips impossibly far, and as Larker watches, an eagle flies from its mouth straight at him. As it surges forward, the golden feathers become a flame, and the bird diminishes. At only the size of a fingertip, it hits Larker between the eyes. Momentarily, he is a serpent smelling the smoke of ten thousand campfires across the lands surrounding, then his world is a sizzling of pain, and he falls careening through the air for an indecipherable stretch of time.

Chapter 3

"I agree, sir. It's absolutely unbelievable. Wilful marauding. The whole lot just smashed and hacked from the ground. The cacti are affright with pointless mangling and the spruces destroyed, sir! And why? For a bunch of jolly fish spears! I found one they'd neglected in the lower paddock between the lagoon and the inner fence."

"Well, how did they get the knives?"

"A hole's been dug, by Jove, under the back store-shed, and they must have scrabbled them out from there. We should yard and flog the lot of them, sir, and see a burning to their log punts if we can trace their stow. Those spruces were indelible to the whole formatting of the optic mood, and we'll not now have more until next spring at the nearest."

"I will not threaten our sanitary reputation, and until the completion of the Canary's exhibit in two weeks, I will risk no reprisal. They may set-up that surliness and wailing, let alone do any more damage to the stock. Chum up a translator, Collins, with biscuit or baccy, and bring him to me at the conservatorium by luncheon."

After his plantsman had gone, the director moved from his desk to stand before the generous bay window. One splayed hand gently brushed the smooth oaken board, pitted with knots hundreds of years old, the other pulled his watch on a chain from a pocket, and without opening it, returned it. Crate loads of native fig trees stood ready in the dispatch side of the square, but as yet unplaced Queensland cherries, in their shining royal robes, amassed in the barked-over area for arrivals, recalled the Director to his ineluctable, monumental scheme.

As he walked toward the drafting bureau, he stopped to study a giant bead of amber hung from the next window. Inside was a perfectly preserved leaf of a ginkgo, a tree species only latterly rediscovered in China, and a generic one-off believed to pre-suppose the first animated stirrings of warm-blooded life.

"Well," he espoused to no one, "at least there's no dinosaurs in the vegetable commons."

Then he streaked the curio into a jaunty penduluming with a flick. As he drew forth the plate he needed, and stone-faced began to mark the cherry sites, a shadow stretched its odd presence — clearly cast from its honeyed tomb by the unblinking sun. The ginkgo leaf played back and forth from the too-browned face of the little man, across his pens and prints, and up to the cornice of the vaulted ceiling like a winged seed drifting chaotic and innate toward fertile sanctuary.

As the sundial in the lawn descried midday, Bullark passed the irrigation plans for the herb gardens, already skeletally delineated by brick edging that wound the whole perimeter of the conservatorium, into Ben's hands. The toothsome Irishman was proving to be his best convict aid, with sharp instinct for both botany and construction. Sure enough, plantsman Collins was striding across the lawn, turning repeatedly to gesture the figure behind him to hurry.

This was a young aboriginal man with shining brown skin who threw out his arms as though walking determinedly until Collins turned, then simply stood, one hand on hip, leisurely puffing smoke about him. Now he half ran, stopped, slapped a leg and laughed convulsively. A smile creased Bullark's face, observing the obvious difference and antagonism between the two.

He sobered as Collins came close enough to stare pointedly from him back to his recalcitrant charge, and walked over to defuse the powder keg of his rhubarb-faced plantsman.

"Thank you, Collins. When this chap arrives, we'll straight for the lagoon."

The man only glared his impatience, nearly setting the Director smiling again.

"Howilly morning, you one."

"This," grated Collins, "is Willy Man Tong."

The careful tapping out and grinding of his pipe ashes, awkward wiping of hands before an incomprehensible ritual, and then the limp grip, but eyes alit with more than mischief.

"Well, I'm Director Bullark. Now, friend, we go lagoon, find paperbark men. You tell them no more chop plants, only he work for me make gardens, me give him tobac, boot-pants, all. He make garden, he get it. He bad man, me call soldier."

"Check. Me tell him, make garden, only no chop garden. Only work boss man you."

"Thank you, Willy, I have met your uncle, Lominkarry. He say you good tracker."

The arms thrown wide, the smile with the front teeth knocked out, then the face concentrating on packing the battered pipe. The hint of a hidden joke in the eyes.

"Well then, Collins, I think we should follow Willy to the lagoon."

After some fifteen minutes of mischievously alacritous walking along the verdant lagoon edge, Willy took them across two swampy springs, one after another. The space, amid pinkly pastelled trunks of the tea-trees, grew more capacious as they became individually larger with saplings fewer. Then they were on the bank of the lagoon, a few purple flowers speckling a gentle slope to the water. Large fish, like oily mushrooms glistening in odd colours of mixed species, declined from a slender spear slipped through forked branches. Otherwise there was no sign of the miscreants.

Willy moved to the water edge, his bare feet bogging a little, and called in a resounding boom. "Ku-ai!"

A heron and some magpie-geese rose in a desperate flurry of affront, but there was no answering response.

"He'd be great to have along for a duck shoot, sir," quipped Collins. Bullark gestured him silent, peering over the wild and reflective deeps.

Then faintly, "Ku-ai."

"Him along soon." With that Willy sat on the bank and chuckled intermittently while Bullark mentally composed his request, seated alongside. Collins, brushing at leaves in clothes and hair, stood aside huffing…and poised in tension. There were three canoes, water-bleached grey, and in the first to round the little promontory a man stood up and cupped hands to brow in the age-old gesture of nautical accounting, until all three drew together. One was riding low in the water, a silvered elder seated nonchalantly behind the paddler.

On shore the fishers waited for the elder to disembark, then the two men wriggled into short pants retrieved from the canoes. The elder exchanged a few weighted words with Willy, while the boy who had been ferrying him squatted naked on the lagoon shore, and cleaned the barbed spears of spruce with wet sand.

"Melanarry say cutting lagoon scrub no good. No spear wood left for him, less water food. Less fish," Willy intoned.

The Director displayed a smile virulent enough to resist the stern silence of the still powerfully formed elder, his cicatrised chest evenly rising.

"Tell him he can keep the knives he stole, trade more better fish, but no more chop plant inside fence."

"Bastard thief," huffed from the background.

The silver one was silent after hearing Willy, and for a minute he stared into the bush as if expecting to see the redemption of his people's fate there. Then he half-turned, signalled to the youth and laughed a few guttural words. The naked youth presented a rope of bark, heavy with fish, to Collins.

"What is this?" he demanded bewildered, while appraising the bounty.

"This one for good spear," came the translation.

"And for good paddle," mimed Bullark, who had noted the ingenious use of the cactus devastation.

Even Collins allowed a chuckle as the various "Yus!" rang from the fishers.

"Well, I don't know how much that resolved," said the Director to Collins, "but I hope I'm not the one chosen to tell them the lagoon will be drained and their river tamed."

They followed a still exuberant Willy back.

Nothing happened for a week, including that the grounds and outhouses remained unmolested. Then, waking from strange dreams, the Director opened the door of his modest home to the scent of smoke and fish. Seven aboriginals were breakfasting around a fire on the lawn; two he recognised from the lagoon, but not the boy or the old man. Bullark was so ecstatic he forgot to mention the burned lawn patch to Collins later in the morning.

"That's enough men to shift the limestone from the river depot and make a bit of space. See if you can teach them to mound some future grottoes, man!"

"Yes, sir. Ah, Willy has appointed himself their captain. He wants a daily wage to translate."

"The cheeky devil. Give him the same start with extra biscuit daily."

Bullark never got to see his limestone grottoes built. When the offer had come through, in spite of being heavily greased with suggestions of resulting knighthood and title to some of the route explored, it was his sheer love of science, of factoring the unknown that made him accept a place in the expedition. When all were assembled, a three-month sail to the central north-west of western

Australia awaited. Disembarking at Exmouth, they would rendezvous with a mule team to penetrate Leopold's country and one of the last places on Earth unknown to civilisation.

He had selected Collins, and the convict Ben to join him, as botanist. A geologist, the two surveyors, four soldiers, as well as the multi-skilled expedition leader, would complete the leg to Exmouth with them.

For that party, leaving the gardens early one autumn morning, while the experimental crops tilted in ripeness, and the growing menagerie of birds and mammals struck a dawn hullabaloo, boarding a punt at the Yarra-Yarra river for their steamer around the bend did not hold fate that they should return — save for one — to see their plantings rise above the lawns in proud obeisance of nature.

Chapter 4

Even to other revolutionaries, his comrades of the Rainbow Realliance Hub, Keevan thinks there would probably appear nothing unusual about this Sunday's Channon market. On ground level, little has changed since the market's inception more than two centuries ago. Peaked marquees, styled as medieval booths, advertise self-help and development insights with their holographically projected unicorns and gypsies — and coloured eyes or faded standards declaim tarot, numerology, massage and clairvoyant services. Though beyond the canvas, the potter knows, await consultants with a firmer foundation in charlatanry than that of their erstwhile peers.

This four-acre field, richly stuffed with tourists, is one of the few places in American South Austral where the poor, or in this case the peasant class, can gather unmolested in a public place — it being free from the usual stigma, both social and official, of those with monetary lack. Growers from shared farms and backyard bakers and picklers still command a milling gaggle around their rudimentary stalls. Owing to the haggling though, which the well-off pursued as a kind of sport, often his stall holder friends covered their production costs and entry fee alone.

At the base of the market hover-stack which towers some hundred metres above the central lawn, a group of security Agents squeeze any impish verve from two teenage owners of an older model hover brightly painted with trees and birds. With sly study, overtly marking price tags behind a mass of terracotta ware, Keevan regards the Agents. The female among them slams a hand under a defiantly shaved chin. While her victim's head is held back, she flirtatiously smiles at her colleagues, who loud and roughly bark their laughter. One passes a confine belt into her hands. This she flips around the youth's arms and upper body, and the security locks close. The spared girl sinks to the ground dismayed, and as the potter watches, her boyfriend is led into the cone-capped, splayed triangle of the security hover. The rear Agent steps from his path to trample across the distraught teenager's shin.

"Do not, Keevan, confuse their lack of numbers today, with lack of vigilance."

Keevan Pufrieg looks at the man who has breathed this advice in such a casual style. He holds no guilt about not telling his friend. Nothing can alter the sanctity of secret knowledge, even friendship. Angelo Hardy is rummaging through boxes of shirts, sequined dresses, and sarongs in his car-boot to find the sizes easiest to tailor for the rotund customer at his stall. Cars still exist in Rainbow County, its odd magnetic flux and persistent canopy making them less a risk than the cheaper style of hovers. The market organisers especially encouraged their use to lend rustic ambience, soaked up every month by the cameras of foreign tourists.

"No, hombre, today I have more important considerations than those games."

With a reassuring smile for his friend, he picks his way through craftily fluted gargoyles and bowls to announce at passers-by in lyrical refrain, "Extraordinary pottery works at a price that's ordinary, folks."

After selling enough pieces to make business seem worthwhile, Keevan leaves the clothing outfitter in charge of his custom, purportedly to make a round of small talk with the marketeers. He is gone all morning, and Angelo, a member of the area's Realliance hub, knows Keevan is not wasting this day on small talk. Market days, impermanent and bustling occasions, are one of the few times in which a revolutionary cell can machinate in heavily monitored and repetitively patterned ASA.

Yet by the time the sun begins to cause shop awnings and the dense shade beneath black bean trees to fill with little huddles of families grouped around icy sugar of varying guise — and clutching too many bags of squashed provender — Angelo begins to feel uneasy. He wonders what Keevan had meant by 'more important considerations'. The strange events all occurring that morning now seem like portents.

An aboriginal elder, who for the last five years had busked the same two dances of an emu and of a kangaroo, had been flitting, arms outstretched, and sinking gracefully to ground or swooping on groups of dumbfounded children. Presently he stands near Angelo's stall, and after letting a crowd build up, announces his goshawk dreaming as 'the sacred dance of my people for death. This fellow peck ya bones, he clasp your spirit in talons, tight now; you can't escape that bird'.

The inevitable harassment of the buxom fruit stall holder opposite had occurred, as it did most weeks, a short while ago. This time two labourers had been going to investigate behind the stall after descriptions of the huge melons they wanted had drawn a stony response. As they edged toward the beautiful woman, a holographic programmer housing had exploded, and both men's legs erupted into flame. They had rolled in the trammelled dust beside the path trying to slap out the liquid hydrogen while the tawny stall holder reached a tanned arm for a water bucket, and calmly tipped it spinach and all, on the shrieking men.

Paramedics arrived and within two minutes the men had been hovered off. Angelo kept expecting investigating Agents, but after an hour he determined their synergy must be impaired. It could not be their communications or transport equipment, and this sort of human error had him narrowing the blame to only two possible causants. Either Curlewalion's Indigoes were throwing up a perimeter thought shield and misinformation catalyst to cover Mist intrigue, or a bomb scare or some such was threatening collateral assets. That latter guess proves correct when, to stop speculating on his worries, he picks a paper from the back of his car.

There it is, just after the front page article of the World American Reform government conference on tidal containment. A Curlew Agent in Acadabourne had rescued three gangers, destroyed five billion of property, but had herself been rescued by what was believed to be a new type of genetically engineered lion. No trace of the escapees or any of the genetic beasts had as yet been found, despite a security cordon comprising five hundred Agents, predicted to grow exponentially until the situation was equilibrated.

So the Enyadding have at last committed themselves to Curlewalion in a temporal way, and nothing will ever be the same again, Angelo muses. An urban legend had been circulating in Curlew for some time, spawned by the few psychics privy the reality of the secretive Aboriginal group's existence. Ghosts, such legend said, would rise up, the souls would be flayed from the peoples of Earth and magmated marbles from space rain upon the planet should the Enyadding make embodied their intercession in the affairs of men.

Angelo knows more of the Enyadding than most. Like others pivotal in the alliance, he knows that it is they who maintain the border storms. He knows the true nature of their bizarre pantheresque companions, common legend across the whole continent. Appraised with facts, not superstition, Angelo had long since concluded that should the Enyadding openly walk the world, the battle front would be etched across the mind of every human.

When Keevan returns at last, Angelo holds up the paper and the two lean on the car bonnet, to all appearances puzzling over a crossword, while hurriedly whispering together with a practiced adeption that compresses their lips to the barest movements, although it is obvious security is occupied elsewhere.

"What are the people's feelings?" Angelo asks.

"There is general awareness of great change in the winds." The thin man raises a sleeve of his coarse shirt to wipe distractedly at the oft-running florid bulb of his nose, the flaw counterpoint to a nobly etched face. He places a long hand on Angelo's shoulder, as always their height disparity making the shorter man self-consciously aware of the other's gaze alighting on his depilated crown, and reminding him of the science of old that saw beams sent down from satellites to the great white receiving dishes on Earth.

"There is now evidence of dissent for the masses, of Curlew's undeniable presence. I have implemented full forward stages for this very night."

"Full forward? Eight months early, Key."

"Yes."

"The Gods help us. What's your thinking, mate, as to why the Enyadding have risked all?"

"I do not know," Keevan lies, "but it is certainly good about the rescue. Curlew shall receive three escapees, with their intricate knowledge of city planning. I think there is a very great deal more happening than we can see."

The two walk to the track and look into the thinning market. Everywhere local people are now hugging openly, in statuesque reaffirmation of life and connection. The air is filled with a thin mist that is only wet enough to melt in the sun, so that it extinguishes in a golden light, or lingers a little longer to burst as tiny rainbows. Peripherally aware of the rare phenomenon, Angelo considers that people seem literally to be embracing the hope lent by news of the breakout. The scrying of a nearby cartomancer carries to him.

"The fool and the emperor again!" The stocky tailor's fleshy face strictures with concentration to hear the next words. "And — death."

Angelo feels it then. The change will be centred here at the market. Suddenly his thoughts ameliorate in lightness and clarity, and he glances at Keevan, but his friend only stares into space muttering acerbically, "Do they know what they do? I think the great ones here miss their mark."

As the aboriginal elder comes past, he looks at Angelo with a perplexed, unbelieving eye and says two words, "Death — dead."

Then the clothing outfitter, with a lineage traced from poets, sees that a goshawk dangles from the black hand. The elder strides through the market, thrusting the bird above his head and screaming in hoarse bursts. As if in a dream, Angelo notices a wind has begun to eddy through the market.

It divulges a strong scent of ripe vegetation, woodsmoke, and something reminiscent of the musty smell of a cave, evoking imagery of rock shelters on sandstone bluffs. Angelo cranes, like many others, staring, trying to elicit the source from which the wafts of burning arise. In the gold haze and through the fractals of rainbows, all he can ascertain is that the branches of the black beans that encircle the market are plumed with wind. Above a cluster near him, their long leaves spin on a willy-willy of growing resolve. He glances again toward his friend, but Keevan has gone.

A knot of people is forming near the strongest willy-willies amid the garden stalls where swathes of pots lie spilled in disarray. Almost everyone is moving now, a few dozen hovers pulling away coastward, with thin streams of agitated people pressing for the hover-stack. A contrary group comprised of some thousand souls is bunched around something he cannot make out. Just as he ascends a grassy rise to see more clearly, everybody in the press sits down, revealing a remarkable man with broad hands forming vortices of energy as though shaping one of Keevan's tall urns on an invisible potting wheel.

The figure claims singularity, not for the cascading rouge of his hair, or garb woven of bark, but for the movement of his body, refining the power of simple gestures with his presence alone. The gapped teeth jewel a smile, even as his eyes ponder some sadness. Angelo wonders how it is that he can read these details, for he is at least a hundred metres distant. Then nothing matters as those eyes stare into his — stars that each have fallen into a bottomless sea. Now the tailor understands the source of the glinting clarity which had first swept him up after the mist had come over the market. It seems he falls from his old mind into a space which is slowed to a present containing all possibilities. He lives vivid scenes of aboriginal massacres, and is connected completely to the beating heart of wonder and calm thought of everyone in that enraptured huddle, before the brief contact of those eyes passes.

By the time Angelo is seated at the group's edge, their benefactor is drawing his hands in rhythmic gestures down his side, drawing all of them into the Earth's limitless comfort, as he sweeps his eyes like a slow question over them. His words resound clear and simple.

"But for a twist of fate, a quirk, I think, these days with all their horrors may each have held promise like fresh baked bread for our spirits."

With a roar the winds now all amass above him and the man allows himself to be spun from the ground a little in their vigorous updraughts. With a yell he pushes the great vortex towards the hover-stack. Sure enough, the tower is soon covered in whirling leaves which swirl into a pulsing conglomerate of light and glimpses of creatural faces innumerable. Angelo watches the scene melt into itself in an impossible kaleidoscope. The man speaks again.

"'Tis this day we'll meet and soothroad, forked by the tongue of today, to hi and bye. I don't need tell you, friends, fires rage now. Their smoke covers all the land, pointless the waste. Be as the deep seed. Remember your essence, and unfurl now through the chaos and the blinding. If the wind comes there will be fair sky to grow into. Be ready."

As bits of stray debris rain from the suddenly becalmed sky, his voice drops conspiratorially to assume a haunted tone, bereft of doubt. "It is horrible, this world, isn't it? A marrow-sucked nightmare prowled by invisible giants, and all too real. If that fate's strands had not been twisted....

"You here gathered are the component to...well, you are simply they who have come to such a pass of time. Go deep. Remember your pattern and if the sky comes clear, never forget the burning, and that your growing may exclude the cloying weeds from the feet of your children. Yes, a bad pass of time is come, but people are the living safeguards of this world. My time is brought ending. Brought ending at last."

The astonishing figure strides with a floating gait from the circle, Angelo noting his fingers clasped around some gold shining thing as he passes close by.

"All people still part of humankind's wild soul must remember themselves now, or the Earth will forget us."

The being of unswayed power walks toward the maelstrom, the entire group following in train as if to ask how. The tailor observes the red-headed man step through the shifting images and lights, then disappear. He feels his words, like a spell flooding his body with a wave of memory and light, and becomes acutely aware of how consciousness alone has given return and resilience to the plunging journey of the Earth across the stars.

The bright spin of snouts and beaks and eyes stills to a turbid frieze, a dull wall of dim colour encrusting the hover-stack that is gradually demarked into several interlocking shapes of giant gum leaves by the spread of green veins of lurid light. In leisurely collapse, the leaves of reflective green begin to topple outward. With their dissolution, a strange shape becomes visible in the background. Angelo is awed to observe that the leaf nearest him somehow encapsulates an image of the exact seeing of his mind, showing back to him both its own integral form as well as another him and the diverse scenes he stares at, before the falling chimeric wonder is finally spent.

With the end of the tricks of light comes a great deluge of people's suppressed emotions. Sobbing and screams, moans and shrills of joy. No trace at all remains of the hover-stack. Instead, a small green hill rises, and standing on its top, about the size of a house and made from some material comparable to volcanic glass, the effigy of an aboriginal woman nursing child glints in the sun.

Chapter 5

Each of the seventy men and women, straight-backed in the white censure room, regard the slowly gliding hover chair above them. Though chosen as much for protein compatibility to moral hygiene boosters as for their brawn, it is not solely indoctrination that keeps all trace of expression from their elite faces. For the man in the black chair circling silently above, the Squadron Leaders is no cranky Zone Command. Known as Man Slitter to his peers, Emmanuel Slitter has been in the Austral territories for over ninety years. His rise through the ranks of the Affiliate had halted at second-in-command only because his ruthlessness could not pluck the kernel of nut at the top of the hallowed tree from the hard shell of entrenched bureaucratic safeguards around it.

Back in America, Slitter's business acumen and inherited private security spoils had given him production of the first automnals — Automated Neutralising Artificial Life Systems. He had personally birthed many of their special features, and the first million plastic cops to hit the streets had accosted crooks with his distinctive grating voice. In 2040, something had gone wrong. Automn bodyguards inside the White House had killed the Vice-President, Secretary of State, and thirty nobody senators — an incident apparently owed to a meltdown of synth-proteins triggered by a new chemical in the furniture polish. Someone had to take the rap, and Emmanuel was hauled from head of military research and packed off to Austral on the next hover.

It had been embittering to have to push up from squadron leader to Zone Command, then Secretary of Operations to Compellance, to finally make Poise One, with his hand wrapped around the shell of the Poise himself. A buoying concession had been his little retreat, one of many of his stipulated rights brokered in exchange for letting himself be pastured out as scapegoat so undemonstratively — a hundred and sixty square kilometres of Kimberley station the government acquired when they annexed Brunei under the W.A.R. banner, along with the Sultan's property. As Slitter bragged to privileged companions, it was the sort of place you could litter one pool with capsized barramundi, and only have to hover a moment downstream to find shooting just as good.

His Chiccargo-accented, bass-toned voice croons in careful understatement, trickling behind the long hair that covers the ears of Victoria's Squadron Leaders.

"Okay. So after two days of plying your strictest efforts, and ALL of my resources, to catch one female terrorist and some dissident blacks, what do you bring me?" He glides down to their eye level and pushes back the head of an aboriginal strapped into a stabiliser unit. "A drunken abo —"

"Hang on," he continues portentously, his lustreless features pitting above his valve-studded jowl, exposing the interlinked math of cell distributors and magnetised muscle beneath the smooth surface illusion. He transits the ranks to stall before a man in the second row. "Donsan. Can you tell me how many field personnel are currently at your disposal for this search?"

The man gulps audibly before seamlessly announcing that 'fifteen thousand Agents and thirteen hundred special reserve are involved. Sir'.

"Right!" Slitter heels his chair, passing along the front row. "And yet, with nearly twenty thousand men you bring me" — he passes by the man on the stabiliser board, and delivers a boot meant for Donsan, save for that Agent's flawlessness of answer, into the prisoner's face — "a drunken ABO! Because he was in the grounds, up a tree, sleeping off his Hempanol, and you equated him with a terror mastermind. Now LISTEN! Find me, please, the naughty girl and her several accomplices, and bring them here alive before tomorrow. DO not bring me any Chinese midgets, ventriloquist-escaped fucking tigers, or inebriated savages. Orderly!"

A white-coated man clacks up to the Poise One from an alcove. "Up his serum. He just may have seen something, and I want him remembering. "

After a minute, the punctilious scientist says, "I can't, sir."

"What?"

"He's dead."

"But that's impossible; he's rigged to a stabiliser."

"I know it's impossible sir, but he's dead."

"Right. Well, throw him away." Slitter glides out the door to his office with a backhand gesture of dismissal. He is sick of impossibilities. Vanishing blacks, unknown mastermind bitches. This one — Sway — he knows is still somewhere in his city. He found her once before and he'll find her again, he determines, and when he does... He wonders how much of a couch a human skin can cover. This whole business is starting to remind him of that phone call one hundred and three years prior.

He had been Compellance only two months when he had received the four a.m. news from the then Poise One. The most critical challenge to his government's regime had been delivered by a tiny group doing the impossible. In the benumbed aftermath, as the regime scrabbled to hold a majority of its geographical control and bulwark the plummeting economy, it had been Slitter's job — indeed condition of his retaining one — to piece together what had happened, and how, on that woebegone May night. There had been interviews with survivors, laborious sifting through remnant surveillance footage, and the soliciting of information in the Asian torture camps.

The night and its prefacing afternoon had seen many battles in both the military and private detention facilities at Pine Gap, but their inception had been at least two decades prior, deep in the jungles of Indonesia. The notion of a plan for destroying American dominance once and for all had seemingly been birthed running within a far-flung tribal region. There had been leaders, no doubt, but they were obscured to history. The motivation was the same as scraggly nationals all over the world — hatred of his government's regime that brought order and technology to their lives — only in the case of the Jepawisat, three-quarters of the once million-strong tribal group had been sunk by World Instated Austral peace enforcers, or killed on their jungle soil by militia activity fuelled by American expansionism.

Two things changed the destiny of the Jepawisat. Their guerrilla combatant expertise reached levels able to repel genocide attacks effectively, and intellectuals and graduates with big ideas began to drift back from the city mega-ports. Under a thousand souls, male and female, were selected and trained rigorously for nearly twenty years in the dynamic martial and technical arts of their people. Even their children were trained in combat, and schooled in secrecy. Of this number, under three hundred graduated to board the Trojan horse along with the engineers and communications experts, all older people, to make the demographics appear consistent. The sacrifice was high, as infants would be lost to separate camps, if indeed they gained landfall. Slitter knew such misfits would have calculated an even chance of life quality behind foreign wire, or in the dying forests.

At a time when the world's eye was once again drawn into a cycle of indignant shock by a media leak of refugee craft sunk by the navy, and a paternal W.A.R. government was promoting its bold philanthropic solution — a side stream of sound business — professional detention centres poured from a mould of utility onto wasteland in high ground the world over, the Jepawisat made their run. Even then it was amazing to Slitter that some untraceable Jepawisat contact inside the immigration department had successfully ensured the bedraggled boatload was incarcerated, minus their infants, in the new detention facility conjoined to Pine Gap. Three hundred and one souls saved with due public acclaim from a rusty freighter off the Queensland coast. The people farmers had brought the wolves among their flock.

Their patience and cohesion of group-mind under the humanity-corroding camp conditions, Emmanuel conceded, was near-miraculous. Slitter first began to pick up the hand symbols of readying preparedness on remnant recordings, a full year and seven months after their arrival. It would be five more weeks before those hands channelled the full efficacy of their training. Only one day prior to the attack, the other four hundred and thirty incarcerates were notified by the Jepawisat of the plan. Mainly African nationals, they pledged to a soul their support, and here it was not so improbable, with nothing to lose, that none played turncoat against their comrades in confinement.

With a combination of simple subterfuge and well-honed *wushu* skills, Jepawisat warriors eventually gained a toehold alongside their enemy, taking the detention facility in a swift, fierce battle before communications could be alerted. It had then remained only for the caterers to be cautioned and restrained, and for the surveillance bunker to radio the adjoining military base two kilometres distant that the shift change was due to proceed. Minutes later, two hover transports threaded through the little opening in the dome of continuous electrical netting around Pine Gap, each carrying thirty-five Jepawisat. The forty warders heading the other way were able to manage only a brief shift as they were greeted by nearly four hundred and eighty celebratory, battle-fevered refugees, many now armed.

Chapter 6

Of the second and most agonizingly bloody battle in the Australian revolution, out of the seven hundred heavily armed American military, and three hundred security personnel, only sixty lived to recount its details to Slitter. The Indonesians had split after entering the base, one hover pulling into the central parking lot. As watching security finally hit the alarms and jammed the doors, too late to stop them from being propped open, thirty-five men and women flowed into the warder's building in a seethe of staunchly calculated bloodwork.

Jepawisat armed only with stun lasers set the dials to high, and after two years of barbarous treatment from those guards, and generations of repression at the hands of world controllers, they lasered their heads into brief sparklers, demonstrating that a close stun to the cranium is terminal.

In one minute, half the hundred warders quartered in the compound had been felled, mostly weaponless. Despite no armour and fewer numbers, the rainforest warriors had gradually prevailed.

Those remaining at the detention centre raced towards the downed perimeter fence. Four of the Indonesians traced away from the dying battle to pilot hovers from the central bay. Each flew to evacuate the vulnerable parties at the detention camp — children, and the ageing, and certain technical crew at passenger loads of around thirty each hover. They left behind them over two hundred of their people trained and willing to brave death. Of the most skilled, Slitter had garnered that forty-three remained to fight.

With the power down, the most fearsome of the Gap's defence systems — high burst incinerator pulsers mounted on the two central towers — were useless. While the warders were being engaged, the Indonesian crew of the other hover had simply driven their craft toward the generator compound, slowed it to a trickle of speed, and leaped to a rooftop three metres below. From there, using flares they had requisitioned from the detention compound, they had blown their hover's magnetic seal when it was over the generators. As the shock blast faded they had unscrewed the roof's iron, removed its insulation, and using a pack of saws and rope, descended to the building's floor, upon which were parked two of the huge earthmoving machines used to construct and expand the warren of tunnels that was Pine Gap's greater extent.

Two of them could operate the metal moles. One lumbered out, expertly accelerating toward the detention gate, the other threaded through the compound buildings toward the central tower. Two guards fired a missile from a hand launcher that exploded harmlessly off the massive hulk. The mole crashed into the tower's base with a force that catapulted the two soldiers from its edge. With another ram to its foundation, the soldiers trapped at its top were pulped in the collapsing heap, which buried the mole and smashed across two satellite dishes. Emerging from the wreckage, the mole had been engaged by a Sacubus Interceptor — a double tiered triangular hover dedicating its lower tier to a magnetic inducer large enough to be able to support heavy machinery and weapons, the same trouble-shooters that Slitter had sent against the Eiterlindt girl.

The warship had descended, until at fifteen metres above the mole, it fired a burst of destabilised ions, destroying the digger's electric propulsion. The other mole had been driven to tunnel into Sector Three, then back out as the swarming refugees plunged into the opening, plugging the tunnel again with its bulk. As though to vent their frustration, the soldiers in the Sacubus fired steadily with diamondised armour-corroding missiles until the mole was shredded. Only then did they guess its pirate crew had escaped through its mounting hatch into the tunnel beneath.

The bulk of the hundreds of soldiers billeted in Sector Two were now flooding down into Sector Three, though some, believing that the threat came

48

from above, were loping toward the open night. Sector Three housed the interlinked computer banks that controlled almost all the satellites in both deep and shallow orbit around the Earth. The backup generators had routed all power. It was a troglodyte realm, its roof impregnated with zinc for psychic exclusion, through which deeps huge python-like cables made a haphazard branching amid projecting spheres of stasis glass for chaotic orbit simulations.

The government force's superior shielding and weaponry were little aid in such a tight melee.

Amid the computer banks, the Jepawisat's gas-masked technicians began to reach their goal from two separate programming consoles. A tall hacker printed out a sheet of paper, quickly secreted by one of the two operatives behind him. He sifted through a flurry of pictures on the oversized screen alongside, making colours around a building pulse intermittently. This was then repeated for other images of buildings.

The hacker on the opposite side of the room worked in conjunction with two women who wore electric clips on their heads, seated at a swivelling apparatus with little keypads at the end of each armrest. They stared into a series of crystal chambers decreasing in size that were hollowed into a metal proboscis mounted just below eye level. From the end of these instruments several wires descended into the floor. As the other team approached to watch, the hacker brought intersecting lines on his screen together until a complex geometric model appeared.

Following a series of feverishly typed information, each line began to glow. Finally a small hologram of a proboscis swivel chair appeared at each corner of the screen. The hacker plugged a cord from a briefcase in his lap into the computer, and began to thermally mould the information on the large module, drawing information across the screen by skimming his hands over cloth pads on the desktop. Suddenly, the screen flashed ninety-eight per cent success. Its body motor whirred, and the two swivels shook, then the screen went blank.

The technical teams then followed their armed detail into a panelled room alongside the main passage. An operator pressed buttons on a tabletop, referring to a newly printed sheet, and a door at the room's end slid open. Four of the armed Jepawisat stepped through, then the eleven technical crew, then two more armed guards. Once inside, the door slid closed, and lights sprang on around the little crowd. All flung gas masks to the ground and looked at each other, those hated eyes wide with knowing, the foreign faces etched in a thick jelly of trepidation, before descending the thin spiral staircase in front of them.

Then had come a new terror. The earth began to tremble and a massive craft rose out of the ground behind the refugees. A war hover a thirty metres high and more wide. From her round, impregnably armoured side laser canons had extended, as though to test their efficacy on this her maiden battle. The Jepawisat inside targeted groups, or single troops on a computer scope before them. Within a minute, only those Americans who had fled on instinct, or who huddled behind the warehouse, remained alive. The rest had been made an ashen powder by a craft that only a double handful of people had even known existed. The surviving five-score of Indonesians and Africans climbed up a rubber moulded stairway, and the hover ascended above The Gap. In a sudden blaze of red-yellow light, she disappeared. One of only three prototype Herovers in existence had been stolen, and within half an hour it had on board another two thousand refugees from detention centres in the Carpentarian Gulf and Western Farm.

As all electromagnetic security systems and communications had mysteriously failed, the warders did not even realise the threat until the Herover had plied the roofs from the northern compounds with her grapples.

"We are going to the New Australia," the refugees were told by the battered crew, "to the land of the free."

There Slitter's account of things became more intimate.

That May dawn, the news barked at him across the phone had confirmed his grimmest fears. Using access to the war-sat system, the Jepawisat had destroyed every inner-orbit monitoring and war satellite. In the outer orbits all units had been shunted off course into a dead trajectory for the remaining tenure of their metal integrity. Even unrelated communication satellites had sustained a ninety per cent malfunction. Without deep orbit mapping, no one could be certain where the Jepawisat had holed up. "But there's a base near Natandy that picked up a large, high speed blip," said the Poise, "looking like a match. And as it seems they've chosen to camp out at your place, you get the job of throwing them back in the sea!"

Slitter had dialled off, his mind a blurred fever with the information he had woken to. Of course nobody in W.A.R.'s intelligence services knew that the Jepawisat's annihilative hacking had not destroyed all the war-sats. Setting out to recapture the Herover, or destroy it and to expunge the insurgents, Slitter had commanded a vast force. One thousand Special Forces soldiers, the pilots and gunners of two hundred Sacubus fighters, twenty Behemoth troop carriers, two fibrillating laser canons, fourteen Agate jets on conventional fuel, and two dozen sniffer dogs with handlers.

At eleven hundred hours, as the sun's heat was beginning to caruscade off the surrounding mountains, Slitter met with his rendezvous of three thousand troops on armed hover-bikes, gathered from the hard desert camps in Quaintsand and Western Farm, and gave his briefing in the valley bowl. Two of the Behemoths carrying the Special Forces would accompany the bikes, while the remainder would be escorted by the Agates until troop deployment was commenced, then scout for the enemy's location. The Sacubus would remain at base camp against the chance they needed to destroy the Herover, which they had been rearmed to do. The craft would probably be recaptured where the monkeying refugees had left it, unable to reconfigure its charge mechanisms, Slitter had assured them.

Before the Behemoths departed he had given his final address.

"As soon as we have aerial confirmation of where these scum are, I want to see heads caved in. Anyone holding back'll wear my boot for a liver. These people have nobly vacated their accommodation for others that will no doubt soon arrive, so we can't be bringing back prisoners to confuse things. And nobody touch my fish or game!"

The bikes were arranged into two columns, himself at the head of one. At eleven hundred and twenty-three hours the columns roared off, with Slitter feeling ebullient. They were a little to the west of his holdings. He knew these hunting grounds. On the escarpment they paused to mount the fibrillator cannons on two eroded mountains that commanded passes Slitter factored as the terrorists' likely routes of retreat, and from where their operators could target any unauthorised movement on the ground below.

Emmanuel had then halted to deploy two groups of dogs and handlers with an escort afoot, so as to capture any seeking escape further afield. At eleven hundred and thirty-one hours, Slitter was triumphant — the Agate pilots radioed confirmation that they had pinpointed the terrorists. At eleven hundred and thirty-three hours, a concentrated beam of atoms shorn of their polarity instantly destroyed the Sacubus fighters where they lay in the valley bowl. The Indonesians had employed their insurance, once again. Their little briefcase controlled the only war-sat not destroyed — the largest and most heinous — Mouth.

No one had informed Slitter of reports which had already begun to come through that morning of the World American Reform cruisers missing from the north Pacific Ocean. The eight battle ships, along with four hundred robotic monitoring platforms that had enforced exclusion zones — cleaning a million refugees from the ocean each year — were no more. The automated roaming platforms were dust, but whoever had operated the final sequencing had deliberately aimed wide of the naval destroyers, the terrorists proven human after all in extending to the crews a fighting chance. The huge ships had been sunk in towering waves rather than being evaporated by space beams.

With float suits and luck, many of the sailors had survived. Though some, Slitter knew, had intimately appreciated those shadowed shapes circling beneath. Before noon the main work of conquering northern Australia and conquassating the world was replete.

Slitter had lost before he had even begun to order the Agates not to engage the huge craft. Whipping through large rocks, with the screams of his troops all about him, Slitter had no doubt been diving recklessly toward just such a fate when he pulled up to take the call from a Sacubus pilot who had escaped. The refugees caught only a few bikes that day, but though Special Forces, deployed along the rivers, were instructed to fully withdraw, only two hundred emerged. None of the missing, or even one of the dog teams, were ever seen again.

Seated before his monitor, Slitter continues to stare, the look of absorption glazing his eyes in memory slowly fading. His palms scuff the thermal pads before him, shifting images from the whole south side of the city. His uncanny instinct for weakness had only failed him once, but never would again. It had led him to luck his whole life, as it had in tracing the Eiterlindt girl — Sway, the data bank had named her. It seemed the sucking Amazon had some luck, but he had the might of amassed technology and a singularly focused population that had entrenched itself in insurmountable security measures since the revolution. She was still on his turf; he was sure of it. Somewhere before him lay the clue that would give her back to him and then he would pare and quarter her brain for use in his new cyber labs.

A day ago, when he had seen all the screens before him narrowing to a figure on a rooftop prison, Slitter's suspicions had been whirring. As he had idly noted the pulses on a map indicating security beginning to deploy their hovers eight floors below, so he began pursuing recent recordings of surrounding buildings. On the front of the file was one oddment listed as exploded solarium, and he saw the indistinct wide-angle frame of pigeons fleeing in fright. But there were four thousand individual recordings of balconies showing the details he needed, sourced from the three apartments surrounding the current crime scene.

He isolated only those with student occupants. He had a hunch, based on what the marshals had told him in the corporate planning tower, that a young assailant meant a student. For some reason he decided that she had used a balcony screening, as improbably remote as the security measures made that. The computer found four hundred and sixty matches with a satisfied purr. He had it show only those which had recorded movement in the past fifteen minutes. There were seven matches.

In the first, an obviously overweight couple were desultorily playing with a head hover. They were making a travesty of one of his game inventions, Slitter thought, as he scanned a man dressed as a king, giving a rehearsal straight at the lens. The overflow of a bondage party, a girl leaning against a rail as another seemed to sleep in the background, and another three that were equally useless. Before Slitter could swear, he had sneezed violently, his hand slewing across the pad, the computer following his involuntary movement. It had blown up the middle frame and shown a girl's foot with a vodka bottle in the background. Just before stalking off he noticed a red flashing cursor in the screen corner and traced its message.

"The bottle in recording 5H9D2 has already been extinguished in waste unit, suggest reappearance contravenes clause three of the domestic litter direct and may indicate illegal reselling as fake commodity."

"No it doesn't!" Slitter boomed. He knew what it meant. A ruse to make the slumped girl seem drunk from a cursory monitoring. His secretary informed him that the suspect was escaping, but wolverine-like, Emanuel Slitter watched the balcony. Shortly a hover pulled up — his personal unit — four men leaping out.

"We need to know where she's going," Slitter instructed into his headpiece: the Agents pounded into the building. In less than a minute he had the news.

"Dirt traces show only one restricted area — the old botanica compound." The Poise One simply gave an order, flicked to a monitor of the gardens quadrant, and sat back to watch...

Now he looks at the same quadrant again, his whole being acerbically reaching for a weakness.

Chapter 7

Cuthpertson tried not to let his fear show. He pulled Windrewally across to him through the smoke of his last retort. As the translator stumbled out of his crouch, and the gloved hands, like some octopus prying open a shell, pulled his black ones from his ears then pinned the bare shoulders, the expedition leader shouted.

"Him no longer come away. He come true and true me give him pot, knife, button."

Windrewally called again, in vain, towards the twisted scrub on the plain.

"Phorcus blight me! That is a droll ensuance. Well, the mules and the two convicts shall become concomitant with the loosed articles." There were only two mules left, apart from the dried bits of the others in the supply. Those three had floundered, lamed by the rocky ground, and been butchered; another had since succumbed to poisoning, plant or reptile.

Ben looked ruefully at the sprawl of water bottles and cookware the trackers had dumped. They had come across the footprints of a party of natives for the second time, these now much fresher. The trackers had cried "yallanded" to Windrewally and turned heel.

Ben straightened resignedly, with a new burden from the pile by which Windrewally stood, transfixed by a look of baffled trepidation. The Irish botany assistant inquired of the lean shy man about the word the deserters had yelled, and Windrewally stirred briefly to eyeball him angrily.

"The Yallanded — spirit takers!"

The indentured convict took his bundle of pots over to the rest of the things by Director Bullark, who turned stoically to him and asked, "All very good, Ben?"

The two had become friends in the last few months of bevying across the wilds, but Ben replied with the honorific, "All very well, sir."

"Only the few steely, polished souls shall brave the unknown tracts, hey?" his master asked rhetorically. They stared out before them across the escarpment his comment referenced. Dry river beds tumbled broken down steep hills into the nearly dry gorge below, and humps of reddled rock trailed in chaotic bleakness back along the stagnant course of the waterway that diverged before disappearing into the blue pewter of the horizon. In the foreground, squat domes of basalt hills were spaced around corroded mountains. Ancient volcanoes huffed rounded heads about the distance, hued smoky black, or a burned umber as their ore meted.

A mule groaned and heaved upright. Major Bindlar threw back his shoulders, crop swishing at the endless flies, and the cavalcade continued its tortuous proceedings. Trusting to the stultified derangement of their noble leader's mind, thought Ben, just as all of Britain tailed scrabbling after the lunacies of order and progress. Ben wondered again for what reason he had been born upon the doorstep of their cretinous asylum. He lacked, though, the energy to curse his fate.

After watering the mules in the gorge bed, they walked upriver the rest of the day through a silent world called to life again only by the knock of stone underfoot, and the flailing swish of spinifex against their legs. In a little amphitheatre of raised sand off the waterway, they stopped to prepare camp where a dry creek bed — green banked from the shadow and seep of the stern cliff mass it clove — met the gorge.

Here a host of butterflies arose like curious fairies among the group, their velvet brown, red, and purple wings luxuriant with the light in the chasm. Even the usually suspicious Collins could see no veiled threat in their splendour. In the morning the Director found more wonders along the side stream. Ben followed him to where he stood suffused in the volatile aroma of white and yellow flowers pendent beneath deep green leaves. Around these the butterflies congregated in a flickering grace. Bullark showed him the spiral trunk where the vine began, then picked some pods of seed which he placed, together with a single folded screed of sketches and notes, into a tin.

"This I shall call butterfly vine, Ben," he declared in a dreamy voice, handing his aide the tin to stow with their collection.

That day the party of nineteen halted early. At mid-afternoon they were divvied on one side of the gorge, where all the cliffs had eroded into blunt intermittent mounds. On the wide stretching sands lay most of the soldiers. Sprawled beneath clumps of tall melaleuca and denser cottonwood trees, they played cards in two groups. A few were horsing in the edenic swimming hole which dipped a deep transparent emerald from the white shore. Amid snorting and splashing, they chorused a ribald song that retorted loudly along the opposite cliff bank. The Director was enmeshed with his sketchbook and an orchid he had cornered. Windrewally and Ben had slipped off to go hunting, both inspired by the taste of a wallaby at lunch, which a soldier had accrued with his rifle. Major Bindlar Cuthpertson, together with Collins and Captain Williams, amid the stone mounds, were pattering about after the geologist.

At each new cave in the warren they would angle a mirror to push sunlight inside, and Spunts would talk appreciatively of these ancient labyrinths, occasionally chiselling out a sample or sifting amid the cave floor. When they came to a place downstream where the gorge had bored a little channel right through the stone, the eyes lit in Spunts' grey-flecked, beaver-like face.

"Remarkable. This looks igneous!"

Collins smirked to hear the man's pronunciation of 'ingenious'.

Just then rang out shots. With ears cocked in curiosity, the men turned downstream. A sudden volley of four more shots had the party moving. Bindlar, armed like the captain, led the group camp-ward at a quick, orderly pace.

"It is ever the sciences, Mr Spunts, must suffer whilst barbaric chaos rules the day," chided their leader over a shoulder, the pale-faced geologist watching ruefully the pebbles that spilled from Bindlar's jouncing shirt pocket. Soon they heard the sound of yelling and through the trees glimpsed movement on the distant beach. A black arm poked through a palm bush, and as they watched pulled a black head and torso over the sand rise. Captain Williams steadied a bullet between the man's eyes.

"Dashed good shooting ther — " begun Bindlar, when next a spear was wobbling in the air where it hung from his breastbone a moment before he toppled on it.

Williams backed toward a paperbark, loading his musket, but a large aboriginal calmly stepped up to him, knocked aside his gun butt with a shield, and swung a long club with a satisfied grunt into the side of his head. As the geologist fell beside him with a spear through the jaw, twitching in shock, Collins stared at the growing number of spearmen angling toward him and began to yell.

"Windrewally, maybe you'll have to cook, like the women, as you not a hunter man," jibed Ben, and then remembering again, he let out the big belly laughs he had been convulsed by for the whole walk back.

"Might come," his new friend agreed half-heartedly, his early fountain of self-humouring laughter now exhausted. Ben decided he should tamp his frivolity as they were nearing camp and he concentrated on the cool weight of Windrewally's spear in his hand, and not the string of game they both took turns in carrying. But it had been funny.

Twice the aboriginal hunter had been done out of his quarry. Once, at a rustle in the high grass, he had dodged, dropped his spear and pounced in manner of a cat. He stood to hold out a mightily struggling perentie lizard. He had the gloriously gilt-mottled creature's metre-plus length pinned in front of him, a hand around its neck and tail, vicious claws forward. Suddenly a brown-gold shadow leaped from a nearby tree and with the slap of one massive wing about the translator's head, the wedgetail had wrenched the prize away.

It was good perentie country though, and Ben had bagged one by the river with his friend's spear. They had stolen along by a stretch of water, shallow and sandy, and Windrewally found what he was after. In a narrow recess of rock a catfish was hemmed with only a marginal route of escape. Windrewally, spear raised, edged into deeper flowing water to cut it off, but had yelled, falling back on the sandy bank and clutching a foot, as with a panicked slither the fish blubbered past him. He had stepped on another catfish. That left a little row of punctured marks with its tail in his tough foot. So Ben had got their two catfish as well, Windrewally laughing by the time the Cork County man had returned, but still rubbing the foot.

How unlucky could one person get? thought Ben. It was then that they came upon the multiply-speared body of Collins. Grimaced in animal fury, the face seemed twisted out away from the body in desperation, as though reaching up for air from too far below the surface of a pool. With each muscle in their bodies attuned to the danger around them, the pair ran in a tumult of adrenaline, recoiling from the spectre.

"Up through that ladder-way, might get it safe." Windrewally nodded to a crack in the sandstone about five hundred yards distant, as they splashed across to the far bank.

Both men had seen the same sets of footprints on the sandy bank, however, and knew theirs was a desperate hope. They struggled in the thick grass and vines of the broken country, tripping on overgrown stones and pulling down rotten logs around them, heaving bodily toward the steeper rocks. Ben had the ironic thought that for the first time in eighteen years he was now a free man. His master and all the rest would certainly have been slaughtered by the massive war party whose tracks were all along the river.

Then there was no chance for thought as he followed Windrewally up a face of vertical stone, bloodying his knuckles trying to find purchase on the flaky rock. On a slender ledge, fighting for foot space with the strap-leafed orchids nearly a hundred yards up, they halted. Ben's limbs felt like they were filled with burning oil, while his heart was an icy stalactite that threatened to crash to the ground. They remained long enough to watch dark figures cross the river and run up below them, yelling triumphantly as they thrust into the overgrown gap.

Ben and Windrewally turned again to the cliff, and each upward scrambled metre was a miracle of the interlocking precision of physics. As their bodies, pressed flat and contorted like appendaged snakes, began in each muscle to overbalance downwards, the stone itself would present some tiny crevasse that their sentient fingers could crawl into, prolonging their continuing writhe. Until eventually they came to where the stone could be grasped by the elbows, and so slumped trembling onto that staunch parapet. The stone beneath Ben's cheek seemed to draw his heaving grunts of supplication down to its roots. Far below, the hunters stalked. Windrewally peered over the edge.

"Might be they only wait we come fall, now come up new place."

Ben could see the band retreating up the gorge and looked across at the aboriginal. Their instinctive urgency of understanding had shifted into one of more tact. Ben's sigh of base determination measured its strength between them. They stood. Thick scrub and rock crowded around them. Ben felt like a child who had become trapped in someone else's dream.

His face was gouged by bushes, legs crushed upon hidden stones as he scrambled after Windrewally. Along a wallaby trail he followed the strong brown legs. It led them hinged-forward beneath the twisting canopy of wattle and tea-tree, or belly-crawling under collapsed dusty old vegetation. He was careful to move as precisely as the dark body before him, so as not to ruffle vegetation or crack logs, though his shoulder-length red hair and beard were constantly snagged by plants: seeming allies of his pursuers.

Once Windrewally, allowing interim halt, showed him a rock-capped well of water trapped in a stone outcrop where they plunged hands to drink. Then on again amid the feet of the scrub and its traitor fingers until they went loping down a gravelly decline, finally able to go upright as the pad broadened through dense but squat cabbage gums, its greater definition owed to larger animals or a convergence of game pads. The rolling hill country scrolled aside its drapes of gum to flourish scattered tea-trees with broad crowns, dotting flower-strewn grasses, and Windrewally soon found a dry creek bed to follow.

At last satisfied, he slowed to a walking pace and Ben marvelled that he had brought them so quickly away from the gorge without pause even to espy landmarks. Lying that night in a hollow between sandy humps formed by the straight ribbon of a dry river, Ben knew their mental and physical reserve was fading, and they had not even a spear with which to point their hope.

In the bright light of late morning, Ben woke to screaming. He rolled to his feet, greeted by the unflinching asperity of four spearmen surrounding him. The closest spoke, each with spear trained still in his direction, in hurried conversation with a grizzled old man. The others shifted eyes between him, the elder, and their spears. Finally, the still-muscled elder approached the lanky Irishman, the hint of a smile offsetting his aquiline gaze. He reached a hand to trace the red halo of Ben's hair.

"Terndi Calutren," he said, turning back to the others, who visibly relaxed. "Uprae Wanon," he intoned. He caught Ben's eyes and nodded that he should come with them. Helplessly, Ben stepped alongside the aged leader. The four spearmen still loosely encircled him as they pranced along the riverbed. The Irishman glimpsed only the inert legs of his friend tangled in some bushes as they passed, but he stepped determinedly through the hummocked sand, imagining Windrewally's death mask one of pride.

Toward night they came to a camp overbrimming with children and unnervingly sly dogs. Here they had reconverged with the gorge, but further upstream. The water was flowing genially; some contributing spring reinvigorating it, and it was across its lively flow that Ben was taken the next morning. To a place surpassing with its magical rapture even the premonitory phantasms of his dreams, its wonders easing somewhat his heart thorn for his friend, and explaining this people's behaviour.

The wrinkled hand of his redeemer, white-haired, coal-eyed Dorraking, had shaken him from those dreams and a remarkably deep sleep beneath kangaroo skins at the chilly birth of new day. The elder's mood had been friendly but expectantly insistent. A fire ripening amid the camp's grass-covered shelters betrayed its tender — a woman bending to get wood in the near distance. She turned deliberately away when she glimpsed them, so only a dingo observed their passage, pattering awhile along the river behind, until they turned up a sparsely treed rise, keeping a brisk pace against the cold.

Before the ochres of the day began to warm them, they progressed through jumbles of rock-crowned hills. At a little defile, Dorraking then steered the stranger down to a bog of cutting grasses and thick scrub, along which they ploughed until another defile emerged. Now the shine of frog eggs lay ever beneath them in the damp, water-smoothed cutting, and except that he could touch either side of the rock chasm, Ben feared that he would tumble head over heels. Where this chute widened, his guide climbed the lesser wall, and they emerged into a thick trickling waterway pitting its course through the great blocks and cracks of the hill.

This larger stream, fed by springs finding vent in the rock, soon became a complication of waist-deep, tear-shaped pools to be waded through, stacked in terraces tinkling with dripping moisture and overhung by rock figs. Now at last it seemed they could go no further, for they stood on the edge of a sheer drop down to a clear green pool — a bowl thirty yards across — into which spilled the runnel of water under their feet that would be a torrent after rain. From this height, parts of the gorge were visible, its floor a sunlit tapestry of curling splendour.

Dorraking sighed easily then raised his eyes comically, and leaped into the deep sinkhole. He gave a youthful bark of triumph as he surfaced and beckoned Ben to follow. Luckily Ben had mastered swimming in the lagoon at the gardens, and after a pause, he too was surfacing next to the delighted Dorraking. The water was cool, only being grazed by sun, but of such crystal definition as to hold an alluring attraction.

Dorraking tapped his chest, then nodded to Ben. He mimed diving under the pool and resurfacing, and Ben watched the brown body frog-swim to the big boulders at the waterfall and then disappear. Marking the spot, Ben dived and found himself, after fear's little press, surfacing on the other side of the rock in a chamber of wildering grandeur. As they sat on the floor of red sand by the hollowly lapping water, bright shafts of purple and gold light played about the walls, and refracting off the ripples, dazzled Ben's eyes.

Along the cave walls grew glowing mushrooms, emitting a thin light magnified by the thousands of crystals projecting from the rock and littering the sand, some as big as a man. Through this kaleidoscope, in patches bereft of crystals, strode a host of whimsical creatures painted on the stone. Dorraking was sitting now, eyes closed, occasionally intoning softly.

The first of the imagery catching Ben's eye was a bolt of lightning that had lodged in a figure's stomach. From this huge-eyed giant, humans received sticks of fire in a long procession. A crocodile rested its feet on two glowing stars while tiny brown figures walked across its back. Women with the tails of fishes, a picture that Ben recognised as pyramids and a pharaoh; hunters around the vast speared head of a long necked, flippered creature — and then he saw it.

Standing in a whirlwind of energy, arms thrown out, was a figure with red hair and a red beard. On its stomach was a long burl of scar — the same scar

Ben traced on his own stomach — the legacy of a sword thrust from a drunken nobleman during the Irishman's early penal confinement.

"Terndi Calutren," said Dorraking, coming up behind him. He shook his head as though to empathise with Ben's incredulous amazement.

Months later he thought of how impossible it seemed that he had been saved purely because a gifted seer had seen him coming and recorded it in time beyond recollect. There were prophets in Europe whose visionary ability had stirred much interest in the tribunes of his day. The fact that his likeness had been prophesied into the cave revered by the tribe had saved him. His new miraculous life was filled now with camp chores, learning the language and culture, and refining his hunting skills, so that he had little time to dwell on other strange things he had seen in the chamber, or on the vortexed halo of energy around the figure depicting himself.

The tribe called themselves Yallanded, which meant not spirit takers, but spirit waterers. Their reputation for fierceness came from an implacable defence of their territory — namely the galleries of the gorge surrounds. Dorraking told him that a great race of ancestor beings had charged the tribe with protection of the pictures they had made. Indeed, Ben had only been taken to the wondrous pool as an uninitiate because of the exactitude of his resemblance.

The Irishman's initiation had begun a month ago, when his grasp of the language had been deemed sufficient. The prior description Dorraking had given, mirthfully malicious, had been a doom of foreboding, but when the grouped men in the stone-ringed clearing had parted for the medicine man, it had proved an agony he could command. Quickly the mussel shell had cut away his foreskin and the mud-pack compress he had been urged to reapply had fallen away to a clean scar. In a few days his naming initiation would begin. With the dark of the Moon, he was to be taken to live alone for three months in what the tribe thought of as the wild — there to survive on his skills.

These thoughts swum lazily as the waters of the little billabong flowed slowly over the sand-and-log flood jam. Indeed less than half of Ben's attention was on shaping and hardening his spear over the fire before him. After ten months among these people, Ben's body was tanned around the loin skin he wore, and his hair, pulled back with a strip of woven bark, was matted like most of the men's. To an outsider, looking across the camp to the main fire and the dozen old men and women talking or crafting about it whilst women and children were scattered along the watercourse under the big tea-trees, it would seem the muscled back of the man on the creek bank, hunched in spear-making, was that of a warrior left to guard the camp.

But Ben knew the tribe saw him differently. He wondered if even his naming initiation would much bridge the gap between them. With half an eye he watched Ngenlin, her smooth-limbed body purposefully gathering river shellfish into a bark bag slung over one shoulder, already sagging with the cache. She paused a moment and looked toward him. Did her eyes relax a little in her long graceful face? Ben knew that the man to whom she had been given was long dead from crocodile predation. Though beyond this seeming availability, a complex of hidden associations silently taxed the natural affection the two shared, muting its acknowledgment. Not the least of these was his status. Uninitiated, he was still a boy in the eyes of tribal lore.

Kederayn, Dorraking's nephew, disappeared over the slight rise. He would travel fast to re-join the tribe who were returning to their gorge camp for the dry season.

The hunting had been good and the fishing abundant in these plains and creeks closer to the coast, but now they needed a more permanent water source. Also, with the greater mobility allowed by the dry, the galleries would be vulnerable to the incursions of other tribes. Ben had been taken somewhere roughly between the two camps. Kederayn would return in three months to collect him, if he survived. He had been assured there was permanent water in the area, and no frequency of hostile tribes. The chance of their encounter, however, remained.

Ben looked around him, breathing deep a conglomerate of scents dominated by hot grass. By mid-afternoon he had found water in a rock ledge from which he surveyed his surrounds. Sandy river beds cut through thinly vegetated plains on which large trees might be quickly counted. In the distance he saw, on a slope of red hillside, the deep green ribbons that would be either rock figs or palms — either meant food, and possibly water.

Next morning he journeyed the remnant kilometres to the red hill and found one tree with a good supply of figs, and two palms small enough for him to knock over and eat their hearts. He used the palm detritus to build a little sun shelter at the sandy foot of a nearby cliff dripping moisture. After warily scouting for signs of strangers, he thought it would be safe to camp a few days and set out to fill the larder. That night he returned with a wallaroo he had cornered in a rock soak on the other side of the hill. He had just enough energy to set a fire and cook it.

When he had marked seven days on his spear, Ben began to feel a pressing loneliness, but also a true sense of independence. He fell asleep with a million stars in his head, the smoke from his neat fire keeping back the bulk of the insects. In the cold before dawn he woke from an unpleasant dream of stepping into a giant rotted pumpkin, and moved to blow life into the coals. With clammy but calm knowledge, Ben knew what was disabling his legs. He had seen big pythons but nothing the size of what had engorged him up to his knees. As though to offset his little twist of struggle, the snake's jaws tensed, then rolled a little further along him.

Ben's spear was out of reach by the fire. His root club lay to one hand and slowly he grasped it, knowing if the first strike failed to kill, the snake would crush with cold coils to silence its prey. He looked beyond the huge head and saw its tail lay in the little cleft where he collected water. He had often pondered as he sat by the fire a certain stone which jutted irregularly from the rock face above this cleft. In a sort of juvenile levity, he had imagined the result should he overbalance it with a stern blow.

He fixed in his mind's eye the precise place on the rock face to strike, pushed up with one hand and heaved his club. The serpent shook him to the ground in annoyance but the next instant his club struck true and a mass of stone slid down the face, crushing the python's spine. In its first moment of shock, he pulled his legs from its jaws and crawled back to watch it writhe, brushing coals from his legs that its frenzied spasms had scattered as its massive head reared up twice his height in a final outstretching convulsion.

Ben's legs were too numb to support him, but he grabbed his spear in case it should wriggle free. It soon sagged though, and as the sun began to rise, he watched the python's eyes glaze. What a fool he had been. He had been cautioned not to camp near rock holes and caves, but had thought it tribal superstition. He wondered of the boy's fate lost in an initiation five years prior. Ben studied his legs and was relieved to find most of the skin intact, apart from ugly red tracts on his feet. Patiently he rinsed water from the cliff drip over the muck on his skin.

When he had cleared the rocks off the leviathan, he dragged it out of the defile and calibrated it at over five lengths of his spear, which was a hand taller than him. In a few hours Ben smiled to himself as the chunk of tail fillet he had cooked restored his energy, and he set about the day's chores. Painstakingly, he removed and dragged the head and skin up into a rock fig where the ants might clean it for him. With a huge string of meat for drying, dripping gore down his back, and entrained by flies, he left to find a camp away from the carcass before dusk fell.

Time passed amid the wonder of the wilderness. The behaviour of the birds transformed through his eye and ear into an extrasensory portraiture of the land. He could tell the alarm for a hunting lizard given out by the iridescent parrots, while the large cockatoos spiralled toward wind patterns still un-manifest upon the plain. Flitting red finches led him to where the wild grain could be stripped into a bark sheath to crush for bread. The webs of spiders spoke also to him, a snapped thread signing the flight of game, a snared butterfly wing betokening a nearby spring.

It was while camped beside one so discovered spring, arising from a chalken base in a riot of reeds, flowers, herbs, and flash of birds, that Ben came literally within a whisker of death once more. A little after sunrise, the six warriors spotted the smoke from his fire, and half an hour after that, Ben's spring was surrounded. He saw them burst through the whippy scrub towards his fire, spears poised in deadly anticipation. But they found only flattened grass where he had slept, and a dying fire.

Sure enough, the scouts he had been expecting soon drew in with report of his tracks crossing the spring in the direction of the nearby rocky bluff. The warriors wheeled away toward the rocky outcrop and Ben threw his spear to the ground and emerged from high in a hollow tree. United with his weapon, he began to run for his life — with the hours his track may have gained to give him hope. As it proved, he did lose the strangers, though he was tracked into steep country, and it was days before he could no longer see their smoke curl above his hunting plain.

The birds had saved him. Gathering fuel for his fire according his dawn habit, he had seen a woodswallow pass some nesting material to its mate, then fly to the water and back whence it had come. Something about the bold ridge on the narrow leaf caught his eye. He was certain it was a pandanus, of which this area boasted no population. A prize from a tatty dilly bag?

It was folly to count on them not already having spotted his smoke, in which case he had known they would surely reach the spring soon. He threw his fuel on the fire, and crossed the spring. He walked the hundred metres to the rocky rise, and scattering a handful of sand upon the stone, ever so carefully walked backward into his footprints — his integration with his body allowing him to refill each step perfectly. By the time he re-joined the spring half an hour later, his legs had ached from the unnatural precision.

He retrieved his spear, and standing on an old log, was just able to climb into the low branches of a cottonwood, and from there shimmy upward by dispersing his weight with equilateral pressure on two whippy tea-trees, and reach the hollow's opening. Grasping thin knots of wood, spear in mouth, he flipped into the rough hiding place. He managed to wedge his spear as a kind of shelf beneath him, and find two tenuous handholds moments before the warriors barged into the clearing. After some minutes his lapsing purchase threatened to spill him into the jagged tunnel, and it was only by thrusting his beard down through a cracked knot that he could support most of his weight with his head until the tribesmen had gone.

Ben heard the loud call of greeting and opened one eye where he sprawled in the sun, head propped against an ironwood, near the predetermined meeting point.

He waited for Kederayn to speak, as was proper.

"Greetings, Tanilla." Tanilla was nameless one. "The tribe seeks your spear arm that it may hunt in strength."

Ben answered that he would return to hunt, and the two fell into carefree banter. As they talked, Kederayn saw the snake skull behind the tree and picked it up in wonder. Ben had saved only a few large strips of skin in a bark bag, as it had been mostly consumed by rats. He recounted his story, and the tale of avoiding the warriors, and Kederayn laughed that such an ugly red brute could easily have scared them away without need to hide.

Ben's rapture at being amid people again was genuinely returned by the tribe. Dorraking clasped his arm beamingly, and his portly old gin had cried, "our red son is come back to us." Ngenlin smiled widely at him while children eddied about, Kederayn's young girl hugging herself around his legs. The nights were spent feasting on hawk and catfish while Ben's exploits were danced.

Muldangan, the medicine doctor, wore the great snake's head and mimed the writhing death Ben had given it. The children who had screeched in terror of the snake, rolled in the grass with laughter next night, as the strange tribesmen were portrayed bursting into the empty camp, while Muldangan mimed clinging to a tree by his teeth.

After some days, Ngenlin sat with Ben beside the fire for a while. She pressed a smooth stone into his palm upon which she had carved a brolga — her dreaming totem. As he did not yet have a dreaming, Dorraking informed him the next day, a gift of food would stipulate their intended union. When Ben passed the wood ducks to her family, he felt so light-headed he brushed absently at a bull ant biting his arm, and then leaped in anguish as it stung him viciously. Ngenlin laughed richly from where she sat pounding reeds. Still it was only when his initiation was complete that he might lie with her. He knew the next testing would be intense, and could take over a year. He felt eager for it to begin.

Ben stared incredulously at the faces of the seated semicircle of elders before him. Once again they had brought him to the dancing ring delineated with stones, the ring where stars were given true names, and where over many long cold nights he had been taught their songs. Only once before had he been here in the day. Surrounded by smoke and dancers with talking bones, the Yallanded medicine man had passed him tiny skeletons; bones that had seemed to speak of kilometres, to yield a sigh, or press of coming winds long before such had blown across the circle.

This was no council of spirit powers or esoterica. It was to homage the totem animals, and to watch rock, dirt, blood and the way of man. For Ben had no dreaming totem, no animal ancestor to bind him to the land and the lore of the tribe. So after all this time and all he had done, they were going to spear him. A portion of him reviled against them, wryly questioning what else he had expected from such barbarous savages. Fundamentally he empathised with their position. They had never needed to ascertain a person's dreaming, it being given by that of the parents, and portents of the birth. It was thought that an animal would show itself on the hunt. The best warriors were assembled, but would arm with the smaller and blunter children's spears. Very unlikely to kill but most certain to maim.

Ben shuddered. This was the reckoning. If he were speared on the lower body, his dreaming was of a small creature: lizard, snake, quoll, the exact totem to be determined by closer examination of the wound and skin around it. Ben's skin twitched. If on the upper body, a kangaroo; if in the middle, an emu for certain. "You see," explained Yatchelomy good-heartedly, "this spear will tell everything truly. Might be you get one near the back, so that's echidna — we'll find out, whatever it is."

The others had nodded at this wise understanding of representative magic. "You can't die, anyway," he continued, "still got to hold a sky fire spirit, like it shows in the rock picture. Or maybe you can, but you come back again quickly."

The hunters had already left, each following a different line parallel to the billabong. A minute later the council gestured to him, and Ben sprang with alacrity toward the billabong to capitalise on his little lead, leaving a rustle, then silence behind.

If he could reach the river safely, his must be a water totem, and he had only to capture fish, turtle or crocodile to find which. He moved cautionless of noise, gauging that the hunters would be well away from hearing, as they had been mandated to walk in a straight line until the signal. Ben now heard that signal — the distant booming of a bullroarer — and the hunt was truly on. He reined his pace into one of steady compromise, vigilant against crushing branches underfoot.

He had the advantage of a lead, and although they knew the land better, he had a cogent point driving him. He did not want to nurse some flaring kidney wound into old age! The yammer of a cockatoo on the flats betrayed the likelihood of a fast runner cutting off the best approach to the river. Ben skirted into rockier country. Running steady, rhythmically, his fear enterprised into constant checks of smell, hearing and navigation. The Irish was achieving clarity, feeling confident of reaching his goal.

His reverie shattered as Mundjerie slipped from behind a rock, and threw straight at him — a blow that could have punctured his chest had not he dived onto the stones. How had the hunter tracked him? He veered off, up the ridge of a small escarpment that was all now separating him from the river. Sure enough, his instinct to shun the trees was proved right by the two hunters streaking into vision from the broken country he had just been in. He had a clear view all around here, and a good lead.

Needing only a descent from this rock to reach his goal, Ben could not remember where the gullies were. He was forced to run close along the ridge edge, so tracking over flinty country and losing his lead. He streamed along a slow decline of stone, chest gory with the little rips from his earlier evasion, hoping he might somewhere here find a pass. A glance showed his three pursuers virtually within spear range.

Perhaps it was that he half believed what old Yatchelomy said about his fate lying safely enshrined in the future, as he calculated the distance to level ground. It seemed the sandy flats of the river plain were around fifteen metres, maybe less if he could slide a little off the lip's edge, or find some slightly lower projection of it.

There was no time. He did not want to be speared. As he launched himself, he imprinted in his mind the conscious intent that he would roll on impact, not trusting that the sandy ground was as soft as it looked. His trajectory was very accurate, and he could see that he would hit the exact spot on the lip of a sloping bank which he had aimed for. As he tried to bring his flailing limbs and sinking belly into fluidity for his roll, he realised that adrenaline or perhaps tiredness, had caused one mistake in his calculations. The fall was closer to twenty-five metres than the fifteen he had hoped for.

He was still falling as the hunters reached the edge to watch. "Recwauch!" His right heel snapped as he landed, then in the roll, all the bones supporting the right knee. As he spindled fully over, Ben knocked two teeth from his mouth with a shin, rolled to the edge of the little slope and sprawled unmoving — but for most of the hour before the elders arrived, he was conscious. The pain was bad, though offset by such joy to have survived his deed. Ben laughed; his totem must surely be a bird of some sort. He watched one, a hawk, fly along the outcrop, safe above the world. From a higher place than it, he had made his leap.

It was the turn of the elders to appear incredulous. As they glanced from him to the cliff top, he saw a light of wonder and respect in their eyes, but on their faces and in their hurried council, there was gravity. They stood at distance from him. Ben gleaned through the pain that he had jumped into a women's dreaming site, taboo to men.

The hollow in which he stretched was one of Tnaldi's great footprints, made when dreamtime ancestors had surrounded the cave at the escarpment's foot with flame and spears. Ben belatedly remembered the fireside tale now. She was a staunch foe, finally cornered, having stolen secrets from all the medicine men. She had transformed herself into a giant, stomping on the fire as she fled into the billabong.

A warrior had rushed into the cave, and finding she had left her magic pouch in the confusion, threw it into the remnant flames. The giantess running across the plain had burst into flame in conjunction with the bag, but because her possum-skin cloak was so damp from her swim, she had smouldered and died from the smoke. When the pall cleared, all that was left of Tnaldi was the contorted shape of the baobab tree — that to this day holds its arms to the skies, frequently burned in the grass fires, but merely smouldering and hollowing, being such a spongy wood.

They decreed to him — those faces that reflected land and secrets — that he might marry Ngenlin. His dreaming totem would be assumed from that of the tribe's medicine man, but first he was to be taken by the women to the baobab plains, there to heal if he would, or reveal with his death an obvious alliance with Tnaldi's mischief.

Later Ben wakened in total darkness, having lost consciousness on the day's long march while the women carried him on a stretcher. His smashed leg felt wet and cool to touch. It seemed it was bound in old leather, dampened so as to shrink and tighten around the limb. His chest cuts had been smeared with clay that must also be under the leather bindings. A few gnats and their whinier cousins worried his eyes. Before closing them to sleep was a brief transition in which he ascertained that the pulpy wood on which he lay was deep inside a tree.

Chapter 8

On returning to his market site, Angelo finds Keevan's car gone. Many another car is likewise missing, and the remaining grist of humanity conjures scenes for the tailor from an antique documentary he had seen. Arms hang out of car windows, horns beep rhythmically, and someone has found a drum-like container, which they play atop a bus. Locals and tourists, stranded by awe, stand in little groups gawping at the miraculously transformed hover stack, oblivious to the presence of two regional police helicopters scouting overhead.

Angelo tells himself he should hurry to the rendezvous, but in the aftermath of the day's incredible occurrence, his direction is made uncertain. An intuitive flare is uplighting within him a flow of thought that snags ever on one point. As he packs the last of his stall, he reasons, *with hearts leaping like this, things are going to stir down the coast. And there's no one down there who can organise a delta pattern or even prioritise infrastructural targets.*

He considers the nature of Byron's buried subculture where their own efforts to organise revolution had met with a hair-trigger attitude. Although the vein of anti-government feeling there was deep, it was so linked to religio-mystic beliefs seeming to arise from the land itself that the Realliance was rebuffed by the medium of chaos at each turn. Many were the stringent government efforts to extirpate mystic radicalism from that hotbed coast that had worn constant failure.

Spontaneously, he drives toward Byron Bay, and is clear of the mountains when some twenty minutes later he sees a Sacubus squadron speeding back the way he had come, malign steel painted in both Nascent Walls and Quaintsand state colours.

It is chilly in the dam wall but the cramped double cell they have chosen warms with the press of bodies. Everyone has made it, excepting Angelo. Keevan puts that from mind as he takes in his sixty comrades, few without grey in their hair. This is it, the epiphany of their preparation, physical and philosophical.

He asks, "Is everybody ready? So we shall tug the rug of our compliance, upon which the warlords tread, out from under them. Ours shall be first defiance, but every Realliance hub shall quickly erupt soon after, catalysing all the way to Syndecide itself." He catches the huge eyes of Jania Vesks, an angular-faced lady and an Indigo, born and raised specifically to psychic attunement. "Please let them know, Jania."

She would now alert other groups' Indigoes, telepathing a warning to prepare for full forward staging to the seven hubs along the eastern seaboard. The puppet Austral government had converted every Indigo they could find to the ranks of their thought soldiery — MIOMICHS — Mind Over Matter In Controlled Hemistatic Suspension. Still, many psychics had slipped through the cruel nets.

Jania is hunched over her hands, fingers tented with the two little ones outsplayed. A similar figure beside her presently looks up at Keevan. The yellow eyes dance in the bemused owlish face. Billy Reet — probably the most skilled long-range telepathist on the planet.

"Curlewalion," he announces formally, "send their greetings and will concert in two hours." He shares a moment of bitten-back anxiety with his fellow confidant, the two knowing just how much rides on the success of this strike.

"Okay, kids," Keevan yells to his motley of rebels, the eagerest of whom already jimmy themselves up the narrow ladders, "Time to burst their storm cloud and bring the rainbows back."

He pours real coffee, courtesy of a hole in the fence at a nearby plantation, from a flask on a tiny crowded bench. He places a cup each before the seated Indigoes, communicating both appreciation and ironic contentment with that mercurial knack his face has, as he regards these powerful allies. Beneath his mask of flippant ease he is consolidating his inward resolve. Up top, weapons are being retrieved from their decade-old cache. He needs to be certain why he is fighting. *The mass tortures of his friends, for one. The sculpting of the social personality —* *no! It had to stop.*

He puts a hand on each of the psychic guerrillas. "Now don't you freaks go falling asleep! We might just need a place to retreat back to in who knows what kind of a state. If you don't recognise a mind-pattern, send the rear-guard to investigate."

Giving a squeeze to their shoulders with his deft artist's hands, Keevan clangs upstairs. In the anteroom, the five dam workers, vastly enjoying their new duties, are constructing barricades out of overturned tables and fridges. Two are very young, yet use their teenage exuberance to extend powerful solidarity over the group. A pair of women look toward where Keevan watches the convoy pulling out.

A few of the cars have been exchanged for impressive dam maintenance hovers, their black capsule bodies reinforced for heavy lifting, with folding-tool legs tucked insectivirously underneath. The ground procession looks like a museum field day, the ancient cars and trucks snaking into the night.

"There go the hippies, off to save the world," says the older woman, a caterer here, Keevan recalls. He chuckles wryly while the young men alongside yell good-naturedly at the departing convoy.

"Go and trip them out, guys!"

"Here," says a voice pressed between optimism and exhaustion. It is Lou, the old dam manager. His son, many years ago, had fallen while laying a bioform on the wall, and been coldly dismissed by the foreman as clumsy. The boy had never been forgotten. Lou steadies a short-range laser into Keevan's hands. "Give them these flowers for me."

Keevan feels reassurance thinking of the little group of workers turned rebels that remain behind. If this night's insurgency fails, that trusted handful — warned by Jania Vesks through their slightly telepathic member, Jamie — would be ready to cover and snipe against any Agency force. The blaster in his own hand seems less reassuring as he looks toward the glare of lights that is Fadtown, and had been Lismore. He would rather be at the wheel than shooting in what is to come.

He looks across at Ellajean; her outsized brown eyes level with his. Her mouth, flushed with a dark tint as legacy of her Cambodian blood, exercises between silent words and a whimsical smirking. He registers a deep hope in the play of those lips, contracted usually in a firm sensual grasp one upon the other.

Blue lights are on all the way along the road, and ground traffic has obediently ceased while hovers spin into the air, or into parking places, and hum down into the sub-city.

"The ponderous wheel slips on its greased chain, even here where they lock the myths of beauty into a permanent suspension."

Ellajean qualifies his comment on their surrounds with, "Lunatic-tocks."

They are in the retail section of the city, and though nearing midnight, a crush of humanity and their robotics and transporters seem to press heavily, carrying fatality like an avalanche. In this part of Fadtown, a wide knifing road is appellated at intervals by denouncements of gaudy paint on its surface as Crystal Boulevard. Along its length, government and corporate development offices share subterranean space with vehicle workshops, while the main government offices, including the Agency depot and courts, huddle distantly along the river.

Pedestrians seethe in a jaunty dance, ears straining for hovers and the striding police automns, bringing their patronage to souvenir malls and cybernetic game parks. Nondescript remodulator knock shops spill flashes of brazen light and seedy allure to those with neural transducers, for whom the recipients of their coin would take on any face and figure imagined. Here, too, are dining and liquid spice booths, pharmacy ponds, automn sellers and refluiders; all the dross for filling the voids that have become people's lives.

The largest crowds shuffle in a cataplexy of meaninglessness beneath magma-lurid screens built into the grey edifice of a completely square building unbroken by windows for its squatting third of a mile of nauseating geometry. The stupendous image frames display scenes from the 'real life' twenty-four hour soap opera, *Crystal County*, its cast chosen for their societal or sporting infamy. Plastic models of giganticised quartz crystals on either side of the screens begin to pulse with light, and from the crowd there comes a hackle-raising shriek, as though the night itself were being cauterised.

"Bolo Endare...landed!" The screens inform, and suddenly are awash with the oily features of a small blonde man, the long pan showing him walking behind security across a rooftop before the perspective pulls back even further to reveal that it is this building — *Crystal County's* managerial sanctum — that the soap's favoured star walks across. There is a flux in the crowd as though it will swarm through the mesh fence around the building, and the two guards before its single aperture — a doorway of blue algalate — tense warily. But then the screen fades, and the theme music to the world-renowned soap opera blares. A few people totter in an arm-jiggling waltz, or push each other in brief exuberance before resuming the loyal shuffling of their vigil.

As the ground traffic starts to move, Keevan feels a wash of relief that his potter's ability had been deemed skilled in the National Reclamative Personality Mandates. Those without economically tangible value had indeed been unlucky...married to vegi-fuel estates, or factories in cities like this, and rewarded with credits useful only for that district and twice-yearly government hover excursions. But in this, perhaps cruellest of the W.A.R. government policies, lay also a seed of hope. Most of the five hundred mandated textile workers that he had just notified through coded phonet conversation of the attack, will soon be a unified force fighting in revolt.

Using the heavily monitored phonet system had been dangerous but the first strike is so imminent as to be unstoppable. Keevan watches as the two buses from their now scattered convoy slip into separate entrances beneath the menacing sac of the Regulative Enforcement Dome. These will shortly choke mostly all access to the sub-levels of the RED, the vehicles becoming barricades which half the buses' crews of six will defend, while the balance attack the institution itself. The major surveillance and armoury of the RED is actually three metres above street level, where four Affiliates sit behind clear algalate with control of two long-range segmenting laz-cannons mounted on the bioform turret, looking to Keevan like some egg of the automated standard attack hover brooding above it.

The RED is a fairly important tactical position to overcome, but capturing it will be of greatest value for a symbolic rally and cry. Its fall would hopefully inspire spontaneous civil tumult to ignite, then radiate across Fadtown. Keevan reflects that if citizens on the street do not join the uprising, the revolution does not stand a chance. If he survives the engagement with the dome and street surrounds, he will push on to join the attack against the Affiliate Compound itself. The initial strike on the compound is to synchronise with that against the RED, and will be undertaken by only four cars and two hovers, but these equipped with most of their explosives.

Twenty rebels in ten separate cars close in on the dome in support of the subterranean group. One of the dam hovers will be involved against the RED. The cars have separated down the five main approaches to the RED. Keevan and Ellajean, well ahead of their backup, move with the hydrogen tang of traffic. Keevan focuses his waltzing mind on the inculcated theory of years of preparation. *Engage police and automn foot patrols. Embolden the oppressed into the bargain, empassioning feelings of resentment in the majority, so their fear and programming is overcome...*

"Start with the plastic muscle, Key…" Ellajean seems to read his mind with regard to overcoming his own programming of the sanctity of all life. "These two coming up on the left. If we get through to cops and Agents, remember they're there because they like it. They like the torture, the ultimate power, the echo of their animalistic views down the narrow slimy canyons of the culture they protect. Remember what we can create and that the family of man has a future bigger than our moral preoccupations."

She pats him firmly on his sternum, and accelerates into the space she had let form in front of her.

"Yeah. When every contribution you make to society is swallowed by a system sucking dry the weak and the marrow of the Earth, the only contribution you have left is to destroy it," Keevan says in a quiet monotone that is lost as the car roars up toward the automns.

Turning with a jerky propulsion at the sound, one unleashes its macro trigger weapons; continually amping lasers that would be impossibly dangerous for a human to use, standing its ground against the brick façade of an upper echelon manicurist with the business name *Quick Ease*. As the other runs down the road toward them, a crushing wave of humanity recoils from the guns. With an incomprehensible curse, the Burmese skews to one side, so avoiding the shot that would have melted Keevan's head. Almost atop the other automn, its inbuilt laser slices through the engine block, then whips past to burst the potter's left ear and bring blood to Ellajean's nose, who manages to swerve directly into the antagonist. Keevan targets the other plastic cop, and in a skilled effort of straining muscles, pumps consecutive bursts into its shield before it explodes.

He has just time to pull his torso into the car when he is winded by an airbag Ellajean eventually cuts from him. After slithering gingerly through the smashed windscreen and looking at Ellajean to check for hidden injury, Keevan runs toward the explosions echoing from the RED, leaping the manicurist's fallen billboard that displays a three-metre long hand, now on fire, its ruby nails raking down a black spine. A bright star of optimism flames in his heart, tells him they will win this position, and his voice follows, compelling with hope. "Don't hesitate, throw down this hate!"

Hovers jostle to flee the laser battles on the boulevard as the boom of underground explosions and plaintive screech of sirens carries from the RED. Keevan focuses on his immediate sphere of action and people begin to respond to his urgency. Some, like the man of patient composure who leans on a car just down a side street, attend in spirit only. Others, like this old woman, warning him of automns approaching through the tourist plaza, then tottering for cover, respond body and soul.

The plastic cops burst through the entrance and mush a robust teenage boy who has just smashed a window front. Most of the crowd desert the area as Simone and Rory, also now both on foot, train their blasters on the automns, keeping them hemmed behind their shields. From the shelter of parked cars or shop doorways, a thin crowd of citizens-turned-rebels yell encouragement.

Then Keevan, calling for freedom, dragging at the maelstrom in people's hearts, notices a tall man in trade overalls step from a car and aim something at Simone, who jerks to the ground, clutching her stomach. He has a nail gun, Keevan realises, as the man's mate ducks from the car, hefting a jack. Keevan waits the space of a loud heartbeat and fires on both of them with fatal accuracy.

Events warp for Keevan to sharp stills of violence: a small knot of people armed with bottles and broken furniture around a dead girl and policeman, handcuffing the remaining cop — and a stray blast from one of the segmenting lasers on the RED that swathes through several hovers and bits of the swatted raining down. A black shape — the dam hover — drops a concrete pylon on the RED's turret and descends to pry bits off its roof with whirring steel and claws. Into the holes rent in the tyrannous structure, mobs of people pour, some awkward with police lasers.

Keevan comes to himself, blasting at security guards who cluster in a defensive huddle near a pharmacy pond, grimly defending their charge. Keevan runs as low as he can to gain the protection of a bus stop shelter. Opposite, a footwear retailer, still brightly lit, has barred its doors with a pile of mannequins, and is blessedly without a security guard. His position is some way beyond the RED now, and he can discern the bridge at the mall's end, above which two automn hovers, without windows of any sort, engage the dam hovers. The robot ships' lasers spark effetely off the pressure coating of the larger vehicles, and as one angles in closer, a flick of a tool leg from a rebel hover sends the smaller craft spiralling out of control to sink in the river. The rebel ships ascend into the night, doggedly traced by the automn.

Keevan retrains his focals to the hunchback bioform of the bridge, perhaps a hundred metres long. Many automn columns cross it from the far bank — the civic quarter — trailed by police fanning out in a dignified scurry from their headquarters close to the river. Keevan sees at last what had spooked the hovers — tanks coming along the main riverside road. He whips his laser around at a figure darting through the mall toward him, but it is only Rory. Always frenetic, his gangly length is erupting with rage following Simone's killing

He hunkers next to the potter and speaks around a quick surveying of the bridge with his own focals. "Only their leaders are silked, the rest are naked. The cheap bastards — though they're stacking them on. I'd say three hundred live, as many plastic."

Two big police hovers emerge, ghosting over buildings on either side of the mall. A retinue of many smaller automn hovers, gun mounts twitching, spreads from the bloated ironing boards. The air thrums with the no-fuss words stamped onto it.

"Ground vehicle owners or pedestrians! Proceed at an orderly pace to emergency facilities outside the area of firefight. Please follow the blue arrows and leave your ground vehicles. Hover owners! Return to your vehicles."

Arrow-shaped streaks of blue light flood down onto the road and into side streets. The message is repeated in several languages by a computerised voice that fails to generate the accent of disdain. Up higher, another hover cruises the rooftop hover parks using similar lights and broadcast to herd hovers from the area. Keevan hears the injunction.

"Magnetic locks will commence across the city in six minutes. All hovers have a five minute window of evacuation only. Please clear the area and proceed to the nearby safe zone. Follow the green arrows."

"Thank god they're putting in a hover lock," Keevan says, relaxing.

"Thank our plan, man," punctiliates Rory.

"And the use of those dam hovers. They just got no idea what we're going to throw at them for fucking once, and they ground their own force to be sure," Keevan rhapsodises, exhausted.

"Yeah, but not yet."

In a flitting shoal, they see the automn hovers skim under heavy fire from within the battered RED. More hovers skim up the road, and Keevan and Rory race across it, the metallic refrain of "throw down your weapons" and laser fire pursuing them as they plunge through the smashed front of a hardware store. Inside, at least a hundred mainly mature men and women are frantically stripping shelves, and banging and clattering at hastily assembled work spaces.

Ellajean straps a belt of spray perfume for priming the urgently constructed air cannons, onto a woman's waist. She looks around at about twenty people she is supervising.

"You need some kind of armour, all of you. The welder's helmets are all accounted for, so use robotic fittings, anything you can find — you've got to cover the upper body from air strike."

Ellajean straps on her own helmet, a modified bike hat with diamond threaded plastic sheeting melded into it, and extended as wings over shoulders and upper spine. It is faintly burned-looking and Keevan jokes with her.

"Hey! They work." He had made them himself — one for each of the hub's core, after forging endless prototypes in his studio.

"You still get the headache. The hover lock is on so we're pushing. So…" she moves a step toward him, turns quickly and jogs across the littered floor.

"So I'll see you," Keevan finishes, as the little group with their air cannons and cumbersome ad hoc helmets, follows their adopted guide into the mall.

A sudden lull steals over the street; the sounds of running and individual bursts of laser fire clearly audible over the final nervous adjustments in the looted store. Faces, old and young, man and woman, are poised in one silent, vital decision as Keevan grades his voice to a matter-of-fact tone, before projecting.

"Don't anyone worry about those bad guys out there. They must want to be beaten because they've dumped their hovers. Okay. We just cross this bridge at the end of the mall, and then we're onto the really bad guys at the Agency depot. Give them arachnophobia — group up — lots of eyes and legs. Don't touch the weapons of the Affiliate — they'll explode. Murder's cold-blooded — this is about warm huge-heartedness, cleaning monsters from the waters our kids swim in, and there's going to be big waves, so go on instinct when needs be. Remember we're only fighting guns on the ground."

"And those noisy birds," interrupts a woman, outfitted with a spinney of knives on two belts crossing her shoulders, as a helicopter whine draws closer.

"Yeah, they're always quick to improvise. But look, don't worry, guys, we're half way there. I hope you can use those things," he says in an aside to the woman as Rory starts to yell. The tall man is bouncing about, looking fervently happy.

"On this mall about two hundred of us are about to reject this system with our bodies. We've already done that with our unbroken souls. So it's time for them to surrender to majority rule, because we've got more crew coming up all the time — a thousand coming up the river. They've got only two hundred and fifty cops up there, a few automns lurking in doorways, some security guards dug in. Just do it, people, look after your backs and one way or another we all wake up free."

There is a yell and a surge as the rally of rebels spew onto the mall. Many manage to press forward while a few are forced to cover behind huge advertising or sculptural works in the wide street. Some are killed instantly by security guards. Their companions take revenge before once more squaring their numbers to attack a thin spread of police and automns in the near distance.

Ensconced behind a mailbox, Keevan sees that helicopters are dropping police onto the roof of a mall hotel. Their shots rain down into the street. A woman falls with a scream. In detached irony he studies the bleeding body and the advertising pillar behind it that declaims: 'When you've got an automn, there's no chance of a fall'.

The boom of air cannons recalls him to his task and he watches a squall of screwdrivers and bolts clatter against a helicopter. The pilot must have been struck, for the thing just falls like lead and a group of insurgents dance around the ground explosion. In another skirmish he assays the bulky silhouettes of Ruth and Fairley, the pair battling against a group of guards to gain entrance to the hotel opposite. Empowerment cadets armed with truthies, as the stun lasers are known, are also targeting the dauntless pair from a rotunda. The artisan moves to back up the fierce lesbians, iconically clad in the red-and-blue-striped heavy algalate suits meant to denounce S.T.D. carriers, the ruse of heavy wear protecting them from more than boys for once.

"Down!" somebody screams, and Keevan hurls himself prostrate as a bright drift of particle ionisers pulses overhead, together with a smell of blood. But the automn has expended its immediate charge from such a massive blast, and two men, armed with a shovel and an axe, each break into a run and charge the machine, flaying it into scrap. Keevan remains intently alert, and as a window of a spice booth smashes outward, he fires on the automn before it can discharge the chaos its partner caused.

"They always move together!" he yells, noting the two grizzled victims of the ionic fire stumbling from the smoking cadavers as a helicopter bulls down the road straight at them.

It travels only six metres above the street, a cop on each side riveting laser rays into the panicked. Keevan steadies for a shot at a gunner, who is forced by the weight of his weapon to hang half from the door sill, but his movement draws bullets from a roof top, and he tumbles toward the cover of a looming concrete magpie sculpture. Suddenly, a motorbike roars up the tail of another giant magpie in the concrete flock and launches from its head. A man tumbles from the bike and lands heavily as the machine continues flying upward. He crawls away on hands and knees as this missile and the helicopter collide, throwing a whump of flames around the potter.

As Keevan lifts his head a leather-clad arm falls on his shoulder, and he stares into a penetrating smile of greeting. "I'm Joust," says the man, at least seventy years old, whose only two teeth are filed like fangs. "Waste of a pretty good bike, that — still, it made a merry blaze. I reckon we could do with another laser, if you'd like to ride with us."

Four bikes pull alongside them, roaring antiques, their riders looking as old. Two of the passengers are vibrant teenagers — perhaps grand-daughters, but for their proprietal grip on their drivers — outfitted in identical sub-machine guns across their jackets and denim shorts that are split-laced along the inner leg.

As Keevan hunkers up behind one rider, the man indicates a screen between the handlebars of the bike alongside, to which Joust has added his weight.

"We'll hit their tail here, Joust, but they're four deep, so we got to really puff up. They outnumber us too; about eighty bikes to our fifty."

"Yup, yup, yup. Let's go get 'em then, Gravel." Keevan's driver hurtles across the mall, the potter seeing the others follow as he relaxes into the centre of gravity while Gravel corners into a laneway. Once through it, they sweep across a deserted hover park and up a slightly wider lane. At its end, two automns appear. Under attack, Gravel veers wildly. Keevan sees four more automns move across the hover park to engage the others, then tracks his laser across their own plastic obstruction. Somehow they win through the lane.

The rear bikes catch them and the little group weave up a greenway, brushed by bushes. As they slow to navigate the overhead vegetation, Keevan asks Gravel, "Who out-numbers you almost double?"

"Our enemy? The Rocks. Corporate bouncers, mate. Drug predators. You want standover? Real blackline, you know. If someone finds a way to milk a Daguerette program, they'll get a piece. They are capital A anti-revolutionaries, brother. And here they are."

He accelerates onto a road, straight at a group of four bikies with slick long hair and red suits; nothing like Keevan's ride. With a deft throw, Gravel tangles two of the oncoming bikes in some kind of cording and throttles away from the chaotic spill which compromises a third bike. Keevan reaps a burst of laser fire across his helmet from the following motorcade, and eyes stinging, blasts blindly toward a haze of bike lights. Two lights from the throng veer toward them but are engulfed in an explosion. Gravel swerves around the inferno but some bits of shrapnel rip past Keevan, slicing his elbow bone.

Suddenly Joust is alongside. "Puff, Puff," he yells, tossing another hand grenade at the Rocks. Keevan fires at an oncoming bike and sees the ray bounce off its frontal armour. The silhouette of Joust and his driver flash by the same bike, which mysteriously spills its driver onto the road, and flips in a perilous spin of steel so close to Keevan's ear that he can hear the whirring of its wheels. Joust is back alongside him, bearing a mad grin, and gripping a long steel rod in his gloved hand.

"Yeah, these guys are shielded right down to half the front tyre, so ya got to shoot at road level, we're — "

Suddenly a metal barb topped by flashing lights pierces Joust's face, and he falls open-eyed onto the road, almost careering his driver's bike into their own. The two drivers give a quick nod and then, while Gravel dips down the steep side of the road toward the hydro station, the other bike shoots along the embankment and leaps up onto a treeway, barricaded to exclude all but joggers and pushbikers — and fiendishly skilled motorcyclists.

The targeter dart follows behind Keevan. "Let's go," he says to Gravel as they streak past the brightly lit filling station.

"I'm going. It must've spat a micro-tracker somewhere onto my old girl. We're coming up to the river soon, and I hope you get a good shot at it before we reach that bottleneck."

Keevan is accorded a good appraisal of the tiny steely assassin, betrayed by its lights on a stretch of unlit treeway. He shoots squarely at it. It dips into darkness but then is glowing steadily behind them, and accelerating. "I'm out of charge!" He is appalled by the irony.

"At your left leg, man!" barks Gravel.

Reaching down, the potter finds what has been jabbing into his thigh throughout the ride. He sights the fresh blaster and lays a storm of crackling red and gold lightning on his adversary. This time it absorbs the assault without even dimming. Close enough to see its intricate transparent triple drive, Keevan desperately recalls a science theory and fires quick volleys to its either side, then strikes it again. With an audible pop, its stabiliser field is destroyed and the targeter explodes.

"Aw shit," jibes the venerable bikie, "we might have interrogated it a little first. Alright. Now I guess we just try to blend in."

They slow, as ahead the battle on the river's esplanade comes into focus.

"Hold on a second," says Keevan, scrabbling out a phone. On the screen he sees that his reflection is smirched darkly with blood from his elbow wound. As they pull over several hundred metres from running figures defying yet more choppers, Keevan clips his words to make himself understood.

"Paulo? Only. Red. Bikies. Nasty. Spread. Word."

"What? Are you trying to ruin our reputation? I'm Gravel anyhow."

"Keevan. If we hang here a little and wait for the word to spread — I'd hate to be a whoops to an angry mob of workers. This is all up to them now anyway, but what are your gang doing?"

"They'll have hit the Rocks back near the bridge. When Joust and us others picked them mongrels moving, we were the only ones near South City. But we've all got good scanners that those scum can't match, so the rest shouldn't have been far off the hunt. I think we slowed their charge enough to give our core a fair chance at hitting them before they spread much mischief."

Cheering resounds from the distance as a helicopter lurches crazily and dives into the river, prompting a surge of bodies along the esplanade. On the treeway, a knot of running figures shy visibly as they see the bike in the shadows. They prove to be university students and establish the pair's allegiance after yelling a quick interrogation. Their buoyant camaraderie folds Gravel and Keevan in a burst of hooting, and with this primal escort of thirty bodies prancing about them they ride into the ferment of battle.

A press of various workers from one of Crystal County's many studios are swarming in and out of the front lines, some dressed in the lacto-silk black stunt suits used for their tedious human monkeyisms. They launch air cannon missiles and Molotov cocktails at the police blockade by the bridge. The students spill to the river bank to join others of their ilk targeting police speed boats from behind shields improvised from old hover doors. Keevan lasers automns blitzing into the gutsy throng from a side street, but Gravel whips back down the lines as a helicopter sweeps in a strafing overhead pass.

A flushed, stolid-looking man with a commanding presence struts up the esplanade with a megaphone, his fine hemp suit an uneasy contrast with army boots.

"Keep going, boys and girls — we're almost there! One for your brother in desperate Luxemburg, one for your mother Earth!" he cants. "Only the red bikies are naughty and nasty. Oh! You guys are sweet as pasties. One for your brother in hard pressed Tangiers…" The indomitable old man passes up the lines and the words fog into the clamour of battle.

Keevan smiles to recognise the man, undoubtedly one of that mad bunch who brought hover logging to its knees before they were picked off for incarceration many decades ago. Gravel deploys himself to the rear to scout, and Keevan edges toward a peskily accurate unseen laser operator secreted somewhere amid a rusty hulk of slumped advertising screens. From the corner of his eye he sees a helicopter curl over the attack. The menace is met this time by dynamic resistance.

A team of rebels, obviously from Crystal County's props department, work a pressure generator that pumps into the sky a rigidly upshooting ladder that must be made of immersulate, expensively derived from marine-farmed copper ions. As the contraption rises, a woman is hoisted into the sky atop it. She sails in next to the helicopter gunner and actually collects him with a stout cudgel. The whirligig beats a demoralised retreat back over the river, and the next to come in is met by more ladder riders rocketing up from nearby the descending woman. Looming suddenly up under its flight path, they hurl paint bombs at the windshield, the riders then bowing their ladders in evasion, swinging crazily away from the retributive fire.

Keevan intuits that the slight give in the rungs means they can in fact be foot-triggered as hinges. As more helicopters approach, a rider falls limply to the ground and Keevan spies the culprit.

The flash of tiny lights shows a targeter dart fleeting towards another rider, who bends from reach, though only for a moment. The potter sprints to the ladder of one of the fallen and climbs halfway up it, spots the dart a little clear of its prey, and blasting true to his training makes of it a brief incandescence. The other ladder descends but Keevan signals his handlers to wait, for the river has now caught his attention.

As though to mitigate the rout of the helicopters, two goliathan police boats, heavily armed, are churning down river toward them. Keevan flicks down his night focals and scans the bank to see how well the defenders prepare. With his augmented height he is able to see the efforts of a small group of people in what he had thought was a stand of saplings, but now knows for a holographic illusion. Looking at the huddled souls, cunningly striving to win the night, Keevan wonders how many more studio crew might be hidden about.

The rebel leader sees them look up expectantly from their deck of computers towards the river, and pat each other's backs as a ten-metre waterspout erupts on it. He laughs as their contrivance approaches the boats in a vortex of noise and foam, and the two marauders flee back upriver beneath the bridge — the water guardian collapsing from where it had arisen.

On the bridge, the human police drag the last of their number back across its span as the automnals barge toward the rebel barricade. The potter descends and hears the new situation screamed through megaphones.

"Be ready for automns. Heavy shields and trigger weapons to the front. Missiles to the rear." And the automns come, over two hundred, in waves to foil the ballistics. Behind them, the massive engines of the tanks shudder into life. Now it is the insurgents who retreat, still calmly, back to the cover of a large amphitheatre on the esplanade. Several automns catch fire from the Molotov's, all except a couple quickly doused by chemical clouds spurted from the mouths of their cyberitic litter mates, as they sweep up to the amphitheatre's inset circle of concrete and wall of screening shields. Two university students, unshielded, belabouring to arm an air cannon, are singled out by the acrimonious plastic — even though, closer to hand, attackers direct laser volleys from behind shields.

"Gas," somebody yells, and sure enough, Keevan notes the canisters that fall hissing among them, fired by police on the bridge. The tactic is more token than lethal. In disease-paranoid South Austral everyone carries a mask. Still, the little pause, the sudden jostle to fit the masks, is all the automns need to break the shield wall.

There is no panic, only a determined individualism, each rebel conspicuous now in the shrunken shoal of their fellows that is no longer able to dart freely about and distract South Austral's force from fully exercising its brutal efficiency. Keevan watches as the infrared senses of the automns guide them to stomp out the lives of those injured or playing dead. The rebels' lasers are too few and their operators too exhausted in the end.

Only a few groups hold back the charge; stunt artists in their silks, able to fire and duck behind fiercely combative allies who wield makeshift clubs, allowing the shooters to steady and attack again. Keevan knows that even had they fifty lasers more, crushing plastic, unlike lasers, is inexhaustible. Slowly, screaming engulfs the amphitheatre.

From that gorge of mud and cluttered pylons and twists of steel like bloated ropes of candy they came. Through the electric fence of the nearby building site, unlooked for by either automns or slowly dying rebels. Their impact is great, though half their number they channel into a defiant counterattack further back toward the bridge.

Keevan's first glimpse of hope comes with laser fire slicing through the side of the amphitheatre, dropping automns. There fights Ellajean with other survivors from the hub, and bikies — mostly overweight and over sixty — casual with their lasers, demonstrative with the chains they smash through plastic heads. A ragtag hundred follow these living antiquities of ferocity, breaking into the gaps opened in the fight, and blasting automns with ready primed air cannons. The newcomers expunge the last of the plastic foe from the esplanade and seethe like ants towards the tanks.

Keevan runs, swept up with all those left alive in a wave of fury, glimpsing on the far bank knots of police converging, magnetised by their threat to the bridge's other end like iron filings. The faces around him, strained but triumphant with life, are three hundred strong of all those thousand who had rallied here. As they come within sight of the tanks, there is a visible cringe among those alongside the potter. He and others of the hub run forward from the skittery, widespread mob, providing a shield of flesh to encourage them on.

Surging again, and still no swathing lasers or bullets, until the tanks are surrounded, smashed on by bars, laughed puzzledly at, and passed by. The mob swings onto the bridge, dozens more from the Crystal Boulevard and from the lesser river way — a swelling bruise spreading toward the tight bone of police at the bridge's end.

Keevan leans against a tank in exhaustion. He wonders if it is the one, and is halfway up the ladder not relishing the thought of opening the giant crypt, when a voice calls from another tank.

"This is it. Wide open, just like they promised."

It is Yatosh from the hub, and as Keevan comes over to him, he sees four more of his friends standing about, but not Flaire, their designated tank driver.

"She's dead," Marnie supplies to his air of consternation.

"Well, fuck!" Karina yells. "What should we do? Curlew can't drive the thing for us."

No, thinks Keevan, but their Indigoes killed all the tank operators, made one of them leave a hatch open. The hidden desert warriors, concerting their minds on the Agency, some probably already comatose or dead from expenditure, and the psychic portal starting to lapse while they stand here wondering what to do.

"Let's just use it as a standing gun mount. It's all we can do." Keevan is interrupted by a scream of sound which has the five Realliancers flexing for lasers, but materialises into a dozen or so of Joust's gang, turning an arc before the bridge and wearily dismounting. The potter barely listens as a grizzled old bikie shakes his hand, tells him the whole east side is in rebel control. He is looking beyond to the passenger in a sidecar, his arm burned away by a particliser. It is Rory. The driver of that vehicle, an obese bald man, catches Keevan's eye and says, "I'm not goan ask how yous caught three o' these. But I'd love a drive, just for memory's sake."

""You can drive these?" Karina quizzes in a desperate hiss.

"Well, not this exact model. Drove Pascals in the war with Madagascar. Conscriptee. But if I can fit in it, I can sure as shit move it."

This is just great, Keevan thinks, more than fifty years ago.

Then Rory is beside him, something more than anguish in his gaze. "Leave this to us and be with the people, we won't be far behind."

With the roadster vacated, Keevan climbs into its sidecar, awkwardly gripping the segmenting laser pillaged from a tank, and the others of the hub likewise find positions riding shotgun. Keevan's driver, all asperity and false teeth, introduces himself as Clatus and then roars up to the battle on the bridge. They cat down to the police courtyard where Keevan sweeps a squiggle of laser fire over a regrouping force, and determines to tie down the massively kicking weapon.

By the time they speed to the perimeter of the Agency depot, insurgents are streaming through the holes torn in its fencing and scattering over the depot lawns. There is a warped hunk of metal between the fence and the stand of feature trees on the lawns. It is one of the dam hovers. Only its magnetic inducing block, melded to the strongest ribbing, is recognisable. From atop its melted mess, a few Agents leisurely laser down insurgents looking for cover.

The potter directs Clatus up the slope behind the Affiliate marksmen. He fires and hits all three as Clatus screeches down the hill. Keevan instructs him for another pass, having seen the lacto-silk absorb his striking rays. He flares the laser fire out into a thick ball and drops the cloud over them, helmets and all. Satisfied, he flicks the segmenter off to let it cool and slumps forward, so exhausted that he lets his nose run against the algaleather of the biker's jacket. They approach the rebel barricade at full throttle, and only at the last second does one of the production crew heave aside an old hover door to allow them within the shield wall.

Five hundred people now divide between air-cannoning Agency lines and maintaining and moving the ragged shield wall forward. Despite the shielding, Agents fire missiles of their own and Affiliate hover-packers buzz waspishly through the tree shadows.

With Clatus supporting the long front barrel of Keevan's segmenter, the pair now ride out through the far edge of the shielding where Keevan trains the weapon on a cluster of Agents moving across a steep artificial hill, attempting to gain a flanking position. The bolt of fire hits the Affiliates and shears out to their rear before swirling back to engulf them in an inescapably lethal vortex.

Now a group of silked stunt workers, with a number of street rebels, some ill-fitted with lacto-silk suits stripped from the vanquished, move at a run through the front of the shield wall. They hold up their own lightweight screens of protection, and covered by the horde in the trees, reach one of the raggedly blasted underground entrances. Using dam hovers, the Realliance had disabled these innately defended positions. The yawning fissures now have to be guarded by dozens of Agents.

The attacking rebel group throw aside their shields, and begin a frenzied brawl with the Affiliates. Kick for punch and baton for wrench, the melee exudes little grace as limbs flay and heads crack. The Agents are highly trained but the rebels' determination is immense. They spit out teeth, retribution howling in their veins, until the Agents are incredibly all down. The rebels snatch up the superior shields, shunning the weapons as they push into the tunnel.

All at once the two groups of guards in front of tunnel entrances nearest Keevan begin firing, each on the other. The Curlewalion Indigoes must have generated amazing focus to cause this. The shield walls of the insurgents flow out and forward as the rebels rush to take the two undefended tunnels. From the glitzy compound itself, Agents buoyed by tiny hover-packs, in concert with helicopters, rise up and fan over the group. Apart from a few passing volleys, this air assault concentrates its menace on the tank that is lumbering up the lawn.

Four choppers launch missiles simultaneously, and as the flames clear the resilient brute fights back. Its pulse lasers explode a chopper from the sky, and while the rest of its prey arcs beyond reach, it sends rockets against positions on the Affiliate Compound. In response the hover-packers whiz in, some laying mines around the fearsome machine, others weaving with various success between the gundecks to lay destabilisers on its roof. As the mines trigger, the destabilisers send their short circuiting flux through its body.

The old motorcyclist riffles a hand through his hoary hair, feeling Rory's eyes bore imploringly into the back of his neck. The rebel has lined up the Agency depot building with the manual gun turret, but with the electrics down, there is no way to fire it. "Okay, son, keep the target hasp steady now." Bunching the folds of flesh on his face in determined concentration, the bikie heaves himself up and smashes an elbow down through the control panel of his stolen craft. There is a boom and the stalwart man- mountain yells with the triumph of his hotwiring.

The hover-packers hum back toward the tunnel and Keevan follows the rest within, the whiff of victory propelling him on into that clandestine maze. He is in a communications room the mob is feveredly destroying when he hears it — a voice in his head where his own should be.

"Get out. Death comes. Get as many out as possible. Immediate retreat. Kaligna Swoon."

If not for the Curlew code at the end of this psychic injunction, he would have believed a Miomich was trying to thwart their moment of triumph. He begins to roar to the hundred or so around him.

"I am told by psychic authority to retreat. Follow me out immediately!"

Perhaps the recognisable insignia of curlew and lion embossed into his helmet lends him credibility. Not much though. About fifty people are fleeing with him when the screaming starts. The first thing that Keevan notes back in the night is the twisted heap of metal, their stolen tank. Then he is fighting through a double line of Agents and throwing laser fire at them more reflexively than gamblers throwing abuse at a dog fight.

The rebels break the cordon back to their own line where a hundred comprise the rear-guard. A few students and punks, all of the effects crew, and some very old and injured, maintain a tenacious resistance. Two more groups break back to them from the tunnels, felled to barely a score by an overpass of hover-packers.

Keevan feels the ship of his hope leave him stranded. Then, through his exhausted delirium, over the shock of battle, he thinks he hears words of assurance. There are three horned figment shapes calling his name, telling him it's going to be alright. The figures resolve into Fisher, Douglas and Janine, crew of the other dam hover. They have captured two helicopters. They can take the core and the injured; Curlew is holding the pilots thralled. They have to hurry, the others can get out through the old service warehouse. The fence is down.

"We'll cover you," announces an intense, greying man. Keevan notices others of the effects crew sternly look on from where, a minute ago, trees had been. As the Realliance leader fires, streaking out of the trees with the rest, he has the disconcerting experience of seeing himself run firing at Agents in four other directions. The helicopters prove to be close, in a hangar rigged to appear as a storage fridge. The people of the city — once again the hunted and oppressed — stream into the warehouse opposite, at least well-armed with the lasers of the injured evacuees.

The choppers launch, swinging briefly above the trees, and Keevan's focals reveal Agents firing confusedly at illusory targets. But something else is loose down there; a new variant of autumn — like dogs, with a saw blade accessory on their heads. In common with all their kind, they have infrared, and as they pull down the masterful effects crew, the holograms fade, then fizz out, so that the Agents are suddenly alone on the bloodied turf.

Chapter 9

Larker awakens from a dream saturated with strangeness. A glistening crayfish, a bird, and a large dingo had each given birth to him at once. They had buried him. First in dirt, then in clouds, and then within a deep river gorge, until their efforts became argument over where he might be safe — but everywhere he lay burst aflame and he burned as well. Always his eyes remained staring at the blackened nothing until an animal mother came to move him. Finally, his three mothers each pulled him in their disputing, so that he tore apart, became words, then each letter of these words, joining similar shapes that were latticed into the patterns of plants' leaves.

Camels came and ate the plants and gained the power of speech. Each time they spoke he flared to life, aware of every ambient detail around him. He tried to tell the camels to hurry before the fire came once more, but when they stopped talking to listen to him, he died back into those two bright eyes.

"Barkin Yarkin," said one camel to its neighbour, and this meant the water is good ahead with plenty of clay people in it.

Thoughts of water now cause Larker to focus his eyes. It is night and hundreds of stars press about him where he lies on a bed. No — wait; the stars actually hang from a low roof and more are sewn into a curtain beside him. He draws it and bright light accosts him in ferocious abundance. As blue eyes master a flickering squint, Larker sees he is in a narrow bedroom with two more single beds alongside his own, and tables between each, completing the austere accommodation. Beside him in a clear bottle Larker finds water wondrously untainted by salt, and steadily swallows half of it. As he replaces it on the table, its contents swish gently, for he is moving. He is in a cart! Standing giddily, Larker throws back a final curtain to gaze straight at a herd of camels.

"What?" he exclaims, thinking he hears a camel greet him by name. The noise draws the gazes of a dark-skinned old grey-beard and an equally Afghani-featured very gracious looking girl who drive the team. When the girl sees Larker, she scowls and ducks behind her own curtain. The man chuckles, patting her now vacant place invitingly for the youth.

He leaps shakily from the dray to the sandy track, steps around the slowly trundling team, and via a sideboard gains the seat nominated by the cameleer. The man nods a gentle welcome, then gazes out into the landscape, his arms folded. Larker matches his study, feeling somewhat of kinship to a first mate, bobbing in the red sand sea.

Low scrub grows on rocky clay pans and persistent gnarly pines dot peaked rises of sand. There is a hill in the distance, dim features running into the blunt trajectory of a ridge top. Larker closes his eyes a moment to sink his mind into the giant spinning planet beneath him. He finds seams of carnelian and a quick impression shows him huge tapers of smoky quartz in ancient limestone. He recognises the geo-imagery from pictures his father made of Northern Territory work. He knows a little of the where he is then, but recalls nothing of the how.

Serendipitously, the old man speaks. "Six days ago we do some trade with a monastery. Good trade. Wine for oil. We are coming early up the track but someone is on the sand. Milgn has shaken him awake then," the old man looks at Larker with baffled respect before continuing. "'Hallo', says the sleeper, 'I'm Larker. I believe you have come to see me through the storm border. May you and the road be one.' Then he is sleeping again, we can not awaken him.

"So we put him in the cart to turn once more for the monastery. But, incredible thing. Will the camels turn around? No. Everyone is yelling. Families, camels…then," he flicks his head behind him, "Senastim, my grand-daughter, says we must take you. So, we know she talks to the wind. We ask the camels to go ahead and they move without fuss. You wake a little for each night. You take some water. Then Senastim says last night, 'Tomorrow he is coming back to us'. Well, I am Joachim and you are a very good hitchhiker."

Larker laughs and wonders briefly how he came to be lying on the track. Trying to make sense through six days of dream fog, he asks, "So we're in the Northern Territory?"

"Yes. Yesterday we are come. To the 'Trusted Territory'." He says the new name with mocking humour. "And in four more days, all going well, we will see the border storms."

The cart suddenly leaves the track and they file behind a dozen more carts toward a distant casuarina grove. Larker notices nearly twice that many behind them as Joachim's cart lurches across the little hump of sand on the track verge and onto the clay pan.

After some minutes they reach the grove, trees thickly massed and greatly increased in this area that is filled with subtle hills and dips. The dense grove is on one of the longer hills, and they thread a path through trees and birdsong to a point halfway up it where the whole eastern contour slumps a bulge of stacked rock and windblown sand, declining to a curling depression of half a mile.

"Ah, lunch time for us," Joachim sighs, and Larker follows the old Afghani for a better view of the hill brow. "Ha, ha, come! Come and see the oasis," the man laughs and jogs down the sparsely treed slope with an athleticism juxtaposed to his age.

Before Larker follows him, he turns to see the clear-featured girl, Senastim, working on the harness of the kneeling camels. When she glimpses him she turns so that the natural mantle of her hair hides her face. Bemused, Larker heads down to the narrow depression.

By the time he arrives several men and women are digging, heaping mounds of red sand, and the finer white, to one side of the depression. He hears the rhythmic singing again, but to his surprise he finds he understands it. It is a song of sand and wind and something about a drink to make one sleep a thousand years. Its haunting tones are of lyric Arabic, a language he did not realise he spoke.

Larker takes the shovel from a slightly bowed Joachim and extends his excavations. The red dirt is soon heavy with moisture and it feels good to re-tension his body for such a necessary cause. A little well of clear water trickles up beneath him, and Larker and the old man cup handfuls of it to their lips. It is sweet, and Joachim fills a flask before patting Larker's shoulder and animatedly demonstrating how he should mound the dirt to make a bath. "And I will bring the camels to drink."

Lying in the cool water, high sun warm on his shoulders, Larker sees camels massing to drink further down the soak. He hears one's thoughts, *'Is it not sweet water?'* He sees a camel looking intently at him, and answers it in his own head. *'Yes!'* He finds he can tune out the mounting babble of their curious conversation and the one who had contacted him merely dips its head to drink.

As he dances his sturdy pants on, he wonders what exactly had happened to him that night where his memory ended at the huge redgum. Another side to him knows it matters not. It is important purely to concentrate on the amazing connection to life and vitality that it has brought.

Larker finds lunch laid out on sturdy sheets of split-bamboo mats fixed to bamboo poles and held rigid by a tight undercross of twine. Most of the ninety people of the caravan are heaping salads, eggs, olives, fresh date chutney onto a plate of rice stew gleaned from two huge cauldrons. Larker pours wine, a rare treat, into a cup fashioned from a coconut. Propped against a big casuarina trunk, he studies the group.

He knows their number without counting, just as he knows their names and language, purely by this new and rich intuition. There are about a dozen children. A similar number of teenagers, among whom Joachim's grand-daughter, Senastim, is gracefully dining, sit with their backs to the shade of the kitchen cart, sunlit faces unusually reposed for their age group. The younger adults number thirty, as do the older men and women. Some few were not of Afghan stock. A Fijian couple, a woman from New Zealand, and an old Irish patriarch whose naturalised son had an aboriginal wife. These eighty-seven wayfarers are the last of a long Australian tradition of camel traders. The Dew, they named themselves, though most called them spit vultures — after their camels' habit. A hundred and thirty years ago their numbers had peaked.

At this stage, for many reasons, American South Austral abandoned its twenty year campaign to seal a desert borderline with over two million troops, from which line they had coordinated the bombardment of the new nation with ceaseless missiles. The government was out of money and weaponry, and fissures were gaping on the domestic front. There was dissent throughout the Austral populace against the W.A.R. government. Vast numbers of climate-change and political refugees were arriving daily on southern shores. ASA was experiencing a rapidly unravelling social profile following the release of thousands of prisoners, and disbanding of jails perpetuated on the world by Curlew at its inception through the brandishing of its irrefutable wild card — the stolen Mouth satellite.

As they had retracted the long coil of desert troops into their coastal bases, the government had covered its tracks with dissemination of the official lie that Curlew had threatened to use its pirated space weaponry on a random city unless the border was thrown open.

Larker knew, through pieces of information his father had uprooted, that the Mouth satellite had by then been three years defunct, lacking the periodic maintenance which its continued operational shelf life demanded. There was little that the W.A.R. government could have done to Curlew at the time, short of building new spacecraft to retrieve the nuclear weapons and archived atomic blueprint that Curlew's initial demands had seen gathered world-wide and sent spiralling toward the sun.

The stringent purge, policed by Curlewans at all levels, had wiped nuclear weaponry from the knowledge of man as thoroughly as Mouth had evaporated every missile and satellite launching facility from the face of the Earth mere hours after the expulsion of Slitter's force from his old hunting grounds.

Manifest ground or aerial warfare against the refugees and their growing thousands of sympathisers was proven to be fraught. The Herover Curlew possessed had a determinable shelf life of centuries, and as Larker's father's research had uncovered, its only two existing counterparts had been expunged by the Mouth satellite before Curlewalion's founders had even looked for a good place to set up camp.

Political manoeuvring and zealous patience were the best that the W.A.R. government had been able to achieve. Revolution had roared through America's new territories in the closing decades of the new millennium, stricturing its efforts to rebuild its military science and space command to a bare trickle.

Larker suspected that the W.A.R. government had no further use for patience and that its spheres of former mastery had once more been re-scaffolded. The world could hope that a new source of plutonium had not been found after Curlew had ensured all known uranium deposits were sealed under billions of tonnes of concrete embedded with countless explosive devices to foil their reopening. There were other ways in which a proficient military might deliver crushing blows. If the W.A.R. government's programs of mass destruction at all rivalled the thoroughness of its interior surveillance — the force that had managed to find out his father and neutralise the threat of his inquisitive mind — then slender years only were left to Curlew's sovereignty. The only thing those early freedom fighters had secured was a delaying of the inevitable.

What a joy it must have been though, when the withdrawal of the greatest W.A.R. force ever allowed those wishing to flee the anarchist state from northern homes — as well as those wishing to enter Curlew from the south —

the freedom to do so. Some travelled by boat while the sea border had remained open. Few south-bound patriots or north-bound new lifers travelled on the three haulways that still trickled with trade. It was too near to the two-hundred-kilometre-wide no-fly zone where both parties would laser down any hover.

Those who brought hovers to the border points, and paid for passage in the haulers, found hauler drivers were a rough breed — and that law did not rule these distant haulways. The roads were pitted and rutted, and only the driver's seats were padded and dustproof, not the makeshift cabins for people in the hauler's belly. Devastating tornadoes were increasingly common in the border area. Drivers braved the risk, and generally three or more haulers, if chained together in time, could not be lifted by the winds — but a caravan of the Dew could pass through hellish gales unscathed.

Though no one had ever witnessed the event due to the blinding sands, both passenger information and government radar indicated the Dew could outwit the fiercest of storms. Experts suggested that because of their excellent desert skills, the sand gypsies were forewarned of storms. They would then either dig specially designed pits in which their own bodies were half-buried as a human wall, or if time allowed, a dune would be undermined, then collapsed at the last second to weighten the caravan or create sudden atmospheric disturbances as foil for the wind.

None of the proffered theories sounded very convincing. The government tried gifts, cajoling, and then threats to get an explanation for impossible data. Still every Dew answered the same — we do not know how the winds spare us. After a time the Dew's skills became just one more curiosity in an unsettled world of drastic change, but safely and cheaply, caravans operated.

It was a romantic and peaceful way to drift towards a new life, easing in part the writhing philosophic divide of a nation at odds. Between the sixteen major desert stations, divided by a hundred kilometres of desert, eight to each side of the border, over a thousand caravans had plied their way. Crewed by at least one Afghani and aboriginal or itinerant workers; a sociographic much like that comprising this last band of caravaneers here before Larker, the caravans had picked people up from their old hovers, and deposited them at one pre-swapped or bought from a station yard across the border. There was now no egress from either nation, some peaceful Curlew psychic force having raised a buzz of sand ten kilometres high and wide across the length of the inland territorial line in 2073 that had rapidly congealed to a glut of debris.

These days tolerance of the Dew was slim. The fact that primitive operators could pass freely through the storm border where elite spies had failed, had not made South Austral well-disposed to the traders. This remnant band was indulged with unhindered passage because they kept the desert wells — that were occasionally needed by far-flung soldiers, miners or scientists — clear. Perhaps also because the government still wanted to know the secrets of their storm navigation. Radars, Larker knew, would concentrate on the group during storm hits, if such imprecise monitors were within range.

Larker becomes aware of the smell of aromatic food and the presence of a keen mind beside him. It is the Fijian woman. She passes him a wooden plate with an earthy familiarity, her regard querying behind his eyes with unflinching intensity. "You will need to eat slowly; then we can talk." As the two settle to their meal, a few caravan chickens bob by, craning necks optimistically.

Larker watches a toddler pick a single flower of the desert bluebell growing profusely in the rings of shade around the trees, then rush over to where the teenagers sit and place it upon a youth's lap. Smelling the flower dramatically, the recipient cries with mock joy and places it on the pile of bluebells he has beside him to show for his enthusiasm. The delighted toddler chuckles mellifluously and returns to the flower ring.

"The desert is lovely on a day like this when the wind is mild. A lot of space for being, space for talking," says the woman beside him, pushing aside a plate too bare for even the chickens. Larker grins around his chewing in assent. He picks up his cup of wine, asks, "How long have you been with the Dew, Esandril?"

If she reacts to his knowing her name, it is only in her answer. "Many things of this good people are no longer a mystery to me. I have learnt their secret recipes, their trade routes, and I have learnt their music since I was very young. But not every journey can be measured in years, Larker."

Larker chews a half egg before her steady regard. A look of resigned trust spreads over her features. Forty, those years number, he knows. A brief vision rises of Esandril dancing at her first welcome, only fifteen years of age, a vivacious, smiling girl with red tints in her hair.

Abruptly she asks, "What is a firefeather?" With the word, the sun takes on a strange colour, enfolds him in pastel doorways; deep they plunge him to where there is music.

"I do not know. But I think it is very beautiful."

Her nostrils flare as if to indicate how good the food is and Larker gasps a mouthful of the ricey stew into his appreciative belly.

"When you lay fevered, many of us took turns watching you. You spoke this word. Also, you called to your father with a great cry, 'They loved you. They have always loved you.' Something strange too, but for which I have to thank you. I had just sponged your face and was about to blow out the candle when you sat up and looked at me attentively. You held my hand, the one I had not used properly since a police automn, whose circuits had fused, pinned my arm too far behind my back. You said in a clear voice, 'You will not need this anymore, Esandril.' I felt a tingling and then you fell asleep. As I walked to my cartroom I knew my hand was better." She thumps her hand upon her chest and emits a deeply inflective sigh of respect.

As he finishes the meal, Esandril, resuming her meditativeness, once again takes Larker's plate. "Well, soon it is time to thread the track once more. I'm just going to see if they need help bringing in the water."

The handsome woman disappears, and Larker wanders to where an earnest babble of chatter punctuated by chaotic squeals indicates the children at play. They have resplendently crafted toy camels, replete with richly embroidered saddle blankets, tied to an imaginary tree. None of the dark-skinned little ones glance up, but an old woman smoking a pipe in the shade throws out an arm in greeting and calls him by name. *Good,* Larker thinks, taking a leathery hand, *this is the matriarch, chiselled by sadness and follies into the emotional powerhouse of the tribe.*

"I am Jesella. It is good you can walk again. It is funny, their game — worlds within worlds. But they are easily pleased. To them a camel is freedom, but only at eleven will they get their own."

"It is always so," replies Larker in Arabic without thinking, "the parents' ways are those of the gods to the very young."

"Yes, that is one wind that blows the little sand grains until they form stronger dunes. You speak Arabic."

"Only a little bit. Yet these kids I suppose see far more than most. Different cultures, both nature and towns." Larker uses English this time.

"A good life, but who knows how long freedom may let us live it." The ancient self-contained woman speaks Arabic, as though warming to an unspoken testing in their conversing.

Larker meets her eyes, like lichen on dark stone, and sees there an alliance; at least of seeking to meter wisdom in these pressing days. "I think the caravans travel one last time," Larker solemnises. Then as he turns his attention to the children, he says in a flurry, "We must make the best, Jesella, of the time we have." At that he rushes with mocking yells right through the children's game, then leaps onto a high overhanging tree branch. He clings there beneath it, like a hairless sloth but for keen eyes which watch the children's shock turn to awe and giggles. A very young child comes from behind another's back to stare, and the whole lot approach this curious creature, determined to see what it will do next.

In the end, as the girls huddle in various stages of chittering hysteria beneath him, and the boys mount an assault on the trunk, Larker springs over them into a somersault backward across the ground and jogs up to the improvised sandpit. Before the astonished, though ecstatic-to-the-point-of-screaming children reach him, he has liberated all their camels and absconded with them slung across a shoulder.

All the while he runs from that shrieking gladness, his mind is a-whir. In it he glimpses a swirling montage of oppressively heavy sensation. As he investigates the first tense images, he finds himself witness to a mining operation somewhere in the south of the Territory. Inconceivably, it is an ore of uranium that is being reopened.

Another image elbows into his view, of the north-east. In a small cattle town, a modern day massacre of aboriginals — shot with their own guns by Agents, framed with drugs. He sees a bus near the cattle town. It is loaded with empowerment cadets fever-pitched with excitement to be pulling into a military training camp at the termination of their school careers.

Sequentially, Larker cannot guess where in time these images lie. The soul of the land itself shows him torments occurring constantly. Poisoning and shooting of remnant desert animals by isolated farmers, soil dug down almost to crystal to make wind barriers, ancient aquifers being drained to water beef for export. Larker blinks and focuses back onto the crescendoing howls of laughter, the greenly gossamer casuarinas.

As the horde descends, he throws himself, pretending exhaustion, belly first over his trove of toys. They pry him off, roll him over, and each takes their prize with a little punch or hug according to their nature. Larker lies back in the grassy sprawl of bluebells, breathing hard, though not from the game. There is nothing, he thinks, for him to do about all these gravid scenes shown in his mind.

There are only the people who come before him, brought as time wills, that he may truly interact with. It is strange to feel no emotion in himself from such visions, yet reassurance to feel his reasoning faculties so honed.

In the radiant blue, sailing clouds coalesce, seemingly from thin air, and appear to pause above him. He watches their beautiful dancing swirls make plains and hills, vales and people. Then he sees that it is this glade they form, and the soak, complete with the Dew and caravan beasts. Larker sees himself in the sky, looking back as a tiny cloud figure between cloud trees. This idol of vapour remains lying, a mirror of his earthbound form, as the rest of the mass rearranges to depict a story in a quick succession of shifting shapes.

He sees that journalists will come to the mining town, a day and a half travel up the track. They will finish filming just before the Dew arrive, and the scuttling of this film into people's homes will canker hearts with its distorted truths and vitriol, entrenching the confusion already present in Austral households into a terrible rage and fear.

The cirrus swirls into wispy threads and then the sky is blue, unchanged once again. Almost a spirit, Larker observes, of the dreamtime, which had always been waiting to show this imbalance point of danger. A message fluent and unmistakable. The camels cannot read dreamtime clouds, he knows; he must explain to them and then to the Dew. As he runs through the trees, a speck of cloud, formed as a runner, follows him a while before fading into nothing.

Most of the camels are being led en masse up the slope from the soak when Larker finds them. He is able to broadcast his need to virtually all of them at once.

'Bravers of the barren lands and fortune of the greatest magi; I must ask you to heed me.'

He feels their attention focus on him as he walks alongside the head herder, with whom he discusses the source of the dates for the chutney, whilst psychically he engages the beasts.

'A very terrible thing is about to be caused by strangers at the next town. It will spread like the worst storm to lay its burden on many souls if we cannot come to the town in time.'

'Then we will reach it,' he hears one of the camel leaders think nonchalantly.

'But we must reach it before dawn tomorrow or we will be too late.'

Now a pandemonium of their ponderous thought forms erupts until a different leader speaks.

'We can do this thing. But if storms come, our efforts may fail.'

'Thank you, my friends. So we will try.'

As they come onto the flats by the casuarinas, many of the camels give a unified bellow. The herd mistress shoots Larker a puzzling, suspicious gaze, to which he shrugs genially, disappearing among the gathered carts. At the mostly deserted kitchen area, Larker prods and nudges people's psyches to make them want to gather for a quick travel counsel. In truth, when he picks up some of the still drying coconut cups and a few grapefruit left on an unpacked table to juggle with, it is only to aid him in concentration, not to enthral the slowly gathering crowd.

Which yet he does. Sitting up from where they lay for siesta, or on the dray of either of the kitchen carts, standing formally arm in arm if partnered, or having just walked up brushing off from a chore, all of the Dew are soon in a loose semicircle with him as its focus. By the time he notices, Larker is energetically pumping ten cups and three grapefruit into a beautiful fountain above his head.

The group imbibes a sort of pressured awe, exemplified by a middle-aged woman who looks around constantly to try to ascertain if anyone makes more sense of this than does she. He catches the eye of Joachim trying to look as if this is exactly normal while configuring hidden meanings. Larker interrupts the musings of the old one and the misgivings of the woman with a flick of a grapefruit to each. He lets the now dried cups drop to the dirt, and catches the last grapefruit. He begins to peel it while meeting all of the eyes before him.

A young boy saunters over to retrieve each cup and brush sand from them before they are deposited in their crate beneath the table. Larker enunciates a greeting and quick praise of the chefs in a hesitant but clear voice which falls upon the Dew in their own Arabic. The body language backing his words is a barely restrained expression of surging energy. As he continues, the sing-song voice and empathetic tones are guiding strengths where the words angle away from logic.

"I said to Jesella today, time is not ours to hurry, but my recent envisaging shows me a time at which our contribution needs to make a big difference. Now comes need to hurry ourselves through our journey to arrive on time. I barely remember who I am now. But if I am lost, it is only to be absorbed as a corpuscle in a greater field, one tenured by hope, and only as hope itself will, once budded in a heart, unfurl without recall to its specific point of gestation. Changed by whatever forces brought me onto your road, the alchemical levers which have worked upon me are merely a forerunner of the dynamo of change set to be unleashed by the climactic workings of this planet's esoteric guardians — renewed in their work upon the world. I feel that you are akin to me, separated by more than the temporality of the passing years from the cradles of your culture's nursery.

"I feel this distance even from myself. But I know of what value there is in humanity. I feel sworn to the treasure of its beating heart; its ability to change and to remember truth calls strength to my blood. Scarcely hidden yearning is in all of your hearts. I guess if ever that yearning strength needs to upwell, it must for what we will encounter at the next caravan stop.

"Even should we reach Curlew, we will need to extend much wary nurturing over the forces of magic that can sing through us, lost hearts of the desert all. This magic you know, for it is in simplicity and celebration. Now we must hold tight to the pattern coming whole, to kindling this good where it may spread."

As he talks he seems to conjure many questions in the minds of the Dew, and then to answer them with other mysteries. Inside them, wells of hope and memories of thoughts and philosophies begin to tremble with clarity; a link of energy surrounds them that has some of the Dew smiling, and some laughing. The young man with the upturned features has spoken so disarmingly, and is now concluding around the suck of citrus juice from his fingers.

"I have asked the camels, and they have agreed to match their strength to ninety-five kilometres before dawn. How or what we shall do, I can't say, but I know that with you stern people it is appropriate, you who are rallied around the last hopes of a rich nomadic lifestyle, that I am accompanied, to try and stop the visions I have seen from making this land divide into an unbridgeable chasm. We must arrive at the mining town at dawn to mete out the light of a little truth, and fight a foe that seeks to temper lies with indoctrination."

Joachim's cart travels second this time, so that the infinitely energetic Larker might be well forward to meet any chance or problem, the old Afghani driving in companionable silence for a long while. Larker lets the journey's gentle symphony — the jangle of harness and cart bells, the soft calls and laughter swapped down the line, and a slow breeze soughing through the trackside grasses — bear him along with its earthy coursing. Gradually, as though carried in a thermal spring along its meander past the palm trunks of its emerald domain, Larker is relaxed and transported.

He tumbles away through all the levels of his mind to a place beyond the fierce conduit of psychic energy that somehow siphons most of his awareness into a streamlining of probabilities. He makes of his every sensation or conversation a study of the wheels of chance, and draws his life as a force of stunning power, one that soon may trigger those wheels. He is still aware of the fragility of life, of its great joy, but strangely that joy seems of no consequence.

He is without autonomy to direct his individual efficacy, except as a steadying of intent, so happiness seems only to serve as an island beach and lure new waves to sweep one from its shore. Beyond hopes, and doubt of his effectiveness in the imminent and ugly cultural showdown, Larker slips.

In a little vortex of memory he finds it lying trapped like a shimmering leaf upon a web of diaphanous beauty. A soothing wave of song, enduring all these years since when his mother had been alive. Larker could not be sure whether the lovely song was sung by her or left by some other chance encounter. He holds it now. Committing its rhythm to his conscious…feels his body hum with pleasure to this forgotten pattern cycling once more through it.

Aftermath to this dreamy mood, Larker notes that the camels, halted as one, are kneeling down — every beast. At the same time Joachim joins other voices in a compelling cry. "Smashlooser! Cover up!" Joachim presses a plastic head glove, replete with a ventilator, into Larker's hand. All around the air turns yellow with grit as a groaning sucking sound, snarling deep into the ear's acoustic chamber, precedes the black muzzle of the storm.

This wind pocket is huge, moving toward them as though it were dark brown paint poured across a horizon made of glass. The debris-laden smashlooser fills the height of the whole sky. Even though to its peripheries the desert is clear, at ten kilometres wide it will certainly hit them. As his world is buffeted by dark and an escalating tormenting roar, Larker wonders where Senastim, the girl who talks to the wind but not to him, is now. Then he is plunged into the thought streams of the camels.

'She is large and hungry and eager to reach the ocean.'

'But not deep, I think; may she carry the prayers of the blameless.'

'May she carry the prayers of the blameless and not disturb the rains.'

'Come, I am first in resonance, one butterfly from the heart; let us begin.'

Larker hears the camel, who had last spoken from amid a team behind, begin to drone. In his mind he hears the sounds that are swept from any other's hearing by the mounting storm. He knows the noise does not need be heard. Its effect is in simply being bounced off the air, along with the other hundred camel voices now droning in the wind. The harmonies make a powerful pulse of energy. The reason they shield the caravan from the smashlooser is very complex and deeply stirring. Larker feels like a guilty spy as he intuits the beasts' secret from their image feelings.

The camels know how much water they and all others have in their humps. In the space left over, a vacuum forms that counteracts the wind. The camel who first begun has the least water, but drones the loudest. At times all the static magnetic energy of the others concentrates inside her hump. They in turn receive the full load of frequencies. In this way a rolling wave of ultra-sonic sound creates a portal around the camels, and charged air particles are momentarily torn apart or forced deep into the ground as they meet this anomaly.

The smashlooser rages by without doing damage, and after a few minutes the camels' droning and the horrific snarls of the wind stop at exactly the same time. How the camels had learned this, Larker could not tell. He suspected it was a genetic memory from an age long ago when freakish winds had also been common. As the smashlooser folds away towards the coast, the camels, people and wagons sway into life again like flowers reopening after a dimming of the sun.

Throughout the night, Larker prays that no more storms will slow them. He thinks the Dew very brave to abandon their delineated trade route for this shortcut and risk annihilating pulses from an automn scouting party. He feels honoured to travel with them and their unique animal guides, and the procession moves now with a quiet dignity distilled into a rarefied poise by his very awareness of their skill and integrity.

This peace is broken as they come upon the fringes of Maroytar. Larker's intuitive fact file on it is short. Zinc and copper chelate mining town. The most northerly South Austral settlement. Residential and subsidiary commercial holdings of course deep underground. Huge slag heaps rise in the dawn sky, dwarfing even the massive hauls that lumber along or lie wasted in rust. Several even larger shipment hauls, twenty-five metres or more high, slowly thread the near distance, heading for the ports at coastal Addlable.

The processing plants appear to run together like a fossilised seam of progress. Massive conveyor belts, crushing blocks, and grading wheels sulk or screech to the day like the long abandoned toys of a giant alien race. Soon business signs betray the centre of Maroytar, and one, blasted into a rock outcrop, delineates 'The Tar Hotel' — their destination.

Narrow diagonal tunnels admit the caravan into the hover yard through a roughly, yet effectively engineered wall, both high and thick. About twenty dusty vehicles adorn the otherwise featureless area. To one side of the dirt square are drinking troughs and rock holds to feed camels. The Tar Hotel accommodates caravan camels along this wall, if grudgingly, and only because it is still the law.

Larker steps into the foyer. Its entryway, a conglomerate of massively hewn stone and slurried concrete, is spray painted with layered obscenity and inanity. A panel of lights flickers into awareness, and joined by Kerfrith, Yorstee and Ramavia, Larker steps into a room through a thin panel that quickly slides into place again behind them. Siphoning dust-dislodgers hum, pulling air into the floor beneath them, then a door to an elevator opens. The four enter, press the only button and are soon disgorged in the vast main chamber some distance below ground.

More smoke than the siphon systems can anywhere near remove is filling the high-roofed chamber from various of the hundred patrons. The scent of 'tough', a nauseating cologne mix of engineered pheromones overlaid with pine and diesel synthetics batters the air. It seems to be working on the few women present, who just screech louder and toss their hair more affectedly on catching sight of the strangers.

The men tense as one entity and a few groups begin pointing and staring in their direction. A barmaid, whose intellect clearly stops at the neatly bowed pink laces on white boots, bustles over from some debate around a table, and appraising Yorstee to be the authority, addresses her hospitality to him.

"What can I get ya? Like, what do youse want for yers an' that?"

To cover for his companions' offended sensibilities, Larker answers for him, ordering that pot of coffee they had talked of in the foyer — and on assurance they stock real lemons, a jug of lemon water. Yorstee informs the rumpled-faced and pit-eyed lady that they require feed for their camels.

"I'll let Harry know to activate the courtyard autommn then," she promises, screeching something at a miner about his meal as he paunches toward the bar.

Finding seats at a long, empty bench near the bar, Larker watches as the Dew slip into a kind of claustrophobic malaise. Another five of the Dew join them. Under vicious scrutiny from the locals, the travellers half-heartedly discuss the price they will receive for wattle rope that they traditionally sold to the miners for marking claims, then fall silent.

Larker begins to talk, essentially to distract his friends from the gauntlet of contempt surrounding them, and the huge television screen that commands the roof, split into four different anguishes. He talks of the journey route to come, draws Trabis out about a rumour that he has a kite for gaining altitude to survey the vista, and recites a funny poem appraising the camel.

In essence, Larker's true focus — his prior intuitive knowledge of it ballooning to a deep clairvoyant revelation — is on the town of Maroytar. It had sprung from a corporate shanty into a civic centre 124 years ago. At the inception of the border guard for South Austral, the W.A.R. government had bought the holdings of Master Mined and leased the prospects, retaining centralised processing. The resultant town had been a foil of distraction and comfort for troops stationed nearby and is still thus on a smaller scale today.

In the town's psyche Larker can easily discern a function more than just remunerative. For this is as close as South Austral came to the Allied Frontier, and as close as its citizenry could come to delving into the mind pool of pathos, swimming in the patois of normal decency, or scaling the heights of heroics.

In some 113 years, the tally of confirmed Curlew terrorists and spies killed by vigilant Maroytarians was ten. Also consumed in the bravado of frontier defence were eighteen misidentified townsfolk out on dark nights, twenty visitors, and a truck load of aboriginal workers from Poygarl who had come to deliver a vehicle to the town's workshop and spend a night at the hotel. They were executed by the dynamite attack of a zealous miner. Maroytar is not an alluring destination for visitors, but miners and haulers earn a good living, thanks to government bonuses.

The group of three men — miners by the contradicting look of muscled limbs and sagging stomachs — who Larker watches idling by the bar, are utterly bent on harm. He knows this well before they surround the Dew pair coming across from the elevators. His blue eyes flit, as do those of his companions, in a quick gauging of the immediate environment. Ritual disdain born of social obligation has given way, seemingly with the end of a rugby telecast, to chaotic, infantile distraction.

As he studies the frozen tableau of mood swing, glasses that dislodge onto the cheap carpet in a jostle of listless elbows merely roll unnoticed under the tables. To Larker's imagining he hears each sharply smash. By the time he slips stealthily along the side of an unlit pool table to where he can appraise the unfolding scene, the two newly arrived Dew have disappeared in a sea of hairy brown arms sticking from tank tops.

"What's that, mate?"

Larker hears one of those in the unholy trinity gasp.

"What did you say, dupe dick?" His friends join in.

"You need to know what Australians think of being insulted," adds the first provocateur.

There isn't much Larker can do as the lumping redhead punches the comparatively tiny Dew. Larker focuses on the fall being safe, and with a psychic squeeze to the underside of the brain cortex causing a merciful rush into unconsciousness ensures the victim does not invite further damage. Larker presses forward to hold a serviette to the bleeding nose as the aggressors perpetuate the lie of being verbally abused by the Dew to a bloating mob of onlookers.

Without regard for any bruised understanding he may inflict among the Dew, Larker, now honed to this towns' undercurrent, looks up from where he still presses the man's bleeding nose and addresses his companion, who is hedged by an even thicker thorn of muscle.

"Hey, Marco, if I look after Punchinello here, can ya bloody check see as the automns aren't scarin' the camels."

Larker magnetises energy to his facial features, making them convey to all those he looks at that this is meant to be. Marco makes a subtle retreat via an elevator. The tough who first pretended insult from the Dew, patently the ring leader, demands of Larker, "What are you, the Kamelkasi Kid? Must be hard to stop those buggers from getting up them at night, hey?'

Those barflies within hearing burst into laughs and savage hoots in response, with calls of 'Terrorise 'im, Terry'. Larker calmly overrides an urge to reply that he is indeed in communicae with the camels, and that their intelligence so far outshone this man's and his mates' as did gold outdo zinc and chelate.

"Nah, mate." He stands and the bar bristles. "I'm just a … hitch…hiker." He accompanies those last words with mime. Pants are pulled mock-painfully up to the crotch, then a little puffing circle is walked, thumb tucked in front of shoulders, his braids swinging wildly. With a goofy look around, Larker sees the tension starting to fold.

From the back foot, his interrogator makes another play. This time Larker has psychically steered the question, and is ready with answer to: "So why'd ya bloody waste your time on them?"

"Same reason you do, mate. They're weird, but they're here in this desert we call a life."

"And the mongrel bloody dupe blokes," blurts out one of his sidekicks, "are so bloody busy with their camels that he gets a total dust-off from all their chicks."

Larker doesn't even have to guide the predictable wind-down, and a couple of old men and soldiers at the bar who had been watching intently now turn away disinterested.

Yet with the man's laughter at his own joke comes a half-clap, half-smash on Larker's shoulder from the huge paw. He is ready for the unconscious brutality, and has breathed into his shoulder muscle so the blow is primarily diffused on the outrush of breath that is a feigned laugh.

The puncher hugs the joker around the head and they saunter away on a wave of corrosive laughter, chanting "Desert desserts" until they eclipse into the crowd.

As the other Dew comes over, Larker says," We best get this poor brave one downstairs." They hoist him gently without fuss, but as they pass by the redhead, his protruding cheekbones lent a reptilian cast, he still exudes an obstinate malevolence. He lets out a soulless "Ahhh," as the Dew pass with their fallen, dropping his beer-can as he stares at Larker, then stagger-turning to bustle up to a group of teenagers, yelling at his utmost pitch in a senseless slur.

It does not seem strange to Larker that many in the bar are drinking at the breakfast hour and have probably gone right through the night. A hard people for a hard time and place. He joins with a group of Dew on their way down to the bunk catacombs, and learns of a number of bags of washing and bedding waiting in the foyer yet to be carried down. Larker assures them he will gather a few. He jokes about how many tips he will be able to collect, smoothing his old shirt, then the Dew are gone in a murmur.

Thoughts pleasantly domestic, he turns towards the elevator and stumbles right into a blunt-faced youth. Others of about Larker's age gather in an oily slither behind him. Larker recognises the face from the group the redhead had sported off to. He watches the acne beneath the freckles flush like the blushing of some male monkey. The tight little freckled lips loosen in anticipation of the excitement of battle, pupils contract to dark pools. The shaman's first impression is that he must be quick and decisive. Still, it is not time to release the disinterested aura of mateship woven so tacitly. He puts aside the vision of bringing his dowsing staff in under the youth's chin. The instant the vicious young face had swum into his awareness he had been musing upon the time he had pulled up his shirt to show Brother Jacobin the tattoo. He lets synchronicity guide his action.

Without pause, he pulls up his shirt, to the titter of a few aimlessly onlooking women, and says to the attacking group, "Er, like a string-bean, fellers." He loudly slaps his stomach. "Totally gutless. More joy's to be had — ha-ha — dropkicking through an old ghost. I'm sure I can spook by you without even making the air move. Backgerk! The amazing feather man," he calls as he passes. The surprise bludgeoning is deflated and Larker disappears into the elevators.

In the courtyard some of the trader nomads are readying breakfast in the little space behind the caravans. There is much banging and clanging of pots, and Larker retreats carrying the laundry. Down in the hospice, singing joined by the usual harpsichord and woodwind comes from some of the rooms. The wild and fluent music seems strange in the clinically engineered warren, with an accompanying bass of groaning water pipes.

The allure of water, hot by the sound of those kicks and spurts in the pipes, generates a sudden weakness in Larker. A room key is priced at ten dollars in the dispensers, and Larker soon finds 'three-one-eight' and secretes himself in its shower system. It is just so vital, he thinks beneath the spiralling sprites of steam, to staunch the flow of hatred here. Here at the merging point of two societies. Ever since the night that he cannot remember, he knows some Earth essence has been growing in him, unfolding into power he always knew was possible. As though the land itself were wielding through him this exact action of consideration and energy reflection, sundering his emotions but trapping his psychic power in a vial of pure expression.

Now he has little more than a morning in which to overthrow a stigma of reaction, inflect a truth of ages into Maroytar. He knows he has secured a little respect of those at the twenty-four hour bar, but the cost of violence to the Dew is daunting. As Larker uses his shirt to pad himself dry, a fluxing chill from somewhere in the cellar block is like a tunnel of doubt. He feels the approach of peril, senses it bodily with the flicker of ache in his finger where a prised-up rock had rolled back on to it when fossicking with his father.

Returning to the bar, he joins a clean and re-invigorated Dew group. A waitress gets through about twenty orders, and Larker's spinach crepes are probably the most complicated. After half an hour of waiting to be served, while others who had ordered after them are already finished, Melliah slips up to the camp. She returns with bread and some dips, mainly to pass among the children and youths. Pelewat calls over the waitress who had first attended them.

When the dark cloud reaches the table, she stands hands on hips and growls in exaggerated slowness, "This is a restaurant. If you want to graze, go and join the camels."

Pelewat and his son stand up, flushed. Larker reads malcontent in their honed muscles. "We have paid for breakfast and would like it," the aboriginal man says.

Another waitress and miner boyfriend come over. A potage of waxy potions covers the woman's remnant hair, which is a continuation of her distorted body, as corrupt as her patois. Placing the dips on a beer tray, she growls, "Ge' them ou'."

Nobody offers to remove the offending articles.

"Got a problem?" asks boyfriend of everyone.

"No problem," says Larker. "It's just that we're slobberin'."

"And too weak from hunger," joins Melia, scooping up the tray. "For clobberin'."

The Dew chuckle.

The boyfriend chokes out, "You's nongs want rhyming…I'll show you dreamtime."

Larker had bent his words from the intended 'knuckletime' to dreamtime. The effect of his utterance is instant. The word has not been heard in the hotel ever, and Larker triggers a mass imagining of being shown the dreamtime. He conjures the feeling in people of the land as an old friend, filled with tales, with eyes like deep natural waterholes. The tone in the bar changes. People talk softly and a woman's laugh tinkles out genuinely. Seeming confused, the man drifts off with the waitress, who tells the Dew that patience is a virtue, and that she'll check with chef.

By the time the meal is over, most of the bar's patrons have dispersed. Those who had gruelled through dawn from last night's session begin to melt into their rooms, while the miners with a hard morning staring into a sifter's screen ahead — now fortified with a belly of beer — have left. Larker convinces three Dew to join him, and as they emerge into the courtyard they see a miner ahead of them test a bark rope for flaws, throw money onto a rug laid before some Dew, stalk to his hover. The camel hair bracelets do not seem to be selling so well.

Silence wraps the wagons, covered in cotton spoils against the heat. Not even the sound of dishes disturbs those sleeping off last night's travel. The four walk toward the entry arch but are halted by a voice.

"One moment." Beside the last wagon, Joachim sits, a long pipe in his mouth. "In such a place we cannot hope for safety. To walk these streets in numbers may at least moisten their dry morbidity."

Six caravaneers traipse from the side of the wagon with little packs overslung by water flasks. Among them is old Tharrin, his Fijian features impassive. Senastim slips behind the group as they leave the courtyard.

"My daughter foresaw that we would be needed," Joachim confides to Larker.

On the street, a sign carved into the base of a hover-steer reads, 'uphold the trust'. Beside is the Territories' coat of arms — the head of a bull mastiff dipped to drink from a trambian pipe. The morning is already hot. Though the red dust is lacquered over with algalate, a biotech triumph of living glue, there is a thin dust rising from the sky, care of the ceaselessly screeching and shuddering crusher giants.

Commerce raises little cameos despite the heat. A bag-laden woman, coming from the supply store, fingers a holster on seeing the group, then stumps away. At the corner, a hover lands, and the proprietor of the fuel store who sells oxygen, bio-diesel and solar slides from his underground stock, steps from the shop to fill the man's oxygen tank and swap languid profanities.

Larker's group passes into the residential zone. Dwellings are marked by massive stone edifices like fallen tombstones, and occasionally by huge houndings that rush furiously at the walkers to bark at the limit of their programming. There is nothing otherwise describing this as a place of humanity. Disgorged slumps of rock and chaotic pits stretch in all directions.

Eventually Larker addresses his eleven companions, now winded of the chant and song that had carried them to the outer limits of town.

"Let's head up this rise. Maybe from the crown we can watch the border storms."

Even before they begin to ascend the bulging slag heap left by the old processor beside it, a tingling all over his body and a sudden fluctuation of the heart as his energy rushes up his spine tell Larker that the peril and destiny he sensed is come. On the top of the heap the three hovers that have been slowly descending, land, surrounding them — except toward the steep bluff to one side.

"I tell you what," says the red-headed Puncher, striding out of his hover, "if one of you druggie spies can stand one-to-one with me and win, then I won't shoot anybody." He pulls a laser from a holster. The other six men are armed. Two have weapons drawn.

The equipoise of the Dew seems to enflame the awkward rupture of a man, recalled to some of them from the assault at the pub. He spins into the Dews' faces, screaming. "The only thing worse than spies is drug-pushing spies. I wouldn't have got my habit if not for you." At that he reaches into a pocket and sniffs from his palm what must be 'race' — precursor to death developed for military uses from a synthesis of all the nasties.

"Come on, you!" he gestures, backed by the semicircle of accomplices and focusing on Larker. Larker cannot even see him. He is awaiting the exact moment to strike again. All of his focus is spread between watching the coils of mesmer spun from the maniac to his henchmen, and the very breath, gaze and hearing of that half-moon of aggressors. He is in body only enough to stand upright. Tharrin saves him, though.

Almost as soon as the Fijian moves, Puncher throws down his laser and bulls forward. Larker had struck while the man had been yelling into the faces of the Dew. He found a word they had for him, his sycophants — "Maddog". He had wound their group-mind around it as a theme, had muffled their hearing to warp the last of the tirade into a shocking "woof, woof, woof," interspersed with snarls. As the redhead had snorted his drug again, Larker made acute their hearing to catch the animal sound, and a few had visibly blanched, disturbed — but by realisation, not confusion.

Tharrin dodges the first blow to catch it on his shoulder, grabs the taller man by his gut, and headbutts into his eyebrow. Puncher lands two blows into Tharrin's liver, and an elbow into the stooping back, but as the solid Fijian goes down he topples Puncher by hugging his knees. Tharrin smashes a fist into each thigh, then both exchange throat clasps and facial blows. On top, Tharrin has gravity on his side, and slips the throat hold to grab a stocky arm and lurch backward, trailing Puncher along his side, and swinging a kick around that over-stuffed frame to catch the base of the spine.

Most of the fight goes from Puncher, and Tharrin pulls the arm up tightly and kneels on his back. The head is pulled back hard, wringing reality into it, then planted more softly into the dirt while Tharrin stands.

"You, boy, are beaten." Before he can brush the dust from his clothes the Fijian falls over the edge of the bluff from a laser blast to the head, to disappear in a little avalanche of stone and dust, swirling thickly up with a blast of wind that is like his spirit soaring free.

Puncher brandishes his concealed boot laser at the Dew, now screaming in shock the charge of coward and liar, but constrained by his murdering instrument to rail against the air. Some among the group are calm; Larker stock still, and Joachim observing the others behind Puncher.

Larker acknowledges the betrayal and travesty at the far distance of his senses, but he must deal with the present. He now knows what he has suspected all along — that this man's powerful animalism and violence hold thrall the other six men, and contributively poison the progress of the town's psyche. He steps forward, hand outstretched to the maniac.

"Now take it easy, big fellow. No one's going to hurt you." He uses phrases and gestures he knows the others will associate with negotiating a dangerous dog.

"No. Nobody's going to hurt me, but you and your buddy killed each other over the drugs security will find on your friends when we turn them in — and you guys witnessed everything, right?", he says, turning to his pack.

Larker amplifies the feeling of being bitten in the other men, makes the words sharp teeth in their sense of individuality, and calls to memory the first time each was manipulated into a pack mind by this brute.

"Put down your weapon now," says one of those with an already drawn laser, now pointed at Puncher.

"Don't you fucking talk to me like that," he threatens, confused by the challenge. The answer is whooshing explosions from two lasers and Maddog falls dead. Larker draws the men's vision to the foam trickling at the cruel mouth's edge, then illuminates their grasping for self-identity, takes them to family experiences, empowering their conviction. One of the men is squeezed on the shoulder by another. "You did well to shoot, mate."

As Joachim negotiates the use of a hover for the fallen Tharrin, and arranges to rendezvous at the security office for a full deposition of events, the tension among these Marotoyans breaks.

"What a bloody morning!" one says laconically. The Dew, clustered in little groups, watch Larker and Senastim leap over the steep bluff, looking for the entire world as though jumping into the border storms that flicker with red lightning on the far horizon.

Larker reaches him first. Tharrin lies on his side at the bottom of the heap. An ugly gravel rash mars one cheek. His hair is singed, but unusually little for a laser strike. As Larker slows his descent, brown eyes open.

"I hope Robian still knows how to put dislocated shoulders back in. What happened to the maniac?"

"His friends killed him," answers Senastim

Larker is stunned. He recalled the laser striking the Tharrin's head, the huge unconscious fall and tumble awaiting. Then he sees the memory field around Senastim. She had rearranged the air, the cloud and the background density around Tharrin just before the shot, causing Puncher to fire wide, and his little close-kill model to explode at the side of the Fijian's face, delivering only concussion. She had caught the falling man in an air cushion, and pushed at his neck-breaking plummet with all the energy she could gather. She is spent now, exhausted.

Larker hitches a ride with Tharrin, Joachim and two miners as far as the Regulative Enforcement Dome, saying he will send Robian for the shoulder trick. Walking to the hotel, he finds himself pondering Senastim and the pendant he had noticed her wearing. He wakens Robian then goes down to the rooms to give Tharrin's partner, Esandril, a quick précis of events.

"He is a rare man. I think I owe him my life."

"Well, he probably owes his to one of those unique talents of yours?"

"Not mine, Senastim's.'"

"Ah. Tonight do we leave?"

"I think so."

"Well, I am back to bed for more rest."

Leaving the capably calm woman, Larker's attention is snagged by a cry on his way across the bar. It is the man he recognises as the manager, who had finally overseen delivery of breakfast with an apologetic air. He is propped on the bar, dishes clanging behind him, but the two are alone.

"Every time I clap eyes on you, you're running around. Sit down and have a beer — on the house."

It is not quite noon but Larker remembers the half-glass of black beer he used to drink with his father. "Alright, but make it black."

The drink arrives before him topped by a thin caramel head. The corpulent hotelier's style is earthy. "I actually do this job because I like people. Even these people. My great-grandfather was a hotel man here before the, ah…succession. So I was eligible to buy this place ten years back. Best place in Austral away from most of the policy and fear-cramming."

"Why didn't you try to get to Curlew? No reality tailors there."

"Chuck it in with the pirates? Not for me, mate. Plus my roots are south. I actually like capitalism — and nationalism. I think true change comes slowly. I realise now just how slow, but egress is banned. I don't really want to speak a new language, live in a hut, and have psychic group minds centre my inner thoughts. Still, some of what they do across the way is a marvel. Feeding that many people…we should still let the information and civic ideas cross-pollinate." It wasn't Curlew who tried to push the border territory deeper and militarised like crazy."

"It seems like it's stagnating here," says Larker. "Trambian pipes will fail in fifteen years or less, then towns like Marotoyar will cough, splutter and die."

"There you are right on the nose, mate, but Curlew engineers who would explain the deep-flow harmonics can't come across. So the Curlies manage to provide safe, clean water, while what we get is both pumped and filtered by unstable chemical interactions. What's happening under our very feet is surely what's important, yet the energy of our townsfolk is being dispersed into some far-gone paranoia about border infiltration. They're a friggin' bunch of fools mostly, but their motivations are simple, not complex like city folks. If the hardliners at the security office could shut off the vitriol a bit, you'd see gold under that tin dust. I hope you forgive them their overstated town pride and I hope you get across the border. You're trying to smuggle over?"

To Larker's nod: "Well, they've bigger guns up at the border than any of the quacks around here, and they'll know every face in the caravans, but if you get through and come this way again, things might have changed a little. So stop in."

"I think they will have. Thanks, and thanks for the ale."

No doubt the publican, as Larker makes his way to the security office, is feeling slightly bemused at his assertion regarding the need to find a working medium here in the middle of things. Indeed the seed the shaman had sowed earlier of dreamtime awareness — and now his psychic underpinning of this good man's awareness upon the importance of water — should combine to make lively conversation at the evening's session. As Larker nears the dome, an idea comes to him.

To maintain security, the building is sighted with a clear view to its north, windblown sand verging the streets, terminating in a cul-de-sac to one side of which a dwelling entrance rises. A woman stands at the entry way of her underground home, looking wistfully across the empty sand of her immediate neighbourhood. Probably, if she was not half-longing for it, Larker could not have sustained the illusion.

Before he crosses the street to the office, he sees them bound across the awed woman's gaze at the clearing's edge; five females and one huge male red kangaroo. Their brief flight is testimony to the magic of this, their once-roamed land, and as he enters the R.E.D., the woman sees them disappear into the heat haze, but her heart remembers.

The caravan snakes out of town while the sun is still high in the sky. As they pass from sight of the mining monsters, Larker feels the journalist's hover go by and descend into the town. His consciousness goes with it and remains to prod the interviewer; to be sure they question the right people, and so his strange power does not help the Dew to slip to one side of the usual border-base entry point. A message from a Dew Strong Talker tells Curlew's vigilant Indigo Mantles — lethal psychic security — that their approach, though not from the usual line, is of no threat, as Senastim pulls tendrils from the border storms to cover them from sight of Austral air patrols.

They are vulnerable, and right until they pass within the main storm, a missile from any of seven bases could have found them. Larker finally sleeps off the tension from a long day. The guards at the closest radar monitors, who should have seen the sigils approximating the hidden organic life within the suddenly swelling storm, are distracted by a documentary about the paranoia over border security leading to a Marotoyan's killing by his friends — his aunt bewailing the vitriolic fanning of his madness with political stereotyping. Watching a publican talk of the need to open trade with Curlewalion for the sake of desert communities; and watching a woman talk of the mob of big reds that had passed through town, bringing a gift of the land's dreamtime. Larker is sleeping still as the first scouts of Curlew come alongside the darkened wagons and happy camels.

Chapter 10

We have lingered in the chambers of the sea.
By sea-girls wreathed with seaweed red and brown
Till human voices wake us, and we drown.
T.S. Elliot

There were times when the tribesman (for such he now considered himself) focused around his endless pain to whimsy after opium, even though that red flower's juice — soul grease of Europe — had been the cause of his penal sentence. For opium he had had to have to apothocare his sister's post-childbirth agonies, albeit that his sporadic employ as a wheelwright's assistant forbade the luxury of its purchase.

Still, it had seemed easy, in a hedged kitchen garden of a sleepy manor, to clip fifty ripened poppies and place their stems in a ewer of water. He had nicked most of the seed capsules to stop the opiate hardening from within as he walked down the lane, but he had dropped the ewer as the gamesman called behind; had run as far as the gardener with upheld fork at the lane's end.

At least this pain brought Ben the memory of its begetting. His flight had been a success. If he survived now, the totem rights were his to claim. He linked his will to this thought as a sailor to a lifeline at sea, and such will remained when the seed cakes and coolamon of water left by the women had gone. With the brightness of light at the tree's mouth to symbol day, Ben crawled out amid tall sprays of golden grass and looked back up at the baobab. Gloriously old, it was distended like a huge caterpillar lying along the ground with impossibly monstrous antennae translating as the mass of leafless branches above. The tree-cave, for such did its trunk form, must go back another six metres from where he had laid, making an upper level that would sleep another five men.

The verdure of the country here enthralled Ben's attention. The riparian corridor had burgeoned after the year's good rain into such greenery, surpassing in its profundity even the hues through which he had steered his boyhood. He could see the creek gushing clearly only metres distant, and as he crawled toward it — the coolamon in his teeth — his hands plunged through a mat of tight green grass up to the elbows, meeting firm soil beneath. As Ben drank, he dipped his fevered head, and with his vision clearing, noted a minutiae of sparkling flowers; red, white, yellow, all along the creek bank. On the laborious journey back to his cave he uprooted seedling boabs whose sweet tubers, cleaned with a little water, were gratefully eaten raw.

In a day on which the claws of heat outside dragged all humidity from the tree's skin, and his, Ben watched bandicoots eating the boab's ripe fruit as it fell. After a long time, he moved. The muscles in his hips contracted into a pandemonium of pain inching him over the rough hallway to flow from the mausoleum's cavity like the first oozing trickle of a flood. A little way into tall straw-dried grass was a baige pod. Ben cracked its seam between his palms to eat the sweet and halky pith around the seeds.

By the time he was once more inside the cool dusty chamber, he had strength enough to ruck a lump of spongy bark in under his head, using his chin to gather the pillow, before he fell into a swoon. Ben saw himself etherealise into the sunlight outside and drift aimlessly across the plain. He followed a meandering river, until at the loud cry of a fleeing brolga on a bend he was no longer hovering, but wading through water.

Looking from the golden sand grains at his feet, peeling slowly into the current, to the skip of water across a fallen melaleuca trunk, Ben realised where his spirit was — at the children's pool, beside the tribe's gunyas. Suddenly he saw

Ngenlin letting fall a coolamon and splashing gracefully across the distance between them.

She pressed her lips to his and crushed her sweet body against him.

"You must study the tree. Become as same-nest with it. All will be well…"

The spirit-Ngenlin pushed a hand against his chest and turned. He caught a glimpse of a great glowing treasure beneath his baobab cave, and heard her say, "Find the tree's heart." Then he awoke, the enwombed darkness and stirrings of little things around him seeming benevolent, undershot with meaning.

Ben rolled onto his side, breathing as deeply as he was able and realised that the spirit he had met could not have been his love, as she would not have been so brazen, even in a vision. It must therefore have been a land-telling, a thing his initiators had told him to respect, and he found himself considering the glimpse of light and wonder it had shown that lay beneath this very tree. Ben allowed himself to be drawn into the little kingdom around him, his acceptance of his fate growing in measure to the engagement of his senses with the tiny rhythmic pulses of life all around. By the next day he found that a cessation in his worry about his totem and Ngenlin had occurred. His focus instead had been singularly on the environ of the tree-cave.

Watching the spiders at their web spinning was the Irishman's last study as dusk pilfered his light. Little bats flew out, too quick for pondering, and he noticed it was to the left again that they turned. Each and each thing to its place. Ben dreamed of the triangles within the webbing, of thrumming strands as tiny legs trod their weave-work. Deeper he dreamed of that light matrix on the tree's roots, of how it seemed to shift like the web, subtly changing.

For two weeks he remained in the tree, slowly attuning to the distillate permutations of five thousand years of knowing. He watched the spiders, neither sleeping, eating nor drinking. The spiders metered great patience offset with decisive action. He observed as wind or blundering gnats unbound their webs, and began to know the force that rebuilt them.

In slow graduation, the Moon engorged over two more weeks until it waited outside the tree-cave, swollen to its fullest. All the while Ben had been learning from the boab, drawing on its strength, and saddling his mind to the radiant math of its deep and arcane life-force. That pregnant night he was drawn, compelled with its sudden shifting intent, out into the world of moonstruck forms under a starry sky — from which he saw a bolt come.

Abruptly as the lightning, his ligneous womb plunged his mind, along with its spirit, into a black secret vault beneath it, utterly inert. As its outer bark was seared by the lightning, the boab's essence dwelt solely in this sanctum, enforcing a relaxation of its system, a deepening, a core unity. Ben slipped through yielding layers of his mind, settling in a poise of centredness, only to have his very blood beats fume out from under him, the darkness stretch him like a doll, and his sense of self fall away like a shore's sand that would not anchor a swimmer's grasping hand.

All at once he was filled with light, an agony of power which he could only master by dropping his mind ever further away from it. He could at last imbibe its glow by subtle shifts of his perspective to mute its excrucia. The tree, remembering again that universal forces greater than it prowled, drew its proud comprehension back to itself; the matrix pathways of its being reintegrating its outer pain as the lightning's nitrogen atoms fluxed like balm through its system, given that the initial devastation of fire had passed.

Ben opened his eyes. They did not feel like his. Before him in the tree's vault sat a thickset tribesman, his eyes staring at some distant world through a nimbus of light that surrounded him. Ben upraised a hand, and from the halo a streak of light transferred into his palm. Suddenly the fierce head of some deadly creature bulled from behind the man's shoulder, its growl an ancient warning as it tensed apprehensively.

"No. Arlyera. It is well. He is Mended now." The creature turned authoritatively, thick russet tail brushing the tribesman's face as it trotted into the night.

The man stood, his nimbus dimming, and stretched in the stooped fashion that the tree occasioned, as though he had waited a long time.

"Good. We feared you might die. The Keeper has taken you deep indeed. Rest, then follow us. Food you will not need, but the creek is a true-flow. Drink of it. Until then."

The man was gone from the boab in a heartbeat, joining more of the pantheresque creatures in silent journey downstream.

"Until then, Maeddan," Ben murmured, curling into sleep without wondering that he could speak the man's tongue or name his true form.

Ben awoke with the pulse of life tremulous for joy in every part of his being. He hunched out upon legs miraculously hale, and stepped as though through feathers to the creek. The land seemed to lift toward him like the arms of a child. All this — the molten sunrise, the slouching wattles and bauhinias and cottonwoods on battered escarpments, even the quoll, whose energy trail he could see as it lay beneath a log — Ben took into his heart.

A smile lifted each corner of his mouth to make another sun as he dived into the creek. He swam underwater with eyes open, savouring the cool flow and beautiful salience of polished roots, and the drooping grass clumps along the banks. Froglike, scoffing to himself for his boyishness, he surfaced to drink deep and noisily at a bend where fallen timber was an impediment. In one breath, with the water's tug to aid him, he had covered more than a mile, and now his teaching tree was a blur in the background as he leaped onto the bank.

The energy trail was wide; that of his new peerage, the Mended. He knew them to be just as surely as he knew their beasts were named marrankur. Myriad colours saturated the ground where they had passed, sometimes spreading out to trees or into rocks and underground springs, intermelding where thoughts had linked. Ben looked down at his own trail; white and yellow bubbles brightly trickling into the earth where his vast-stepping feet lightly touched the ground, leaving only the barest trace of a print. The marrankurs' prints were more discernible, huge paw shapes on the sand, though surely only left as a trace of corporeality for his assurance. Ben willed the sand over his and their tracks with a thought as he passed.

To a distant observer, Ben's journey would have seemed an awesome sight. A tall and honed man, evenly smudged red to brown but for the blaze in his locks, seeming to hover above the ground for four full strides of a tribesman, until a foot touched down softly and kicked off again. A wonder moving quicker than the kangaroo before a hunter's scent. The head rested calm on broad shoulders, looking at the ground or straight on.

But no mortals witnessed such a sight. At the limit of the time field, only those akin to himself could watch his grace. Only the Lellying Enyadding, who were gathered around the age-fire on a blunt escarpment, looked occasionally to the figure several kilometres distant. A woman with gold eyes spoke as if to the air, her hands idly engaging a marrankur where it lay on its back, dodging its swift paw strikes to chuck it beneath the chin.

"So he has come at last, the fireseer. Will it be enough, I wonder, and will he be able to cuspidate a Spear?"

Lakellewan looked across at Brawyndy. The way her excitement sheened her skin — a luxuriant caramel, striking even among the Enyadding — kindled a memory of the love they shared, two millennia cold. She had left him to try to conceive with Gadruin, but the child had been rifted. Gadruin had been expunged too, long since. They were few now. Only the fifty-three gathered here at the Iridestine age-fire, eight scouts, and the stranger. Brawyndy had voiced the concern of them all. Soon they would see. Below, the one of the prophecy was shimmying up the cliff.

Ben noted the face leaning over the precipitous edge with an interest greater than that he gave to his feet, which moved free of his need to guide them, propelling him upward by their slight purchase on tiny knobs of stone as though each of the cliff's knuckles was a wide stair. The flow of power and sense of immersion with the universe, although only just birthed in him, felt as integrally part of him as a limb.

The face, broad and snubbed, which lowered itself toward the climber represented a little mystery, soon dispelled by the drawing of a muscled body level with him. Ben had wondered how the pets of those who awaited him — those like himself made Mended and in mastery of gravity — could follow such beings into this terrain. He watched the back legs as the massive creature climbed in apparent nonchalance headfirst down the cliff. The russet limbs ended in opposable thumbs and these dextrous digits it shifted to grasp chinks in the mountainside. Then the front paws slid forward, their thick claws bracing the creature's slinky passage, the hinge of its hips allowing the anchoring back paws to search sidereal along the cliff face, so that for long after Ben reached the ledge to stand in silent smiling communion with the tribal-looking immortals, he was pondering the disparity of an animal so huge being able to move like a spider.

Many of the Mended, coming to embrace their newest member, expressed a brief wonder at his wild hair and beard, their own grooming as immaculate as their feather cloaks. They wore no ornaments, save that in most the skin and broad perfection of the features was a beguiling dazzle. Ben steeled his sensitivities so that this new world's intensity would not overwhelm his grasp of the deeper mystery beneath it; that of why he was in it. Once, among the Yellanded, he had briefly mastered the drone pipe before the shock of hearing his music coming back to him with its own free will had made him lose the breathing technique. He strove for a relaxed concentration. Even so, as he clasped arms in formal greeting with an especially beautiful immortal woman, he felt himself humming internally, magnetised like a bee to the viscous malt of her eyes. A huffing and panting at his ear broke the spell.

He turned to stare into other eyes, inken globes of expedition and black blaze accosting him from behind an oval muzzle pouted by two shearing incisors protuberant from the top jaw. He was literally at a stand-off with Gawn, leader of the marrankur pack, although in truth, the marsupial had to drop its neck to stare levelly at him. Propped on the bow of its hind legs, the creature rose straight-backed, its long tail twitching across the dust, the shorter front legs hanging at each side of its raised flanks. Flexing thick nostrils, the brute yawned, then stepped backward several yards as Ben found himself drawn by a Mended man to one side of the group.

While the Lellying studied the plains below, over which slipped stars and a new morning, Ben journeyed through a hundred and eighty thousand moons to know the story of immortality. It was Maeddan, the immortal he had first met who linked his mind to the Irishman's, transposing memories and knowledge threads from the tribe to him.

They had been philosophers, born on a vast chain of islands. Retreating from society in a movement of some thousands, a fraction of the numbers of their peaceful kin had established themselves on three main islands. Theirs was a response to the increasing complexity of the world around them, of the endless seeking of their countrymen for new knowledge. The islands' forests had fallen exponentially to yield material for the boats, vast halls, fixed rafts, and laboratory fires — all the elements comprising the quest for ever new medical formulas, food storage techniques, and the juggernaut of salt crystal labyrinths that both modified their climate and served as criminal adjudicants.

In this striving, the breakaways had argued, the sovereignty of the individual was forsaken. With those who had heeded them, they had retreated deep inland, away from the roiling port towns, to follow their own intuitions of life's secrets. Secrets they believed best discovered by remaining still, and hearing the voice of the land that had birthed them. Some decades later the great learnedness and acquisitiveness of their countrymen had been given its sore testing. Not by the breakaways, but by the rapid onset of the ice-age fifteen thousand years ago.

Hundreds and thousands had sailed out in search of a safe haven and been lost to antiquity. The branch of natural philosophers, however, endured. They had eventually retreated into volcanoes, and there, over a dozen generations, had altered. Close to the dynamo and intelligence of the Earth, they had kept warm while the islands grew bleaker, and in the peak of the freeze had replaced corporeal sustenance with an etheric substitute. The formidable rhythms of their land's evolution, and its latent store of universal star seed, weaned them from the old path of compulsive human survivalism. Needing only pure water to survive, they became the Mended — in their language, the Enyadding.

Undying as the Earth itself, they had become telemantic, invisible, and rulers of time, custodians of knowledge prophetic and panaceal. As the freeze yielded, they had been called — all three Enyadding races. They had sailed out across the thawing seas, encountering vestige peoples dispersing toward the warmth, and succouring them with hope where there was need to reveal themselves. They had made the Heart-finger, the Aleris; a great crystal embalmed with their will and interwrought of essences from the trine of volcanoes.

It was to serve as beacon for the children of the Earth, to guide them through future planetary upheavals. Its dual function was to bring safely through the mighty oceans those who traversed them, and to dissuade the wayfaring of those made restless or craven.

So they had come to shore on their first and final journey, some few thousands of immortals, on the vast land of Australia. A place of pure upwelling and ancient rock; of gentle creatures and subtle song, and of tribes endowed with patience, improvisation and gratitude. The Enyadding had made themselves known to these authents, became part of their legends, and in turn absorbed tenements of their lore — wisdom perhaps handed down from others like themselves who had worked deeply with the Earth in times distant. Often the Enyadding looked to sea and felt the Heart-finger; as all who travelled on the water felt it. The moons of many centuries cycled, the world in a harmony of renewal. Then had come the ones sailing up the rivers of the Enyadding's adopted homeland, questing for gold and minerals. The immortals had been unconcerned at this exploration. The Aleris had not hindered their passage. Like the Enyadding, it knew that their leaders sought security of trade in their blooming society to build gateways to the universe's spirit for augmenting designs of great hope.

There was one on the ships whom the Aleris should have envisited with some vision to cause him to fill his lungs with water and ensure his soul was cast back to the gods. A priest. Certainly the Heart-finger had brushed his consciousness, but while the malice in him had been dormant. The priest's sleeping malcontent had been fattened on visions of wealth that the successful mining had conjured, the man grown stretched and bitter under the pressure of power and the nausea of home-sickness.

His hold expanded over a decade, as his hold on his own soul slipped away. The original conveyance of a religion for guiding the body's sleeping serpent of creativity became a power lust, and as many of the mining deposition left, he became the highest remaining command. Then his irreligion had become blatant, his consort of priestesses broken to his whims, and themselves mined for their psychic power. Wrayten's thirst for the vampirism of souls would have come to little if a deeper lead had not uncovered a thin deposit of the most momentous alloy.

His priestesses had perceived it quite by chance. Once they understood that their envitalised dreams were triggered by a specific influence, they had found it very quickly. After the first deaths among the miners, Wrayten discovered a simple way to handle the firefeather. Firefeather was the name the land breathed to the Enyadding for the blue crystal burning with its own inner flame of silver. To the land the crystal was enmeshed, somehow reaffirming the finest and subtlest of the continent's life expression. It permeated Australia, giving the soil a colour written in spirit, a tint of song to the air, and a poised blitheness to each plant and creature upon it.

Firefeather could take into itself the properties of almost anything, seen or hidden, and transform them a thousandfold — blurring dreams and substance, the mind and the elements. Wrayten found it of great utility when deliquated, in which state it lost none of its inherent properties, and then set in gold. Fully encased in gold, it was dormant; a part-casing gave reasonable control over its volatility. Over three years the High Priest had ordered thousands of coins minted, with inside a weight of firefeather. On the front was the head of their ruler, on the transverse, a serpent; for he who would rule once the firefeather was activated back in their homeland.

From the first time it had been mined, the Enyadding had stirred, their number little grown in nine thousand years. Under four thousand gathered to view the fortress rising flawlessly to its high apex by the dock, mooring a trio of ships — prime engineering amid other lesser buildings and temples that dotted the mullock-heaped hills.

The Enyadding studied the great white sandstone edifice, contemplating the devastation imminent for the land's spirit, and for humanity should Wrayten succeed in removing the crystals. The first immortal group to attack was the Lellying. Tall — but not nearly as tall as the Marrafar — garbed in feathered skirts, invisibly they swept upon miners or soldiery, and slaughtered bare-handed each they found.

Wrayten had grown guileful over the two decades of his rule. He had designed a single entry way of weighted stone to function as doorway to his lair.

144

Upon divining the furore of battle, he had instructed his bodyguard, sealing them inside. From behind spyholes, the High Priest and his coven had looked out on the plain, afraid and amazed, intently curious.

Out there the last knots of soldiers, eyes rolling like trapped cattle, fell as they stood jabbing spears at the lethal air, dying back-to-back as some unseen force twisted their necks to the side, or stopped their hearts with the sudden constriction of a pressure point. For a while the High Priest peered out on a plain filled only with sunshine and the languid feasting of hawks. Then the stealthy forms of huge beasts became apparent, shadowily inter-crossing the hills in packs of hundreds.

Soon after, Wrayten perceived his enemy, and saw why they had not needed to throw their pets into the attack. With their minds concentrated in three fanning spearheads, a thousand formidable men and women used their psychic acuity, which had destroyed the soldiers, against the stone door. Controlling their every muscle, the Lellying began to corrode the huge slab to rubble. Having to work within matter-time to induce such a stern task's success, the Lellying were vulnerable. Though they split rock with their minds, they were vulnerable.

Even as they flowed back into outer-dimensional time and entered the breach, the staggering of a Lellying woman, skewered precisely through the head with an arrow, showed them just how exposed they were. They knew a great force interceded against them, never guessing it was the pendants of the priestesses, each of gold half-encasing firefeather.

The priestesses had studied the Lellying while they had been visible, and intuited many of the inter-dimensional matrixes encoding their power. They had learned enough to beam the matter-time matrix back on itself such that the attackers were visible. Arrows did not easily kill Enyadding, save only where the priestesses tore at the immortals' connections with the Mend essences, from where the subtle focus of their sinister priest husband could shear through immortal defences. It was the Lellying's numbers that won them through the bodyguard. Supremely agile, powerful and fearless, they dragged the soldiers down with their bare hands.

Wrayten's coven imported to him the very patterns of power which the Lellying had been sourcing. The diabolicist struck precisely, slaying in an instant all before him. Those hundred Lellying still outside perceived the peril and acted instinctively, perhaps rashly, in the teeth of self-annihilation.

They magnetised the ley-lines of the land to the Mend flows and stripped the energy of eternity to become briefly disembodied, re-emerging variously along the thinly pulsing lines of Earth-power. Thus they learned of the fate befalling their kin, and of their mistake, through a blurred and indiscriminate land memory.

The huge Marrafar Enyadding, shocked at the Lellying annihilation, realised the bane represented in the priestesses; they who had channelled to Wrayten the knowledge to kill the Lellying. The giants had advanced, battering the priestesses' defences with precise mind-links until the priest's coven began steadily to topple. Unable to see them, or grasp a firm vision of their power conglomerations — subtly different amid each of the Enyadding races — and without access to the links provided by his priestesses, Wrayten could do little. Transforming into the serpentine form of his soul, he writhed, a monstrous snake, grotesque fangs striking at the dust.

Just before the most erudite High Priestess was vanquished, her body exploding to decimate part of the inner wall, Wrayten had received her linking of the intricate design with which the Lellying had escaped to the power lines; of the terrible realm of blankness, of the un-manifest, the limbo-field through which they had travelled to reach the powerlines linking them back to inner-dimensional being. The Serpent's eyes glittered, firefeather flared, and the Marrafar, unable to steady their plight through the exhausted power lines of the land, were banished to a soul into that ocean of void that laps the shores of the Earth in a few places, and from which they could never leave without such a key of ley-power as the

Lellying had possessed. The squatly-statured remaining Opsweyed Enyadding began to retreat.

Wrayten, not to have his triumph vitiated now he knew the secrets of dimensional sundering, sought the immortals. Towering mightily on his coils, he spied their flight before any, save one, had retreated the necessary kilometres to safety.

Jermourlvah, a powerful Opsweyed prophetess, had sensed what would occur and had demurred from battle. She had found the Lellying weeks later and detailed what had occurred on the plain in the mirror of her mind, hidden kilometres away in the hills.

Remorseless, Wrayten had thrilled at the alignment of pattern in his mind. Suddenly the Opsweyed Enyadding had ceased to be. Collapsing into his true temporality with an exasperated roar for the loss of his army and coven, Wrayten had rehabilitated several of his surviving soldiers and ordered the detritus at the entrance to his lair to be flung aside.

His outpost had been the last vestige of the mining operations, and he would have to sail with only those very few men and trust in his own skill. Now that this strange place had moved its ghosts against him, he wished nothing more than to be gone. It would take some days to load the coins and provisions for his ragtag crew. He did not care who his attackers had been — they were slain, else banished beyond time, and he thought no more of them.

They met at last in the land's heart at the huge rock like the red egg of some bird god. It took the Lellying, escaped to the power places, five days to regroup from all ends of the continent. There were one hundred and five left living. Like disincarnated spirits, they could feel the presence and suffering of the time-sundered Marrafar and Opsweyed, and intuit the horror that had occurred. For two days they mourned their slain friends and their doomed kin. Then they renewed the fight. Eternity awaited their grief. They did the only thing they could. They activated the Aleris for war.

With a singularity of focus, they called to the Heart-finger their need. For three weeks, fierce storms pushed the fleeing ship toward the deeply trenched place in the ocean in which dwelt the Enyadding's careful crafting — pushing the vile one almost within reach. The Lellying watched, their Mend skills creating a modular picture on the air as Wrayten's ship nearly foundered. Suddenly Brawyndy, the Eagle's Whim, spoke of her misgivings.

"No more than needs must should form the Spear to kill him. He may yet reach us even here, though he cannot see us. I will engage the Heart-finger with nine others."

"No, Brawyndy. You could not cuspidate the Spear, and you have no autonomous defence glyphs to flex in. But you are right; we must risk the minimum only."

Focused behind Gadruin, they honed the Aleris and shattered the ship with a single blast, but Wrayten was tenacious, his wrath almost tangible through the seeing as he uncoiled down into the depths.

He traced the Aleris, knew who and where his assailants were, and redirected the Heart-finger power back at its own creators before the cuspidate could summon another blast to slay him. There was a stand-off. The Serpent churned the waters of the seeing as sweat steamed from those in the formation on the rock ledge. As one, the Spear raised their hands in farewell and became dust. To call upon the astral forms as they had done meant that their astrality could be harmed — slain. The body could not endure with the astral vessel broken. They sacrificed their minds fully to the Aleris, and it repulsed and slew the Serpent.

Transfixed, Ben watched through Maeddan as the Lellying recovered the firefeather from the fortress and used it to set the age-fires, setting the land surrounding these out of sync with time. Thus were the Iridestines created, sanctuaries invisible from within the third dimension, but from which glades streamed a surge of replenishment and nourishment to the ley-flows. A time of wonder and harmony for them and the continent stretched for countless days, though ever there was that stark, abiding thorn; the horror perpetrated upon their brethren.

Ben's seeing continued up to a thousand or so years previous, at which point flashes of a great serpent of the sea featured in the unravelling of time's story. He watched Lellying again engage it with their astral selves, and again fail to return to their physical forms. He saw the foretelling of his coming, of the desperate chance he was to be. He did not understand; Wrayten had been slain. He had to ask the Lellying what this meant, and as he groped toward a conscious autonomy he saw glimpses of their world in retreat: Lellying unable to gather at some power places to rebalance the leys, the spirit of the land waning once more, not yet recovered from the robbing of its firefeather, and now laid siege by an invasion that should never have been possible.

"The Aleris failed?" Ben gasped on his resurfacing to a world of dawn and those strange, gathered eyes which held the final answers to the immensity of his transformation.

"The Heart-finger did not fail," answered Endralion, her silver hair signifying her as one of those who had not been born into the core-field of the Mend flows, but changed by them while still mortal. "You know that the Aleris was a guide, a song and following breeze to those lost at sea. It was a promise to the Earth's people that although hard times might come again, a pulse of warmth and light would meet the minds of those who journeyed soothfully."

Gistoan took up the thread, "The Aleris was comprised of three essences, ever replenished through the hearts of our own people."

Ben began to understand.

"When the others were time-sundered," Gistoan continued, "cast to the limbo-field, it was thrown from balance and forced of need."

Endralion's commodious features nodded a heavy accord. "We knew it would feel the loss, but also that power vents in the Earth itself could nourish it. We saw the Heart-finger began to draw from afar what it needed to rebalance.'

"Know this, fireseer," belled the powerful voice of Skyather. "The firefeather within the sunken pendants worked always to transpose that nourishment to itself, but imperceptibly to our vigil, for it was infused with Wrayten's cunning. We were deleterious in our assiduity. As the Aleris drew of the Earth's store, the pendants began to reassume their programming of malice. It was an incremental process. The pendants fed most of that initial energy gain back into the Aleris to accelerate its recharging from the Earth's power, and establish a hold upon it."

Gistoan resumed the narrative.

"At some point, the Heart-finger became aware of the interloping warped firefeather. The corrupted mineral's menace had become tangible, and while never quite a danger, it was an unsettling presence. It determined to release the excess power that the pendants were cycling to it, to bleed itself and the parasites dry — and over generations succeeded. In a fashion, the redirections of energy were a marvel, yet they sowed the seed for calamity.

"The only way the Aleris could siphon off its energy was by providing either doom or inspiration to travellers at sea. Instead of mere winds and whispered guiding that used an instant power surge — not the steady draining it needed — the Aleris created living thought–fields that drew energy when they interacted with the minds of sailors, even with their dreams.

"Mermaids were born, and sirens. All the while the pendants diminished. The Aleris risked a change. In winter, and other stretches of time, few seafarers came near it. It began to reach out to the minds of men, to spark the desire to sail, to explore. Those of pure heart spread wondrous tales of the sea's creatures to the new lands they visited. But those of ill intent were not always sunk by the Heart-finger. Perhaps it had become confused, trapped in the web of its own fantasies. War came thick to the lands of the Earth, but a worse pestilence arose that we now fight — that you must fight."

Ben groaned and forced himself to drink from a water skin. "But what is it, this Serpent?"

"Slowly the gold corroded from much of the firefeather coins. The neutral essence released was usurped by the still-contaminated pendants, and they overcame many of the Aleris' defences. They cannibalised the Heart-finger's energetic conduits, leaving only the innate seed of the Aleris unsullied. A succubus form evolved to model the indentations on the coins — a serpent, with sometimes the head of an emperor.

"The Serpent and Aleris have linked; a chaotic mongrel neither wholly bad nor good that cares for one thing — power. Always in internal conflict, it has become a creature reliant on a web of illusions created through the conduits of fantasy that the Aleris first hybridised to defend itself. It consumes electromagnetic emanations with an exponential hunger. The energy stand-off between Heart-finger and Serpent is mercilessly self-destroying. One part wishes to remain in balance, the other to master life. If this part erodes the Aleris' seed memories, life on Earth will be torn asunder. As it is, the resonances from the sea floor pervade the subconscious mind of humanity, creating a lack of satisfaction and a maddening struggle between security and brutality.

"It was predicted by Jermoulvah, now rifted, that one would come among us whose ancestral memory carried the knowledge of the Aleris' compulsion from his people's endless wars — one whose clarity was honed by the Earth itself. A man whose knowledge of injustice and slavery would deduce the truest action. A man already a serpent slayer."

Ben dazedly fingered the thick bracelet of python skin which he had cut to gift him luck before his final initiation. His gaze was compelled to meet Endralion's.

"It is the Earth herself that has made you one of us, but your hair is sign to yourself of your powers, and we have studied five hundred years since the foretelling to follow you into battle. You are not Ben who will lead us in this grimness; you are Enanyetem."

"Lightning's brother," mouthed the reborn man, realising for the first time that his hopes of life with Ngenlin were as ashes' warmth to a freezing man.

In the first days of his Mending, Ben yielded with rarefied wonder to the cloud of fate sweeping him southward amid the Lellying. Soon even the last of his mortal conditioning fell away to an open recognition of the fifteen-thousand-year old allure of Brawyndy. In her, the dark coppery skin of the Enyadding was infused with a caramel tone and her hair — a similar startle of brown hues shot with scintillas of gold — fell long over the poised muscles of her spine.

After three days the vast sand stretches fell away to a terrain of dun-and-bloodily-shouldered hills multiplying into ranges. These the party crossed only where well known routes exploited vanguards of stone.

On the third day of their journey, they halted a little after the six remnant sisters of the Pleiades had faded, their impromptu singing and harmonics filling a wide, naked valley. Ben walked a while with nostalgia; then stood stark in a thunderous nausea of longing. The frost, thick around his bare feet, took him back to all the pasts now gone forever from his unfolding. Sobering to view himself from a distance, Ben realised his ache for a simple life as father of Ngenlin's children would never cease, and that his new life was inescapable. He was the balance point of the world, and the hope-of-time to destroy the Serpent, as Maedden had that morning reaffirmed to him.

"A land to make even me feel young," observed blunt-faced Pyregiss beside him. His deportment was a portrait of sardonicism as always, and expecting only bleak conversation, Ben did not comment as they walked back toward the distant fire. The Lellying had not sought out an age-fire, the terrain being too open and unpopulous to warrant more protection than that afforded by their own power and four-legged guardians.

Two of these, curled up sleepily, suddenly disentwined themselves — the female emitting a low snarl followed by a high double-staccato scream like some bird of night. The male, darker and heavier, raced into the gloom, and Ben watched Gawn, the leader of the pack, lope cautiously after him. Suddenly a woman's voice cried out from the blackness, "Hey, Valyssian! How are you, boy?" followed by a man's, "Gawn! Well met." The trysting scouts had returned, their time-dimensional veils flowing into the greater of the Lellying group-mind.

Valyssian settled to once more curl with his mate, who uttered the low, cavernous hum of marrankur contentment, which reminded Ben of the underbelly protests from the hell steed that had bucked him over six months' sail to the new colony. The Lellying milled to greet their peers, and those marrankur not out hunting reposed with a disinterested air after a few quick yips at those of their kind just returned with the scouts.

Ben let his body navigate the curious, beckoning doors of consciousness to his own, until he stood amid the scouting group and was greeted as wonder and welcome and hope by all save one: short-statured with skin flaws and a receding hairline each side of bushy black curls, marking her originally initiated, not born to Mending. After removing a possum fur hood to swap names with the Irishman, she kept her face screened by it. The others, all with the flint-of-diamond faces native to the Lellying-born, told the scouting tale.

"There is very great passage on the mother-river, and she runs with mud past the age-fire in the hill-seat. We had need to kill a cluster of horn walkers to give rumour to foul plants near the sacred gullies, and thus spare the wanton forest losses to grass-greed, with their rotting warning," volunteered one, with a descriptive mime to match. More reports followed; one quietly spoken but intense woman's words caught Ben's attention.

"The tribes are everywhere pressed and sore. It is as we feared; the invasion is rooted in war and does not see itself as slowing before a span. The new harbours are congested with soldiers and sulphur. We sundered the partial memories of a party hunting tribe's members far up the mother-river, and turned them around. But such is fleeting effort if the madness blows to seed."

At last the hooded woman spoke, her voice raw with feeling and strained.

"Things are grim. Disaster's spectre grins ever more widely. Yet would I question two nuances of our beliefs. First, that we have here the ability to measure what this misery of the lost Englishers may become, or how quickly may the Pattern be undone by this fraying on its weave. For we have never since the Journey observed those removed from their place. Second, as for the prophecy concerning the fireseer, there is an incompleteness regarding time scale that we cannot deny. It is worded that one, red as the flame he wields, will come to bring down the Serpent, but not when. Maybe were those of the Opsweyed still in the realm, or even Streeborad, we could cast another prophecy. One which might reveal that in two hundred, four hundred years will the time be ripe, his skill be ready. The danger looms to a total unmending…"

She was cut off by four Lellying, running their words fluidly into a single sentence.

"We hear you, but tomorrow we make the attempt."

The fight leaving her voice, Lornahe observed, "If we fail and survive, the Serpent will be forewarned of our resistance."

"If our fate is to linger overshadowed by the corruption, we shall be pressed hard to hide from mortal incursions into our balance. Tomorrow we shall know. Come, we are eldest and must set an example of focus," replied Eadralion, his face, like Lornahe, flawed with scars.

As the gathering drifted apart, Ben was enthralled to feel Brawyndy's hand on his shoulder.

"So, Ben, how is your feeling for your doom?"

"A part of it is gift; another heartache," he offered through a smile, and held his hands palm up, searching for the words. "I am held captivated by the marrankur and a certain other beauty among this party."

Brawyndy's hand trailed a shower of sand into one of Ben's palms. "Forgive my boldness, but we Lellying have a fondness for drawn-out language, perhaps to fill our span. 'Ben' seems too short for my tongue, yet Enenyatem somehow too formal. The story of your Mending within the tree called by the English tongue baobab or boab, is a great one. May I call you Boabben?"

"Yes, I like it very much." Boabben. It carried much of the tree's strength, he decided.

"Well, Boabben, do you feel your life has prepared you for this coming bleak thing?"

Boabben gave her a quizzical look. Feeling perturbed by Lornahe's misgivings, he directed their conversation toward the marrankur, and so gained from her, almost oblivious to the joining of their hands, the pieces to the puzzle of the great beasts.

When they had first arrived in the singing land, her consonous voice told him, it had taken many decades before any Enyadding glimpsed a marrankur. Their concealment had three allies: one was the rugged and dense nature of their chosen habitat, another was owed to their physiology, sublime stealth and nocturnalism, the last the Enyadding came to identify as a faculty for dimensional veiling. The beasts achieved a kind of redoubling back into the environment, their external senses moulded to the feel of a place and influence over other creature's perceptions and decisions. The Mended had since confirmed this to be a glandular anomaly.

When the ingress of trade with the great fishers from the Sun Islands had climaxed to include such treasures as ache bark, air-stone, and sea maps, the first marrankur had been brought forth by a tribesman. Killed by luck or cunning, the outcome was devastating to the huge marsupials. Soon Sun Islanders traded exotic tribute for rights to hunt them on tribe lands across the north. The leopards they brought, trained for the purpose, were rarely fooled by the dimensional Veil, and enjoyed the insides of skins painstakingly prepared on the journey home as trophies for kings and medicine men.

The Enyadding befriended the doomed species. Pair by pair they hefted them, mesmered, from danger, and patiently developed psychic rapport with the beasts. Eventually more than a thousand hunted under their protection. The marrankur enjoyed natural longevity — being selective hunters, not scavengers — and prospered beyond a century in life span. They guarded the camps with fierce loyalty, as in turn the Enyadding guarded their health. The shared dimensional anomaly of each had established a unity surpassing the sublime, one that Boabben had rarely glimpsed.

"So the ten dozen here are the only remnant of their race?" he enquired of Eagle's Whim.

"Of the northern type, Boabben, we are certain that is so. Once, before the sundering, there were so many — hundreds with we Lellying alone. But the bond is too deep. They die when their bond does and will not breed beyond Enyadding available to bond with. Yet there is a southern marrankur form, smaller, yet numerous still in the deepest mountain forests.'

Boabben wondered of those southern wilds he had only sketchily seen, and pressed Brawyndy for a tale of their essence. For answer she kissed him long and deep, then guided his hands with her eyes to the fastenings of her feather dress. His fear of clumsiness beside her immeasurable experience was soon dissolved in a rhythmic sinuosity that had no tangible origin in either one of them. The roll of her starlight breasts was like a hearkening of the universe to a joy that danced up from below them both, and then they were folding onto or into that earth in the waking dream that may come on an Enyadding around dawn.

Returning to his six senses, Boabben found her gone. He was psychically aware of her, helping her bond pair track emu in the direction that the rest of the group soon pursued. The Lellying travelled slowly to cover the hundred and fifty kilometres to the place in four hours. Its walls arose amid sandy dunes miserly garlanded in spindly trees. The incongruously round uplifting of sharded hills had an eroded opening, and they soon gained the crater's floor.

Once inside, the fireseer promptly felt the otherworldly power of the site.

"Yes," affirmed Maeddan. "The age-fire here laid is the most powerful; comprised of the largest firefeather crystal we retrieved, and saturated through millennia by the star-knowing still reverberant from the meteor strike."

They sat, the sixty-three immortals, in an out-fanning wedge on a shelf of sandy rock shaded by tall seed-trailing wattles and squat eucalypts, their russet bark camouflaging the onlooking marrankur. Thuriskaen draped a gum leaf of gold around Boabben's neck, while psychically instructing him to leave the gold on the skin. "When your Mend power touches the firefeather," intoned Thuriskaen as he sat behind Boabben, "it will be melded to your form forever, and this age-fire will no longer shine its protection and land balancing."

Boabben considered what the Lellying Spear would attempt. It had been discovered with relief that Boabben did indeed have the nervous disposition necessary to cuspidate a Spear. They would spear to separate the Serpent from the Aleris and destroy its parasitic malignancy. If separation was impossible, both must be overcome. He did not feel any knew how they might succeed, only that they must. As the Spear intensified, a focal projection began to ripple on the floor of the crater, hazy images appearing upon a whitely luminous and moving blue and green backdrop.

The immediacy of each of the Lellying's astral bodies became a tangible presence in Boabben's mind as he fused into the defensive alignment of the Spear, and bridged doorways to yet untapped niches of his power. Suddenly, what had been merely a wave of light through which he saw himself and the Spear rushing, individuated sharply as Boabben's awareness came fully into his astral body, and the raw immensity of these last immortal beings was revealed.

There was Thuriskaen's Sphinxian Irrefragability of Splendour and Maeddan's Red Light of Primality among the defence, while Brawyndy's soul flashed in a scion of talons, whirling in a magnetism of danger among dozens of fearsome shapes forming the attack, urging and guiding his own lightning into readiness.

Boabben was aware of himself in two bodies in which he could employ all of his senses, with the difference that in the one in which he flew before the Spear, he felt himself to have unlimited movement and strength. It was a larger body, and its substance seemed comprised of turbid, shifting flocculence through which flickered blue, purple and white light.

From behind his other body on the rock shelf came Thuriskeaen's voice. "Now here, in your flesh, you must be only as an eye-of-air and gather all of its other power into unity with the Spear. To the Spear!"

A seethe of sundry psychic expostulations rose around the lanky Irishman as he complied to place all but a fraction of his awareness into that other powerful body.

"Think not of any place of age-fire, lest the foulness survive to remember."

"Shift recognition to the dawn-dream. Try to draw the vile one into the base fractals of living organisms."

"My beloved Opsweyed, this day shall the reckoning be made!"

Across the baking valley of the crater bowl fell silence like a sword falling through air before it strikes stone. Perhaps the marrunkur, still but strained in alertness, and one other watched as the ripples and colour in the valley coalesced into a richly stained ocean, bruised at its depth, and struck with light and darting shadows that must be shoal fish at its rim just below the feet of the tranced immortals. At the bottom of the ocean synthesis, Boabben that was eye-of-air looked on as the Aleris smouldered with wavering light. Wrapped coil on massive coil around it was a vast, vicious serpentine form.

Even in this mentally moulded projection it was stunningly huge. From his body that was merely eye to gauge his strike, Boabben glanced at the crater Serpent while the predominance of his being hovered astrally over the real ocean with the rest of the Spear. He gauged its actual length might top a mile, comparing sharp, shaped flecks swimming along the crater's floor beside it. Without thought, Boabben reversed the gold leaf and assumed the surging quickening to his strength that the firefeather gave. As dozens of coloured forms dived through the ocean around his astral self, the valley simulation glowed with the descending menace of the Spear.

Boabben felt toward his enemy, and with the rhythm and precision of the hunt, sped also into the sea to take his place at the head of the Spear's spear.

The ocean grew darker as they plunged, but Boabben's vision gradually adjusted to penetrate the gloom. The Lellying had implanted directly into his mind all knowledge of the Serpent accrued in their long struggle against it. Boabben now allowed the Mend flows to animate this archive into a picture of the Serpent's current ruminations.

He could discern that it had not forgotten who had sundered it from the Earthlight so long ago and destroyed its human vehicle. He studied the way it poised in attack upon the Heart-finger, bringing forth energetic titbits to nurture the great crystal, as though some nesting brood-mate.

Deeper, and Boabben began to brush against radial threads of the Serpent's energy network; feeders in scout of new power sources, and snares to prevent the Aleris rebalancing. The Spear slowed, and Boabben felt the Lellying instinctively wanting to bombard these threads. Instead he led them weaving in careful avoidance down toward the nightmare colossus of their enemy's physical form. Risking a glimpse from his body consciousness, Boabben saw the Serpent still heedless of them, swooning in its aeon-long power dream. He slowed the Spear into an imperceptible downward glide until they heard its million tongues of sibilant madness, enflamed with hate, a daunting numbness spreading palpably around them. They propped a half mile above it, and Boabben became certain of its true weakness.

Slipping in through the still intact hibernative programming of the great crystal, the fireseer began to undermine the Heart-finger's outer defences. The black nothing between the stars he wove around his crafting to conceal his hand from the Serpent. Carefully he burned away the crystal's harmonic field until the Aleris light waned to a dull amber. Suddenly, the Serpent was presented its long awaited chance; it believed somehow it had breached the Heart-finger's integral protection.

For the first time in thousands of years, the Serpent allowed for only what was before it; the Aleris and its waning light. It tuned its emotions, quelling excitement. It relaxed muscle after muscle, preparing for the jolt of power it would ingest.

As he inched closer to the monstrous peril, Boabben drew on the only frame of reference for the abomination that his experience knew — his victory over the python. He waited until its jaws were over the massive crystal before moving to float immediately above the wriggling hump of its end coils. With every force of his will and every iota of his lightning being, magnified by the firefeather and the Lellying Spear attack, he scorched through the bone of the fiend and sprung away from its paroxysms of despair.

Instantly, residual serpent essences retaliated against Boabben's astral form but its physical vessel was destroyed. The huge body floated limply. A dark Serpent form settled on the sands, the arching spasms of its dying stilled.

The residual forms were numerous. Near transparent serpents flittered in thousands around the fireseer. Boabben's soul spun thought glyphs that hedged the attackers into balls that he ripped apart with constraint harmonics from deep space.

Several Lellying veered from defence links to engage a restoration and rebalancing of the Aleris. Boabben glimpsed their ministrations of wonder and finesse just before he realised his folly. He and the sixty Lellying still linked to his mind screamed to the others; *the Serpent lives!*

It had passed into stasis from Boabben's blow, alert but paralysed. Now it sent from its recovered body torrents of compulsion and non-being at the surprised immortals. It was binding them into the Aleris for its later delectation.

Boabben sourced the only defence he had. Severing the Lellying Spear link, he broadcast onto the Serpent the whole of his power filtered through the vibration of a bacterial form known only in the meteor crater, and so unknowable to the firefeather. In agony, he felt the pain of whole worlds dying. Still, Boabben channelled his will through his outer consciousness and engulfed his foe with blast after blast of scything light.

The Serpent was only confused by the tactic. It was prepared for the fiery one's cleverness now, recovered from the genuine fear it had been dealt before the Lellying had recharged the Heart-finger and assured its own energy recovery. Boabben felt its regathering strength, and the instant he judged the Lellying all safely withdrawn he layered a final wilderness of geometric mazes on his being to cover his trail and fled back to his body.

Boabben stared grimly ahead, an indescribable chill upon his spine, as though minute icicles were birthing ceaselessly from it. The ersatz ocean was gone. At the periphery of his vision he was aware of a column, a vortex filled with lightning — purple, white and blue — that pierced the sky above him to an unknowable height.

As it slowly faded, tribespeople who had watched it swell over the past hour began to head toward the crater. Had the nearest European eyes not been three hundred kilometres distant, focused on gun barrels and the plucking of chickens, they may rightly have named the sight an omen of the world's end. Boabben had failed.

Two marrankur lay sprawled a little distant, hook-legged in early rigor mortis. Maeddan's voice came softly at Boabben's ear.

"They were Anuisiht's bond pair. She was caught between the Heart-finger and your alien glyphs. Not an instant death, but painless. You fought bravely, Enanyetan. There is no apportioning of blame."

They burned the marrankur at dusk. Anuisiht's body had crumpled to ash with the passing of her spirit. Before the dawn-dream, a disconsolate council made a simple précis of facts. Skyather deliberated.

"It is not defeated. Who could say how this may be done when it survived the power of the fireseer? No doubt now it is slowed, a setback of maybe a hundred years to its full recovery we have dealt it. The Aleris was returned some harmonic accord; Lakellewan believes he may have even realigned it some..."

Lornahe interjected. "This is a victory sorely bought. We have now one more to avenge and must repair to the north with our task more pressingly on our thoughts. Soon the invasion will be considerable." There was no evident sting or gloat behind her words.

"We have learned more about our enemy," Skyather continued. "More yet we may intuit. This indeed may have always been Enaneytan's role to fulfil in the prophecy. A seed rather than a climax solution. In any event, we must now assure our defences. Among the crocodile songs let us dwell some time before we penetrate the south to assay the cataclysm of the colonist's cities."

"Yes, the marrankur have hunted adequately for emu and bundle rats. They will obfuscate us on our trek to the warm lands that we may calm and harbour our energies to fullness once more," said Maeddan.

"Then we must part," intoned Boabben. "My way lies south to the lands I have yet to roam. I am wearied and soul-sore. Not again will I face the Serpent."

His words caused no discernible dismay amid the group. On clammy psychic channels came brief farewells.

"Ways part. Who knows, but yours may yet be a role in future victory. I shall watch for your wild light in the dawn-dream."

"May your streams be pure till next we meet."

But there was one voice, plucking in snatches at his deeper centre. "You did well. My path is north. Yet trace for me of a time. We shall be joined once more. Be equal of care and joy, Boabben. You are my honour and your choices ennobled turn."

Brawyndy. He let her feel his essence without replying. He touched the fresh welt on his chest, shaped as a gum leaf, where the firefeather had seared into his being. He quickly crossed the battle-sea of the valley, and she did not watch him leave.

Chapter 11

Mendez stands as the captain shrugs around in his chair to clink bottles with Enrique and Sean, and then himself. Four freaky fish fleeing, a part of Mendez's mind riddles, screening his heart with drifts of nonsense as his younger self had done through the real nights of Spanish orphan-hood.

"To warm waters," the stoic nautilist intones. He stretches across his collar, too stiff from thirty hours' vigil to stand, but is just able to pluck the source of their group focus from its wall bracket.

"Twenty degrees, lads!" Twenty-three counting the ones Curlew will honourly instate on you when we...hold that!"

The captains' face, light-hearted for an instant, is already blanching as it turns from Enrique's' clutch of the thermometer to a small light pulsing on the console. A switch flicked beneath it dulls the pilot-screens' crowding of sonar imagery, and a final bio-pass on the ghostly screen brings ethereal forewarning into substance.

Five dots move brazenly toward them. Captain Tabaveres draws a long draught of beer before leaving the bottle on the metal floor. "Well. Looks like we're in for a good old-fashioned scrap, kids. No backup within eight hundred kilometres. I hope you know how to surf."

This feigned light-heartedness worries the exhausted Mendez, who had remained sleepless from emotion on watch beside Tabaveres for most of the journey, studying the pale-skinned man. Mendez had been privy to irregular, precise commentary on Austral's coastal defence systems and the way in which Knocktwice was made to appear as school fish to the many predatory eyes of ASA radars, their seeing blurred as Tabaveres' computer transpositioning cast an echo of each radar onto the other.

Throughout all of this, and even when a routine sub patrol had forced the captain to deploy two missiles into a sand wall — bringing it down on top of them until a camera probe had shown the prowler gone — Beaumont Tabaveres had been detachedly alert and economic. So it is for good reason that this new expansive jocularity and bravado alarms Mendez. It is a flimsy mask over terror.

In the end, mercurial of action, Tabaveres pursues the only hope. Backed into a tiny crevasse with nose and shoulder sloping out, they could hope the convoy might pass unaware of them. At least it would have to attack within a clear line of Knocktwice's torpedoes.

"Right." Tabaveres faces the three assembled in all but the final touches of their diving gear. "To get to shore, hand compass only, I'm afraid. Their scanners will track anything computerised. Twenty-two kilometres, so you'll mostly have the light. Lasers for hand-to-hand; they won't budge the subs, and if one of those comes after you, split up. I should be able to slow them down, but three peckers isn't going to more than halve them. Let's see which way they're going to dance this before you pick an exit line."

They await, like bizarre sprinters wrapped in weights and gear belts, for the starting whistle. Soon it is apparent to all of them what Mendez has been musing on for some time; the fleet is not turning around. Finally the captain stirs; the whistle is one of relief.

"It's no trick. Somehow they've missed us. The cocky bastards can't have even been running a peripheral pulse. Get changed and get happy, guys."

Mendez contentedly notes a return to candour in Beaumont, and a strict economy of manner as the gangly blonde sets the Knocktwice northward. Mendez questions him as to what they were up to.

"I don't know, but in half a day we'll find somebody who will."

The Curlew border; Mendez cannot even conceive it. Changing in his cabin, he looks on Sean's permanently-aged, but almost peaceful, drowsing face and realises that sleep is a hole almost completely beneath him. As he falls into it, he thinks of a great storm with gyres and vortexes beneath the ocean, and dreams of Sway — his love — kicking submarines across the sea.

Tacleara pours off a cup of the fragrant brew. She will need the shineark for what is to come. Saturating the coffee undertones are herbs unknown in the continent before the insurrection. An eclectic mix brought by the boat people of the world, they had proven the greatest boon in the beginning. Her life had been saved under the triumphant bark roof of her hippy parents, anxious-eyed beneath guerrilla paint and emaciation frowns, administering crane wing, do-neit, gorgon tussle. She sips back into the present, imbibes the heart-lustring view before her — the stunning eclipse of reality that is the everyday beauty of Ja Junction — the nation's capital.

Beyond the massively hewn decking, the verdure of the billabong traipses across her eyes, blurring infrequently into one of the hundred or so fishing canoes in lonely languid labour. No one swims. The Indigoes who specialised in crocodile pacification are absent from both the watchtowers that trestled up from amid the lilies. On the far shore of paperbark forest, Tacleara can just discern children in frenzied acrobaticism, exhibiting the style that serves as the nation's fighting technique and cherished sport.

From somewhere wafts the alarmingly evocative scent of smoking fish, base and complex odours entwining — and also the whine of mosquitoes. Reluctantly, she slips within the sonic field repellent and steels herself for this hard thing that is not of her choosing. As she makes her way to the Homager, Curlew life flows out at her from the vast-scaled Earth tables, roughly constructed circles entirely celebrating function and tenaciousness, except for a blue-and-green-tiled mural of the planet upon each.

Adroit conversation, performance, children's games and stories, agricultural consultations, and coupleting in all stages from seduction through to collapse, skip stones across the silken atmosphere of the Tryst Common.

Often she hears her name called in greeting or is caught up by some peaceful eye and regaled with sentiments about the weather. Tacleara's empathetic skills allow her to respectfully keep moving. A hundred or even a thousand greetings in a morning has become part of her life, and she knows she is the most celebrated member, partly due her longevity, of Curlewalion society. Indeed the closest, heaven forbid, that the anarchist collective has to a leader.

Her celebrity had begun before the deaths of her parents, who prior to the revolution had been frequent visitors to the north amid that band of palaeontologists pursuing with zealous care the skeletal echoes of lost history in the gulf country. Rallying around the banner that was their painstaking reconstruction of that first great fish so worshipped in such circles as progenitor of all backboned life.

The needs of establishing a new nation forbade them continuing their work in the Gulf or in the founding capital. Taking inspiration from the dilapidated fish, they in turn became important progenitors for the framework of Curlewalion society. In Jandamarra Junction they had branched their scientific enquiry, helping consolidate deep-flow harmonics into a sustainable aqua harvest that delivered fecundity to the land, and had also perfected tropical nutrition and natural medicine programmes.

After their demise, Tacleara's empathic skills had come to the fore while she negotiated with the burry sensitivities of pirate hordes to whom Curlew had willingly ceded its northern peninsula. It was by following her parent's work in herblore that she truly earned her fame. Remarkably, she had stalled old age, maintaining the rickety good humour of a seventy-year-old through her dedicated application, right into this, her hundred-and-twenty-fifth year.

Cleara thought of herself as a cloud passing them all by, yet one somehow struck with inescapable subtleties that served to magnify feelings in people. She could elicit from them tears, threats or joyous paroxysm, and they could activate either the warm or cold current of her passing, though she had largely mastered her outgoing emotion. Her mere presence could incite in people a clarity of feeling, and an awareness of the emotional dynamic and potential of a group situation. Her own emotions dipped into nadirs and were cannibalised by new emotions complete with their own fresh insight; a constant parade through the minutes of her life.

She was generally adept at hiding them, a thin but effective screening to keep any awareness circuits in the crowd from channelling her worry.

Most of what Cleara vies toward is perpetually screened. Her cloud floats, awaiting the gathering power of the gale — war with South Austral.

She has always felt Curlew's stratagem of sponsoring localised insurgence to foil Austral's militancy was aptly insightful. It had been so integral to all efforts undertaken by every Mist and Indigo action or liaison that it had been a tacit subject for many years at Homagers, like a big tree that grew steadily to maturity, providing continuity during any number of garden overhauls.

Not only had it promised the surest breaking of Austral's grip, but having roots inspired amid the populace ensured a grass roots morality emerging in the bloody aftermath. The resistance cells had grown painstakingly in their first ten years. Even though South Austral had long since tightened down on all civil liberties, artificial feelings of security and prosperity still translated as a nationalistic blindside in its populace.

Over the last twelve decades, dissent had swelled inexorably to the point where the first revolt was nearly ready. An emissary of the Lellying had shown up five weeks prior bearing news of near-strike capability in Austral's hybrid nuclear program. Before they had destroyed the war-sat, Curlew's forefathers had used its leverage to ensure a closure of the world's uranium mines. Existing warheads were sent into orbit on a path for the sun, and in preface to Mouth being programmed to follow them, a final effort to destroy all long-range missile equipment on Earth had been undertaken.

Only weeks after Austral's completion of a three-year endeavour to string border bases across the desert, missiles had begun to rain upon Curlew.

Curlewalion Mist destroyed launch sites where they found them and kept the destruction minimal, luckily spared the burden of combating the W.A.R. government's occasional launch of a satellite by a rigorous and adept cleaning of the sky — undertaken by the technologically profligate Anarchticans.

For much of her girlhood, Tacleara had been in missile attack zones, so it seemed to the understanding of last fortnight's Homager that it was not inexperience which had had her argue to bluff awhile against Austral's trump and merely bring the date for revolt forward. The destabilising tactic was initiated while the planning details for the uprisings remained nearly a year short.

The Fadtown flashfire and upheaval, calculated to catalyst the whole northern seaboard as far as Signdecide into galvanised action, had been crushed. Indigo Mantles are monitoring a fraught leadership in Byron; its fate would trigger a nationalistic backlash of attack across their northern border, and maybe from Maroytar. Tacleara's face relaxes; the creases across her full features smooth. She does not know if they can survive open war with South Austral, but is beginning to realise they will not survive without it.

Tacleara parts the light blue cheesecloth and steps down into the lowered circle of the Homager. The three Indigo Mantles seated in high-backed chairs around the group show not even a flicker of their closed eyes to attest that they have noticed her return. Tacleara feels a tendril of their awareness loop back into their fierce psychic ward, hermeticising the Homager's discussion, an insular privacy immune to the prying or suggestion of hidden minds.

She seats herself as Furrow's voice continues in unbroken efficiency like the line of his body, muscle-honed from years at sea. Cleara comprises the twelfth member of Curlewalion's information continuity exchange — its Homager. Furrow is the fixed representative for external security, a sort of general by right of his untiring service of forty years at sea. Lans is the fixture for internal security and Saliska, a gifted radio telekinetic, represents psychic development. Her own position ascribes to community integration; some would say a difficult one in a nation fleshed by all the world's peoples and all of its liberal tastes.

They in turn are advisers to a chaocracy of seven — randomly chosen by computer ballot from any of the populace who desire inclusion on its data bank — and it is these who vote on Homager contentions, their consensus becoming gnosis. These gnosis are still ghostly laws until disseminated among the community via theatre, poetry and discussion, whence their support or rejection could be established through the efforts of Gaian Screamers. The Screamers are the most trusted adherents of the shamanic code arising from a deep magico-spiritual undercurrent in the Gaian Aboriginal Merger lands.

Once incorporated into the Charter of Ramification, a deliberate flouting of an accepted gnosis could result in only two outcomes — banishment or death. For some of the Ramification articles it is difficult to enforce a penalty. For instance, the acceptance that all warm-blooded animals are equal to humans means that someone who kills an animal for food can refer back to the Charter for the Ensurance of Human Survival for their defence, or claim kindred association with the Gaian Aboriginal Merger who are exempt from that gnosis, as are inhabitants of the unpopulous locale, Omnivore.

Most often, anti-social activity is ramified, and always by the Lion of Lion — an ascetic warrior cult that is also internal security. Planned or sustained harm to a person's body or psyche means facing Lans or a similar tracker, as well as the pride of big cats with which each senior member of the cult holds a rapport of quicksilver. Such activity is rare and never attributable to mental imbalance. The healers of her land, Cleara thinks, have made of such a thing an anachronism. Truly, this society is a ripening fruit tree on the shores of time, but to protect its crop she has to conceal her deception. Furrow has finished detailing the latest Mist reports of Austral movements, and recapitulating their position. The lyrical, self-effacing young Pangtrek has begun to speak. Still, guiltily, Cleara remembers.

That night, she had sensed an urgent presence moving down the wynd-way connecting the research allotments. Even at such a moon-dipping hour, her inspired neighbourhood was to urgent presences as seesaws in sunshine were to children, and she had continued her meditation seated in the amphitheatre within Ja Junction's botanica nursery. It held hundreds of thousands of herbs upon five stepped shelves ringing the mile wide bowl of mature seed trees and ponds.

The largest of the ponds and its water plants was before her, the Moon's light amid the weaves of riotously textured aqua flora. Tacleara saw only the emanations of the seven herbs on which she bent her study, daisied together in the single pot wherein she had planted them a week prior to make assessment of their etheric compatibilities.

Though deep in meditation, it was stunning that he had walked almost up to her before deliberately letting his presence be felt. The Lion of Lion apprentice had explained that the Lellying wished a private liaison with her, and that Lans would guide her from a prearranged location to them.

Did she know the Plethora Outcrop well enough to approach it along its largest westerly dry wash by hover, by night? Probably — it would take her just over an hour if she left now.

"Lans will light a signal," The apprentice had handed her a sheet of melaleuca bark with a pattern of six dots charcoaled onto it. "He will expect you in just over an hour."

As she piloted her hiccoughy little prototype, she had mused that for a Luddite cult the Lion of Lion sure knew their distance times for a hover's travel. She had soon found the six fires, by chance or design appearing like a flaming eye, and set down nearby.

His conversation constrained purely to the task at hand, Lans had stressed his neutrality and role as middleman in the meeting.

"None can come to Yellanded lands by hover. The soil lode here is peril to the magnetic drive. But Unilion can find paths in. Come, Cleara."

The Unilion leader had seated her on his Ra-king, Tanbyss, and then led her over dead-wooded hill brows, slowing to patter alongside his Ra-king in narrow, vine-strewn gullies. Somehow, he was unfaltering through the rock and thicket chaos of the night, eventually whispering careful instruction to Tanbyss as the massive lion bearing her descended steeply into a gorge. Here another fire had awaited, two aboriginals rising in solemnity to stand delineated with hands raised in greeting.

"They and dawn shall guide you back to your hovercar. See you at the Homager."

Without thought to consider the ability of the Unilion, Cleara was spellbound by the venerable couple formally taking her arms, nearly as venerable as she.

Tacleara could sense an aura of wildness still extant in these people. Nearly pureblood, which was rare. She felt a great pride and graciousness coming from them. The man passed her a dark cloth and daubed her forehead with ash.

"Okay we get to take you spirit-givers, isn't it! All the same, we got to do the proper one. Only little bit for now. It's changed now from old days, only we can know spirit-givers. But you have to put that blanket on your eyes. That's it. Don't worry 'bout that fellow. You can still see it? Just for more proper."

The woman had helped Tacleara tie on the cloth with surprisingly dextrous fingers, and it was through the gritty sheath of this blindfold that she came to glimpse the path to one of their kept places, a glimpse that for so long would have meant death. Then had come a light and a voice of greeting. Taking her blindfold off, Cleara's heart had skipped. She had met Lellying before, but never on a personal basis.

She was somewhat mollified to recognise a face she knew among the three immortals as she crowded closer to the eldritch heat of the woodless fire and observed its bizarre light upon their features.

"Thank you for coming, Tacleara. Strange now, that every minute counts for so much. I must begin mid-flight, if you will permit me." It was the woman who had come to the Homager and held a day's counsel some months previous: Tawbyn.

The silver-haired immortal, her frame sized much as Cleara's own, was lent strange contrast by her two kin. Both of those men were statuesque and flawlessly featured with hair as black as Tawbyn's skin cresting their coppery bodies — as though their peaking manhood had been cast in suspended animation. Laying aside the mystery, the empath had considered the first time she had seen Tawbyn, looking then, over a century ago, as now. There was no doubt, despite silvery hair, that the Lellying woman was as immortal as her companions.

That first time, Cleara had been riding back from a day exploring and gathering river herbs near the third bridge on Chesceykance Red when she had felt a rapid fluctuation in the emotional field. It continued; a current of danger and violence so great that, had she not been in her headstrong youth, she would have demurred approach. About halfway across the eucalypt copse through which she rode toward the source of the emanation, her horse had refused to go any further.

Proceeding on foot, Tacleara had reached a rock strewn flat where stood a man, clearly Unilion from his superb physique, caruscading dreadlocks and necklace of lion claws. She could actually sense his pride — his stalk — scattered in the grass nearby. Facing him was a man Cleara could tell to be aboriginal, though this character's back was turned. Both were at a stand-off, spears raised.

"Now come on!" implored the Unilion. "It's not up to me, but it is tribal business. You must return with me and answer to them for the killing."

Then Cleara had felt a new energy, quite different, like that of a dry wash about to be inundated. From her prone spying position in the standing straw, she had seen a woman simply spring into being on a rock above the pair.

"No, Teb, hold! He acted for us. He is fully pardoned. Come, we must talk."

The silver-haired one had seemed almost to float down to the Unilion, and they had left the awed aboriginal man to go his own way. Tacleara had also left as she felt the consciousness of the stalk, free from its focus, suddenly brush against her awareness. She had been shocked, the rumours true, after all, and the Lion of Lion knew the immortals.

Neither beast nor immortal had scared her since she had reached her womanly majority and the fleet unfolding of her powers accompanying that time, but what the Lellying before her, garbed in a finely felted, short robe of bark stitched with sugar gliders' tails, had said in the gorge that night brought fear back to her heart.

"I am glad indeed that the world can birth such a versatile soul. Many are the things you can do that we, no matter how immune to the ravages of time, have never known. Yet most essential of your abilities to our need is perhaps the simplest. We require your complicity and your power of influence to facilitate a diversion for us."

The intensity of the three immortals' wills had increased, and as Cleara strengthened her own, she sensed the aura of desperation and pain suffusing the energies of the Lellying.

Feeling cornered and now angstful, perhaps from apprehending the undercurrent, Tacleara commanded her nervousness by gazing into the oddly reassuring phantasms of rainbowed flames emanating from the very ground itself. Looking through their hypnotic swirling, she saw the two tall Lellying men. The one furthest from her, seated on a log and glistening goldenly around his bark robe, snared her eyes with his. In powerful serpentine aspect, he extended his whole body toward her, head to toe inching in the dust, and spoke.

"Your society will, I think, go to war. It will be less than a month before the impetus soon to be begun breaks on Austral. We intend to exploit that disturbance to wage a war of our own. A last saga in an ancient struggle on which all life teeters. There are two factors we must overcome to be able to succeed; two fruits, if you will, that we need pluck, guarded by same thorns.

"On the one branch, a delegation of our kin will shortly be conducting broad scale psychic activity to locate a traitor and then establish the depth of his betrayal. This they must undertake along the populous northern fringe of coastal Nascent Walls. On the other, a Lellying group now wend their way into the heart of Acadabourne, seeking to extract a weapon from the very maw of the Affiliates. We are all agreed the atmosphere of internal stability and technological guardianship in these areas is a lethal threat, even to immortals.

"We are poised to fall from the see-saw while our enemy extends a grasp across the schoolyard of humanity. The Lellying scouting groups are locked to their chosen courses for better or worse, but unless we can all reunite to fight together, hope is lost...Austral must be destabilised immediately!"

Tacleara, flummoxed, found herself staring at a strand of her own grey hair pressed between her fingers and asked, "But what can I do?"

The other Lellying, delicately hooked features and light grey eyes lending him an air of a stage magician, clapped his hands sharply.

"Trigger the uprisings. The Realliance. Send word to one most trusted among the Rainbow Hub to bring the revolt forward to tomorrow evening. At the latest."

"What?"

Tawbyn implored her, "They will be fighting anyway, exposed and swept up in war. What difference now or in unison with Curlew's inevitable attack? Unless we can reach our enemy in time there will never be an end to war."

"I don't understand. There is to be two wars? Who is it that you Lellying combat, and how can two wars come to rise in similitude?"

Tawbyn, with a muted shake of her head, as though sorrowing for a dissolution of innocence she must bring, had answered.

"Tacleara, the world is not as it once was. The seed we planted to direct its fate was uprooted and warped such that it conspires now against humanity, working to hurry it — to harry it into a technological prison derived of feeling. The essence of violent imbalance that we fight is mirrored by the human manifestation that all free people must disdain. The signs of a faltering resistance in the guardian of our hope are bold.

"Exponential has become the Earth-suffering in the lands we do not intensely shield. The citizens of the Reform Government fret, and there are those who would exploit the barbarousness which hungers in them, not knowing what it is, to create a mindset of hatred on this planet that will be its final human memory. We can no longer contain all the fronts of fraying woe. Our chance is to gather for a concerted strike, to extract the root while hope yet lasts — though it is a fraught task."

The third Lellying, Palathos, spoke cogently, and Cleara crumpled beneath a weight of despair.

"Our brothers and sisters have been sundered from us. There are so few of us left now. You must aid us. Before night tomorrow the uprising must begin!"

Finally the head atop Tacleara's husk straightened, and nodded. Tawbyn took her hand and her eye. "Send word via a trusted long-range Indigo only. Have them reach Billy Reet — I believe to be the connection aside the Fadtown cell — and impel him to extend full and careful explanation to the leader of whatever group is to begin it. Thus only you four shall know, and we may yet claim the initiative. Your guides are here. Look to the coming of the Dew; they bring news, if not hope. May we meet in the ice-orchards or before."

Cleara turned to the old man seeming suddenly to appear before her. Just as suddenly she had felt the Lellying energies vanish, and without looking back knew they were no longer in her dimension.

Tacleara returns to the present, having partially followed Pangtrek's analysis of Curlew's slim options and the ostensible capacities of Austral for attack, whilst spelunking through her memories. His obtuse style of ending his statements with a questioning air is actually quite compelling.

Tacleara glances one last time through the cheesecloth, symbolically a filmy blue for the colour of communication. She is glad to note that the youth who had been asserting himself so ribaldly, pushing the limits of social grace with both loud and demonstrative verbosity from his chair closest to the Homager, is nowhere in sight. She had known what had so affected his nerves — two girls at a distant table whom he had been unable to choose between. Knowing the problem's solution, Tacleara reached it by empathically suggesting to the girls that they make clear their true intent…that neither was interested in him in the least. They currently talk with a group of older men. Cleara smiles to herself and heeds the rhapsodising man of Chinese blood.

"…in being aware of what is the climactic approach of Austral's hybrid nuclear capacity, I cannot conceive of a defence-based response — it's sort of like trying to dodge your reflection in a mirror, isn't it? Even if we could survive and the sky filters performed to test standards, the implications for the Anarchtic region, the Horn of Drums and pockets of Unopean Punkture resistance are heinous. Return to nuclear capacity for the W.A.R. government will engender a refugee crisis that is impossible for us to mop up, yes?

"When my parents left China, they were barely amoebas, bereft of all but bare life, desperate for a vessel in which to articulate their culture. Here now, we stand as the culturing dish for the cells of humanity. We are obliged to protect ourselves aggressively, to wrest control of human destiny from the claws of a few individuals. Strikes against extracting facilities with the Herover are no longer an option. The new qualification of enriched ununtrium would seem to mean they have already enough raw materials cached to wreak devastation, wouldn't it?"

"Actually," Furrow interrupts, efficiently conveying apology and ominousness of revelation through a level breath and glance at all their faces, "we do not possess a Herover. Although the possibility of the W.A.R. government's nuclear rearming and return to mastery of ground-based attack was premeditated by Curlew's founders, so was the dire possibility of the Herover being retaken by Austral or rogue forces. The power plant for its engine was built into our continual energy cogitator, whilst the time that Austral has poured into development of anti-Herover technologies has shown the value of the ruse."

Tacleara draws the unalterable truth of their situation into the group awareness, and she notices the rodent-featured young Bistani's agitation dissipate into acceptance.

Pangtrek continues. "We are informed that an attack upon the launch facility in the Southern Bite is a fraught action due the presence of near a million troops and automns at the conjoining base, Mjolnïr. The Mjolnïr pontoon docks one-half of the W.A.R. navy, but a glimpse of hope is given us via the safe transference to our shores of three ex-prison gangers with explicit engineering knowledge — this is truly right?"

Tacleara answers his metronoming eyes with a nod and the added detail that the one-time students had been forced to labour deep within the Hills of Hypertrophy, in which mazed buildings the Mist had confirmed the hybrid research laboratories to be housed.

"Well, I therefore support a pre-emptive attack on Austral's northern coastal bases as counterscreen to tactile operations by Mist in Acadabourne. I think we might have to pray a bit that our allies will lend us aid, but in concluding, I remind myself and the Homager that we are not comprised only of words and thoughts, but of the instincts also of the animal. Let us revert to the fight for life with our nostrils flared, our spines straight and our eyes wide open. My parents always said that once a buffalo herd has charged, it is too late, but if we yell and growl and attune with our primal nature when Austral thunders down upon us, we may spook them into chaotic action and confusion for long enough to destroy the labs. So 'Wrraghbubbaliyagor!'"

Pangtrek shakes the expostulation from laughing lips and returns to a focused repose. Plain of face, but aglow with self-harmony, greying Satino Cavern now signals her intent to speak by holding the conch that both the African Saote and wildly pithy Trev have ceded in its circular passing, their silence tokening assent.

"I was born here. My children have here been raised to a peace perhaps never bridled by any society of human history. A harmony based on equality of all beings and ideas. If I purport to the validity of open war, then this is a peace they may not live to mature in. Or, if they remain here, in tenuous safety, then they may clutch it only as a veil, whilst their peers suffer travails in the realms of the corporate overlords. Yet as much as my heart mourns injury to Austral's misled citizenship, and even the fate of its warrior minions and the Riven, I believe South Austral's menace must be removed — even as fear is removed from the heart, with full vigilance, and without hope of final success. I cannot countenance the destruction and mindless intimidations of being that American South Austral has engendered any further. Therefore I go to war, in honour to the blood that bore me, and with the unanimous support of the blood which I birthed."

As Doherty Park and the elderly Dianne Prior also voice their assent, Tacleara takes pride in the way each of the Homage have kept their minds and hearts unified and calm throughout their deliberating on the nuclear crisis. She does not notice Bistani give his self-conscious and final voice to the need for war.

A jolt of wrongness in distant conversation flow has inured her attention to all else. She concentrates on the woman speaking, too far away to be conventionally audible, but easily discernible to Tacleara's refined senses.

"…I just think it's great. You know, for the first time he's linking hovers in with maintenance and harvest of all our crops. I just feel like god among the corn, I really do. You case a weak stand of regrowth and you can actually direct sow into it, and all that water goes into food production — the regrowth diminishes, but for a few harvests we can claim the water rights of a forest producer because it's mapped according to our needs, not some unsubstantiatable 'Earth morality'. Ha, you should see what's happening with the combination rituals; we become fused, his power shows us the transparency of the flesh and a mind that is walking in the readiness of modernity."

"So is Avery actually there?" asks one of the gusher's companions.

"Avery is present at all modernity combination rituals. You have to come, it's…"

There was that name again. Avery. Avery…Farmer. Cleara remembers hearing the name some weeks earlier. And here was the same feeling of compulsion in yet another person talking of him. The conversation had been innocently agrarian, but it is the yielding juvenility of enthusiasm in the listening women which seems uncanny to Tacleara. Before the empath has time to discern their susceptibility to energy subversion, Dianne's hand on her shoulder recalls her to the dispersion of the Homager. She farewells the woman and the other six until only Lans, Saliska, herself, and Furrow remain.

The dignified head of security passes her the conch gravely.

"You must inform Curlewalion. Ostensibly we are at war. If the populace shoulders this burden, I will deploy five thousand Mist in the first waves of the attack. Saliska assures me one thousand Indigos will be also ready. Lans has given assurance that two-thirds of the Unilion shall break the Austral holds on our bordering lands. Have no fear that your — our people will be unsupported in battle, Tacleara."

As she gulps back the emotion hatching in her throat, the centenarian hears Furrow enquire anxiously as to the whereabouts of the newcomers and Saliska's assurance to him that they will meet here shortly.

Summoning a calm she feels divorced from, Tacleara walks across the Tryst Common and blows a short note on the conch. Her voice pitched low but steady, its rhythm increasing in tempo, she addresses the intermingled thousands over the solar speak system, her words graced with a silence through which a baby's cry strangles from laughter into satisfied moans.

"Today the Homager formed a gnosis that we need to attack the northern bases of Austral in open war." Tacleara feels the interlinked awareness of those gathered cock its eye toward her, magpie-like, hunting for the meat of her announcement.

"We feel Curlew can no longer contain, through covert method, the threat of Austral's human and Earth-violating aggression that has found a return to its expression of capacity for nuclear warfare. Bards and playwrights — let your souls be thrown bare! Such an hour of malaise has never been upon our land. Though many of us may survive a missile attack, only a concerted army dedicated to pursuit of our beliefs may prevail in offence! The task is grim, with victory's chance a shadow. Gaian screamers and windchanters, let your voice tremble in the tongues of the Earth's knowing. In three days we must reach a consensus. Cast sleep to memory, and seek out the remedy for our crisis of conscience. Let your souls shift to the dictates of the land, and may our decision be bound to the consciousness of the future and the flexibility of the present."

To Tacleara, watching the emotional reaction beginning to ripple on the surface of the stillness, it seems certain that the populace will galvanise for swift attack. She sees a mass of the flying colours of realisation swirl out and merge until, like a budgerigar flock, it iridesces into single entities, becoming aware of

181

all the terrain that their souls must face on the coming journey. The energy descends, and people begin to scream, sing in low voices and to disperse, huddling into little groups, senses poised to give meaning to this new reality.

"We are the sum of our study of time. It seems strange so much of our land's time may now pass into destruction, the fires of the soul warping into destruction of fervour and entropy."

"It may, Lans, but you have always been more a pugilist in action than a slick conduit for philosophy," Tacleara observes.

"Well," interrupts Furrow, "we need to set up a contemplation window between the four of us tomorrow. Say midday at the old canoe workshop? It seems I've got a busy night ahead of me, we all have, but at least things…ah!" The man turns sharply away toward four men trudging through the puddling of intense discussion circles and holds up a hand, crying, "Beaumont! In the cinch of time, you fluke."

Tacleara watches him shepherd away the three prizes and their procurer, feeling great respite wash from the nautileer and weary enthusiasm flow from the hearts of the young men.

From these, then, will come the stones to cast back into the Austral glass houses, these ones of forbearance and pain. Something in the image reminds her of the brittle tardiness of the woman she had overheard.

"Lans. Has the name Avery Farmer come to your ears?"

The etched features of the blazing-eyed man retain neutrality as he summarily answers. "Avery. Moving big amounts of people through his design exchange, and large amounts of food, but he has always equated his watermark. Enjoys ballooning. There's nothing distinguishing him from any other agrarian except that his social profiling tends to mean discussion becomes forum wherever he goes. He seems pretty firmly earthed though; in fact he tracked down a Unilion through thick country to tell us about this double murder some two kilometres along Lurallerelly Green from his tribute."

Tacleara's inner watchlights flare at this mention, yet she needs evidence to support her intuitions that he represents a scuttling menace, so demurs, her lever poised to upturn Avery's rock, pursuing instead the actuality of the hunt for the two fugitives, once croppers, who had killed a neighbour and his wife, leaving a pile of ash in place of the homestead.

"In nineteen days, there has been no rumour among the prides of their apprehension," deliberates Lans, his flinty gaze seeming restless, as though to catch some glimpse of a black tail flicking above the reeds that might betoken news.

"Samut and Cyskuah both track south-west, toward the outer regions."

"Not both. Cyskuah has turned west."

At the sound of the voice, Tacleara's heart soars, and she turns to run excitedly and hug Tharrin and kiss his wife. The Dew's elder, Jesella, comes slowly through the meeting hall, and Tacleara intones the customary welcome, "Well met and safe memories," before seeing her seated.

"What news then is this?" pursues Lans of Tharrin.

The big Fijian explains how they had met Cyskuah two weeks prior, on the main border road, after his learning of a bloodied frenzy in a tiny town, purportedly orchestrated by those he pursued. According to the tracker, dozens had been slain as some fraternity of malcontents had overrun and fortified the town's underground cellars and library. They had spent the night with Cyskuah and his pride. Tacleara considered this would have been interesting for the Dew's camels. Then the Unilion had headed to Bunyuree, closer than Ja Junction, to alert a boma of Lion there, whilst they had journeyed a fortnight straight to the capital. Samuk remained to monitor the situation.

'Thank you. You Dew seem to excel at timely encounters. If you'll excuse me?" Lans is already too distant in his loping stride to hear their murmured assent.

Saliska also slips away, her eyes fogged, and Cleara knows that their understanding is mutual. The radiotelekinetic will pursue information on Avery Farmer and array any unusual details with a small team of Indigoes. There is nothing now to do but wait. Softly talking at a table near the water's edge, the wild vitality and unique insight of the Dew buoys her more than her cup of shineark. Even their hushed talk reverberates across the meeting hall, empty now save for a lone bard squeezing gestures through the air with a hand as he scribbles furiously.

When Tacleara confirms their suspicions about a gnosis for open war with Austral, Tharrin whistles through his teeth, and Esandril sheds a single tear.

Jesella, non-reactive, speaks. "The hatred is growing out there. Not a sandgrain of romance can be exploited from the disharmony and suffering any longer. The Earth stirs in her chains, Smashloosers swell, and the soul of humanity recedes. It is well to meet these transgressors, although our people will not join the fight. Our allegiance is to the journey alone, and it seems its springs have dried at last. Who can say what will become of us, of any of us?"

And then Cleara sees it, a sort of wonder mixed with fear.

"Yes," intones the aged Dew, as if sensing her thoughts. "A world opener has travelled with us. He will be waiting to meet you among the herd. He has become very close with them. Can you find the way? I think these two are keen to pursue the roof of old friends."

"Certainly," Tacleara says as she stands, brushing her skirt in measured movements to hide her sudden excitement.

"Then I will stay and bathe. The old ones will not trouble with such dried flesh."

Larker's amelioration of a strange, tumultuous fortnight within Curlewalion lands, of experience ranging from sublime to wholly unnerving, is nearing completion with her approach. The swirling field enfolding him has brightened since he became aware of her some time ago, its underlying components have sharpened — the colours, impressions and language comprised of laughter — though he is no nearer a kinship with these phenomena.

He knows she is the one to free them — the beings from his visions of the ages-old time rending, whose disturbing images had been accompanied by a glimpse of himself, somehow facilitating another to undo those horrors. He had thought himself suffering a crippling malady of the mind when he had first witnessed them after leaving the caravan for some solitude, loping hazily through the desert sands.

Giant, hirsute beings barely touching the ground as they walked, and the smaller statured ones just as hairy. Then he had come to espy fragments of their ways: the energies of air they worked at times, that pushed up spouting winds as though bursting from a cage of ether; the language they shared, vastly mournful and wise, the meaning of which he could not decode. Only ever two or three, and some days they were not to be seen. Then his vision had occurred, and he knew with numbing certainty who they really were, these yowies of legend and folklore. Once most powerful of humans, now comical characters of shaman's tales, startling apparitions to accost the traveller with a sharp eye for higher energies.

His earlier visions of war machinations and the hungry of soul had continued and intensified, buoyed by the powerful spirit of this land. Great was that essence, raw the forces and compacts of Earth that yet made their home here. He had thrilled to heed the elemental connection of man and nature as a thriving, revelatory thing, had followed birds to sacred pools and heard the story of ancestor spirits and stars upon the breezes that played over Curlewalion.

Now she was here, and already so wounded by it all, but he could give her no respite. If she believed in the land as strongly as he, she would surely flex with its need.

She feels him long before she spots the camels sprawled about a seasonal creek basin along the alluvial rise to the hills of Gatha, where trees thin just enough to glimpse their overhung crests, feels him like a river might sense a precipice, yet rush toward it anyway. The day is lingering before fade, and as Tacleara moves through the nonchalant herd, grasshoppers disturbed by the browsing ruminants are struck to a reflective whir of blue and green wings in the striated yellow light.

Larker: the air breathes the name to her. To make a heavy thing light — an apt name for this youth who makes even difficult yoga seem carefree. She watches him seated lotus fashion on the sward in blue denim shorts, brown hair merging with the tan of his skin. Cleara sees muscles ripple in unison along his light frame. His breathing seems to go all the way into the very Earth as he practices some internal chi refinement.

On every long outbreath he emits a combination of guttural drones. There are flowers unknown to her, Tacleara notes with awe, that grow in a wide ring all around him. As she looks on, a long blue manta orchid unfurls right next to his leg, and Cleara apprehends that the whole of nature is giddy from his presence.

The pan boy indicates the ground before him, eyes still closed. "Please join me, Tacleara."

As she settles on the meadow, Larker stirs, smiles and looks mutely upon her. There is something behind his dilated eyes that he shields; she can discern only that it is growing.

"So gladdening to see you, but before we walk the little dream together, I first must thank you, thank all of Curlew, for balancing these lands and guarding them, for facilitating their beauty. It is not really my part to praise you, others with greater lineage may truest speak thanks; the tribal peoples, or even the little things that flit here once more, still far rarer than in distant times, but tentatively returning."

The youth holds out his hand, and upon his dun palm stands a very tall beetle with intricately patterned red, white and black markings, its body gently quivering. She extends her hand and the beetle walks onto the cup of her fingers and begins to vibrate, swelling her whole being with joy and invigorating her every nerve before it flies smoothly away.

"It is a guchiehay in the aboriginal tongue, a wondrous creature, so very rare. They feed only on the pollen inadvertently brought them by native bees, which cannot resist the plink-plonk song and free massage. You have been guchiehay to this land, refreshing its people, taking a measure from each and binding the whole in focused vibration."

"Thank you for friendship, acuity and sincerity. I must ask though. These flowers, the very air around you…are you aware of…the otherness to you?"

Larker leans closer, his blue eyes focusing on her brown. Cleara is fascinated and appalled. There is not a vein of emotion emanating from him. No wisp of whimsy to impede his concentration. There it is! She can see now the creature-forms which she had felt eddying around him; one is perched behind him with great hairy ears and shining eyes that are similarly devoid of emotion.

Then, watching the reflections in her eyes, Larker sees the hob. They have not wanted to appear to Larker and risk their presence, or the heightening of the firefeather within him that such would provoke, for fear of drawing Enyadding interference with careful plans. Now that Larker has safely met the one who can bridge the gap, Fortusenay has appeared.

Bowing graciously, the ancient creature considers the humans, its facial colours and eyes shifting wildly, then it begins to talk. It is mainly for Tacleara's benefit. With that first reflected glimpse in his companion's pupils, everything had come rushing back to the rhabdomancer, and he listens now to his psychic benefactor explaining to the woman how imperative it is that she trust and align herself to Larker's will, of what noble soul and blessed ancestry he is comprised.

Larker notices Fortusenay makes no mention of the firefeather. The firefeather; Larker assays this dragonesque force that he seems to be — not contractual to, but a part of. He can glimpse its vastness, a delicate beast, though of earthy alliance and brief scouting fights of wonder and daring. It seems to him he is the tail, the twitching of which brings the dormant form into soaring being. Of a sudden the hob studies them both intently, saying, "I doubt we shall any of us see each other again. May the openness be you."

The Hobgoblin bows once more and fades from view. In the little space of the bow, his thought pattern had come to Larker's mind. "Forgive us for what you have lost, but already you have saved much, true-worker. You know what you have to do, our authority will guide you in both tasks."

He is surrendered a vision, momentous, but not like the chilling abstractions of past weeks, and one which might marry him with an end. Then, feeling the firefeather swell within him, he turns to Tacleara, speaking solemnly.

"I have now to show you grim truths, friend. The world as we know it will change and shudder in the days to come, yet humanity that lives and plays on this land has a slight chance to endure, regardless of whether you choose to face the dark and lend your aid. I implore you to attempt the role cruelly cast for you, and which I shall give preview now to you.

"Whatever you choose, that wilder way which swells in you is the key. Now is not too late, but the time is past for mediating politics with your feelings alone. The work of herbs must be swept into your embrace exclusively. Whether you use the teachings to ease your people's coming travails, or as a wrought stone to plug the gap that I will show you yawning, hot and vicious, is the choice you face. You are the only one. Ligature of the forgotten marvels to staunch the crisis nearly here can be plied with your hand only. Chance may yet prevail, but if after this first seeing your soul decrees it so, then into that gap I can take you. Awaken now to the true dream, Tacleara Guchiehay, and wander by me away."

All of a sudden Larker's eyes are portals and she is falling through their green world, deeply conjoined to an energy that supports her emotions, lifting and qualifying them into free things of her choosing. Fused utterly, for the first time, to her consciousness, avoiding the far yearning places of wonder that she glimpses on the edge of those green tunnels, she attunes instinctively with humanity's need and plies the patterns that reveal it to her.

The peril is vast. At almost every turn her shock is nurtured into focus as she gleans the truth from shifting imagery. Robotised humans, she sees, capable of breeding and near completion in a Texas sunken workshop; a vast tube sunk into the earth near Greece, the purpose of which is to draw direct star energy, using the Earth's magnetic powerhouse for ground warfare; a Chinese hyacinth-computing team, close to being able to patent time, charging for its non-standard usage.

Nearer to home, threats to Curlewalion are staggering. Toxic waste-filled automns creeping in their thousands along Pacific Asia's coast, screened by artificial storms; a lightweight device for blocking empathic and psychic energy, completed somewhere in American Tropical Territory; thousands of brain-altered ex-prisoner assault troops some hundred leagues off their western border, housed in oceanic cave systems and programmed with berserker-inducing frequencies in the Washington labyrinth. After the missile strike, the W.A.R. government intends to leave no trace of Curlew's existence.

She dives a little deeper. There is a pyramid where a gold-masked man faces a group of what she knows to be Lellying Enyadding. She feels their sudden anguish as they simply disappear. Another group, Marrafar Enyadding, faces and is destroyed by the vanquisher, now in the form of a Serpent. Then the Opsweyed Enyadding. As they evaporate, Tacleara sees how she might be able to save these beings, that this is Larker's 'gap'. In a second she comprehends what would have to be done, but even in her state of current equipoise, there is a nausea in her being at the notion. She soars forward to a near future in which she sees the whole of humanity enslaved to a war machine with interplanetary design. She does not need to look any more to equate the redemption of the lost immortals with the only chance of derailing that outcome of despair. As she comes back to herself, the hills of Gatha are cast in a last light, a light of endings.

"Take this; it will give you stamina for your journey, Guchiehay."

She chews the long root, sharp but clean tasting, that Larker gives her.

"It will also lead you to the wondrous ones of its missing kin. Do not seek to force a decision. There is some time yet, a half moon, before I can open the gap, so let your heart lead you until then. And do not let the visions disturb you, the coming battle is a thing that must be, a saddening that must be cried. Go with chance. Go to your wild path and let the hard angles of the world turn a little while without you. Take with you this drop of friendship. May it illumine the spirits of honour."

Larker slices his thumb with a grass blade and squeezes a drop of blood onto her palm. It dissipates instantly into her skin and suddenly a searing rainbow light shines from inside her hand.

"You have only to think of the light and it will return."

As the rainbow fades, the brilliant realm of the stars opens above her, and Larker rejoins his meditation. Tacleara's heart is like a thorn with knowing as she follows her feet towards the hills, towards her wild way. The magic of the herbs she can sense dotted through her lands closes over the thorn like the richest rose.

After a long time Larker stirs and watches the Moon's horn disappear among the stoic camaraderie of the camels. "I think it is time now. Two of them are coming and I must go to the place and remain there indefinitely."

"Travel well, our friend," thought-links Judjuerrachal, matriarch of the herd. "We shall wait your coming, and our hearts with you muse, though we cannot walk the high ways."

Larker smiles before thinking back. "It is not so little an obstacle, and yours is the un-walled land, and the wait between breezes. Your road leads to other waters."

Mendez shifts in the big swinging chair that depends from a high bough of the silky oak. Duncan had said that they planted it for someone sorely missed. The Spaniard traces its line of symmetrical branchings, penduluming now with no thoughts — now that it is done — but for her. Duncan and Prelisya had found their bed, after such stories as to make him forget her for a time.

The grace-light from the reflection hut casts a dim lucency across the lank lawns, not enough to sully the stars poised in patience as mentor and wonder to his soul. An unheavenly serenading chafes from the hut — Sean, reacquainting himself with the oboe. Sudden wild squawks harken to each new round of Duncan's mango liqueur. Enrique had deserted them after the play at the nearby Tumble, a black comedy carefully threaded around that dreadful spectre — war. The smitten consort of his handsome friend had dressed her Malaysian limbs only in bells and a blue scarf, and might never give him back. Mendez smiles blurrily.

There it comes again. The surging cry is mournful as a wind lost at sea and rich as morning clover. Glad he had been for shadows across their group, beside the tiny fire, when Prelisya had answered his earlier query of the call's origin with "Curlew". He had known his tears could not spirit her to them, would not secure her safety. Memory loomed so vividly of the student dreams they had shared about the vagrant, fragile bird and the wild, warm lands that were its last refuge. Happiness one could yield to on such a night, or at least dance against its shoulder for a while. The heady draught had probably blinded Sean to the worries driving their hosts early to bed; those concerning their child, and the sharpening scythe of war.

War. Here was a land where contentment, abundance and the sublime had merged around members of every culture of the world. Here daily discoursing came rolling from the tongue in many accents, but all in the expansive Lonan dialect that was the nation's language; as though a voice at last had been given to answer humanity's great puzzle, solved with its uniting for common need. Here the little flowers of impossible chance had begun to bloom, and yet here, in less than a week Furrow had said, must their gardeners prepare either to hide from the sun or face death to earn the right to continue feeling it upon their faces.

Mendez knows life is ironic, to just what extent is now revealed to him. Here he was in Sway's parents' own home, yet still not safe and still not with her. Here was his life's freedom restored him, yet seemingly little chance to survive it. Yet his existence had made a difference, so Furrow had assured him, enrapturedly considering diagrams the three of them had sketched for him that dusk, plans Furrow believed might yet prove the greatest succour for Curlewalion.

The Spaniard studies the contraptions hanging from the tree about him. The fearsome things formed part of Duncan and Prelisya's training instruments, and the couple had assured him that they would familiarise him with their full functioning the next day. But Mendez knows that no clever device exists which will take away that inner hurt, the gnawing of his soul for her.

He tries wearily to shake his mood, to see that at least he still holds life to fight, unlike those poor townsfolk in the uprising at Byron Bay. But there is no rallying in him, as there would be no retreat underground, commended for his help, if war came. Leaving philosophy to the young possum, uncertain in its rasping investigations above him, Mendez tucks his feet beneath him. With dawn's light, he will begin to search for her.

Larker walks steadfastly away from the herd and tracks his quarry for many kilometres. After some time he can hear them as well as see their lights; the bio-lantern's orb and the great blue spiralling shapes from the occasional whimsy of music that the two express. As he prunes their lead to earshot, the mad abandon of their song ignites in his soul and he realises that he is walking in rhyme with the swelling of their tune.

He calls out. "Hail, Peacebeats. Wings to your hearts and no finishing to your completings."

The little light goes out. A mighty seraphinic voice appears to start right before Larker and then to wander along the plain until it seems to whisper from the distant escarpment.

"Do you child the fleet joys and flee the chiding melancholy? Do you bring music, or speech clenched in muscles?"

Larker taps the gaps in atmospheres around the two, creating rapid tinkling explosions of bell-like rhythms, crafting endless exotic melodies, sculptured somehow to yet one thrumming note.

"I seek aimlessness, imperfection, a raining roof and child's reflection." Larker projects his sincere petition calmly into the empty air from where the bells had sprung.

The light comes back on, and a gangly aboriginal man with a didgeridoo blasts an echoing of Larker's melodies while striding in frenzied circles as his friend takes up the rhythm on his own cornet, turning somersaults capuchin-like, as he plays. Larker approaches the pair until he can see their enamoured faces, eyes transported in delight at this new song. Due to the turbulence of their joy, Larker has to dampen his soaring essence, focusing on an utterly still presence. The music stops.

"Hello, sky-player. Hello, hounding hornwinder," he says. The two seem shifting, as though wishing to still be channelling music, unimpressed with this formality. "I seek guidance to the Tear of According and a song-still According."

The strange men with a scampish air look at each other. Then the cornetist declares, "Guide we shall trade you, in fairness for the melody, but you must ask the music for According at the sun maze while the soul shines yet from the tear."

"Then we must hurry," says the aboriginal, "for we sought to travel widely, caressed by firmament and strange lands before returning home."

The three begin to run over country that rises steadily, skinned with a strew of rock, until the stars are almost erased by the tors which tower above them. Larker squats on his heels, looking up at the stretched verticality of stone. In the hush before dawn, only the deep labour of their breaths can be heard. Then softly his two guides begin to sing — an unearthly harmonic that spreads into the night and is punctuated by a nattering whine, nuanced with protest, in what sounds like the aboriginal's voice. A rhythm forms, folds on itself, then loops insistently faster, though not louder, until a great slab of stone in the cliff base eases open. The lantern flares to light, already throwing the aboriginal's shadow back down the two metre high tunnel as he plods ahead.

"Hurry, hurry. I'm Red, by the way," says the fellow with the beard, as Larker precedes him, and the panel rolls shut behind them.

"Larker. And I suppose you're black?" he queries of the man in front of him.

"I am actually. Name's Cory, though. Pleased to meet ya."

They jog through the tunnel for some minutes, which twists rarely except to bypass several floaters of granite, the smooth walls quartzily snagging the passing light, until they come to another panel.

"Just nudge it," offers Red. "It won't bite."

The Peacebeats giggle as the panel slowly rolls forward in response to Larker's shoulder. It is quick to close, though, and Cory, who is last, whips the didgeridoo from near obliteration and shakes it threateningly at the offending cliff.

"Oh," says Cory and extinguishes the lantern, for a thin meniscus of light now rests on the land. The three stand on the edge of a massive swamp crammed with water ribbons and the odd lotus. Behind and to either side are stern bluffs of the eroded escarpment. Beyond the swamp is a hill of black stone and tailing it, a mountain, also of the same heaped, dark boulders.

The doorway behind them opens with a faint crunch, and an Indian man and woman, he with a sitar, she with finger cymbals, emerge. The man smiles and the woman holds up a henna-patterned hand. Larker is aware of several people scattered in the lee of the cliffs, though the light is not yet enough to reveal to other than a firefeather mage more than the basic landscape. *So this is the Tear of According*, he thinks. *The place will do. It will do well.*

With a marked brightening of the day, Larker now witnesses what none but initiated Peacebeats ever have. Upon the universally green surface of the swamp, glowing paths, winding with the shape of a treble clef, suddenly appear — the sun maze. Joining the others, Larker steps onto the nearest path that leads, as do the rest, to the hill of stone on the far shore. Larker has wondered about this leg of the journey. He had seen the cliff tunnels in a vision that had shown only their termination at an impassable quagmire.

Cleverly capped just centimetres below the surface, the bricks on which they walk are wide enough to make their navigation easy.

"Bricks, so it's a good effect, bruz. Bio-luminary," Red explains softly over his shoulder. "They only glow for thirty minutes after dawn and before to dusk."

About a kilometre into the swamp, Larker sees that apart from the dim dozen figures crossing from the escarpment side, twice the number employ the paths from the other direction. The whole primordial bowl is silent, except for the electric trill of frogs and patchy laughter from kookaburras. Then comes a long trumpet call, winding high and mournful before fluttering in shaky cries and finally smoothing into a rounded melody of silken notes, each bracing against the air to hold open that path for their fellow travellers on the ether.

Now every instrument in the valley entwines, a tumult of lyrical yearning and screeching with a great thrumming of drums booming in unison, then in overlapping succession, their tempo dying now into a whisper, then shattering forth as though mirroring the stop-start of a hailstorm. The air literally feels alive, as the reverberant cliffs echo with marvels of sound, the frogs and kookaburras lifting their own efforts to match the frenzy.

Every time Larker thinks he catches a melody, leading instrument or vocal, all the sounds are sutured by echoes, and new tunes begin, the old seeming never to have begun. There are three wondrous female voices — almost as though the singing trine on the nearing hill of stone are channel to the muses. Larker can see a great many people in the shadow beneath the hill and understands that it is from here the drums come.

The foremost figure, advancing head on along their path, has almost reached the fast-paced Indian woman in front, whose flute-like voice carols over cymbal beats, crisp as hail. The newcomer plays a harp; the Peacebeats would say the instrument has chosen him, for its melody seems to hunt a longing from the very air. All at once, Larker understands. Perhaps the harp has helped.

He has spotted the uniting principal of melody for the entire According.

His bursting atmosphere of bells begin again, evoking the response of a second rapture from the frogs. But this time he makes his slower notes stronger, almost like cow bells, so the reverberations are blunt, hinting at the enticing code of rhythm but never completing it. Around these he threads his other tintinnabulations, nuzzling into space between guitars and banjos, oboes and harp, until there is not one of their rhythms that he cannot predict. One by one the instruments fall silent until only his bells and the three musicians sing. They fall silent, the foremost calling, "You are apportioned a song-still."

Around him people stir as if awakening from trance, and Larker moves forward, beginning to make his plea, watching. Peacebeats nearby shift carry-straps to shoulders, and those on the far shore arch back to view the radiant sky whilst hearing him. His words fill the valley in a low and steady tone like the echoes of boots on a fog-blanketed night.

"Entwining many fates and forces, I come to you in a time of war; a travesty from which you Peacebeats have thankfully redeemed the charging trumpet and marching drum, and reclaimed their innocence. Not even the harmonic of your devotion can stop the coming horrors, and maybe not even your sanctuary can outlive them. However, it is for this I have come to you. To tell you that, with your help, I can protect 'the Crescendo Vale'."

He passes the Indian woman, a hand to her shoulder in affection.

"From the black mountain I can weave energies to protect Curlew's peoples from either radioactive damage or the surge of an army. I will wrought of these hallowed kilometres a place that will survive even until the last denizen of the Earth persists, so that music flowing wildly might make final human transcendence if the planet casts us off in the doom that approaches.

"To do this, I need you to study unremittingly with me, to observe the humble tenements of my authority, and to here remain until such time as freedom breathes once more, or people are in need of a last refuge, whence you shall guide them here. Will you undertake to aid me in ensuring the defence of humanity, Peacebeats?"

After a pause, some fifty voices sing a word in unison, "Yes."

Then all those from the tear of the valley, now restored to a thickly-lilied swamp in wait for dusk's lowering light, gather to watch as the three muse-voiced women come singing down the hill of stone, their spell opening a passage mid its boulders. Larker threads through the eerie shaft with the group, who move in a mill-pond calm, oblivious to the pressing weight held apart only by the command of sound.

Small clay and stone huts dot a blossom-filled meadow, triply cut by a deep clear river given rise from springs beneath the stone mountain. To either side of the lush vale are endless untrammelled wetlands, their purple-lit ponds stuck with islands of emerald trees.

The Peacebeats had chosen the place not only for its inaccessibility, but also for its highly charged magnetic field, originating deep within the mountain, that kept any hovers from possibly disturbing their revelry. Suddenly there is a boom that clarifies into a river of sound, a thousand voices singing in a hundred languages, a rolling hymn of the word peace.

Of course it is the Verse, the According being only the ritual of music for those passing on the Tear's sun maze. Truly strengthened and awed by the thousand strong choir, Larker lies against a tree trunk to ponder the precise dimensions of the fortress to be built. Soon sunshine shifts the Peacebeats' focus from music to swimming.

By afternoon, they are making music once more.

But this time Larker aligns the singers in the ancient formats for the energy channel, the bass and treble instrumentalists guided to exact timing by his bells. As the huge stones levitate — those already positioned aglow with the rainbow's colours — Larker can see the spirit forms which work at the massive task of broadening the mountain's base. Elephant gods, giants and trolls, every mythic memory of the cultures of man. To the Peacebeats, though, it seems only that the rocks move and glow from the power of the sweetest music with which their tumultuous joy has ever been resonant.

Chapter 12

He feels somewhat foolish and impotent as he turns off the relatively deserted highway and heads through the beige snarl of tourist apartments packed row on row along the flat ground, spilling up into the hills like blood that has rushed to the site of a bruise. Still, he remembers that crisp timeless clarity in the seer's eyes, and Angelo's focus returns anew in an acuity of balanced electricity, pulsing him to a view through the very eye of the universe. As it rises along his spine, he breaks from his doubt like a swan from an egg. He knows where he must begin now.

Proceeding along the coastal road, it is uncanny to see the leisure seekers continuing in giddy abandon; they seem pointless manifestations of being in light of what he has just experienced. A huge karaoke screen squats in a fold of hills flashing magnified images of nerve-strained jaws and eyes. Wave pools trap a fluorescent-clad army of surfers, watched by reclining crowds on lawns hillocked into mounds styled as huge breasts. Tidal cannons launch people sky high to fall onto padded mats across the ocean, as restaurant flotillas lend the cheers of their diners from a safe distance.

Cutting inland past the service warehouses, a high-rise Densitution, several streets of muzzled houses with tiny lawns, a small vege-fuel estate and metal reworking plant, he slows to scan the front of the retirement home. High, razored fence and two guards, a man and woman, plus the one behind the tinted glass gatehouse. Retirement villages! Behind the government image to the contrary, they were prisons. Some, he supposed, might still be designed on a rough sketch of aiding the elderly. Yet as he swings away from the facility, he recalls the words of his friend, Luke, after their visit here a year ago. They had come to see his friend's father, and on the drive home, Luke had put on a bluff face to hide his grief and shock.

"These old cats were only teens when the ASA New Zealand war ended and the anarchic backlash flared in its wake. It took the world rulers most effort to stamp out that spark right here, man. And they remember it. That place is just pure draconian efficiency. It's like holding a razor to hug him in there…still, funny to think of them all upping the ante, living before the personality mandates…"

Angelo considers how quickly had life become a thing for breaking. Any citizen over seventy could be compulsorily brought behind those high fences and indentured six hours a day to the conjoining recycling and fuel estate. Officially, the work translated as a 'bolstering of self-worth and mental acuity'. In reality it ensured a fast track to death, suiting a regime reliant on youth and glibness to drive its economy. He remembers seeing Simeon that year ago just returned from his 'age bridging' or 're-education' daily lecture. Staple fare for any in the village with a dissident record. There was no doubt their purpose was to break the spirit quicker than labour the body.

Angelo prays that Simeon's spirit is still whole and that he will be one of those selected if they take the bait. Sheer greed should factor the inclusion of the big, devout anarchist in any labour team, if Angelo's plan to appropriate one succeeds. He parks on a side street, changes into his boiler suit and walks a wide loop back behind the recycling facility to come at the retirement village from that side. As he nears its gatehouse, he quickens to a jog, signalling to open the gates. They part and Angelo stands, one hand on a hip to talk to the guard, gesticulating wildly toward the plant.

"Look, mate, we've had a really big order come through, and we're backed up to the warehouse chutes. This is gonna mean a guaranteed Asian flow, right — if we get it right. Now I need fifty men, and not the usual piss-pants — big solid blokes that can think on their feet — from now until forever. Rations for three shifts, full tool kits, intercom and some first-aid kits. And we need them an hour ago."

"Hang on, where's your clearance? You're not ID'd. Who are you?"

"I'm the guy turning plate to pure gold. I'm the guy paying for your fucking job, mate. Every second you stuff me is three hundred kay gees lying idle. I didn't stop for ID or for a dollar to call your supervisor from the nearest phont."

"Okay. Hang on, I'll call dispatch."

Five minutes later, after much pointed pacing and spitting, Angelo is leading a group of men across the road and raving on about full actualisation of remelt assimilies, a yell of "Hur-ry up!" gusting from the bellows of his orotund chest. Once around the corner, he confirms with Simeon that none in the party are reactionarily barbed. With an arm around the greyed giant, whose craggy face holds still alacritous brown eyes, the descendant of poets begins where he stands.

"Listen, this is all a load of crap. I don't just mean me pretending to work at the plant. I mean the whole society which has eroded the soil of your life. Something happened today. You don't have to believe me, but I saw a man turn a hover-stack into a sculptured aboriginal using purely the wind of his will. Now when the energy of that happening spreads, men and women — your sons and daughters maybe — are going to awaken, shaken at what has become of this Earth, and take to the streets to fight for their lives and their town. If we let them stand alone they will be mown down, cleared from the throat of business-as-usual. My name is Angelo Hardy of the Realliance, and I appeal to your maturity, wisdom and skill, and beg for your aid."

"That's right," says one proud-jawed fellow with long hair more blond than grey. "Up against the Affiliates kids don't stand a chance. I'm with you, mate."

With that there is a flood of acquiescence to help and fight, and much curiosity about the market happenings, to which Angelo replies that if they live through the night, he will explain in the morning.

"But," says a hulking elder with thrice-broken nose and interlocking stars tattooed on his forearms, "how come we're the revolution?"

"The whole thing is a mistake of circumstance. Realliance is right now trying to raze Fadtown, but the cells in Ballina are the ones primed to go on its success. Byron was never calculated in the revolt. There's no doubt, after the display of hope and power today, that people are going to act right here, so we're in the middle of it. I came to you because Simeon, who is a friend, has told me of the old days — "

"Well, I'm not with you," says a calm, bitter-faced man.

"Oh, come on, Geordie. Lighten up, mate. Take it easy, bro," ventures Simeon.

The protagonist shakes his head. "It's alright. I don't care for to roam the streets fart-arseing at cops, but I don't care for these fools running my retirement holiday either. I've no intention of getting lasered while this little jaunt fails, as it will, but I'll be quite happy to sit with some whiskey in the process shed if you lads are gonna plan to smack everyone out the way, like."

"What is the plan, anyway?" asks a man, his eyes deeply set, who continues with no uncertain irony. "We waylay the wherewithal of recycled metal, whacking future sculptors from winning over windboy's work? I am with you, having waited a life for this moment. But what do we do? We should keep moving at a dispirited shuffle and plan en route, I say."

The group's commendation of the notion is shown in their mobilising back into a shuffling caricature of dispiritedness to approach the gates. Eyes dart to share swift understanding as Angelo talks loudly with Simeon, the crash of the plant no doubt annulling any voice-recording devices.

"I'll deal with security. How many are there, two?"

"Three."

"Yep, okay. Any other personnel we need to round-up, then lock down out of the way. We need a solid couple of vehicles, three somethings that make a really big boom, shields, armour, helmets and weapons. I'd say we have a grace of two hours before it all goes nuts, so we wander in, make like monkeys with finding bars and things to exert our authority, then get on with it. Where's the security detail?"

"Normally there's two on the rounds, one on the gate."

"Okay. I'll stick behind you when we approach. Just tell the guard that the village sent you for a double shift."

Within minutes, the fat prosaic guard is walking to the main offices, heavy boots spraying gravel, having instructed the group to remain. Angelo's fingers shake as he jimmies the door of the gatehouse with a little bar he has set aside for the purpose. Sure enough, a hand gun is in the second drawer, loaded. *It* is a duel, he affirms, slipping back out before the guard has trudged more than a hundred metres. *That* fat one has insulted the honour of equity, slurred my land's heart. However, he thinks it through, there is no way beyond this glitch of morality. His shot is accurate into the broad target of the man's back, the gun's retort absorbed by the cacophony of machinery. The gang of elders disappears quickly, and left with only the splayed and gore strewn body to ponder, Angelo gags, chokes for air, and falls to his knees. The needling of the gravel through his hemps cuts through his sensitivities. He moans, pulls at his face, then sobers to drag the awkward weight, hiding it from sight.

He does not have long to lurk, secreted inside the gatehouse cubicle, before he steps out, gun upraised to meet a guard returning from his patrolling rounds.

"Hands up in the name of the Realliance!"

The slack features of the guard contort in defiance as he goes for his weapon, and Angelo feels feathers of molten ash rain through his heart as another body falls before his feet.

"Thus is the lineage of poets brought low."

He stows the corpse and throws a shovel of gravel onto the dark stains in the road before locking the boom gate down, not that any traffic is likely now by road, and hopefully not from the sky.

By the time he hunts down the remaining guard and reaches the main processing facility, his ageing rebels have herded all the workers into a storage room, two bleeding from face wounds. Bran of the deep-set eyes, with still a thin pate of red hair, explains that his friends have 'encountered the audacity of youth, but are tough enough to handle it'.

It takes them two hours to assemble what they need, the skies still as moonlight in a river. Angelo, loading the explosives into the three company hovers, sleek but light models, can only marvel at the skill and enspiritedness of his allies.

They have even constructed bulky cannons from reworking handheld compression units. In head-to-toe plate silver armour and modified welding helmets, they look like a fierce crew of space explorers. The heavily moustached Kite gives Angelo his metal protection, and the tailor-poet observes that a rough insignia of the curlew and lion has been copper-soldered onto the chest. He knows that it is time they leave — the battle in Fadtown would be drawing to a climax, and theirs is overdue for beginning. Rising above the slave sector and severely marginalised area of the town these men had once so loved, Angelo feels they may able to claim it back.

There is no guarantee that what they are doing is legal, yet with the amount of passageway tattoos his employer bears, Saul doubts that anyone would be coming to stop them. The man had credited his account in advance with a fingertip, pocket-size transactor, and only the mega-rich could move funds instantly with a fingerprint. There were two more days of work as guide, the Spanish collector requiring human aid in addition to his automns in such perilous country. As well as navigating magnetic flux and giant stinging trees, Saul remains vigilant against other things than snakebite.

It is probably as much of a thrill for Syeric, now studiously cross-checking a plant his automns have found, to be bagging the last of these specimens in the world, as it is for him to be hunting in such a landscape. Saul hears a yell and rushes out from behind a cedar tree downslope of his charge, a huge repeat laser thrust forward.

"Don't shoot," Syeric scoffs in his taut Latino accent. "It's a narrow leafed palm — believed to be extinct."

The next instant, a shovel extends from each of the automn's arms, and they dig the whole metre of soil from beneath the man-high plant and fit a latex pot around it. After watering it from a pack on the hover platform, they stow it with other specimens and the safari continues.

Saul is ever watchful for gidditeas. To most people who have never been to a wild area, he supposes, they represent simply a bygone tool that had done a good job. One of few things, people would perhaps think privately, that the World American Reformational Government had done well with. Saul knew differently. People in forest areas knew that the gidditea, initially a by-product of cloning research on Tasmanian tigers, had not died out at the inbuilt prompt of its cellular programming. A gidditea was bio-engineered like a small leopard, but with hugely powerful jaws capable of complete vertical opening, this feature modelled from the thylacine gene.

Released into bushland areas across Australia, it had been estimated it would take twelve years for them to reach sufficient numbers to do their job, for they had been designed to hunt and eat only feral dogs, cats, pigs and deer. Saul remembers having seen a picture of the environment minister patting a laboratory breeding pair. Now it was a decade since the recessive gene was meant to have kicked in and wiped the species out. They had eaten every dog, cat, pig and deer from the wilds, yet somehow they endured, their protein processors adapting to other game.

One day his girlfriend had been dragged from the road by one as they walked home. Security had made a big show of looking for a homicidal vagrant after he had told them, meanwhile operating a private cull around rural towns of the area. It is because of his vigilance that Saul now sees what occurs. Over lunch he has been watching Syeric with one eye, as the Spaniard leans on a big fig tree eating a sandwich. Suddenly Saul sees the tree beneath his boss become semi-transparent, rippling like water. With a gasp, the Spaniard disappears into the opalescent jelly which had been trunk and roots, then the tree re-solidifies. As it does so, huge vines lift from the soil, and with a determined leathery reach, wrap around the two automns and smash them on the side of a boulder until they are demolished. Saul straps on his hover-pack and speeds pale-facedly away, wondering where he can hide; for this time he knows security will not believe him.

As two of the security hovers fire at him, Saul realises that for once his pot-induced paranoia is not misguided. He had lit a joint almost as soon as he was over cleared land. The weed was grown expressly for business boffins and visiting politicians by government farms, and was known to cause virtually instant hallucinations in the uninitiated. Saul, who liked his smoke, went through black market contacts in the Nimbin precinct, the most entrenched in South Austral. He had decided that blending into the tourist press in Byron was his best chance, and that from there he might ship as a guard on one of the fishing boats foraying along the northern border.

When he first crested the hills surrounding the bay, he had assumed there was some kind of festival going on. Floodlights at both ends of town showed a crowd of grounded security hovers, as well as big armoured police buses. The fat bald man reached the periphery of town just beyond the water recycling plant before his pea-brain discerned he was in trouble. Too late he realised the crowd of fast moving vehicles in the sky was not some display or gaggle of joy craft. Then the laser blasts flared by him.

Saul dips and manages to make a narrow defile between two high-rises. Shooting out the other side, he is forced to weave between trees as the pursuit tightens. Realising that he cannot outpace them, Saul alights close to the top of a stately Norfolk pine and unloads his own laser at the nearest security hover. The effect of the striking rays from his high-powered weapon on the hover's front is devastating, and it plummets from view. His only real skill saves his life, as he manages to wing the other one, hearing the bang of its differentiation drive failing.

Saul is now swept by a mood for shooting security hovers — his last stand! Though, as he puffs on a roach, he ponders how they could have found him out so fast. He has done nothing wrong really, and with the strength of the righteous, he culls three more hovers before coming over town itself and observing, to his astonishment, a roiling seethe of people battling two lines of forty or so police and Affiliates with little more than paint bombs. Finally understanding, Saul knows it is a battle he wants no part of and takes his opportunity to buzz toward the lighthouse and safety.

Considering what they have achieved, Angelo knows things have gone as well as they could. He still grieves the first hover that did not return from its deviation to bomb the police station. As it had dipped low, poising to drop the explosives, automatic ballistics had strafed it with laser fire spewing out of the lawn, and the hover had banked and been engulfed in a sudden fireball as the station exploded, the hover's bombs deployed efficaciously after all. Angelo's and Simeon's crews had levelled the security building, avoiding the automatic laser cannons, the knowledge of which had been bought so dearly, and had then landed three kilometres apart at opposite ends of town. The plan had been to converge on the council chambers, removing security and private or public resistance along the way, whilst inciting and streamlining rebellious factions.

Angelo's group had arrived outside the chambers first, with fifty or so locals in tow, all but a few in their teens, who had spilled from houses and hover cars to join them. Two of those silvered comrades with him, whom he thought of as elder knights, had been killed en route in a fight with Affiliates. Simeon's group arrived with a large tail of a hundred and twenty people, many among them aboriginal. From where he is sitting on a rooftop opposite the chamber, Angelo can see that the most frenetic resistance comes from the aboriginal fighters. He glimpses several of the elder knights, but has not seen the distinctively gargantuan Simeon for some time and is certain his friend has fallen.

Simeon had been fierce in flank attacking the council security that had Angelo's mob squeezed in a trap. When Angelo had first converged on the town centre, many hundreds more people than he had predicted were already engaged in a revolt they were losing — to which the mass of sprawled bodies below bears testimony. The tailor and his knights had steadied the horde once they had broken through, delineating targets and forming shields with their bodies until hovers could be moved for the purpose. They had nearly eliminated the last of current forces arrayed against them, including two wedges of crowd control at street level. Many rebels had gained the sanctuary of the thick stone council chambers, and others, like himself, had climbed onto rooftops to discourage hovers and scout for advancements of security.

Angelo recognises the shapes moving in across the ocean, two triangulated helicopters of military origin. He has barely time in which to radio the sighting and bemoan the evil luck. As the black forms materialise, he knows his handgun is useless; the choppers are prime war machines with manoeuvrability, weapons and armour. Just above the roar of their rotors, he hears swearing and sees a fat man go rocketing overhead in a hover-pack, straight into the flight.

A bloated laser ray flares out from the mad image, and one of the choppers plunges into the building next to his. The other helicopter is now turning, firing at the unlikely target buzzing out over the ocean. Incredulously, Angelo watches him fall away from his hover-pack, a mile high, and collapse straight into the sea. Then he remembers the ocean padding out there and finds himself willing the man to survive. Heedful of the returning monster, he jerkily gains the street and ushers everyone inside.

From within the chamber's security room — their captured command post — Angelo and his knights study the monitors that depict the street-scape and immediate sky around the building. The chopper, with nothing but the dead and severely wounded to confront it, spatters its bullets into these. Then it is challenged. A young woman rushes from a building opposite to hurl a Molotov bottle up against the craft. It burns for the briefest time before the unscathed helicopter fires a rocket into the community drug clinic from which the attacker had come, shooting down the fleeing woman with a lazy ticker-tape cough of its guns.

"Obviously," broods Angelo, "they are hesitant to level this one. It works for us that they so love their collateral, but we have a very slight window in which to do something, I'd say."

"Pani says she's found the services map to this block," volunteers Teller, a very young woman who has emerged as a leader. Angelo and the two surviving knights crowd around the beautiful Indian girl's monitor. She highlights a possible attack based on an oversight in the civic planning that three people might exploit, then the tailor urges her to go and advise the four hundred souls in the reception hall to remain where they are.

Up again. To the roof of the council building this time. Angelo runs through the workings of the heavy but ingenious cannon while on the last step, then he edges open the door. There it is; as Pani's hack had shown, an ionisation unit immediately outside, behind which he huddles.

A crackle on his intercom brings Girt's voice and the message, "I'm ready." The tailor breathes deeply, then rushes to the roof edge where a quick glimpse shows that Girt has done his job. The helicopter has turned down the street, responding to the knight's ruse of laser attack. Hidden behind the roof edge, Angelo cannot tell if the brave elder is still alive, but his ploy has succeeded, and the helicopter poises at the street corner as if uncertain of further action.

"Get ready," crackles Bran's voice, and Angelo shoulders into the stone balustrade, priming his weapon. Having followed the service tunnel, Brannagh now bursts from a shopfront across the street, Angelo watching him maintain a steady fire on the chopper while being hit by anti-personnel bullets clacking from its gun racks.

The gunship corners the elder in the little cul-de-sac, and now Bran has only to entice it a little lower. The knight dodges under it to fire, and the craft flips then dives in a vicious arc down at him. From a corner of his awareness, Angelo sees the big man collapse, but he is concentrating solely on his target, firing at the methane line on the street below, where the computer had showed its above-ground seam.

He has a tiny window of time, and though strictured even more by need for accuracy, his shot is steady, the chopper exploding to slurry as the methane becomes an inferno, paving blocks erupting as the fire roars back to the mile-distant header tank that sends forth a resounding clap of chaos that pursues Angelo back downstairs.

Reinstated in the security room, the tailor is elated to see the safe return of the big Irishman, Bran, but the fall of the bright-eyed Girt lies heavy and unspoken between them. Angelo takes up the public announcement microphone after conferring briefly over some computer statistics, aided by the dynamism of butch young Teller and a glowing-faced, but eye-of-the-storm-calm aboriginal man, Napirya.

"Records in this facility indicate that all local police and Affiliate forces have been overcome. The army has most likely already sent the only aid it can spare, and with the victory of the Fadtown uprising, the area by tomorrow will be judged too risky against further deployment. Many of you are here this night in revolt because of miraculous events at the regional markets earlier. My suggestion is that you now gauge between yourselves the import of such an event, and celebrate our victory with what sleep you can get. However, we need to disable all telecommunications, so anyone with due experience should meet in the green room in five minutes. Tomorrow brings us work; asset re-apportioning, community forums and the expulsion of cyber- emotionalised individuals from our town. I am Angelo of the Realliance, and I believe that this day on which we bring the storm will be hallmarked to commemorate the time that the rainbows could arch once more over free lands."

An hour later, a radio message reporting the successful destruction of a transmitter tower brings other news to the rebel quarters.

"What is it?" demands Teller of Angelo's shocked countenance.

"Empowerment cadets. Six hundred, rallying on the town fringe. Finalise the barricades and mobilise everybody."

Reports of two smaller groups of cadets come in, as well as a column of automns, a hundred strong, emerging from an underground repository near the charred security building.

"Man," sighs Napirya, "we couldn't have known about the automns, but we should have factored on cadets." The aboriginal is cool, the levitation of eyebrows all that betrays concern.

"Well, we are now," Angelo notes, grinding knuckles across his scalp. "Let's find a way out of this death trap."

The automns strike first, ripping through the barricades and atomising the chamber doors. They enter with lasers poised and infrared scanners buzzing. After combing the building for several minutes, their computers indicate the service tunnels and they predict a flight path. There is a brief altercation between man and machine as the mechanoided lifeforms convince the cadet leaders of the folly of egress through the tunnels, and the minions of order spill back onto the streets toward the beach.

Angelo has nearly secured the four hundred and fifty rebels when the first wave of laser fire breaks upon the rocks and hastily begun walls of sandbags around them. They are hunkered in a labyrinth of breakwall, a combined effort of four generations to stop the hungering tides with a variety of reinforcements and boulder piles. A little party of wounded stumbling along the grassy shore is pulverised by automn cannons. Angelo takes the legs out from under a sheeny-faced cadet cavalierly trying to close along the sandy flat. A sable-haired indomitable lass leads a counter-fire with three other women.

The rampart ensconcing the quartet is a jutting tumble of enmeshed concrete, girders and boulders, overlooming the cadets gathered on the sparsely treed lawns. All the top of the shore levee is higher than the lawns of the town level, but lacking in the big hollows beneath and amid those giant rocks embedded in the sand around Angelo.

As the tailor goat-hops along rocks toward the front line, he glimpses bolts of fire thrown by the woman and her three cohorts, all rebelliously sporting short-cropped hair. They have formed into pairs to work their weapons, trained upon their adversaries in a merciless barrage of brute fire. Only intermittent and inaccurate fire curls from the slim portion of unscathed enemy lines, but enough that Angelo must continuously duck into a hollow between rocks while he records the sprawl of bodies and automns that already litter the lawns. Other laser strikes confound their foe. The clustered rebels have almost enough weapons to go around, though no charger, Angelo reflects.

The abhorrent bark of hundreds of exploding grenades rends night, thought and limb. Angelo sees the four high defenders shredded into plumes of fired flesh, propelled across the night like discarded rags, before a ricocheted burl of rock slams into his chest and knocks him down. Recovering, he finds a cadet skipping lithely over boulders toward him, her truthie raised. A rebel, face blood-spattered beyond recognition, lasers her dead and scrambles to repel the attack on the front line.

Screams and the blaze of lasers warp the senses. After nearly blasting an ally, Angelo holsters his laser, glad to reserve its charge, and bloodies his fists instead. He crawls under a rock and soon snags a uniformed leg, unbalancing a cadet to squish headfirst onto stone. He works his way to the exposed northern flank where protecting tide and rock are separated by sand. Here he finds laser work, aiding a staunch huddle of aboriginals who hold off an unremitting advance of automns. As though another tide, the automns' plastic forms begin to overwhelm the little group.

At that moment a furore of rays strobing into the back of the foe precede the shining, though dented, armour-clad forms of a group of elder knights. It is a remnant half of the crew whose hover had been felled by auto-lasers at the police station, presumed lost. Standing amid the wrecked dolls of oppression, a knight looks humorously on Angelo's anxious face.

"It's alright, mate, we brought backup."

As they complete the tasks of rolling rocks to create a more permanent bivouac and of propping up the scores of dead presentable enough to seem still living, Angelo is heartened that the numbers brought in by the knights now swell their ranks back to about three hundred. This unexpected force of stragglers, armed mainly with shovels, had decided the battle for the breakwall. With the injured bedded down and the still hale gathered in the gloomy shadows of the boulders, Angelo stresses the priority of staying together to a subdued audience.

"We sit here at least until dawn. Then we can make assessment of our ordnances, tap into some feeds of more support and scout the opposition."

A thick-jowled aboriginal youth, one of those who had stood most implacably against the automns, opposes him.

"No way, man. We've won. We should free those other olds at least and start purging the tourists out, smashing the mansions while the hand of chaos still favours us."

Joining in, a short man with sunken eyes and Unipean accent begins to foment. "Yeah, there's a place just down the way where the bureaunauts are experimenting mind drugs on kids. On kids! That is just to say what I know of, imag — "

" — First of all," Angelo delivers gratingly, "We have not won. We have survived. Secondly, we are tired, nerves are frayed. We need time to think and sleep. If our unity crumbles and things fail up in Fadtown, the light of resistance is gone. We stay here." Like the growls from some alpha wolf, his words quell the dissent amid the rebel pack, and people settle to sleep or their night tasks.

When Angelo hears the sentries' screams of 'incoming', he rolls awake from a humped sleep on a purloined leatherveg bag to a world of dark that is striped with flashfire. Slipping and straining up to the little bastion where an elder knight and contrasting teenage pair, all working cannons to stave off hovers, he trains his night focals on the sky and knows full well what the outlines of the speeding shapes represent.

"Agents in hovers. Military on the ground, two hundred plus!" he screams over a shoulder.

These are Fadtown hovers surely, the spick regiment like nothing Byron possesses. Angelo ponders this significance, and having read all the Affiliate manuals, recalls that Agency forces can only be employed ad hoc from a depot within fifty kilometres of the trouble spot. Therefore the Fadtown revolt has failed, for other than Byron's tiny, already subdued security post, there is no other Agency depot in the vicinity. Numbly, he begins to count the hovers, and as the levee snipers are destroyed, realises it will be less than an hour before the twenty-two assault craft overrun their position.

Napirya is despondent at the makeshift strategy counsel which Angelo calls. The mercurial, athletic aboriginal had just pulled the body of his nephew from a sniper turret. By contrast, Teller, the energetic young lady of bi-coloured eyes and previous leadership initiatives in the council chambers, is as straight talking as her name.

"What you doin', man? We got a pickle here — a big sour one!"

"I'd rather be here with good rock and the ocean by me than die in some building from a single explosion," Angelo says to her, then raises his voice against the twisted cries he hopes are coming from amid the opposing forces. "Okay, let's double everyone up. Spread the word, Bran, tell them if a partner falls, they stay under a rock. Geordy, stage a bluff retreat on the south flank. Put some kids in the rocks there with a couple of cannons in case you catch a hover coming in to bail out whoever falls for it. Mirusta," Angelo turns to a broad Asian woman, tightly sashing her dressing-gown with a gesture given credence by the awful authority in her eyes, "be a kind woman and go along with Napirya to kill people on the north corner..."

Two big lads and a severe, bronzed woman dump a crate in the little clearing. The youths unsling their rucksacks while the Amazon states: "That's our reserve. Twenty lasers. The paint. A hover shield."

"Okay. Nape! You're a native-born shield waver. Shalade, get some fit friends, take the lasers, wait in the rocks until the first wave breaks, then you will be inside their lines and you can give them some Shakti. If you three start bagging this paint, I'll start sending people back for it. Tell them to employ it on soldiers only; the hovers are video-imaged so a dirty screen won't slow them." Already running, his last words jar along a disembodied trail behind him.

Angelo moves among his desperate band, flapping away fears and slapping at backs and weaponry as though a rooster premeditating his flock's usurpation by a newly come rival. Amid the sonic sizzle of the home-made cannons across their front line, he urges people to conserve laser fire until urgent, then selects a boulder against which to steady his rapid focal-scanning of the shore. Clamping back fear, he reins in on the three shapes that ghost across the sand and out to sea.

Shale pontoons, unlike craft with electromagnetic differentiation drives to power their anti-gravity, exploited a delicate relationship with sodium electrolysis to maintain above-ocean hover buoyancy at a level close to the surface that would be treacherous to other hovers. Angelo feels himself falling further. It can be only pure fluke that the pontoons were in the area at all — perhaps to be serviced — as their expense rendered the Affiliate zealous in confining them to their big northern bases.

The rebels' only grace lies in the fact that the craft have come from land and will need time to charge their segmenting lasers as the drives stabilise through the changeover to chemical catalyst. The pontoons prop beyond the range of home-made cannons, parallel to the rocks of the shore levee. Angelo wavers, self-doubt misting the windows of any reason through which he might spy a way out of this trap.

"Angero! Hang on son to your hat!, whimsies Jumo, a Chinese teacher, grunting back against the rock beside Angelo and lifting his focals to the impending fate of their brief resistance. Suddenly Angelo is laughing. The oriental man is dumbfounded.

"Is not that funny, isn't it? Get to be brasted all over rocks. Wish I am raughing this way, Angero."

The contrary leader only deliberates on some hallucination.

"He might just sink them from there, crazy loon."

As the conversion banks of the Shale pontoons flare to green in cannon preparation, he directs Jumo to a bald floating head and the solid repeat laser muzzle snouting up before it.

"Ho, ho! Sea god, isn't it? Oh! Look now. He-hee!" His companion eddies in a wild dance and skitters back to the battle as a pontoon explodes, igniting another one and cannonballing the third into a flying arc. Without pause to consider the effect of the devastation upon their saviour, possibly the same fat survivor from the earlier daring mid-air hover-pack evacuation, Angelo hurries barked instructions across his radio.

"Tamsyn, get the wounded down to the beach, and a couple of cannons to cover for us, over. Simeon, spread the word to flee the levee in two minutes, head to town and disperse; everyone for themselves." A cluster of people soon slink out from the rocks, the three ragged figures with cannons looking little better than the five wounded being shepherded along by Tamsyn.

Brannagh and Simeon lumber up the beach while Angelo looks over the party of maimed gathered by the spidery Tamsyn. He converts his wash of emotion at the knight's loyalty to stern injunction for the aboriginal woman to flee. She flings her hands around his helmet, and reaching up to raise the visor and kiss him, whispers, "How 'bout that young girl?"

Angelo glances past her at the traumatised youth clutching her charred torso, and says, "She won't make it."

Tamsyn nestles the girl to the sand and presses a knife into her palm, then flashes into the night. Angelo hefts a limping woman in his arms and staggers behind the desperate party that threads its way along the wet sandy concourse between the boulders at the levee's foot, forced time and again to diverge into the sea around obstructions of boulders. As they gain the open beach, the knights exchange laser fire with some miscreants hidden in the rocks, and the wounded, the tailor and the cannoneers stumble on, wide of the conflict.

Angelo turns at the sigh of segmenter fire and sees both knights fall in flame smote upon them by an assault hover. The cannon team is assiduous in reply, a frail faced girl robotically loading the pipes with shrapnel from the last in her sack. Tenacity harvests reward. The cooling vent on the front right gunnel allows some slim object to pass through and pierce the drive. The hover slews down into the line of breaking surf.

Amazingly, Brannagh picks himself up. Angelo suspects he is the last of the once sixty elders, now that Simeon is a twisted sculpture. They scurry on, the bunchy silhouette of Napirya still fighting madly around its upraised hover shield, fighting for nothing but perhaps a distant memory, certainly not the hump of concrete on the edge of the break wall from which he throws down his assailants.

They crawl up to the beach lip and across the now pitted park lawns as the six remaining assault hovers bustle like the steeds of sky cowboys, their lasers the lassoes with which the fleeing rebels are rounded up. On the rubbish-strewn ground beneath a casuarina stand, Angelo's group catch their breath. He motions the ammunition-less cannon crew to flee with the wounded while he and Brannagh crawl back toward their oppressors.

Dawn breaks like a guilty lover returning to home's door, dragging its feet and the light that will aid them. The wispy brightness lends Angelo several vague demarcations — soldiers unchallenged on vantages about the shore levee, soldiers grouped casually around three hovers on the lawn, Agents strapping prisoners to hover trestles. Angelo turns to his companion.

"It's over," he states.

"Not yet, mate," Brannagh replies. "Not after losing Simeon and the rest, and all those kids. Maybe light'll burst this scum like vampires." The doughty Irishman is up and running, and together the pair rake their lasers across an unprepossessing group of soldiers. Angelo rolls beneath segmenter fire from a vigilant distant hover, then serpents his body around to face the hazy outline of an Agent among the prisoners to swiftly annul it.

Before he can sight another Agent, his shoulder blooms in pain, and he drops his blaster, a bullet shrieking in his flesh where it had pierced the frayed armour. Laughter approaches him, and he looks up at two soldiers, one of whom places a lazy boot on his sternum, pinning down the armour. The other flicks up his visor, and Angelo feels his facial skin squirm and tastes the bitter synthetic alcohol of army issue as it runnels into his nose and mouth. Blinking stinging eyes, he hears a cigarette being lit and the satisfied sounds of in-drawing.

The instant his vision clears, a rock bounces from the smoker's head and he drops backward, only to be pushed forward again by the buffeting mass of a leaping horror, to fall across Angelo. The lump of furred muscle slams into the other soldier, Angelo's stunned senses witness to a mastiff ripping the South Australman apart, its paws skittering across his armour — the fallen soldier atop it — to impel its purchase on the neck of its victim.

Angelo stirs as the beast patters off, turning his neck and a burning eye to see Napirya and Brannagh alive and concerting a string of stone-and-club-wielding defiers against the surprised military. A huge hover prop catches his eye, swarming with figures levering off masonry and building detritus to smash down atop the grounded Agency hovers. The soldiers form riot blocks now, but Angelo knows they will not bluff their way from this impasse. The resistance they face is sourced from the fabric of the oppressed townsfolk, and now that they have tasted freedom, only blood will be the sweeter. The strain of being Byron Bay's default rebel leader for the past fifteen hours suddenly catches up to the little tailor, but as he fades he wonders at a strange noise, so long it has been…since he heard…the sound of galloping horses.

Angelo awakens to a hubbub of voices, and by coupling the distinct slap of waves on rocks with the explicit aromas on the air, concludes himself to be in the pool garden of a certain lodge some three kilometres north of last night's fiasco. A voice, respectful but strained, rises across the others.

"Now look. You've got a perfectly good balloon here. All the makings of ascending over the terrain of oppression, but without a viable plan there's no gas in it — it's just a colourful skin. We've got to move off the coast and set-up in town. I reckon in the sunken theatre. They couldn't bomb — "

"No!" The rebuking voice is Napirya's. "On the coast we can see what's coming. This ground gives sacred power to my people. Bring up a few dozen boats, that way we're mobile. We can't be surrounded, and we can maintain a roving base without being sniped at by patriots."

As the patiently measured voice proceeds again, Angelo slides the cloth from his eyes and opens them to pain and knifing spring sun. He contracts his arms to push upright, but cool hands press against his shoulders. He bunches ineffectively against the nurse's admonitions to lie down, but then an excited slim body is crowding the woman away, and he is swept into a hug, his name an exuberant yell on the lips of Jumo, the Chinese teacher.

A neatly groomed hand is extended to him, and he finds himself hoisted face to face with an aged man, gold glinting from his smile and green from his eyes.

"So this is Angelo." It is the voice from the debate.

"Petard Gilder, we need to talk, my fellow." Angelo humours him with a smile and a nod, asking Napirya, as an aside, about survivors, while letting his eyes rest on the soothing blue commodiousness of the stranger's hemp suit.

"There's four dozen survivors from the shore levee, Cap'. Half of them are wounded, and that includes those five you stashed under the bushes, and yourself. But that bullet went right through; we already found some olivacea to patch you with."

Angelo plumps into the chair that Jumo draws for him, considering the figure of Petard and his estimable suit. "So then, you brought in the cavalry. Literally, or was I dreaming?"

"Ah well. The equines were Janine's and her cohorts' from the riding school down at beach seven. My contraptionry was less organic — one of the hover-props was from my wharfside business. Trader by inheritance, I'm afraid. Been waiting on this day a long while, comrade. My friends Greiger and Wayne brought props from their own endeavours, and together we ferried six hundred. From the bonfires along the southern beaches, and the transition houses, not to mention the street camps outside the welfare baptisma. Our number was matched by the trickle of twos and threes, locals who had traded word, waiting on the battle fringes for dawn."

"Amazing."

"Yes, and what's more, we nearly all survived."

"How many are we?" Angelo cough-starts himself to his feet to look around, and fends off the nurse.

"A thousand twenty-eight, including your battle-hardened circus."

"Armed?"

"A bit lapse there; but gas masks, goggles and radios to go 'round. Shields being made as we speak. The three big hover-props are an asset, if I say so myself. In addition, we've got ten hover-bikes from the police impound and just had confirmed three laz-cannons that our hackers tracked to an automn-deal house in town."

After a half hour's conversation, Angelo is satisfied with the decision to remain on the coast. The fallout of Petard's lobbying is that sixty rebels have gone to instate themselves in three well-vantaged and defensible buildings around town. The hover-bikes have been dispersed more widely, carrying roving teams of scouts. Napirya smiles slackly at Angelo and gazes out on the ephemeral coastline with its distant jungle-clad volcanoes. The two drip-dry upon the sand, having disdained the lodge pool.

"You know," says the aboriginal, "this is the first time I've ever looked across my country freed of the bridles and bits of leisure pursuit. My soul is freed."

Angelo busies himself towelling water from his neck to disguise the lump in his throat.

It is about halfway through a huge and diverse late afternoon feast, sourced from raided kitchens in the abandoned and barricaded establishments across town, that the radios begin to crackle. Angelo tests his shoulder and hoists up the long-range laser at his feet as he listens to first Petard's, then Napier's communiqués with the fixed and roving scouts.

"Right. Just get out of there. Get out of there!"

"Yes, I understand. Hunt your ass back here, mate."

There is a brief dissemination of the news, and then all the twenty gathered battle coordinators are running. Except Angelo, who shuffles determinedly among the hodgepodge of defenders to enlighten them as to the impending attack and dispel their fears with an earthy rhetoric. In part, his fanning of their courage is well founded, for the day's work has raised a vast wall of piled old hovers and containers, with even a few small freight ships all keyed together by a requisitioned algalate. The speedy hovers along its foot hiss into life as well as the big hover-props, purring resonantly.

Each prop houses sandbagged ballistics nests and a laz-cannon. Napirya stands harnessed into one such bulking chrome voodoo finger of destruction, his arms and features stretched toward the sea. Petard moves alongside the tailor-poet, his hemps exchanged for a black lacto-silk suit, a pair of antiquated shotguns slung in a crossing brace over his back.

"I made the shot myself: bit of a Luddite at heart."

Angelo stares at the seething anthill before him.

"Man. They're going to suffer when they hit this bunch. Why do this?"

"You know why. They can no longer question their loyalty. And they are always suffering. To them this is fun, to turn on their own people. To uphold honour." This time, Angelo thinks bitterly, it is no martial faction deployed against them, but the actual cogs forced to grind out the smooth hell of South Austral life.

The Belief Brigades, 'the Riven', as Curlew and the Realliance called them. Tradesmen and bureaucrats, largely all with behavioural streamliners willingly implanted. Initiates to a sort of bionic masonry, giving them linked understanding, social rights and petty power. Addendum to these lost acerbic souls will come the security guards, bus drivers and butchers — all the specialised hands inculcated to believe the world could not possibly turn without their dour presence.

Thousands, the scouts had said, probably massing with the Agency's covert blessing and flooding in numbers from up and down the coast. He wonders if they will suffer all that much against this unproven mishmash of brave ants. He hurries down to the beach defences, imbibing a brave air, but noting gladly the few dozen flat metal punts moored offshore, their camouflage netting ready to drape over defeated townsfolk for an evacuation in the dead of night.

Leon looks about him at those fringing this circle — all associates and mates of his boss, a butcher. They are focused on kicking the poor thing, the last that they had caught after the daguerrette had swept them, one hundred pigeons, from the rooftop of the Byron Plaza hotel above. The gathered minions of security guards, phont workers, couriers, had laughed, then roared to see the little things with their clipped tails awkwardly hit the ground. Sadion, well known from appearances on the station called Interface, had intoned.

"There are vermin loose in this city. Please see them exterminated. "

Immediately, the bizarre pigeon-stomping ritual had begun — now winnowing as most of the circles concentrated around their tortured victims break up with nonsensical bellows or catch-cries from various daguerrette advertisements. In the space allowed him to think, behind a mien masked into a snarl of excited confusion and timidity, the little ruddy spy named Leon censures his pale eyebrows from rising in sympathy with his realisation — he had been right all along. This has been no mere bloodlust but a clinical eliciting of all-pervading barbarity via invisibly inked symbols etched into these men by their daguerrette handlers.

The Curlewalion Mist have long known the dangers of the daguerrette's conversion schemes, and Leon's mission here is to destroy as many of their leaders as he can unroot. He had always maintained that it was not just the big bio-implant groups of electricians, builders and plumbers over which their powers held great sway. Destiny vibrators, Reality Coordinators, Pathos Virtuosos. Several were the Austral names for the many-suckered arms of that sharp-beaked creature that ruled a virtual society from the throne of people's minds.

Camouflaging into the ocean of citizen's reality constructs, into the emotional urging driven by body chemicals, covering its tracks with the inkjets of cultural credos and ever-shifting refinements to its clues at winning the game of societal acceptance, the thing that tailored mass hallucination and applied incomprehension was rooted somewhere in the entertainment industry — but was sleekly muscled, beyond the restraint of even the Affiliate. Leon knows now that some terminal velocity of its power has been reached, allowing it to annex ever more subtle sciences to the management of its psychic dairies. In Curlew the creature was known as the daguerreotype. Or just the Ipe - Incubus of Psychic Exaction.

No doubt the power of the daguerrettes had entrenched through imagery and the encapsulation of the ego possible through television, and had then spread to control speech, taste, feelings and the meaning of a smile. For those with bio-implants able to access social hormone maps, stress alchemisers and the like, there were response options for every situation in social life, with the assurance of knowing how peers would interrelate. For those in the big trade groups, there was the Ancestor-of-the-Guild chip bestowing, in the privacy of one's own head, salt-of-the-earth humorous benedictions and advice about specific points of the trade.

For the others, whose group identity accumulations weren't large enough to make bio-implants a thrilling prospect, there was always Interface and the electro-node and endorphin kit that allowed one's face or voice to super-impose as the hero of a soapie or the captain of the rugby.

There were generous glimpses of information, hidden in the commergils, for a low-cost, self-mirroring serum to extract from them knowledge of what colours to wear, the place a potential partner might be found and what to eat or drink. In such a retinue of food combinations were chemicals designed to enhance social buzzes and the personal signposts of societal success. It was a mutable world of manufactured emotions, hemmed in by a maze of thorny fair-dinkumness into which Leon had to walk, and now need tread more carefully than ever to maintain his footing.

Rushing forward, he stomps on the pigeon's head, reaffirming his group identity thus, but sick of its suffering anyway. The fine balance of surviving this four-dimensional maze was in pushing to a peak in the group supra-structure, then retreating back to its hazy deserts. Several are the bodies of young apprentices lying pulped to the ground around other circles, their indecision or chemical upwellings as body language having signalled some weakness and drawn the wrath of the group-mind.

As the snarling screams abate and the focus turns to him, Leon casually scuffs his soiled boot against the tarmac, triggering an outer layer to peel from the self-cleaning footwear in a predetermined outspringing of rubber, leaving an origami-like crumple beside the bird, styled as a skull with an arrow through it. The appropriateness of the motif and the funny little trick — even though only butchers and plumbers could carry off the self-cleaner — has quite a few men patting him on the back. His boss's hand, however, comes down in a short chop into his neck.

"Phlescher! Killin' our fun! You can walk the five blocks to the beach and be last to kill a traitor for all I care. Let's get to it, guys!"

Roaring off with the other hundreds of hovers, the leering faces of his boss's mates press laughingly against the silicon menisci of their own crafts, while he dashes along the street, trying to look aggrieved. By the time he reaches the battle, all the illusion of mateship has fled from the blue-singletted Belief Brigades of plumbers, electricians and builders, and the white-singletted ranks of the more diversely specialised groups of workers.

None of those felled by the laz-cannon fire and shrapnel projectiles fountaining from the hover-props above the walled-in resort are aided by their friends. The minions seem in a climactic frenzy to reach the front lines, all wearing fixed hyena grins as they advance on the smoking wreckage of the foremost plumed-in-fire hover prop. Intuiting the cause of the smiles, Leon casts around the battle fringes and spies the filming bubble afloat at a little remove. He recognises the blond puff-pastrified face within: Anita Morass, mainline reporter for Interface.

With a sudden sickening lurch of his being, Leon is overwhelmed by this whole invidious nesting of illusion into people's hearts, rendered consumable for a blinded Cyclops doomed to feed on itself. He stalks toward the eye-spy sphere and presses the remote in his pocket.

It would make a nice explosion, the terrace lodge some kilometres north that he had sapped several nights previous, having traced its use by several daguerrettes liaising with the Crystal County film set on the beach near to it. He considers the transparent bubble tracking aslant through the air before him. It is composed of the same gene-fungus as the new highways and greenway bridges, but fed an alkaline substance to render it see-through. As he watches, laser fire is absorbed harmlessly, and various hurled objects bounce from it. He has to dissolve the half-metre thick, stronger-than-steel wall of this co-operative organism to have a crack at the mini-hover, Anita and the two camera crew. In Curlew, Leon was taught to dissolve flexi-fung.

He lobs his incendiary grenade to explode in a sheet of flame that engulfs the floating dome. He pulls a gun from his calf–holster, a window of seconds to make the shot. Under great heat, he knows the organisms comprising the shield will crowd towards metal, seeking to renutrify. The bullet's clean hit is evidenced by the whole casing shucking to the ground in a burning pool, leaving behind the naked and ascending mini-hover.

Leon glimpses two Blue Brigaders working a laz-cannon from the roof of a destroyed hover and sends a bullet into each of their long-suffering brains. Gaining the cannon, he etherealises the eye-spy and several other brigade hovers before his back roils in liquid fire, and he glimpses the running forms of vengeance surrounding him. As he is torn apart by their fury, he realises that nobody will warn Curlew now.

Slower hovers dump a ballast of blunt heavy objects onto the edges of the wall defences, or onto the rebel's constantly shifting positions in sandbagged bunkers along the beach, then track back over the defences under cover-fire from swifter flanking hovers. The bombardiers wheel away now, and Angelo holds the seven able defenders with him from firing at them, not wanting to alert them to the fact they are now fallen back to the last bunker before the inner defences, and that the rain of destruction had fallen only upon decoy hats and coats placed within their previous position.

From the overrun bunker some hundred metres away, a hoard of men in blue shirts pour forward, only slowing to angrily kick the decoy lumps and leap the obstructing sandbags, bearing down on the rebels. Angelo stands and fires at them, noting the plumbers' insignia of hourglass and cross on their shirts.

Suddenly, a figure streaks out from the shadows of the wall base, running diagonally in behind the foe and mowing down their whole left wing, while able somehow to dodge the lethality aimed at him. Angelo calls to the rebels to stay put and leaps over the bags to meet the oncoming charge. He is aware of the aboriginal elder, Peonie, by his side, but they are both able to discharge only one blast before she is slain beside him. The tailor ducks under a cowl of rays discharged point blank to dive blinded at the legs of two attackers. He grapples and swats at flesh, while a roar of hovers thunders overhead and suddenly he is dragged backward, his vision clearing to reveal the plumbers in disarray retreating back up the beach, pursued by rebel hovers. As Angelo plonks into the damp pit beside the others, his rescuer — solidly brown-faced but otherwise undistinguishable in the dark — says, "Beg help, man! The radio — we need aid!"

Angelo raises Duterra, Napier's confidante and leader of the hover bike crew.

"Actually, it's…a bad time. They've just taken out another…hover prop."

"We need to hold the beach, Duterra," he tells her. "Just send a couple of bikes, and quick."

The next wave of bombardiers halves as it slips over the wall, with about eight hovers heading toward their bunker. As they purr closer, Angelo's focals reveal fidgets of movement from behind the overrun bunkers, where brigade forces are amassing steadily once more with Brigaders who have sneaked through sea or leaped from hovers to get around the wall. Then the bombardiers are stung by the daredevil attack of the aboriginal hover bike crew, their ballast cast out as they flee from the five darting shapes. Barrels and furniture thud upon the sand like an invisible giant's footprints, tracking within metres of the bunker.

The heavy building hovers lift away, and their sleek vanguard roars in to tussle with the bikes. A disabled hover spins to earth, its occupants leaping out to fall, still firing. A bike explodes before the fight wheels away over the wall.

Angelo's rescuer hitches up his pants and whispers passionately, "Okay. Let's drive these monkey asses off the sand. Cover me!"

Angelo is foremost among the half dozen scrambling after the valiant Mexican, but his fleet, diminutive figure draws ever ahead. Angelo plods onward, feeling heat glance from his armour, and sears a laser ray in the direction from which the strike came. He stumbles on a slain rebel, dropping soundlessly in front of him, and targets a shape hunching over the brim of the nearby fortification.

Lasers flare across the sandbags and delineate the nimble swarthy man leaping high to flip fully twice before sailing into the bunker. A massive blow rips Angelo's neck muscles and he falls, upswept in agony once more. As he clamps his teeth to lever up his head, he sees the little man dive into the sand before him, and with those brown hands clamped around his shoulder armour, the surreal character tells him they have secured the bunker.

"Now you're injured, so if you can, crawl to the wall defences. I'll keep these hovers off your trail."

As he turtle-drags himself up the beach, Angelo is aware of the man's hoarse screaming and two hovers at the corner of his eye that stall, turning to battle his ally's indefatigable bravado.

After a few minutes, Angelo comes within sight of one of the wall bunkers, from which defenders issue to ballistics mounts above. A dim silvery form rushes toward him, and the tailor-poet finds himself swept against Brannagh's solid shoulder and trundled up to the bunker. Hearing of the beach crisis, the knight takes two defenders and ducks from the doorway, leaving his friend propped up with a first-aid kit. Angelo squeezes an instant brace onto his neck, and taking a deep breath, clambers wearily up a ladder to the wall's top.

He sticks his head from the cannon-nest. The last hover prop is busy as an eagle in a rookery; huge holes everywhere corrupt the wall, and most fortified positions atop it have been destroyed. Grasping the radio, he reaches Petard.

"Evacuate all the wounded and the reserve. We've got to use the punts. Activate the manual repellents in three minutes for full evacuation."

He teeteringly descends to the beach, blasting away at the Blue Brigaders who have now overrun every outer defence, while the dozen defenders from the wall embattlements clamber down, slipping inside the door to the inner defences just in time.

Within this lesser wall, protecting a sliver of beach right down to the water, a group of twenty horse-riders are gathered. The big side doors are flung open, and the laser-wielding riders crowd out, without the intention of return. Above, the first of the tine slings are cut — strained catapults bearing a fright of glass-tipped bamboo lances designed to spear out across the wall.

There is a frenzy of activity around the metal punts, with shooters taking up positions on the beach and alongside the wounded and other evacuees in the first crafts as the engines are started. Suddenly, Petard is dancing among the boats, compelling their engines silenced, and gesticulating frenziedly toward the horizon.

Angelo's focals come to rest on the horror. Like prehistoric sharks, the five submarines poise in lethal vastness. As the parties are laboriously returned to shore and the southern wall is breached, Angelo barks out his predetermined fall back plan and turns aside the panic of the last of the four hundred survivors.

"We head north half a mile, then inland past the water reserve and make for the hills."

The big hover prop comes overhead, clearing the way northward. Angelo oversees the bundling of those unable to walk into the last of the undamaged hovers, escorted by an armed column of four hovers with the instruction that they head north and wait in thick coastal swamp across the border.

Then he dinks on the back of the last hover bike, targeting the brigade hovers that already skim over the fleeing crowd like rogue dogs among livestock. He is dropped off at the little track opening through the dunes that is central to his plans. Here he plants his makeshift flag, then stumbles back toward the sight of doom approaching the forlorn group. A wave of hovers suddenly part from their encirclement of the prop, and three automated hovers, already alight, careen exploding into their last hope.

With the threat of the prop removed, Riven on foot spill up the beach behind the routed rebels, and death rains indiscriminately from the sky. Many Brigaders have overflown Angelo's position and out-spill to close the trap to the north. Even as the first escapees begin to trickle up to the track opening, the flimsy vanguard is targeted by hovers lurking above the dune trees, cutting off escape that way.

When their bizarre redemption happens, Angelo pries off his helmet and sits on the sand, his mind numb. Those with him hug each other in fear and wonder. The noise is agonising. At least thirty big trees have grabbed every hover from the air behind them, their branching fingers now grinding the metal plate into shrieking jelly. Vines snake through the air to wrap their trophies in tight death hugs. Two big old banksias rear back and thud a passing hover to the ground in gnarled unison.

There are twiggy wattles shambling over dunes and down toward the massed Brigaders now halted to fire in panic at the determined, flaming balls of attacking greenery. Then a thing of the very sand itself leaps up before Angelo's watching focals to drag down a brigadier and disappear back into the beach.

There are dozens of sandlings, almost impossible to see, picking off Brigaders, herding them back to the flaming bushes. One stands up at the very edge of the shocked and elated group of rebels. It walks toward Angelo through the two hundred survivors, and he sees it has a human face — a face with the most amazingly childlike and vivid expression that thick hair and beard cannot obscure. Then Angelo understands; the sand is a camouflage, artfully arranged.

"Come," says the man, in a warm ebullient voice. "We cannot linger. The trees are no match for the metal monsters. We must retreat inland."

"Yes, we must," Angelo agrees in a dream, turning to signal the survivors to follow. "Thank you...but, who are you?"

"We are the Welving. We make the little weaves. What has been released is a wonder that we must heed. So we return from our hidden webs and the world wreckers now, my friend, shall weep."

Chapter 13

For two days Boabben travelled south through a featureless land of dunes that burred into clay pan, presided over by a glazing heat that did not remit until dusk. Boabben travelled at night, and spent the hours of sunshine sweltering supine beneath a tented shade of sticks and the bark cloak that Maeddan had gifted him.

As the third dawn broke since his leaving the crater, he heard pulsing on the breeze the chanting song that the Lellying had bound into the ley-flows of all Iridestines. The fireseer increased his pace, the fortifying energy field of the nearby age-fire drawing him, invigorated, across the last few kilometres of pilgrimage.

A flock of a hundred emus rose from sleep as he approached, alerted despite his almost undetectable presence. They scattered about him like errant plumes of horizontal smoke. Maybe the unusually large flock had also felt the power beneath the earth. Boabben slid down through a narrow fissure in the chalky stone beneath sand and spinifex, using a clump of the spiky grass to dangle his weight into the shaft and drop a few feet to the time-smoothed floor below.

The immortal's vision did not differentiate between night and day, and he pursued the dry, cool passageways. After several turns and switchback tunnels the light of the age-fire flared in acknowledgment of the fireseer's aura. The corridors began to break into sandy chambers, linked to each other only by a crawl space.

Finally, in the splendour of the age-fire cave, the immortal drank from a clear pool and sat on the soft sand listening to percolating drips fall into the million-year-old catchment. The place was familiar. Instead of the natural crystals in the waterfall cave on Yellanded lands, here stones placed by the Lellying over millennia threw back the age-fire's nimbus.

Diamonds nestled between the blood rumours of jasper and glaucous spills of agate that was also propped against the chamber's walls in broad sheets, sliced and planed by some violence of subterranean tearing. Black multi-headed crystals crowded, large as footstools, and imprisoned stars of green and cerise in their depths. Lumps of gold hobnobbed in haughty remove from flaky purple rocks peppered with a blue and red shine, as though they had been fired from a gun barrel. Everywhere were pebbles and eggs of a beautiful milky blue, glowing with an inner light like a melding of moon and ocean.

Here too were pictures of the Enyadding's world, as there had been in the cavern. There were precise depictions of desert animals — the bundle rats, dwarf emus, rat wallabies, intricate star maps — but also a frieze of the Serpent priest and his transformation. Boabben dropped his study to his hands. Over a year ago he had first glimpsed artefacts of the Mended world. It seemed a span of time no more pronounced than that between a butterfly closing its wings on cloud-shadowed ground and its unfolding them to the sun in the next instant. More and more, he realised, years would come to seem as moments. If he could find clean water and no caverns collapsed on him, he would endure as long as the Mended essence itself.

An eternity alone. For though Mended, he was not Enyadding, shared not their emotion forged by countless years of experience. Though initiated, he was not a tribesman, could never go back to the Yellanded. His fate was to continue ever-peerless, with the hope that one day he might hear Brawyndy's mind-sending on the ether. Discouraging himself from contemplating her, knowing her image would not nourish his loneliness, Boabben focused on the sand grains beneath him. He felt himself enter one of the deep side streams of the Mend, a tunnel of layered possibilities arranged in mandalas of light that constantly shifted as they incorporated his new experience. Deeper down his spirit was borne, aware of the buzz of healing and rebalancing undertaken by flagellate-like patterns that spun webs of cleansing — pooling at one edge of his consciousness.

Extended before him was the overview of Mending in which all of his magnified senses seemed to have a voice and a personality. He lingered in a sixth sense like a fine web onto which thousands of raindrops of potential causality fell, and he knew that though the Serpent was wounded, it was supremely confident in its spirit. He saw where he might focus or relax to better hone a future attack, and he felt the Mend shifting to try and align a power flow to his needs.

He saw there was no moral impellent to make him face that suffocating horror again, for there was wild joyous innocence in all the Mend fibrillations, a vibrancy heedless of human projections. Into that wild space the fireseer flowed, vowing to himself that he would enjoy this beautiful world with all the vivacious bounty of being that his new awareness gave him. Before he slipped into the dawn-dream, to be in strange worlds modelled on the life processes of Earth's great forests, he received a vision of a tribal group close to the south — and the tinge of a warning.

Boabben's path was overspied the next day. The dimensional Veil was no fool against sharp eyes belonging to five crows flappily pursuing his swift steps, plumping down onto the bugs or lizards stirred by his concourse. In Ireland there had been those who claimed to talk with such birds, and in a way, Boabben could as easily guess meaning in their croaks as he could in the sighs of wind catching in the desert pines. After a little, thoughts of signs led him to remember the vision of a nearby tribe. He stooped and slung a knot of wood at a crow's non-existent ear. Heeding his language precisely, the birds arose to find other sport.

A few kilometres on, over a dune, Boabben spied the tribe. He was glad of distancing the crows, which might have revealed his invisibility to a hidden scout. All the tribe's focus was tuned on the depression, grown with ragged desert pine below, where a stew of ill will was about to over-boil. Boabben's horror of the spear bite would haunt him for a while. The fireseer dared a little nearer to the group of tall and stony desert nomads. The unconscious man, who fed the sands his life with a trickle of blood from the spear-rent in his side, was the lover of the girl the old women now surrounded. Boabben's knowledge of the Yallanded tribal speak plus the Cundamble of the Enyadding — itself composed of many aboriginal words — gave him clear grasp of the conversation.

"The girl is mine by way of family track-craft. Besides, the spirits will no longer child her for you. It wastes our blood circle."

"The winds lay before me my due. No more they will release it than you might grow a pouch, Corriwiban."

The two greyed truculents seemed to Boabben to have little separating their generative powers, though the muscles in wrinkly arms still tremored tautly around grips on spears. Boabben could guess the journey made by the young woman slumped at the disinterested feet of the old women. He could intuit the love between her and the now dying fellow outcast. It had led them to flee to enemy lands and escape the taboo on their suitability — and he could see within her that she would kill herself before the night was through.

The two patriarchs were ready to fight for her. He could tell by the air of forced relaxation settling around the younger men. Boabben thought of his own Ngenlin and did an impulsive thing. He walked into the press of pent brown bodies, and dissolving the Veil, held his arms up and cried 'No!' Old women erupted into wailing as a dingo ricocheted away from the youth and made a quick warning rip into the immortal's leg. Likewise, the lunge of the oldest protagonist's spear was more emotional compunction than anything, ending centimetres from the redhead.

"There is only more suffering for the tribe if the girl cannot go free."

"You know this?" asked a wide-eyed warrior.

"I have seen it," Boabben bluffed.

"But you are not a Creator spirit." The grey-hair was staring at the blood around Boabben's calf.

"No. I live in my own wind. I am man, with eyes to see, passing to my next waters. Please leave me with these lost ones."

"This is greatly odd. I sense that we should do as you wish," the younger claimant slowly mused. "Yet if you are found on our lands tomorrow, you will die. If you prove a Brundi and any of us falls sick, we will hunt you down."

The tribe simply drifted away, weapons and baskets and babies on backs, the latter giving proprietorial stares at him as though a food they would return to try. Boabben staunched the male's wound with a little chewed grass and ochre. Now that he was alone with this ill-fated pair, Boabben suddenly felt futile. Nothing in his power could save the man, and he would die before they could reach an age-fire. The girl began to keen, and Boabben stepped back, chasing the thin shade. He stared up at the heavens in a listless union with life's grimness until the racking gasps of the girl broke his reverie. She was lifting a branch to impress her heart's ache upon her scalp when Boabben, motioning his hand, took consciousness from her.

He walked for three days, hoping that the primacy of action would denude his grim thoughts. In the age-fire glade, lassoed by startling coloured hills graduating from umber to chalk blue, he finally contented himself in knowing that the homeless tribesgirl would survive a while longer. More than that, he could not guarantee her, though she would quickly become a formidable warrior. Boabben had given her the entire spat of his tracking and weaponry keys to flesh the new identity he had woven her; changing the reason for her outcast status to a fierce desire to hunt and be independent.

Boabben pondered the butcher birds and swallows dipping into the soak to snatch water. Before long, he was copying them, bouncing along his chest on the water and landing in an ungainly crouch on the far bank, the swell and hush of his body a teeming joy. Staring into the water, the immortal watched calmly as the vision unfurled, even as he was struck to numbness by the feeling of danger and imminence it carried: a party of white men, leading donkeys and heavily armed. Although the age-fire here was dimensionally Veiled, it was rare that the Lellying created an Iridesce of illusion around an entire age-fire glade, and even then only in areas heavily populated by tribes, because of the drain on their group-mind that such illusions drew. If this party found the spring, others would return periodically, and harm might incidentally befall the firefeather crystal. There was no chance he could remove the whole glade into another time single-handedly.

From the edge of the bluntly eroded hill, he could discern a plume of distant dust. They would arrive before darkfall. The beasts would lead them here, pursuing water's smell, though such beasts could not complete the climb. He could not allow mortals to come near an age-fire, and prepared to greet them with the only defence he could conceive. Deep in insistent study of the Mend flows, Boabben finally found those he could use as a brush, and he fanned the hibernative power from the crater's firefeather to a glow within his cells and soul, melting the ink from his own essences. Quickly he imagined the scene. An imposing stubble of dead trees, a certain mood of oppressiveness, a greatly slipping soil, rank spinifex instead of feathery grass. When he was done, his back to the trunk of a regal redgum, he watched the four men approach.

"Must be water here someplace."

Two men looked right at him, seated there amid flowers and ancient trees on the hill of natural power, and saw only dead trees on a hummock pervaded by an unnerving discordance. Boabben knew the spring would not be far below the powdery ground on which their donkeys kneeled, and at his psychic nudge, the men unslung shovels and soon struck water. They and their beasts slaked, they moved off again in the dusk to find 'more firewood and a better feeling spot'.

As Boabben continued south, he peered back at his crafting in the dawn light. The illusory enchantments would hold, he knew, until one Mended should care to repeal them. Three more days Boabben journeyed, until the power of the ocean was a tangible presence along the Mend flows. The Mend, hinged as it seemed to be on a play between land and sea, coursed excitedly through his blood.

As he forayed over the rusted saltbush plain, once an ocean itself, Boabben dwelt upon what he knew of the Mend. It was a force made from the distillations of every emotional response throughout history that had been unable to complete itself within the field of the originator. It was a repository for links of consciousness which scarce knew they had been birthed, but which the Mend held in an envitalised stasis until transforming them in the utility of pure energy.

Much about the Mend and what had passed into its mighty store was unknowable. It was possible only to utilise the Mend's knowledge or use its energy for self-enhancement as far as the keys of one's perception allowed. Boabben could see, as a blur, the trillion-seeded essences of emotion which had swelled it, but could only explicate specific knowledge from it if that information was already benchmarked in his experience.

He could walk with utmost efficiency, but not fly. He could glimpse, as he journeyed, aspects and correlative facets of the Serpent, because he possessed an experience of that horror. No fraction of something of which a mind did not already have a gleaning could be revealed by, or changed through the Mend.

The Enyadding believed that they had been the first beings to be granted tenure of the Mend's vast astral riches; that for countless years it had been a vital force beyond recognition of the five senses and discovered only when chance had drawn them to each other. Yet it was eerie to Boabben that no Enyadding could ever know if they had been first to chance upon its infinite provision, that past aeons of possible interactions could lie swallowed by its cryptic sea.

As Boabben continued, refining his rhythm to a comfortable vibrancy that massaged every muscle of his floating and gently setting-down legs, he likened the Mend to a gusset. A patch could be stitched to any garment of possibility to allow it to fit the wearer. It was an oddity to Boabben that its influence could both strengthen five-sensory reality and at the same time allow one to undo the laws of that reality; it was a matter of reworking their pathways into a different integration. The juxtaposition of the Mend was that though it was a coagule of emotional essences derived from sentient creatures experiencing the intensity of gravity and death that underpinned their lives, the collective field such energetic reverberations made had the ability to sustain immortality.

It amazed Boabben that he was privy to the secret that emotions could never be lost or exiled into lonely solitude. He imagined a monkey as it had learned to scratch its back with a bone, only to forget such agreeable pleasure, distracted by a bright bird. Or a woman who had briefly collated the whimsy of her youth and the circumspection of age into a meaningful self-love, only to have the feeling stripped away by death. Though mostly unknowable, the individual strands of unabsorbed emotional essences must have been countless throughout time, to form a drift deep enough to fertilise the autonomous force of the Mend from their accumulated fractions.

Feeling humbled by the majesty of the force that had changed him, Boabben contented himself merely with focusing on the movement of his limbs, not attempting to engage his creative thoughts. Through the repetition of mile after mile in simple attunement with his physicality, Boabben gradually gained an awareness of the environment, quite extrasensory, as though watching it from another self, or several selves. His seeing, touch, taste, smell and hearing deepened in partnership with his focus, and through this heightened synthesis he was able to intuit the landscape beyond his immediate vicinity.

The Mend needed only his recognition of a faraway smell or his understanding of cloud behaviours to unfold the hidden kilometres all around to his extrasensory body, so that he could precisely feel the land. He had found the Mend Map. Boabben deliberated over his way, squatting in the sandy dirt. Resisting closer study of the scroll-like tracks of lizards, he concentrated on the Mend Map. Eventually, he stood, drank sparingly from the water skin and squared his shoulders to the full moon. He had travelled a month since leaving the Lellying. He did not recall how long since separating from the white world. He would not backtrack to the age-fire calling only thinly from the north. Tomorrow he would reach the coast and the world of restless men. Before autumn's end, and with it all chance of the direct passage he sought to Melbourne. For it was to that first issuing of his new life's circle he was returning.

It was not for either a speedier or easier journey that he hung, upside-down, watching the corners of slyness along the edge of Port Adelaide's docks and the crew's unconvincing casting-off movements below him. The five of them seemed to slump the further for each part of alcohol the toil sweated out. Even from high on the larkspur, Boabben could see the captain's activity in the wheelhouse. Whilst one handheld the tiller, the other daubed vinegar over the syphilitic blisters on his member. Boabben swung upright and climbed around a clammy-faced crewman locking yards into position. A breeze luffed tardily in the sails, then the helmsman squared his tiller, and the sails billowed true, and men scrambled below deck. Boabben kept his eyes on the horizon. Before she reached Melbourne, the 'Enfant' would be surrounded everywhere by ocean. It was a sight the Mended stowaway anticipated happily.

Seeming to dip its head at him, the huge starlit bird glided away to hunt above another part of the seethe. For hours it had hovered near Boabben, plucking fish stirred by the dolphins. Those creatures, with their music and ebbulience, stung Boabben's heart. Perhaps it was a good omen they travelled in much the same line as he, at times filling the whole horizon with their strong and rhythmic swimming. As he studied a young creature suckling while swimming steadily alongside its mother, he slipped into the dawn-dream.

He did not get long. Almost on top of him, a man retched over the rail, implored the dolphins to eat it, and then disappeared. Fifteen minutes later a brass pot was struck repeatedly, the clamorous announcement of breakfast supported in its cogency by the smell of gruel from the galley. Why the sealers were being roused so early was a mystery to the fireseer. Their cargo of lime for the return run had been safely stowed before Boabben had first found the 'Enfant' at the tradehouse. Perhaps the captain feared for his clutch of rum and silver against the unlikely chance of pirate incursions. Whatever the case, the crew, a surly grab-bag of nationalities, was soon sitting on crates about the deck and gripping hot bowls against the cold. The dolphins had thinned to sporadic groups comprising fifty sleek bodies, but still riveted Boabben — seeming an exaltation of sunlight as they belly-rolled in turning dance.

"Those fish wag they Jack to breathe so easy the Davy," observed a man with lips modelled on the cockles he had no doubt eaten many of; they were shellfish-like, offset, with only a bubble of foam to keep them shut.

"Well, what do you say, Troy?" He punctuated his question with an elbow. The young confidant, on the crate beside, looked around silently, nodding while old Cockle-lips continued. "Bet theys fish wont wag so if they drunk my half of whiskey, ho!"

Insipid laughter came to Boabben's ears from the younger sailor, followed by his determined slurping. Cockle-lips slunk off to return with a shark line, one end of which he knotted into a slip. From a nearby barrel he extracted a whole salt fish and baited the line.

"What an' ya co hardly miss a dancing fish, Jocran," observed the young sailor.

"Trove. But now we can catch two on this line…gather here."

Boabben could hardly warrant the whispered plan that he heard. However, the young man, constrained to his part, wandered down the deck, slip-line in hand. Jocran threw the bait overboard and the younger conspirator looked

242

back to him. At the fierce nod, the youth dropped the slip loop over the cook's slumbering head. Just as the surprised man wakened, the line went taut. The cook screamed and fell to his side, sliding slowly along and clawing at the line.

Jocran was torn between doubling over to laugh and straining up from behind the barrels to see. The first mate came on the scene but was unable to cut the line. His abuse of the youth was so mighty that the sailor backed away, leaving the mate to take up the tension until another crewman loped over and wrestled the slip knot from the cook's head.

"He's dead."

The purple-faced man was indeed.

The mate ran at the slight youth, stabbing him repeatedly and pouring him backward over the rail, telling the flailing body in the waves, "We don't kill the cook!"

The interceding helper, meanwhile, was winching a small dolphin over the side. Coming up to him, the first mate said, "OK, Kenneth, you're chef. You better get this chopped up for tea." He booted the dolphin's head to expound his point, leaving to check the housing on a nearby lifeboat. Boabben visualised an albatross wheeling in starlight, while Jocran's laughter spluttered out wetly from behind the barrels.

For three days they ran south in good weather, passing near enough to Port Adelaide to see the lantern light of its trade houses, but the ship did not reach Melbourne. For this it was Cockle-lips to blame again. One day Boabben followed the man, alerted by his slinking deportment, to the wheelhouse. He heard a grim exchange. "Ho, Cap'n. Well, we chasin' blarney and put to it, Captain, to make speed. But with the food Ken serves, it seems the crew gets punished, 'stead reward. Would do all well to take on a few women. Sell 'em off to some bloody whalers and all the better for another fur run."

"Aye, well, Jocran, you might have the right of it."

Boabben listened, hidden amid clubs and gullet knives, vats and salt bags beside the brig.

"We've made a clipper speed with these southerlies. We might find a place a little along to send some boats. There's a good tip from the 'Zachary' puts coastal blacks on a river near here."

Hours later two longboats were dropped alongside. Boabben slipped into one, not wishing to swim the half mile to shore. He had noted the plethora of sharks throughout the trip, of several different types but certainly all brute enough to be unselective over mortal or immortal fare. The 'Enfant's remaining seven sailors set out, those in his boat dullardly unaware of the prow dipping more than usual.

On shore, Jocran rejoiced to find footprints, and the captain, tamping his rifle shot, nodded sagaciously.

"Here they are now, like seals for skinnin'," guffawed a young deckhand, his skin a crackle of blisters and want. Three tribesmen and two young girls stopped on the sand to stare. The captain raised his rifle agitatedly, but the first mate interceded. "Those two would sport well, but we could use more. Let 'em all come out first."

Eventually the tribe did come gently from the thick scrub. Proud and inquisitive, the warriors moved forward. Boabben contemplated it all as though a tormented dream from where he sat on the damp shelf of beach, still exhausted from his work.

As one, the sealers raised their rifles against double their number. Jocran screamed, his eyes blinded. Muted yells accompanied the retorts from the guns of the others, all clutching hands or necks where Boabben's fusing of the firing chambers had caused the blow-backs.

The warriors smiled uncertainly at this flippant dance. Boabben stood and unleashed his final trick. Out at sea, flames roared over the 'Enfant'. The tribe stared amusedly as the young deckhand screamed.

"They're witchmen!" His knife outdrawn, he charged down the beach. Women quickly shielded children away from the violence, and likewise the immortal began to walk south, disappearing around the distant cove as the last of the spears fell and the ship was slowly claimed by the water's cool redemption.

Boabben told himself he was not heartsore at the impending doom of the tribespeople. As for the fate of the sealers, he held no account against his repudiation of evil. The response thrummed through him like a force of nature — and as innocent. If ill did not confront him, he would not it, but there was a difference between killing to protect hunting and water rights, and that done to serve the whites' greed. The tribespeople might die now that the Aleris had betrayed the world balance, but all things changed, by nature, as the land beneath his feet testified, the beach turning to cliffs.

Leaving the rocky shore, Boabben wandered inland brooding on his philosophy. Trees crowded in an understorey of every shape and smell, such that he sought the more navigable treefern glades or sprang along highways of logs that might run a quarter of a mile if two canopy giants had fallen, domino fashion. These roads he shared with wallabies and wombats and many varieties of snakes. From the holy rooftop above, song leaked from a rainbow of parrots chiming in gregarious praise of the high seeds.

Everywhere little rivers coursed. Home to purple crays, water rats, platypus and large black fish. As the country gradually gave way to swampier areas, rioting life expressed itself in magpie-geese, ducks, pelicans and gorging roos. Boabben was astounded to glimpse his first koala colony and chuckled at his blood countrymen taking the measured dusky arborealists for bears. Nights brought the enchantment of flying possums, and quolls frenetic in their canopy

245

hungerings. A divergence of owls was unified by a shroud of deathly precision — silent wolves amid the tree herds of insanely voiced possums.

When the coastal hills began to turn to mountains, ever laid in obdurate rain partnered by sailing mists, Boabben realised the going would have been easier along the coast. Two factors induced him to the west. He knew there was an age-fire about a hundred and fifty kilometres inland; also the country itself enthralled him, containing fresh wonders for each stride. His pace of necessity slowed as hills yielded to mountains. The wet place which engorged him glowered in a perpetual twilight that roared or croaked with the shifting of white, black and grey cockatoo flocks. Though caparisoned in cold and fog, Boabben sweated. Unable to see over the deadfall of trunks thrice his height, he used immaculation of willpower to make upward progress.

At one point he covered a mile along the twisted mass of vines plaiting together the understorey. Inexpediently they gave way, and he landed heavily, head centimetres from rock. The trees tightened their gargantuan stronghold as Boabben advanced over three days, until he could no longer. Beneath the snagged trunk overhang of a giant, he lit a fire, feeling at odds with the curious part of himself that had led him to such miserable straits. Weary through, Boabben looked from his steaming bark shirt back to the trunk of a tree otherworldly.

It was almost wholly grown to mossy tendrils and dangling ferns and flowers. Where the tree laced into another of its kin, halfway to the far-flung tops of the gums, the immortal thought he could detect an odd flurry. His mood, though, turned immediately inward, and he studied his dejected state by the flames and realised he had no right or ability to interpret anything in this sensual jostle of ancientness. Summoning his will, he stared hard again at another of the dark-trunked sentinels likewise swamped by hanging vegetation up at the height of the moister air. Seeing the creature there, he marvelled to feel the strength of its emotional manipulation, watching the black marrankur leap twenty feet out onto another tree as it came to feel his gaze, and vanish. They seemed smaller than the northern race, but more compactly muscular. He attuned himself to their presence during frequent halts in the slog of that day and night, but glimpsed nothing more of the creatures.

Before dawn, the fireseer drank deeply from a rocky spring, filling his skin. Soon he descended a long flank of land, and through the clearing afforded by a tree fall, saw laid out before him, finally, a country into which the mists could sink or be blown away. In the far distance a broad plain receded around volcanic hills, glinting with large lakes. In half a day he cleared the mountains and came to game country where firestick had pushed the jungle into stubborn creekside patches and cleared the understorey beneath brooding grey-trunked gums to a knee-high ferny sward. Boabben rubbed a handful of wild raspberries on his face, feeling their sugars stimulate the pores of his insect-bitten skin. He let the calls of ducks and swans draw him toward the lake.

As the canopy thinned, slender trees interspersed the ferns, including one with seraphim-scented blooms which odour pursued him to the waterside, where the scent was undermined by a corpulent rot. Boabben soon came upon a puzzle. Concerned to take a closer look at the burial platform, he climbed up alongside hawks and kites, the shining-eyed bliss of their feasting becoming a tattered whoosh of commotion at his intrusion.

So many bodies upon the frame of thin saplings told him something was certainly awry. The bullet wounds were mainly intact on the two-day-old corpses. Enough so as to ascertain that the four warriors and two elders had been shot at a handshake's distance, and the others from behind. Ten others. A mixed family group, including two young women, indicating the slaughter was motivated by land greed.

Rich volcanic soils. Copious water. Boabben could hear the pastoral officer's pitch. He strode abruptly to the lake shore, a dry bile rising through his throat and settling in his lungs like the restless canker that had attached itself to the promised land of these blacks. The feeling of abhorrence for his countrymen that had been building since boarding the 'Enfant', had since become an unremitting mourning for the curse of soullessness beneath which his blood kin were bowed.

From beyond the wide lovely lake, the age-fire beckoned him. Usually he would need only the slight surface tension of the water to cross straight over it to the just visible far side, but not trusting the emotional body of the Mend to make up for the shaky nature of his own, Boabben followed the shore.

A forking path led him up a slight rise to a cluster of tribal huts that he perplexedly discovered to be comprised of stone, with snugly capped mud and thatch roofs. All about were the trappings of village life — beside cured eel skins was a big basalt rock pored by countless holes and furnished with a deep hollow in which lay a small amount of mustard seed. There were reams of tea-tree, stacked for translation into spears — but no people. As he continued back along the shore, Boabben saw the richness that had led to this unprecedented settling of the tribe. Wallaby and kangaroo. Bread-reeds. Water cress and shadows of fish fatly lurking where rivulets coursed into the lake. Turtles and every type of waterbird abounded in its azure embrace. Plains bustard and yam-daisy, numerous echidna and bandicoots.

Coming to the bank of the largest creek he had yet found meeting the lake, he saw that squatters had pegged their claim. An obviously overworked draught horse had been used by the party to pull huge felled logs into a crescent, fencing a hectare along the creek that was the deterrent to escapees on one side. Their hundred or so sheep drank from the lake shore, and as Boabben passed he saw it was muddied and scummed with algal explosion from their droppings.

There were traces of human faecal matter along the creek's bank, and Boabben lingered only long enough to observe two drunken tribeswomen with the three white men at their camp. A little apart were gunyahs, outside which a ragged family sat, covered in flour bag shirts and smallpox, and smoking — even the children — from a reeking tobacco pipe.

Boabben was tired. The European crush upon the land was like wind-driven dust clogging his senses and bowing his head. Before him, like drowning sailors, worked men waist-deep in scrub. They were the ragged wraiths of his former life — convicts. Apart from those piling scrub, others were hewing roadside trees. Several toiled behind a selector's cart, propelling it through the mire of the roads. The track was boggy despite thousands of treefern trunks laid in twenty-yard lengths upon it. The cart lurched forward past the immortal, the hooves of its four horses crackling and squashing through the fern graves.

Boabben's brain felt dull. Perhaps he needed very much the deep spring water that oiled an Enyadding's eternity. He stepped onward, the ache in his calves giving him a cool empathy for the indentured men piling roadside boulders further on. He suppressed the bilious feeling in his soul. It had risen an hour ago when the road passed a neatly fenced sheep paddock, its front rails lined end to end with eagles and owls nailed to the wood.

Where the roadside widened into a smouldering, stump-littered clearing, Boabben quickly discerned, in the pitched tents and staked horses, a soldier's bivouac. It was time to leave this ghoulish thoroughfare, diverging for the direction from which he could feel the age-fire. The extensive soldiers' clearing, gathering afternoon mist, appeared a good short cut into the forest. Two slavering brindles met his sneakery with an apoplexy of rage, each jerked short by a chain metres from him. Boabben moved further off with relief, hearing the rough soldier banter with half an ear.

"See, it's set 'em off again. I say we kill it."

"No! Tomorra it ships for the museum, boys, and that witch-cat is a-goin' to make a new spell. One what gets us gold."

"I suppose he is a queer enough thing. Well, you best check on him then, Pat."

His senses taut, Boabben followed the man away from the tents and along a trail through some residual scrub. It was in a packing case with one wall knocked out and replaced by bars of slender tree trunks.

"I know you're in there, even so I can't see you, witchy. Now don't you go upsetting the dogs." He emphasised this stricture by banging on the roof with a stick. A yowl came from within.

"I knew you were in there." The soldier poured a large kettle of water into a receptacle behind the bars. He crossed himself and spat at the cage, then stamped off.

Boabben kneeled before the bars, peering through the ingress that had accommodated the kettle spout. The marrankur was young. Only a little over a metre long, not counting tail, with dog bites along its head and flanks. It had probably been found injured when tree-felling was done.

It shrunk back in the cage, but glared defiance at him. Gradually, Boabben allowed his spirit to merge with it. In exchange for his telepathy, he began to receive a commentary of colours that equated to emotions and thoughts, and a few pictures. Boabben did not hurry the delicacy of trust-getting, and it was night before he snapped away the bars and took the hurt one in his arms.

"I do not fear the noisy, snappy ones," he sent to it, ducking around a netting of vines. The country opened beneath a colonnade of vast grey gums, and Boabben strode north-east, the marrankur soon asleep in his arms. Eighty kilometres on, in a thick patch of rainforest, Boabben poured the last of his energy reserve into a coursing of healing light that closed the young one's wounds and steadied its breath. Then he sank into a wide-eyed stasis with his back against a tree and the marrankur warm in his lap.

The immortal's Mend grafts roved close to the Mend's dynamo, partially restoring their frequencies, bolstered enough until the ley-power of the nearby age-fire glade and sharp piquancy of its fresh firefeather could re-sculpt them in perfection. As he stirred in the dawn-dream, there was a strange uneasy astral splash of close human feels, but Boabben knew his body was still tense and dived once again into subconsciousness. Slowly he journeyed back up, his cells finally restored by their primal bath, until with a rush he came into his body consciousness as the sun joined the forest floor. He blinked, instantly awake after the extended dawn-dream, like a lizard suddenly quit of hibernation.

The marrankur stretched its face up to his and coloured into his mind a picture of many men and horses. Just then came the sound of a tree smashing to earth, followed by an intense booming and ripping and the thunder of cataclysm. Boabben dashed through the forest, the marrankur at heel, instinctively recoiling from the noise. They flowed over obstacles like lion-driven gazelles.

From the corner of his eye the fireseer saw the monster rear above him, then come smashing down through the canopy as he outpaced the marrankur, mentally urging it on. A mortified ancient slammed in front of them and they leaped its great bole while it still shuddered. The ball of lead — vast marble of chaos — struck into a rocky patch and ricocheted to hit three large trees at once. It bounced up through scrub, sailing across the hollow that the escapees had just crossed, before landing to riot along a valley waterway and roaringly exhaust its momentum somewhere in the distance.

Boabben lay with his leg pinned to the ground by a branch, almost its width, protruding through the sinew and bone above his knee. The marrankur licked at the blood. Boabben motioned it back while a lone tree creaked in entropic acceleration before bursting upon the understorey. The road razor had done its job. The forest lay obliterated for a mile, as far as Boabben's shocked inner vision could tell; all the way back up to the hilltop where the men were gathered with the scores of horses it had taken to initially set the devil's orb rolling.

He was skewered one metre from safety, at the high edge of the swathe along the gully. The immortal's Celtic grey eyes flashed through blue, then black, as he made a fire within, disintegrating the wood impaling his leg. There was a cloy of burning flesh, and then the gaping ruin filled with light and was hale.

Boabben staggered, then straightened purposefully. They had to leave this place. The marrankur lifted its thick tail under his hand. Boabben was blind, having used the power of his vision to transduce the healing. With his Mend Mapping in spasming shock, the fur beneath his fingers was his only guide, as for eleven hours his ally led him unfalteringly toward the age-fire. Finally, they completed the nine mile journey, and Boabben lay sucking up spring water with the last of his consciousness. Then he, too, was felled like some innocent tree, prostrated beside the water.

Boabben wakened to look on dawn's tangerine leaping — his vision was restored! The spring rose through a golden rock shelf twenty paces wide, upon the edge of which the marrankur flicked his tail in acknowledgment, stripping every shred of meat from a wallaby's bones. Boabben was also hungry, and he plunged his arm into the rockpool and swallowed a dredge of sand followed by the clear essence. As he repeated the feat down along the rill with a handful of clay, the marrankur's colours formed in his mind, questioning, "For bone and inner eye?"

Boabben assented, asking that it conduct them to a good lookout. The marrankur ran through the bush with an impish testing of Boabben's speed. They raced along the open forest floor, littered with slatey rock and a profusion of herbs and grasses. Finally, there was a steeper climb and a bald tor giving a commanding scope every way but south, where massed buttresses obscured the skyline. Behind that obstacle, Boabben could feel, lay Melbourne. The thin morning sun clouded over, and the marrankur bunched beside Boabben's crouch, its thick shoulder ruff pressed along his neck.

Together they looked over a tableau of green flatlands. Grey-green wavered rarely into limier patches where rainforest sprawled, for it was predominantly open country. It was under attack. Stark, cleared paddocks dotted the scenery like amoebas threatening to join into larger entities. Plumed smoke rose beside bone-white twists of felled trees. Through the rich and fraying lands below, two roads knifed, angling north-west to the goldfields.

Not expecting such an unremitting pace of advance across these wilds, Boabben was stunned, though he should have known that a culture capable of producing the abuse he had seen on the prison ship would attack this land in a joyful flensing. The age-fire here would not survive. Most probably it would be blown apart by dynamite with the spring's enlargement for more stock.

Abruptly Boabben felt his throat parch as if emulating the slow future death of the waterway. As his vision filled with red, he realised he may not have fully recovered from yesterday's shock. Fevered, he fell onto the soft foil of his bond mate and began to see imagery smudging across the red desert of his mind. Within a minute his future-seeing had ended, leaving him in the calm certainty that he must move the two southern-most age-fires from their ley-lines to places where his prophesying had showed future need of their sanctuary.

He decided to move this one the next day to where his visions had shown, thankfully only fifteen kilometres distant. Over to that deeply broken country southward, which might hold out nearly forever. The marrankur stretched languidly, propping on two legs against him as he stood, its midnight muzzle not yet reaching his face. The flash of colour along its gums suddenly brought to Boabben's mind the stone tourmaline.

"I will call you Tourmaline, then. My shining shadow. A hard light we must be, now that we have only each other and enemies a-glut."

The juvenile marsupial imparted a colourful pattern to Boabben's mind which he interpreted as, 'we have the whole world.'

"You are right Tourmal," Boabben sighed, looking out. "But for how long?"

It took most of the next day to navigate the steep blocky gorges and set the age-fire into the top of one. Boabben selected a tumbling spring with a deep pool that had no traceable re-emergence downslope. Around the waters he layered the illusion of starched bones and dead thickets of wattle, enough to deter idle curiosity a time. From just beyond the lip of their sanctuary they could see the smoke of Melbourne. Across those eighty kilometres, Boabben's vision could discern even the masts of ships that anchored in the rivers.

Boabben and Tourmal journeyed towards the town, reaching the volcanic plain below just as dusk brought the ecstatic imprecations of possums and flying possums. Soon, their way joined a kind of track, and wagon ruts became common, along with occasional barking carrying from some homestead. Boabben measured the easy stride of Enyadding walking pace, Tourmal loping alongside or into the night's fringes. In no hurry to reach the city, Boabben was glad to feel his healed leg respond well. Suddenly Tourmal's dismayed colours probed his mind. He found his bond pondering over a bloodied lump of fur beneath its paw, and explained psychically.

"They are part of the human hive: tame hunters. Cat. I don't know what they taste like though." Boabben smiled and moved off. The marrankur caught him after a minute, contented feelings plushing its aura. As the Moon sank, they came to the city fringe, with its river obstacle. It was quiet but for the shufflings of rats in a storage warehouse which made Tourmal flick his ears. In the end they crossed the wide water by leap-frogging off three closely moored ships. Then they came to the town itself, much bloated since Boabben had last seen it.

A night watchman passed close by them, but Tourmal kept an easy, if fascinated calm that endured when a drunken party spilled onto the street amid the broken plates and bottles outside a hotel. At an intersection a pack of dogs lifted mangy heads towards them under the dim lantern light. They growled as the pair passed, preoccupied with the mostly gnawed bones of a long-bogged bullock team, their humped skeletons trailing the shaft of the dray.

Soon reaching the erratic bows of the Yarra-Yarra River, they pattered briefly across manicured lawns into scrub behind the botanic gardens. Boabben lay back in respite. There were few stars, and he revelled in the fine musky smells of the trees and the virility and gentle feeling of the earth that seemed — across this coastal river plain called Melbourne — to be imbued with a warm glow, despite a cold breeze and mizzle that made Tourmal snuggle closer. Tomorrow he would seek the other age-fire and attempt the thing revealed to him as his task.

In the pre-dawn primalcy, walking with his great floating steps, Boabben scoped the gardens, feather cloak latched beneath his beard. Tourmal was off hunting water birds, so Boabben was able to devote all his attention to the changes wrought in five years. There were temporary humpies newly erected beside the staff quarters. Many more monkeys were caged between the long glasshouses he had helped construct, and Boabben counted no fewer than twenty types of antelope and goats, as well as a zebra, in little enclosures about the lawns. The directorate house had the innovation of a bulky ship's rope draped double around the flower beds as a kind of border. They had moved the river.

With an engineering trail announcing supreme effort, they had done it.

Vast sand bags and concrete ditches and levees chaotically scarring gentle hillsides choked with fallen vegetation were one testimony. The absence of the sandy-beached, pink-tinged lagoon was another. Boabben sat beneath the old gum that had not changed. He felt himself drift over land that still breathed in solidity, pressed against its sister, the sea. He felt the land across continents and the fiery emanations of space and the world's spin through it. But nowhere did he find redress for the moving of a river.

Such a thing! They would move the timeless beauties to create a greener lawn, level a forest to give light to a flower patch. Among such a treacherous gang of conquerors, how could the Enyadding protect an age-fire? Yet he had been shown in his vision that he must place an age-fire in the vicinage of Melbourne. Boabben coupled his intuition with those mounds of limestone he had seen that morning, an imitation of karst, and planted with cactus, and abruptly he knew what he had to do.

The invaders would mould this park. They would smash it and cherish its remnant shards as natural inheritance. Within he would plant the age-fire.

Watching the work gang of aboriginals for some minutes, it became obvious to Boabben that Willy Man Tong was no longer their leader. It was an old man who, with an economy of gesture and golden tints in the grey hair and beard that lent him authoritative portraiture, handed out baccy and biscuit to the eight men. As they rolled smokes and looked grudgingly from the cold-handled tools to the pile of rocks and dirt beginning to represent their last cactus grotto, Boabben stirred a melodramatic mist around him until all eyes focused on it. He unthreaded the Veiling and manifested before the nonchalant curiosity of the group.

In a mixture of lingos, Boabben explained that he had been sent by the late Director Bullark to ask them to make a circle of rock unlike the other grottos, in that it be open to the sky, so that the Director's bones could be placed within and look out to his gardens. He guided them to the place, a few stones defining the small spring he had earlier found, a little distance across from their predicated work.

"In exchange for the burial site being made," Boabben concluded, "Spirit had asked that I heal any of your family who have the white rotting. Please send three men to camp to witness that this is done."

By afternoon Boabben looked over distant hut-lined roads jostling toward the township from atop a cleared hill planted with fruit tree sprigs, their last clutch of golden leaves backlit by the lowering sun. He was tired, but the light betokened only greater hurrying. The task of burning smallpox from two women and a fever from a boy had been a crushing drain. Yet such miracles were accomplishable for him. The shifting of two hundred tonnes of rock and dirt was not. The work gang, in concert with others of their tribe, would attempt such under cover of darkness. For the tribesmen it had to be done in one night. Boabben, in his guise of spirit representative, could not be kept waiting in a request for fear of offending the Creator.

Inland, Boabben looked on the slight mountains at the feet of which, somewhere, he could feel the pulse of the age-fire. After a twenty mostly flat kilometres, the country flexed wild claws, fielding vast jungle eucalypts and close rainforests. Boabben understood the Lellying's choosing of this place before the English had arrived.

Springs rilled to join larger streams skipping through the plains, and tree-ferns clustered, their damp, unfolding green pinions ten times his height. The trees soared in a crescendo of flinting growth, and between their ancient turrets vines that reached the venerable canopies depended in the misty silence, their massive ropes a conspicuous black against the creamy pregnancy of the heights.

In the exhausting navigation of the green riot, compounded by fallen trunks like small hills, Boabben dreamed of gaining the solid serenity of the treetops and a clear view of the way ahead before dark. Prohibitive to climbing, each totem pole rose some forty times his measure before its first branching, and Boabben slogged forward, imploring all his strength and Mend instinct.

"I have to find that age-fire, Tourmal, and get it to the garden by morning. Strange that it is vulnerable even here." For to that unassailable grandeur, he knew encroachment would soon come. They had crossed no vast hills or rivers that might impede the conqueror's axemen.

The marrunkur found a sort of path, constructed originally by wombats or wallaby, challenging to Boabben's verticality. Yet along it the plains gave quickly to uplands as stars candesced above the trees. Boabben sensed the age-fire pulse very near. Finally they negotiated a gully stream, flowing beneath an accretion of every possible blanketing green, at the top of which they found what they sought.

Boabben spurned the supremacy of the view and finer details of the bubbling cascade as he placed the firefeather talisman into a pocket of the feather cape. As the last energy of the firefeather faded from the former Iridestine, Boabben and his bond had already descended the gully, their strides trained upon the town. At the edge of the night, they crossed a bridge over the Yarra-Yarra where it deployed from the last of the little rolling hills and sped across the conquered plains of Melbourne.

When normally he could have replenished in the dawn-dream, Boabben instead ushered Tourmal off to hunt, his weary arrival at the gardens intercepting the day's light. They had finished the open grotto. Twenty tribesmen sat around a fire, sharing the haunches of what looked suspiciously like a rhesus monkey. Old speckled-beard greeted Boabben's apparition with proud familiarity and the whispered confidence that the entire tribe was leaving that day, though all present had sworn to secrecy concerning the grave.

They had done a fine job. A mound of stones ten yards high now ringed the spring, studded with the transplanted cacti from the old mound. All that was left for the fireseer to do was to create an illusion of grass and leaves where the old mound had been and over the tracks between the sites. He positioned the firefeather pendant in the rock circle, binding it to the life of the underground spring, then unable to dimensionally autonomise the ecological keys to the site and create a fully hidden Iridesce, he crafted a roof of illusory rock and cactus to cap the mound, confident that the garden's maintenance would not extend to anyone climbing up to attempt to water the hardy clustered illusions on the non-existent top. He had made for the Lellying a town lair, and Tourmal and he were overdue to leave.

Boabben found Tourmal on the river bank, napping in a sheoak tree near the old cascades, recently dynamited. The marrankur's thick coat was stretched by a comfortable bulge. As they walked, the marsupial's mind colours excitedly relayed how it had scaled the wall of the meatworks to eat the naked ones on skewers. Boabben thought of the half-eaten sheep the workers would be mystified to discover, but he was glad his bond had passed up the offal that the shambles disgorged into the river.

They followed the Yarra-Yarra for a time seaward, then struck out across the weedy backs of pomped or parlous houses clustered accordingly. The Mend Veil kept them hidden from the actors of the early morning's scene. Maids and grooms on errands bustled by, market carters plodded with their bullocks, idle children kicked stones.

As they passed through an orchard interspersed with men hefting pruning saws, a skiter leaning against a tree muttered about black devil cats between sips on his bottle. Maybe, Boabben considered, his intemperance had given him a deeper insight than the oblivious antfolk, and he pulled the Veil tighter around them.

Until noon Boabben kept the eastern Pacific to his right shoulder, then his Mend Mapping took him inland to scorn the labyrinthine coast around the smaller muddy bay of the original settlement. In this folded country, sheep milled with an afflictive stench. They passed the odd shepherd, haggard-faced men staring always vacantly at the clouds or their flocks. Mostly they just saw sheep in their millions, surrounded by an imbecile legacy that the immortal knew could never be repaired.

Eroded landslips blunted the hills. Waterways, choked with dirt, had outspread to wash away valleys or trickle greenly-hued and viscous. Biting things and flies abounded. The stink was overwhelming, although Boabben found Tourmal's eye-rolling hilarious. For a time they passed through tall forests of thistles with only the Mend Map to guide them on. Finally they scented a sea-breeze and hastened over a rise to be greeted with rolling valleys filled with blood.

The soil was dyed a purply red and Boabben found the bodies of earthworms, as thick as his arm and twice his length, torn by the plough's first taste of this land.

Following a ridge, the two eventually came to little frequented lands. There was a cart path, but one styled to ever-wind in avoidance of gargantuan eucalypts. The ocean was visible at times, and stopping where a treefall had cleared aside vegetation, the pair looked across sheep paddocks rolling to the water, and further, to the island in a muddy bay and brooding wild mountains on a far promontory. Boabben sat on a gnarled rainforest tree's trunk and scanned the vista, his eyes narrowing and then lighting up.

"That's exactly what we were looking for, Tourmal!" he declared, greatly pleased, and they jounced downhill toward the coast.

The duo swam the quarter-mile out to the flotilla of fishing and military sloops, as the shore parties dozed in a camp darkened save for a fire large enough to keep the sentries warm. At the water line, Boabben grasped the anchor rope of a military supply ship and vaulted onto the deck. He let down a buoy for Tourmal to climb into and heaved the marrankur smoothly aboard. He dried them both with a trickle of firefeather power, laying down to hum old childhood sea-lore rhymes while the nutty smell of his bond steamed around him.

By the time it was fully light, Boabben's chosen salt nag had skipped out of the rugged bay into a broiling sea at the head of eight other vessels. Two ships trailed off to the south, laden with koala and platypus furs. The vainglory of the northern-bound merchant craft seemed even flimsier to Boabben as the sea loomed in a redoubled afternoon lust while the shoreline whisked the wind over blue-silver dune growths before it was swallowed in the immutable breast of vine-tangled rainforest.

The soldier-sailors around him seemed unwarrantedly proud of the speed driving their mission. The merchants in the other sloops had mastered scurrying to and fro to drive away the cold, Boabben deeming their industry might be more to do with dispelling the risk of learning nature's truths from the shoreline's unbroken mirror of primordia. Around dusk the flotilla anchored off a long sandy coast, steeply shelved. A greeting party with lanterns helped those who had rowed through the huge waves to alight safely on the beach and showed them to pre-pitched tents.

As Boabben and Tourmal slipped to shore on a boat heavy with supplies, the fireseer cast his seeing out along the Mend Map. When they had skirted the camp and attained the top of a slight dune, he saw that the map had not prepared him for the grandeur and allure of the water body he had sensed. A vast lake spread back southwards, locked by dunes to seep its fresh waters into the sands. The Mend Map had revealed that the lake system wound parallel with the ocean and up inland hollows for hundreds of kilometres.

They followed this furthest northern fringe of the fresh waters inland, beside reflections of a dully purple sunset. In the hills was a little settlement of four or five families, to judge from the rumour given forth by the barking of dogs. Tourmal flashed through a reed bed to take a swan, and suddenly the lake was a giddying outcry of mourning swan sorrows and buffeting wings that stirred the voices of ducks and brolgas, herons and cormorants, rails and magpie-geese, and a dozen more reed denizens into deafening verse. Boabben was transfixed. Something in the richness and sudden shock of life here seemed almost to overmatch the natural elements put into it, evoking another world entirely.

After Tourmal's meal they continued along the natural road made at the cusp of the lakes and rainforest. In this margin of cyclic flood, few plants were able to obstruct the path beatings of kangaroo and wombats, though occasionally a tendril of vine as thick as a man looped erratic spirals over the track and sprawled in the reeds where its supporting host had long since rotted.

In the middle of the night, the dense spice-redolent forest species fell back beneath a majestic gum cluster. The doddering royalty and their protecting captains were about to be overcome by the smother of rainforest plants, their weapons of inflammability annulled, their final seeds doomed to rot, unable to produce heirs amid the lightless understorey. For now their sheer size held back the patiently advancing usurpers. They held a ridge of land circling a spring, their venerable forms demarcating an aboriginal campsite.

There was no sign of the most recent contributors to the vast midden of charcoal and shells. Boabben wandered the wispy lawns beneath the trees, pursued by memory and loneliness. Touching the eldritch trees soothed his pangs, as did the placid silhouette of Tourmaline seated in study of the water, an arm of the substantial body they had left, pulsing with a little current from some inland flow.

Among the remnants in the midden was a turtle carapace of medium size and unlike any of the specimens known to the northern tribes or recorded in any of the fauna sketchings he had perused on occasion in the Director's home. The conical shell rose steeply in a singular lime green. Nearby was another puzzle. Bones of a massive width stretched in segmentation before him. This was a hunter's trophy! The dorsal section indicated an eel, although the head was missing, and truly he did not wish to see such. The strength of a six metre long eel would put even the python he had killed to task.

Boabben joined his bond mate where a stream flushed into the channel with a soulful trickling sound, at a place marking the end of their unhindered shoreline path. Rocky nodes upflung suddenly; a flinty overhang teetered beside them. The aboriginal camp sheltered in the lee of the rise, and no doubt there were tracks passing over it. Yet a minute's swim around its base through the inky waters that faintly lapped the stone would bring them to the rocky continuance of the path their nocturne eyes could see lying ahead.

A spirit of apprehension passed between Mended and marrunkur, and a moment later a long wave split the waters at the cliff edge, revealing a shadowy form, swallowed again by the depths.

Come on, Boabben mind-sent to Tourmal. *Let's climb over this fishing hole tonight.* By noon of the next day the immortal had found an age-fire, the most isolated of all those placed by the Lellying. Here they tarried while winter deepened and fewer birds greeted each dawn. The springs, gushing from the mountain, soothed Boabben's pent indignity at his birth people's excoriations of the land.

On their last day at the age-fire glade, Boabben looked out, knowing the place would long reign secure from the defiling hand. Via a gorge and a dizzying spur they had been forced to access it. Everywhere rose mountains radiant in their pregnancy. The view of sky and of green failed only where it was split by two rivers. Along the north-westward flow he could feel the stirrings of a large settlement. Yet it was the road they had to follow, for the river led toward the wild place that Boabben had felt calling his heart through nights past.

Tourmal had bulked sufficiently from the travel to be immune from all but the most savage dog pack. The marrankur was someway down the rocky flag below, his shoulders hunched supplicant against the same swallows that, earlier, he had made the source of his delighted games. The unusually sunny winter's day had seen Tourmaline leaping at the birds, their spectacular flexibility only just exceeding his own. Now they had rallied to turn the attack on him in a stream of a hundred flickering wings. Boabben laughed, and his smile was reflected in the shining cheer of this high world. By dawn, he and his bond were dots in the westerly river valley, moving with the grace only joy could lend.

Boabben surveyed the grotesquery. Moonlight splashed across the scene. It was a timber-getter's camp. Hillsides had been made into slipways of logs from those species deemed commercially undesirable. Small piles of dressed logs surrounded a clearing on which propped several shanties. Smoke rose from fires that great swathes of fallen branches awaited to feed. Under the press of persistent dog barking, a lantern guttered alight. The travellers moved off to rest in a patch of tattered rainforest where they could no longer hear barking, but instead were serenaded by the alien bellow of distant cattle.

In the daylight, Tourmal coloured *little hurts* to his bond mate. Boabben found the ticks, not yet bloated, but innumerable on the marrankur. Within a few minutes they were all removed and Tourmaline recovered his dignity. They journeyed only another short way, however, before Tourmaline collapsed, his legs aquiver. *Inside fire*, he coloured, and Boabben's efforts at the slight Lellying healing he knew finally prevailed. Under his hands, the marrankur drew steadying breaths, but Boabben felt the poison suddenly surge and his friend slipped into a coma.

Riding the waves of adrenaline ahead of the tumult of despair he knew might come, Boabben hit upon a cure. In England they had used apis, made from crushed beestings, for insect poisoning. He charged off to find a native hive, losing valuable time before he remembered they were stingless. For a few minutes Boabben ran back toward the timber-getter's clearing, hoping all the while that this was the worst a marrankur moving out of its habitat range might suffer. Boabben anchored a thought matrix of ragged clothes and shoes to himself, then stepped into the clearing.

There were three men sawing branches off trees beside a horse team and two carts. One of them alerted the others to the stranger's presence, and an elder rotund fellow slipped a rifle from the cart and leaned upon it while the immortal approached. The two ghoulish-looking young men, all cuts and bites, eyed him up and down in slow study. One turned away to cough and they returned to sawing.

"Sweet Bathesda, man," exclaimed the portly elder. "Where were you comin' from, and what were you wantin'?"

"We have a farm over the mountains." Boabben cocked his head, swimming a look of anguish over his features. "Our daughter is dying of exposure, and my wife thinks as she won't take food, she might try some honey. Is there anyone keeps hives with you?"

The man stared, then shook his head. He put away the gun and retrieved his saw.

"See that hill? You follow that, take the third branching stream in the gully west. There is a lad up there, he got hives. Watch out for his dogs; they roam all these trees." Boabben strode away as slowly as he could bear, then raced up the gully.

At the stream intersection, he picked up a rock in case of said dogs. The country here was largely unscathed, owing to the plummeting slope. An attempt to salvage a patch below him had been abandoned, and over the regrowth Boabben could just glimpse the timber camp below. Further up, a few trees had been taken, and Boabben struggled through the resultant damage from their colossal felling, dense regrowth and snagged trunks making a thick barricade.

Soon a fallen trunk, into which steps had been hacked at regular intervals, intersected his way. The trunk path joined another, and Boabben scented woodsmoke before sighting the roof of the hut, built off the end of the log. Here another gum had landed during timber snigging, its double trunk held well off the ground horizontally by the weight of its root ball. Bark sheets had been laid over this, which now leaked smoke. Boabben cooeed and descended via the notches on a much smaller ladder trunk.

A very drunk man, invisible in the gloom to eyes other than an immortal's, reclined inside the log cave. He had a rifle trained on Boabben. The man skittled out into the light, asking, "Came all the way up here to die?"

"No. I came because my daughter's dying. I need honey for her."

"You seen two dogs? Yea big, brown?"

Boabben shook his head, recognising the man suddenly as a runaway from his original convict workgang, escaped after bribing a soldier with rum. He was later rumoured an aboriginal killer. Any second, the fireseer knew, he would have to step inside the delay caused by the wet powder his senses detected and break the man's neck.

"So you want honey? That way." Boabben did not think he would get honey if he turned around.

"Put the gun down, come on. I need this medicine."

"Yeah. What you going to give me? You want to suck my wag-staff?"

"How long would it take you to reach the nearest bank?"

"Two weeks, mate."

Boabben placed a thirteen day illusionary glow over the rock he was holding and drew it from an illusionary pocket.

"You can have this. It's all my wealth but for my wife and little 'un."

The man swooned at the sight and feel of gold, biting it. He mumbled a help yourself and ran into the bush.

Boabben grabbed a cigarette case from a log and soon filled it with a dozen bees. As soon as he arrived back, he ripped out their stings, squeezed their little sacs of poison onto a ball of gooey ash and wrangled the medicine down his bond's gullet. By dusk Tourmal was looking perky and colouring *hunger-happy-hunger* to Boabben.

Boabben made the marrankur stay on sheets of bark to keep him away from ticks. When he returned it was with three pigeons whose hearts he had stopped with a flare of his blended fire. It was only a snack for Tourmal, but enough so that they could move again.

Through the length of two bright but rain-flecked days, they continued higher into the river's catchment. Boabben had left the valley with the first hint of a traffic-bearing road encroaching through it. He had meant to cut back north-east anyway, to negotiate passage over the mountains to the place that had called him these weeks past. He could feel it clearly and even envisage its colour and living treasures, but the most his Mend senses could tell him of the route to reach it was that the going would be imponderably difficult.

They came to a marshy stream intersection that had been pulverised into slurry by the hooves of cattle.

266

I think you best start hunting the tame ones, Boabben sent to Tourmal. He was serious, although a cow path over firmer ground hastened them along their way very providentially, grass abundant with bestrewn flowers and a grazed understorey providing lovely walking.

As they reached the bottom of a declivity between two hills, Boabben froze to admire a most strange apparition. A woman was sketching in the bright sun of the cow path, her easel propped on a log and her features beneath her plaited blonde hair trained studiously on the myriad flowers. Boabben found himself wanting to linger and sat with Tourmal on a hill's slant to watch the artist. There was something more than her obvious beauty that beguiled him. She would have been an outcast of sorts to be this far from clamorous humanity.

He had a daydream of going up to her and introducing himself, and lay against Tourmal, shutting his eyes in a brief yielding to other possibilities. Then he ruffled Tourmal's nape and they continued around the woman, just close enough so that the immortal might glimpse what she sketched. Boabben drew in breath, closing the gap another fifty yards until there was no mistake. The charcoal picture depicted himself and Tourmal reclining in the sunshine.

"Hallo, golden one," the woman called, brushing a hand across her finely freckled nose and inadvertently smearing it with charcoal. "I'm Nancy. Nancy Welving. I would so like to meet your faery cat."

Boabben dissolved the Veiling and Tourmal trotted over.

"This is Tourmaline. Tourmal, Nancy."

"And?"

"Boabben."

"Well, it's a lovely day. I don't suppose you'd care for milk and cookies? Let me guess. You don't eat; I'm used to your type but the influence has far from worn off onto me."

Nancy busied herself with a little basket and Tourmal got most of her milk. Boabben asked if he could look at her work. She assented, while stooping

267

to fawn over Tourmal. The pictures proved astounding works of imagination. Over the flowery ground lounged small beings about two metres high with narrow bodies and delicate upturns to all their facial features. They had mahogany skin and woven rough clothes with sometimes a girdle of shells or a bone-handled dagger in a snake-skin belt.

"Nancy, your art is wondrously creative. How fleet must be your mind!"

"But I don't imagine it! You dear magical man. They are your people." At the look of perplexity on his face, Nancy stared from him to Tourmal. "If you're not a faery, then what are you?"

"Faery. Miss Welving. Do you actually mean…"

Suddenly, Boabben saw a cautiously approaching armed party of intent small beings. The vision had him wondering if this was some elaborate trap at the same time that his world paradigm was shattering in awe once again.

Chapter 14

Sway rouses groggily but with a thrill of girlish expectation. Her lover is safe. She can feel it! With a lurch of dizzying recollection she realises she does not know her whereabouts and begins to gingerly probe the area around her laser scald with her good hand. It is swollen and tender, but the bone is untroubled. The arm has been healed! Sensing eyes on her, the brunette turns and looks beyond the strange fire — its radiance seems to be the source of the colour swirls on the roof — to an extramundane figure beyond the beatific to describe.

The woman regarding her does so with her head resting on the side of one of those fairytale marsupials. Her eyes, gazing calmly at Sway, are like the lush inside of a hive remembered from a school economy forum, but the honey in these is lit from within to a molten iridescence. The woman, whose skin is a caramelised version of dark copper tones in the man who had rescued her, shifts her focus to Sway's arm and ruffles the fur beneath her own, eliciting a low hum from the sleeper.

"Your arm. We have mended it, Sway." She continues assuredly, "I am Brawyndy and you are filled with questions, and doubts."

Sway keeps her own counsel with a non-committal smile and an elastic stretch that affords her a quick scan about. The number of semi-naked dark ones in this intricately holographed cellar does not premeditate escape. Even should she deconstruct the illusion, find a door, she doubts her chances against three or more of their numerous beasts at a time.

Suddenly the woman is by her side. Sway startles. Her reflexes must be sapped from exhaustion, and she tenses slightly from the golden-skinned touch on her arm.

"Sway, you must trust us, please. We need your help and you ours."

Sway constricts her thinking into disciplined channels. Somehow they have fixed her arm; perhaps a bio-surgeon is in their host. They rescued her from protracted and ignominious death. Yet there is nothing to attest they represent a friendly faction or even that they are not government automns programmed to interrogate her for information on the Mist.

She looks on the animal rubbing itself along Brawyndy's back where she squats on her heels. It seems to be sharing some apprehension with the woman, trying to reassure her with the soft butting of its broad, blunt head.

"Sway. These animals are a unique species, not a genetic hybrid. The one who gave its life for you had another six decades to live, as does its mate who will now take no other. It is moot that you should trust us. Be calm and assured of our honour. "

Sway realises that she does trust the woman before her and reaches out, brushing the animal's head to display her new vein of feeling.

"Tell me what you were doing in the gardens, and where I am now. What is this place, Brawyndy?"

"We were waiting…seven hours ago for you. We had wanted to contact you sooner, but your undertaking was of pre-eminence to our need. We are still in that place you call the gardens, but in a time dimension slightly offset from the present. We can penetrate some dimensions at will. But to hold open such doorways as this Iridestine, we use the age-fire which you see before you as a magnifier of our ability. It is a derivant of unique crystals only found on this continent."

Sway studies the lights or flames curling sideways, spiral fashion. There is an outcurling of evanescent vapours, smelling much as the marsupial creatures of only wild green, subtly infused with eucalyptus burning. The age-fire warms her to the comfort level of her blood. The closest comparison she can draw to it is the beautiful yet entirely inconstant light of the aurora borealis.

"Sway. I know you are not Indigo. But to tell you our story, which is so long beyond measure, and to also better assure the safety of us all in flight from here, I must ask that you allow me to open your telepathic centres."

Sway accedes, and Brawyndy's warm hand on her neck brings no pain or sensation, just a high ringing in her ears. Then her mind fills with imagery from Brawyndy's own. The changing clime, she sees, fifteen thousand years distant. The encroach of ice-age over a people hunkered in the Earth's deep. The interaction of minerals in those sunken streams with the bio-rhythms of the volcanoes, a process that somehow changed three races, immortalising their proteins. The journey to Australia, and the battle with the Serpent priest. The marrankur; Boabben's coming and the failure to free the Aleris; the destruction wrought by the conquering interlopers and the disaster looming. The plan to Mend her and harness her martiality.

Mostly, Sway wants to cry. Her own pain is as nothing compared to the revelations of the horrors smiting these peoples, but after all she has been through — to learn that even her own skill cannot reunite her with Mendez — better to sacrifice her heart for a chance that he will have a world to survive in. To help redress the balance, she has to leave mortality, ally with these people and the frightening force that pervades their blood.

"I don't understand, Brawyndy. You Enyadding are immortal. Why do you feel you possibly need me?"

"Many Lellying do not believe we do. Those of us here trust in the conviction of my son."

Sway now sees a dim figure shift from the background and advance into spectacular apparition. The startling man before her is very tall, with his mother's eyes and rich skin, topped by golden-red hair.

"I am Aruan, warrioress. Son of the fireseer. In my dawn-dreams I have looked to your coming since before you were born. A week ago a vision, a prediction cast by my father, led me to the corporate planning building. I was hidden witness to your mock attack and knew you were the one. Your reflexes, Sway, are ingrained in your very blood. They are the one thing my father lacked against the Serpent. You shall fight, as the flowering of my raw power and yours will be the hand to crush our foe. Sleep again. For after the dawn-dream we shall flee this Iridestine."

Sway searches out sleep, its coming devilled by memory of Brawyndy's telepathic aside that accompanied Aruan's vocal exuberance.

'Have no fear for your abilities. If you accept, your advantage will be strong. Much essence of Boabben's firefeather command passed direct to his heir. Still, the task will be opprobrious of slightest weakness. You will be instantly Mended, given all of Aruan's power that he will leak to you before the battle in a merging of your fields. If the experiment fails, then his sacrifice will be for naught. Yet we dozen Lellying here are certain that in this frail thread is the knot-fasting of hope.'

Warm by the age-fire, with the feather cloak Brawyndy had given her as pillow, she turns restlessly on the soft grass. All over again she must steel her heart, must temper courage with conviction. She knows she cannot refuse Aruan's sacrifice.

In what passes for morning in the strange womb of light, woken by padding paws and feet, Sway mind-links immediately to Aruan her accedence to his plan. She glimpses Brawyndy as she sits up, the woman's eyes momentarily more beautiful for the tiny wave crashing across them. A man passes her, his scarred face a curiosity among the unblemished group, and disappears through the hazy fringe of the Iridestine.

He promptly returns before Sway has finished saying back the rhythmic names of all the immortals gathered in formal greeting. Many had already offered tentative mind-links of welcome last night. The scarred man holds forward his hand, the last.

272

"Lakellewan." Then he addresses them all. "The world is thick with Agents. We know we must travel as a group to protect Sway and in some measure, ourselves, in such a place as this. But the marrankur we cannot trust to bolster our Veiling. They must keep open the way for our passage. It is vital you keep your pair bonds within the established Veil which we cannot maintain beyond a square of fifteen metres.

"Turquin is grieving after Iltigh's fall last night. His will not be a Sending focused beyond his own need. The marrankur are overstretched. Shundry must look to her cub; Alawry and Seffern need to interchange to bear Sway. Nineteen alone can will their Sending. I tell you all, keep tight your minds around the Veiling as you would your face to shut out sand. I know not if the Affiliates have any dimensionally sensitive equipment. If they sense us, neither Sending nor Veiling will help. Thus we move quickly.

"Too much delay is engendered by the marrankur swimming the river. The bridges are fraught in their narrowness — we must risk the tunnel. Any delay in the madness of Acadabourne will weaken the Mend integrity. We are aligned? Good. The magnetic disruptors will initiate soon, removing the greedy camera eyes. Let us set the pyre and leave."

Sway stands with Brawyndy, as the Lellying gather bark and wood from around the vast boles of the trees, their tops merging beneath the roof of haze at the Iridestine's apex. The immortals stack the pyre beside the stream and lay Iltigh's body upon it. The sight recalls in Sway the terror they all face, and she clasps Brawyndy's arm.

"Hey. Why can't we remain here? Until the danger dissipates enough that we can slip through?"

"Time is doubly an enemy. The Serpent may assimilate the Aleris within a moon. Also the water of the Iridesce spring, which is our one requite for life, is here filtered by the geometry of power glyphs overlaying the age-fire crystal. This filtering is sustained by our feed into the Mend to transpose as pure emotion

273

here, so in a way we are merely consuming ourselves, not drawing replenishment. To stay much longer will mean our demise. Trust my bond pair, warrioress, their will is great. Speedily and true they ride."

The two marrankur approach, the fluid movement reminding her of sharks, their powerful haunches — geared around a levered propulsion of the hips and a sinuous enfoldment of the pouch in the female — move at odds to an angulated torso and the rigid muscling of the forelegs above the paws. Regardless of the appropriateness of a parallel to sharks, there is no mistaking their deadliness.

Sway hefts herself astride Alawry's back, grasping the ruffle of fur over the solid muscle of his neck and slipping her feet into stirrup-like knots in the fur beneath it. Synchronising with other marrankur at the Iridestine's edge, her marsupial pony bounds forward and springs skyward. Sway's backward glance reveals Aruan's hand rising casually toward the pyre as it ignites in flame. Alawry comes down on manicured lawns, a metre from six jogging Agents. He springs straight over their heads and lands marginally clear of a police dog team running up the slope toward them.

Metres away the frantic German shepherds begin to bark fiendishly, and Sway feels Alawry tense. Uncannily, there is an eruption of nearby barking, back inside the research garden's fence, and the handlers intently steer their dogs toward it, oblivious to their snapping jaws — centimetres from Sway's Veil-hidden leg. Like ants to sugar, a great many police Agents now stream uphill toward the marrankur-coerced disturbances.

Into the midst of operations tents and trailers dotted all around the cactus-choked Iridestine grotto, the Veiled Lellying emerge. Sway watches them follow the marrankurs individually downslope. Even though Brawyndy's telepathic revelations about the immortals' history had told her something of the massive animals' psychic abilities, she is amazed to see the creatures miraculously opening swathes in the officious flurry. Her own position in the chaos is still

274

quite hemmed, however, as Alawry and Seffern pause to survey their next move. A rapidly descending Affiliate hover whirs through elm branches, descending in a straight line above their heads. As it levels with the lower branches, Sway expects Alawry to bound away, but he holds his position. Inexplicably, the hover halts, then rises to disappear among the foliage.

Most of the marrankur and all the Lellying have crossed the tiered lawns and crime-scene-restricted jogging track by the time luck allows Alawry to follow and Sway to catch her breath. The others surge up the side of the silicone tube covering a greenway as Sway and the bond pair break clear. Alawry bears her onto the thick tube wall, and Sway sees the intermittent pedestrian traffic coursing through the giant steamy oesophagus which links the northern city fringe to universities along the river.

Flanked by Seffern, they dash to the waiting group, then across the three hundred metre wide rim, pelting down the other side. This area, between greenway and river is largely devoted to hover parking, and though many of the gravved vehicles are of the Affiliate, normal city life here proceeds, muting the Agency presence. Lightning generators click and whir, orchestrating the colour schemes for this part of the river. From a bridge nearby, the underwater coruscations are watched by a group of business women, spiky-haired, and German tourists in floral smocks. An octopus-like robot — a river plucker — works away, for all the world a holidaying aquatic alien but for the barges it tows, one for hard rubbish, the other refrigerated to store corpses.

Sway observes it all in a compact Veil blur as they race toward the tunnel mouth. An old car route, dankly leaking, it now supports little stalls and fashionable cafes and is busy with bicyclists, buskers, automn patrols and Japanese tourists. To navigate fluxes of lurid bicyclists zipping by, the group stretches up against the edges of the Veil, allowing the chaotic meteors to pass through their midst. At the tunnel exit, the Veil becomes a tight wedge, flowing onward along an enclosed greenway. The marrankur will their Sending upon the crowd to allow the three-metre wide group constant passage. Within a minute of entering the commercial heart of Acadabourne, their going slows to a fast walk, dictated by the multitude of the crowds.

They plough on, the marrankur vigilantly defusing hazards. Hence an old lady collapses before Sway's eyes, clutching her heart and drawing the elderly tour group to her aid, where before their doddering had hindered the Veil. Japanese tourists suddenly hem a horse and cart operator, begging pictures — two obstructions neutralised simultaneously. Reciprocating the workload of their marsupial allies, the immortals maintain the Veil with grim faces, shielding them all.

Sway's training discipline imparts to her the necessary detachment as she threads amid thousands of souls atop Alawry's metre of height, sometimes bare centimetres from boredom-ravaged faces. Her marrankur's leaping of parked hovers or wild dodgings to one side recall to Sway the bruises of the previous night.

The rejuvenating ministrations of the Lellying had healed her arm but not the deep, aching sense of misalignment around her neck and chest — result of over a dozen laser impacts. Her legs and arms are stiff, several muscles locked or spasming from combat fatigue. Sway harkens to the guiding principle of martial arts — no presumption of differentiation — one. She focuses on becoming one with her pain, enters it implicitly. For oneness she had demurred to flee her homeland and find her parents, for oneness loved unceasingly Mendez. Now she hones into the alliance of new cells which goad her pain. Summoning the resilience of her inner being, she begins the raindrop-falling-in-storm meditation to prepare for internal kung fu breathwork. With biting severity, Brawyndy's mind-voice brings her back to the city labyrinth.

"Beware the street meldings!"

Sway sees at once what will happen. The impending disaster is prompted by a new company, 'Bodylift', marketing their implant products across micro-screamers with topless male and female models extolling two-for-the-price-of-one on breasts.

People flood to the Veiled section of the street like oil spreading on an ocean. Sway watches a group of lascivious lads run past her and does not think the marrankur can be much help here. With a fury she works on unlocking her muscles, plying them with deep breaths, as her fear is confirmed by a voice — recognisable as Lakellewan's booming inside her head.

'We cannot stay together in this. Push forward by all available means, conflict or concealment, but do not get trapped in a crowd mass.'

By the script of people's faces, Sway gauges the exact moment she and the marrankur pair are forced to leave the Lellying's Veil. Expressions of passers-by contort into grimaces of fear and choked screams, and Alawry and Seffern's muzzles curl into snarls from the sudden attention. The marrankur leave wailing children and a fainted woman in their wake as they duck through the ogling Bodylift customers to bound up and over the dirty marble foyer of a building.

Sway sees a press of men fall dead, their heads blackened, and in their midst, a Bodylift model stares at the still-smoking stump of her arm in a confused daze. Alawry and Seffern press on by the grace of luck and speed. About half-a-dozen marrankur are visible nearby, and all are being targeted by automns. They regain the street in a less manic place but are met by laser fire.

They turn at the next intersection and a human officer steps from behind an eave to sight Sway point blank with his enforcer. Then he merely lowers his little laser, staggering beneath the marrankur Sending, and uttering a feeble 'Halt' as she passes. Converging from everywhere are the glittering shapes of automns. Sorely, Sway wishes for a laser and prays it will not be long before they unite with the Lellying Veil.

'*And* all their valliance was no availance,

'*Gainst* automn persistence, without their Veil friends...'

Sway had long indulged a secret love for the barding style smuggled to Austral as a dangerous intellectual artefact, had in fact met her love at a clandestine poetry club that struggled to keep the art alive. In prosaic terms, though, mind-warping would have no effect on the mindless.

They are forced to the main way of University Road, a greenway diverging from it that is blocked by massed automns. Their vulnerability attracts not only sprays of laser fire, but missiles thrown by workers on roofs and a pot-shot from a passing tram driver. As Seffern leads them past a row of doorways, a briefcase flies out at her legs. Alawry trots disdainfully from his course to find the cowering culprit and claw out his throat.

Only a little further on, they are forced by crossing laser fire to shelter in an alcove as a pair of automns close from twenty metres. Sway feels certain there are no roof snipers yet, and slipping from Alawry's back, bolts from cover. She dives, rolls, and runs again to mount a perpetuating body flip until she feels her legs connect with one robot's arm joint. The wiring is exposed, and she kicks the unit in the chest, catching its shoulder with a jerk at the last second to twist the weapon arm away.

She dances the automn into its partner, but it lunges aside for a shot at her. Somehow both units erupt in flame; indeed, every street unit is falling in sparks.

Aruan's voice rings with respectful urgency in her head. 'Alawry is down. You must ride Seffern in continuance along the street, taking the laneway second left. We're going to go over.'

People stumbling about the area raise their hands submissively or shy away as she charges back to the marrankur. Alawry lies just visible beneath the collapsed awning, and Sway throws the rubbish from him, watched by the wide, suspicious eyes of Seffern. The crossfire has merely clipped him, but it has done a jolt of damage.

'Hurry, Sway. Hovers are coming.'

The male marsupial is imperilled not by countless lacerations, but his fractured shoulder. Sway impulsively digs a foot in under his ribs and leaps backward, catching the limb above the paw as it reflexes out in pain, pulling his foreleg against the brace of her feet. As the joint cracks into place, Alawry rolls upright above her winded position and rips his teeth along her arm, but there is a respect in his eyes beyond that pained lapse of affection.

Sway snatches a cloth display sign from a shop fringe as she flees on Seffern's fresh legs through a jumble of people blundering helter-skelter amid the burning automn mounds. While she binds her arm, she notices Alawry runs with a stumble, but then they arrive at the laneway.

As his hover streaks above the street toward the escape route of the two bio-bots — one wounded, and the girl — Gunner Templeton is excited at the prospect of her termination. With cold control he decides to use the laz-cannon in favour of the machine gun, as a mostly demolished building before them is the only collateral material nearby. Seffern's mind finally slips inside the craft. The Affiliate Agent abruptly experiences an abject horror of heights and runs screaming in acrophobic panic to the navigation console.

Aruan watches the marrankur spring wearily up through the gutted levels of the high-rise, noting with approval the hover exploding from its rapid impact with the street. Brawyndy and four of the Lellying at once encircle Alawry, and Sway witnesses a healing process accomplished seemingly by fingers in mime of the movements of weaving.

Below, Sway can see streams of automns herding people away from the building in which the immortals and their company shelter. Mini-hovers begin to cloud the sky, some landing on the roof near to the Veil, or on the roofs of surrounding buildings, discharging scores of Affiliates. The Lellying, now restored, leap away from the landed Agents around them, busy in their attuning of targeter dart control bands, and are soon traversing rooftops, passing quickly through the medi-space boroughs. Eventually the Veil descends to follow an uncovered greenway west, largely deserted save for a group of hiking school children and the odd grim pensioner pushing a hover trolley.

The speed of the immortals, undaunted by a sprawl of steadily rising hills, is remarkable to Sway. Less than an hour after leaving the rooftop, the city is a far distant fugue. Trees diminish to scattered bushes in the higher, drier ground. The Veil crests a ridge that flutes away to the north and south, and the party stops in mortification. Just back from the ridge line, an Agent blockade follows the landform as far as the eye can see. The net extends vertically to dozens of hovers strung like poisonous fruits upon the sky.

Immortals and marrankur shun the greenway, leaping the fences of an ostrich farm filled with pitiful birds, genetically blighted with stick-thin necks and heavy bodies. They clear a tangle of fence obstacles, cutting south, but it is for nothing. The line of Agents continues along the brow of the hill they reach. The Affiliate ranks, intersected by police and overtopped by hovers, run in an unbroken chain.

'By the stars!' exclaims Brawyndy in all their minds. 'The Mend Map shows a ring locking right back to Acadabourne, aspecting to the west. Somewhere we have a capable enemy.'

'There are dogs right through the line,' comments Fliteal.

'We must go on.' Aruan says. 'A second line closes from the city. I see, among its barbs and hooks, astral frequencing delineators. They mean to unearth us.'

Crowding together, Sway and her rescuers approach to within hearing of the blockade. Dog barking erupts, and Sway feels Alawry tense beneath her. A team of beagles rushes along the hill, an Affiliate officer hover-packing to conference with the handler. At the Agent's word via intercom, dozens of hovers begin to converge above the Veil, descending slowly to optimum range for laser strike.

'If they just start blasting, we cook,' Fliteal mindsends.

'They are too disciplined,' comes Brawyndy's cool reassurance. 'They will not shoot at chance and rumour'.

Sway feels the energetic fabric of the marrankurs' Sending brush past her as the marsupials pit their minds against the dog teams. The furore of barking down the lines shows their success, and the marrankur needle forward as the dozen nearest automns explode from a willing of Aruan. The marrunkur pack bursts from the Veil, streaking shapes leaping around Sway, who clenches tightly to Alawry. Then they are clear of the blockade. They sprint through piles of building slag, cabling, and crushed cars, the detritus occasioning grim shelter from dozens of pursuing hovers. The Lellying overtake them, and the group cuts invisibly back toward the high point of the ridge. At one stage, Sway sees Aruan turn and raise his hand toward numerous trailing dogs. As they burn, more hasten to fill their place. Aruan rushes back to the fleeing Veil, mind-sending to split up. He locks eyes with Sway.

'Follow me,' he commands, and together they race across the hills.

The lorn pair thread through farms and densitutions, Seffern beside Aruan and Alawry beneath Sway, still untiring. She hopes the other Lellying are alright, now that they have split to the four winds to hinder pursuit. Five grainy hours pass, and Aruan's promise of nearby sanctuary still seems remote, albeit that the land is here more open. They flit by yet another dog team and down the thoroughfare of a Densitution, the occupants of the little building's stacked cells busily cooking their various renditions of boiled mush.

Aruan leads her along the sordid rear of this conurbated hell, amid tangles of broken hovers, overflowing toilets, and finally through a tear in the Densitution fence. They mount a near-vertical hill, all scree and the stubs of thorns. Once atop it, they climb a shoulder toward a ridge, the sky above cluttered with the holograms and approach signatures of a hover-fill, though distant enough that Sway cannot hear the painful customer-wooing lullabies. She glances at the land below her, eroded to rock and thistles, cadaverous as the rib-cage of some long since scavenged animal.

They come to another fence, forbiddingly tall and capped in triple strands of razor wire. It runs along the bereft gully squeezed beneath the shoulder, and is marked with signs declaring: *Hazardous Waste – Keep Out.* With an effort, Alawry bears her over the obstacle and they trek along the gully's slippery side. The dusk has begun to blur into nightmare when suddenly an intoxicating vision of sanctuary rises around Sway.

Gurgling water trickles off a shorn basalt shelf, pooling in a rock pond threaded with the contented bulgings of smooth, steely roots. Beyond the Siamese-grown gums on its edge, the water fades into a bog riotous with ferns. Predominantly, the Iridestine is dry grassy ground, speckled with flinty lichens upon which the marrankur stretch exhausted.

The Lellying sit around the pool, some on the loops of vine hanging from the bulky rock slab. All seem distressed. Then Sway realises.

"Wornjarren," Araun says simply, and Brawyndy nods. Fliteal's female bond.

"She was stunned by some kind of electric trap, exposed to automn scouts. Jendari was first to Mend-Map her plight. When he alerted me, rushing to save her, I called him back. They had already taken her."

Aruan looks at his mother wearily. "Tomorrow my fire shall be rekindled; we shall see what they reap for this."

"Drink now, my child. Simbrel and I go to watch the Iridestine boundary."

Sway sits enervated but wakeful in the dark, soothed by the water and by Alawry's big paw on her lap. Then come the bizarre spectres of the transparent Agency hovers, ghosting right through trees. There are numerous phantasms of men and dogs soon after, tracking up and down the coomb in nebulous, silent commotion. Star-softened, Brawyndy at last returns with strange news.

Apparently a great many more Agents had entered this gorge country, narrowing their search ever closer to the age-fire, when inexplicably the land had emptied of their vileness. On all her Mend Map, there was no number left of them that was large enough to register. With the turmoil finally subsided, the Lellying stretch in reprieve and Sway lays her head by Alawry's snoring repose and is soon thicketed in sleep.

Chapter 15

Nivat passes the Common Tryst, mostly deserted now, usurped by the preparation of dried and dehydrated food rations for the galvanising armies of Curlewalion. Youths stream to and fro upon the powerful backs of their perenties, carrying messages out to farmers and smiths or bringing in full saddle bags of supplies. The reptiles bearing them had thrived on the boom of rodents and snakes accompanying the original densely urban and hastily construed settlements of the nation. They replaced outmoded dogs and cats as affectionate companions for the young, and had responded to Indigo suggestions and allowed small children to ride them.

Over a century they had changed in other respects, as the community's awareness had enmeshed with the land about it, amalgamating with the beautiful gold-and-green mottled lizards. Young Curlewalions took on perentie-like aspects: quickness, agility and ferocity. The perenties seemed somehow to swell in more than their spirits at this and had swollen physiologically as well. Selective breeding resulted in a strain twice their initial three metres of length. Fed mineral supplements, they could bear a man tirelessly. Nivat, for his part, enjoyed walking.

After he wanders the Fealswon Swamp a way, he commends himself, as always, on negotiating the narrow rampway of logs interlinking bulbous paperbark trees. It comprises the path through the heart of the reedy morass. By the time Nivat reaches the area where Musa made his reche, he has been challenged by the individual appearances at ramp junctures of five lion and six lionesses, who had interrupted their lounging in the trees, and only after a long stare had decided him to be no threat.

His muscular and ebony skinned brother is seated in lotus meditation on his reche — a wooden platform, raised just above the reeds, covered in mats and a thick, shady roof also of that abundant material. The part-Icelander lets his much slimmer body down from the elevated path via a rope ladder slung from a melaleuca branch, and stands staring at the water — adjusting his diluted blue eyes to the dimness, and smelling the thickly alkaline scent given off by the ochre on his nose as the protective clay swells in the cooler air.

"Hello, brother!" beams the Unilion, rising fluently to hug the smaller man and brush a cloud of midges from his eyes. The Lion of Lion was a strictly ascetic cult, using no technology and eating only what they caught or gathered. Orphans, they had grown up together on a desert farm near Sibill-Abong that traded in bamboo and was known for scientific prodigies, one of whom had made manifest the theory of deep-flow harmonics by using precise patterning of shafts and acu-point tapping of the water table. A more recent discovery was in anti-gravitics, yet to be fully expounded, but said to be capable of fielding hovers independent of magnetism.

The two had been among thousands of orphans in the happiest of childhoods on the bamboo farms. There they had learned the mapping of the stars from the Lesbian Sectariat Astarte, who gave name to the locale and in whose parentage one could find an enumeration of mothers — and the one father, Sun. At age eleven, with the Sectariat's blessing, Musa and Nivat had journeyed to Ja Junction, where Musa gained apprenticeship among the lion and where, at Mellode Flows during gnosis testing, Nivat had drifted upon a barding talent.

It was not uncommon for non-Lion to visit the reches — although petitioners traditionally approached the Pride Vale — but Nivat was the only non-apprentice or Unilion to maintain a friendship with a member of the cult. That was how they liked it. The intricate approach over logs was not solely to ensure undisturbed meditation. Orphans were favoured messengers of justice, precisely because they had no real family to be held against them.

"So you have heard of the gnosis for open war? I suppose the Screamers tell the Bard Board even before us. Have you come to wish safe travel on me, or recite a farewell betokening? That I should love to hear, but there remains another Speak Out before the stalk is due to leave in two days' time."

"I will not wish you farewell, brother. I have decided to go to war for my nation, Musa. I want to travel with the lion." The straw-haired poet sets his rounded jaw to forestall his brother. "I need to be amid the stalk, to gauge the true opposition against us and leave clear record for the survivors. There's another factor. I don't like that we're all pawns. I want to discover what the Others are up to."

The Others. Musa knew, as did all Unilion, of the great ones who controlled the border storms and possibly the fate of the world. If the prophetic ability of one of their mothers was to be trusted, this war was all about fighting an altogether different enemy than American South Austral. Both brothers had heard the tranced words of Conaine as they had been working with her to separate edible shoots from timber in a moso patch. Her eyes had rolled back to assume an eerie half-blue, half-pink taint.

"At the eve of the final decade of this century, the hidden ones shall be made seen and Curlew war in a fight that is not war. Fire son shall war with Serpent king. Curlew shall fall, yet hold while the world is destroyed."

They both remembered the prophecy. They had been taught to honour and record the trance state but had dismissed it as more fey riddles, until that day some decades later. Musa's first pride had engaged the hunt for a gang of skit addicts and smugglers returned from previous banishment to once again grow their genetic crop in the north of the capital. Four of them had escaped Unilion retribution, later raping aboriginal women on Yallanded lands, desecrating sacred sites. Only one had survived the tribe's wrath, and Musa's pride had cornered him in a vine and pandanus thicket.

Nivat remembered it. He had attended the stalk to make barding of the event, a thing sometimes permitted the nation's unofficial press, his first work of gritty social commentary. The smuggler had long since exhausted his laser crystal, firing at feinting lion without a hit. Still, Musa held back the stalk. Nivat knew his brother sorrowed at the pitiful man; the prematurely old face and skit-blighted skin thankfully hidden in the gloom. One of the Others had appeared by Nivat's shoulder. Obviously distraught, with a rage-broken voice, the beautiful enchantress had addressed Musa, who had evinced no surprise at the episode.

"I lay this burden of blood upon you, though strike now or I shall. There is nothing so hideous as they who sell themselves for illusion. His crimes are greater than you conceive; malignancy rules now where once was man. Fear such as these that subvert the Earth and their own minds for power. Pursue them with vengeance, and lend them all of your mistrust — even as do we the sea-serpent that has crushed our heart and our hearts."

She had promptly vanished, her final reference a slip of the tongue which was duly noted by the pair. Musa gave assent to the restive pride, and the brothers observed the efficient flurry of dark muscles around the suddenly silenced figure and waited while big Jerexil brought the corpse before the Unilion. Musa had strung the wrecked body upon a tall tree and burned the seal of justice into the log at its base.

Nivat continues his case. "They mean to fight it. The Others. Through these portalling eyes now gain porthole, to their witness known no other mortal."

Musa knew the passage from his brother's composition alluding to what the bard had guessed about the Others' secrets.

"I need to be among the prides to pursue the truth and act independently of the Totem Companies."

His brother resumes his meditation position, holding Nivat's eyes with the corners of his own. "I have the safety of four Indigos to oversee, as well as orchestrating Pride Slumber's wellbeing. I will not look after you."

"I can vouch for myself."

It is true. Up until he turned fifteen, Musa had been unable to best the slighter opponent in bouts of Khorustaming, the national fighting craft.

"You will not be able to keep up without a Ra-king. Travel as a Venger. You will still have utility, and you would qualify."

Vengers would be selected to pilot Curlew's scant hover equipment into the heat of battle only from those who had directly suffered at the W.A.R. government's hands. Nivat's parents had drowned when their ship was sunk by an ASA flotilla.

"Sanfel will bear me. You said yourself he was ready to Effulge. And you know we have a rapport."

True again. The squat black-and-tan's energy was often heightened when his brother was around. It seemed Nivat could mind-reach the beast, though he had no other psychic skill. Musa enters meditation, searching for something amiss here. Nivat feels himself magnetised into the inner power of the warrior, his own breathing slowing to match that of the Unilion. After some time, eyes still shut, Musa says.

"I'll send Sanfel to you this evening."

Nivat rucks his yams quickly from the coals, scritches the excess stain of the fire from them and slices their white flesh lengthways in his bowl as he walks, eager to catch the last light. He adds leaves of fennel and beet, oregano and basil, snatching them from the goat garden spread about him, and takes the steps two at a time to the simple mosquito-meshed platform atop the cellars.

Glad for the chance at solitude, due to the continued absence of Darton's two sons, the bard sprinkles some feta over his dinner and chomps the baked roots as he adds a note about the ant-nest he has seen colonising a cherimoya tree to his conspicuously small list of observations for the day. For the promise of keeping these observations he had traded Darton his own cramped quarters at Bard Board, the man having decided he wished to trial a more erudite life among the twisting tongues of the poet's commune.

Whether the Bard creed would induct him remained to be seen, and Nivat had wrangled the swap knowing that his job as an extra set of eyes here — as well as extra cheese taster — could end at any time. That had been months ago. Darton's predicament while he waited to be accepted for creed membership, was this — should his tribute fall into disrepair, the next round of goat-herders would shun it, beginning the process that would see him lose his land. If he could not get the milk for his cheese, if his production stalled, then his right to hold land and work it as he chose would be revoked under Curlew law. In any event, that particular article would be repealed for the duration of the war. Still, he suspected that Darton's sons would maintain the tribute in trim enough condition to allure the goat herds and keep up the flow of excellent herbal cheese. It was to be greatly hoped so.

Nivat composes his thoughts, enjoying the view across the field to the distant belt of trees. In a handful of days he will be among Musa's stalk, striking the early blows of a war that could not bring resolution to Curlew's dilemma, only postpone its doom for a couple more generations.

What of the Others? Could they bring enduring peace to the world? Or was it they who kept it at odds to suit their own interests? The latter is hardly credible, he knows, the possibility of their representing a malcreant force obviated by their help in the form of the border storms. Nivat does not know the riddling of it all. He scrunches a clump of blonde beard in his hand, thinking of the many factors, other than his own death, over which he must prevail to learn the truth.

A blotchy shape pads into the yard clearing beside the cellar entrance, a shape with a mane of tightly-curled black hair.

"Hey, Sanfel. Remembered the way. You eaten?"

Nivat perceives the hunger of his old friend and newly become Ra-king, and cuts loose the strung hare he had killed an hour prior. Sanfel gives an almost sardonic grunt and slumps to the ground over the rag morsel.

"It was either that or feta," mutters Nivat, lapsing into consideration of the great beast and the similarity between his own journey to Curlewalion with that of Sanfel's forebears. Both he and the lion were here through surmounting great odds. Both had come from lands far away to reach safe haven, but in terms of guaranteed safe crossing for lion and man over the wide sea, the similarity ended. The first of Sanfel's progenitors to arrive had been at the end of a long process of sophisticated planning, the other had come in a craft superior to most on the ocean. Whereas Nivat had bobbed — a toddler in a tiny float suit amid the jettison of a poky craft put out of its misery by an ASA patrol — and had made landfall still breathing only through the intercession of the luckiest chance and the most skilled of Curlew's mini-sub scouts.

By the time he was old enough to know what they were, Curlew's lions were a dozen generations entrenched. Each had the characteristic length and black mane, if not pure black body, as well as the massive stockiness of the northern African species — the Barbary. Barbary lions had been believed extinct in the wild since the mid-twentieth century, survived only by a few odds and bods of DNA carried in captive individuals descended from Haile Selassie's private collection.

The species did endure in the wild, its final stand and subsequent recovery a favourite story after dreamdine at the Bard Board, and for good reason. Throughout the modern era, in a remote Ethiopian valley, a Rastafarian tribe protected a patch of woodland by force, a terrain on which still hunted God's messengers — Barbary lion.

Three years after Curlew's declaration of sovereignty, the whole tribe and their sedated, semi-divine cargo had ferried safely to Curlew. Several years later, a party of Ethiopian royalty — distant relatives of Haile Selassie — had sailed to Curlew in a seventy metre yacht. Its hold contained the finest Barbary from a preserved collection.

Enshada. He was a pure black storehouse of the species' original power, weighing close to the six hundred and a quarter pounds a Barbary could reach. Interbreeding with the wild females from the valley, he had sired the lineage of Curlew's mighty prides. It was truly an amazing happenstance that these beasts — that were often twice as heavy as the biggest of the southern African variety — had come to bear willingly the burden of Unilion warriors with no more thought than a horse might give saddlebags.

Nivat, with his long legs, is glad that Sanfel's height nearly matches that of his southern cousins, rare in Barbaries. With a sigh as relaxed as his Ra-king's snores, Nivat — happy that the first stages of his plans are succeeding — turns his attention to his craft. As though it were a lion he would ride into battle, Nivat carefully grooms his memory as he runs over pieces that might work at tomorrow's Speak Out.

Nivat leaves Sanfel a mile from the Speak Out glade. If any of the tens of thousands he has passed were curious at seeing the bard Effulged, none had commented. Probably none had noticed. Though Curlewalion was well prepared, war had come suddenly upon its people. The Speak Out offered great hope of solace for they who would volunteer to fight, and for their husbands or wives, children or lovers or friends facing an uncertain future in two days' time.

Nivat drinks in the dusk-saturated slopes around him, all the more precious for knowing it may be the last sunset he will watch in caress of this country. All the land seems steeped in a preternatural beauty, as if registering the deepening appreciation by its many denizens who might soon know it no more. This had all been fairly barren three decades ago. Now coconuts and black sapote soar over thick canopies of mangos, their swelling fruits heralding summer. A myriad of other fruits in startling hues burst in close ranks upon the hillside. Everywhere wattles and grevilleas bloom goldenly, and a mellifluous hum lingers over all. Rambling beans and pumpkins sprawl up the trees. Below Nivat's feet, water gurgles in little rills.

The track floor is a constantly accumulating pile of wattle prunings stacked about two metres high and wide enough for two perenties to pass. A huge old amethyst python slides its way a metre or so below. Vines interweave the pathway of branches, the springy mass protecting the earth from passing feet. The bard pauses to break off some overhanging wattle sprigs and add these and a few dead branches to the hillside path. Thousands had done likewise this day and countless days before.

Along the path he passes old African women singing prayers to the flower spirits and children gathered to eat the thickest fruit coruscate in little giggling groups. It is an inherently Curlewan saying that the journey, not the destination, is important. A large crowd is gathered at the Speak Out glade; his appraisal calculates three hundred thousand. People mill about the lawns, sharing fruit and wine beneath the gloriously orange-flowering ironwoods, or are settled already upon the high rock ladders with their living tree seats. Towering infernos lick skyward in the bon rings and, though tempted by their heat, Nivat settles within sight of the conch parapet, further back than other bards he recognises.

Somebody offers him a pomelo and he engages a very tall and comfortably featured Unipean woman, Nyssa, in conversation about a fruit bat he remembered helping her extricate from a tangle at the weaving compound some months before. However, a much focused exchange nearby between a cavalier bushrangery-looking man and another, part-Chinese, portly but elegant, gradually drains them of their friendly banter and silences a little circle all around the verbal sparring.

The shaggy interlocutor is heard to ask, "Given that you are reclined in a woodland on the pillow of your expanding boots, and that an Austral patrol coming your way is spotted, what do you do? Newles has given the ability to quickly gain the canopy with his focus threads — indeed all vertical endeavours are safely aided therein — but with a TMJ you get to race into battle with a pillow."

"To be rested is an inestimable boon associated with the transposable material juncture, however, the shielding taprocore in the device will exempt laz-fire in small bursts when tented over the vulnerable rear organs and skull. Also, a TMJ may be complemented to a laser's crystal, heated in its circuitry, and transmogrified as a blanketing glue, gripping to anything after fifty metres acceleration."

"Focus threads give you illegal hitchhiking options that gluey pillows don't explore."

"True. But you can't bring down a hover at fifty metres with a yoyo on a long string, no matter how organo-retrified its design."

"These things afford reach — and strength in hand-to-hand."

"Unless you're hitting a carbonised plastic face with a saw for a mohawk, like the rumours say we'll face. Look, Filbert, just accept the transposable material juncture has been produced by the apticycle operants in favour of a dozen other inventions aside from Newles'."

"Well, I don't accept that fighting will be static. To realign fabric junctures demands a margin of leisure we just won't get. We need frenetic aids."

"Only time will prove that."

"Well, time's run out for the focus threads, thanks to the wondrous over-stuffed handkerchief."

Both interlocutors laugh, and the spiky arches of Filbert's eyebrows lift as he flicks a root-like weight soaring from his wrist to catch an overhanging branch. As he is hoisted upward, dangling by a thick leather wrist band to which the in-reeling thread is fixed, he calls back down.

"I think they're bloody palanquin, anyway!"

Nivat becomes aware that a bard has begun, his words shaking through the air on cliff echoes as naturally as if they have always been there. Only slowly do others become aware of the subtle barding, employing the rare feeling mode, in mimicry of the unseen process by which connective group ideas mooted into the universal mind. Nivat knows it is the man's psychic empathy as much as his training that allows him to pull threads from thousands of conversations into a poem.

He feels a familiar tremor, reviewing his material for the evening, and a surge of respect for the unfaltering improvisation of the current bard. Long fingers of a downy blonde arm, each hair delineated in the glow of the tall thermal lamps, pass him a huge, tapering joint. It is a medicine finely wrought, laced with lungworts and native stimulants like the pituri wattle, sealed in banana leaf paper. Briefly, his eyes scan those of the frivolous girl who reclines again, embracing her lover, as her burden of socialising is removed by Nivat's hand.

He is tempted, but offers the reefer to the lungs of the Unipoean. Marijuana was used by the Lion of Lion to heighten rapport between man and beast and to relax muscles for combat resilience. The last thing he wants is for Sanfel to pick up on the plant in his system and shoulder his way into the glade to investigate. Just then a big hand falls on his shoulder, and Musa slips gracefully between him and Nyssa. His brother produces a joint of his own, and Nivat accepts it, realising Musa must already be training beyond his muscle's endurance. The young, inflective voice of the bard abruptly achieves solitariness as the huge audience, reaching critical mass in their awareness that the Speak Out is begun, immerses with it.

“...

But no expression

Without evolution,

Conscious offering on the road

Of this life...”

Then a rolling applause, leaving silence but for the simple calls of people exploiting the focus to make public communications across the glade night.

“Marcia,” proclaims a woman’s clarion voice from somewhere. “I think that’s enough rollinias for you, sweetie-sweet. Come back to the red pillars and see me.”

From the far distance comes a protesting, ghosting answer. “Mumma! We’re just putting the faces on the faery statues, and they want us to finish all their fruits. Anyway, I bet you’ve had too many smokes on the joints.”

From nearby Nivat, comes another woman’s humoured but stern injunction.

“Adults are allowed to do what they choose.”

Then follows a cheeky chorus of children’s screeches, in which Marcia is indistinguishable. “Alright! Alright then!”

A brief introductory mock-serious poem announces the next poet.

“The wrong person always winds up kissing everybody goodnight.

Always kissing everybody goodnight winds up the wrong person.

Kissing the wrong person goodnight always winds up everybody.

Everybody always winds up kissing the wrong person goodnight!”

There follows laughter and a great wave of whoops, ululations, calls, animal imitations and joyous screams. The bardess continues her enigmatic word play, and as the mood of the evening deepens Nivat proceeds along the conch parapet. Seeing no one in the cavern wings, he waits for the current bard's disturbing short stabs of words about destruction of the environment to be dissolved in applause, then climbs the last stair, greeted by his aboriginal precursor with a studied, deeply considered nod.

Nivat realises that the style of the evening is in succinctity, and consigning his planned ode to some distant time, instead puts on an artificially dramatic and woebegone voice which quakes forth:

"Mercenary, un-contrary...

Morel grimaces, feeling surly, although knowing he cannot blame his old perentie, Giggara, for that beast's reflexive nature — causing further insult to neck muscles already aching. Giggara had just lurched aside from Curlewalion's major and dusty arterial, his quick, twisting lunge snagging a plains bustard for delighted jaws three days without the taste of a large meal. The bustard is certainly that, yet beneath his tall rider, Gig reduces it to a limp bundle with a rapacity of chomps, and bolts the bird with an accompanying rumble of wind, while Morel probes what he is starting to think of as his poor neck to ensure it is still in place.

Because the wayfarer stations between the Om Trine and Ja Junction were overflowing with volunteers like themselves, journeying to flesh out Curlew's army, he and Tamziel had decided late the previous afternoon to seek out more romantic solace than the crammed bunkhouses could provide. Tamziel had insisted she knew of a flet quite nearby, and the prospect of sleeping on one of the spartan but comfortable tree platforms built by the servers of the seal had seemed a pleasant prospect to Morel.

Tamziel's navigating had brought them to the place with enough remaining light to discern that the palms, planted by the servers at all flet bases to provide thick, clean matting for the open weave platform atop each rope ladder, were missing from this site. Decimated by wild pigs, no doubt misbehaving due to their hunger in the strangely prolonged dry season.

They had used their saddle blankets to partly make up the shortfall, but by the time they had strung their mosquito net above the platform it was full dark in the fig tree, and romance had wandered elsewhere. A few whining pests came in through holes in their contraption, but when Morel flinched in the middle of the night and pulled the crawling thing from his ear, it inflicted an abysmally painful bite to a finger, and he had automatically flicked it away. The enraged and large ant stung what it landed on, which was the thigh of Tamziel, who was unconvinced the act was not revenge for her earlier circuitries of flet locating.

As he watches, she disappears into the distance of the road with a haughty cast to her features, while Morel convinces Gig that the reptile can digest and move forward, leather-bag limbs to follow. An hour past noon on this third day of their journey from Omnipotent, Morel catches up to Tamziel, only to taste her disgruntled disdain and be forced to ride on the other side of the road from her.

Dust and braying about eight kilometres on announce a gathering of the group responsible for maintaining the road — Donkey Charmers. The arterial is here a sandy plunge over the high flood-wash embankment of a riverbed, and at its steepest, the concourse is crammed with hundreds of donkeys. They are being made to walk slowly in harness, bracing the tension in great wooden turfers through which ropes play out, that in turn are hitched to a massive cart, descending in shuddering bursts. The Charmers' cart moves on rollers fashioned from trunks of trees and is crammed with their gear: rough-made saddles, tied bundles of dried vegetation, a giant straw effigy of a buffalo with an outsize crescent moon in lieu of horns, and numerous wooden chests.

The remnant of the cart's contents, numerous children and several elderly, mill about the hillside. Donkeys bray, as do their handlers, deep startling cries of vigour, man and woman. Many of the Charmers have one thing in physical common — they are mal-conformed.

Where five fingers should be, there are a miscellany of digits, where eyes should look forward, they are askew, or an arm is missing, a back bowed, a face hung without any of its muscles seemingly aware of its neighbours. Some shared osmosis had linked Curlewalion's early Charmers — those with genetic or radiation-induced birth defects who had migrated to the revolutionary land — in a seeking of further journey, to the margins of their new society. The spindrift of lonely wanderers in search for self-identity or an answer to fate had seeded and grown into a little band of roadside dwellers.

The simplicity of life travelling upon or pioneering the roads, Morel reflects, with their moods of shifting loneliness alternated by the diversion of passing travellers, had struck a chord with the Charmer's needs. Curlew's peoples had aided them to build homes, dubbing these smiling and different ones Charmers. Soon, strange sculptures and shrines had sprung up near the colourful abodes where wayfarers gladly left tribute.

In their self-imposed exile, time wrought of Curlewalion's physically disadvantaged an enigmatic and resourceful sub-cultural group which exploited a nomadic mainstay — a lifestyle liberating its followers to pursue the mystic revelation many sought. It was a group in powerful commune with the land's herds of donkeys and water buffalo that the Charmer's pastured in a semi-wild state. Some beasts such as these before Morel, the Charmers had domesticated to tend the nation's roads, and used when they wandered in from the plains to stay in their roadside houses. At this time they extended the sculptures of their shrines, structures that were both convolute and as simple as a mass of boulders around a fruit tree to protect it from grazers. The Charmers had raised countless young trees along the roads, lovingly watering them.

Morel greets a broad-backed boy his own age, questioning him as to the Charmers' movements, but receives only the rudimentary reply of a grin. The Omnipotentan is not surprised; the Charmers welcomed many with Down's syndrome to their tribe, and from these there often sprang gifted Indigos, normal in all ways save the dint of their mind's far reach. As Giggara sways in a contented waddle down the warm sand of the hillside, Morel notes that the cart they bypass is the same as he had seen the Charmers use in stabilising roads, their sheer weight crushing vegetation sprouted in the wet season. This one is without the winged blades with which they were often fitted to lift gutter silt.

It takes some ten lengths of his perentie to pass the vehicle, and at the last he sees one of the open chests is stacked with antique rifles and discerns what he had presumed firewood in piles beneath the dried fodder is, in fact, a numerous array of bows, fletches and quills. The Charmers are going to war!

Morel sights Tamziel at the base of the hill at the same moment he sees that another cart blocks the bridge across the river. There are hundreds of ass and buffalo milling behind it, and on the opposite hillside, a team of donkeys waiting to move the burden. Suddenly impatient at the delay, Tamziel nudges her mount into the wide, unrelenting flow of the river. A cry rises in Morel's throat as he kicks Gig to a gallop. Years ago he had seen at least one large croc in this waterway by the bridge, but as they reach the bank his imploration dies on his lips. On the far bank are some dozen Omnivoreans, their dyed orange faces and arms animated as they gather, feasting around a smoky fire.

It is obvious even from Morel's distance that their fare is a medium-sized crocodile. The carcass of another is strung from a nearby tree. Now the youth observes a party of river fishers slowly moving a net through the downstream current. The orange backs of their arms and short, sharpened clubs slung across their shoulders mark them, as much as the daringness of their hunt, as Omnivoreans. Each of them in the heavy midstream flow are harnessed back to another with an end of rope upon the bank.

For a people known to go many days without food of any kind as they watched the heavens through 'desert gateways', it was natural that when it was abundant they should pursue it single-mindedly. Crocodiles were taken also because of spiritual beliefs, and Omnivoreans would just as soon hunt them alone in turbid waters as join the netting. They believed they were already dead and would soon reincarnate on a golden planet they called Rustelie. It was their lore that to kill a crocodile would translate as great powers when they returned to the orange sphere of home, visible in the night sky only to those who had undergone the desert hardships.

The river before Morel, Amsequill Grey, is the last on the western edge of Omnivorean-sanctioned hunting grounds — Tamziel will be more than safe. Sighing, the youth plunges Gig into the flow, soon having to swim alongside to allow the lizard to cope with the fast water, in mirror of Tamziel up ahead. Being a strong swimmer, Morel draws quickly near her, the blue-gold current sweeping them downstream to a point half way between the hopeful hunters and the feasters back near the bridge. Inexplicably, Tamziel yelps, then disappears beneath the water. Morel's heart unconstricts as she bobs up again, swivelling her head frantically as her flaying arms drive her in a wide circle.

Sighting him, she yells, "It's alright. A snag. My foot." She goes partially under again, fighting to get the panic in control. "I don't know what I'm caught on," she laments, as Morel treads alongside her and the perenties pull themselves ashore. He dives, disgusted to find she is literally a victim of fashion.

"It's the cording, Tam," he splutters, "those ridiculous rope cordings you girls insist on bracketing onto your pants." He spits water, supporting her somewhat against the tug of the river by clenching the canvas of her shirt back.

"I've got to strip that gear from you; shouldn't have left the knives on the perries."

"Okay." Her smile is strained, but her panic subdued. Morel holds her against him as he winches down the pants, the shrunken material resisting his efforts. He digs his toes into the waist hem, pulling the canvas down over her lower thighs with his legs as he braces them both with one arm. Tamziel is pressed awkwardly against him, her hair and gasping mouth caught against his torso. He dives and yanks the incumbency over her knees and begins to lift each leg out of the material.

With a final jiggling of her trapped legs, he extricates her and soon they are ashore, Tamziel rubbing her current-strained calves. He looks across at her semi-naked predicament and they both giggle. By the time they follow the perenties' tracks up toward the Omnivorean's fire, they are in hysterics. In the distance, the kerfuffle of the cart moving still resounds. Morel studies Tamziel's thighs as they walk, trying to remember which was stung, but can see no welting.

Instead his gaze is caught by the pale scantling of wet calico affixed by a single waist string, rising in time with each step before pressing back against her mound. Tamziel, sensing his regard, gives a low, feeling-charged sigh and the next moment flings herself upon him in a smothering of kisses.

Between installments of her passion, she whispers, "You…rescued me…from …death."

They walk, half-entwined and oblivious, along the bank, as though one creature with three legs.

"I'm as cute as your dad?"

"No," she elocutes more clearly.

"Oh. Well, Tamzy, who's going to rescue you from me?"

Roaring, he scoops her into his arms, melding his hands into her waist where it is cinched against his own. They stagger on his two loyal props, become one breath of shared desire. Their beast of ardour comes to rest against the spongy bark of a melaleuca for a flurry of kisses before it stumbles giddily, Morel aiming for a half-glimpsed patch of sand on which to sprawl. Instead, he trips on the tail of a dozing perentie and they come down heavily, Tamziel underneath.

As though they have landed in a liquid sun, streams of orange erupt around them moments before wild laughter. They stand amid the gleaming-eyed watch of the Omnivorean group, Tamziel's legs and Morel's arms dripping with the orange dye from the mobile mixing pond into which they had fallen — the thick mixture intended to replenish the sacrament of the feasters before they continued to the capital. The lovers apologise and slip, part shocked and part mirth-filled, toward the road.

"Hey!" A woman calls, running after them with what Morel judges a fierce look. Gazing behind, he sees for the first time the spectacle that is become of Tamziel's derriere, now entirely a lurid orange.

"Hey." The woman calls sternly, catching up to them, seizing Tamziel's shoulder and yelling back to the others. "See, she is self-chosen as sacrifice. To uphold our law, tomorrow you shall be staked for bait in the river hunt at dawn, first to be given to any of our men, or women, who desire you!" She finishes in a zealous screech as Morel bristlingly interposes himself between the two.

"Over my dead..." he begins, as the woman doubles over laughing. The Omnivoreans are in uproar as the young pair retreat to their perenties. Among other oddities, the gold-faced ones are inveterate practical jokers.

Morel studies the delightful suffusion of tone in his now-clothed blonde lover's complexion while she excitedly details her theories about why the Donkey Charmers are sending such numbers to the war effort. Then he sees it again, the barest caress of disturbance through the high brown grass. Again comes the faintest riffle through the standing straw and Morel, all scanning-curiosity now, does not observe Tamziel's perturbed look at his disregard.

As they crest a rise, need for accusation or explanation is severed. Toward them rides a stalk unlike any that has ever been, staggering in its massing of martial power. Column after column of Unilion; hundreds. The pair can both discern the lion that slip as its innumerable vanguard through the roadside grass. The youths rein to one side of the track, instantly recognising the approaching lead rider, by dint of his infamy, to be the first white man to head the cult.

As his party of advance captains come alongside the youth ahead of the main stalk, all in the same pigskin shirt and pants and armed only with spears and knives, Morel sorrows that there is no sign of Cyskuah. That greatest Unilion of all legend was known by several distinguishments, including his gargantuan three-metre frame. The boy waves disconsolately and rides forward along the oncoming stalk.

His spirits soaring, he shyly smiles at the massive man sporting the very rare arming device of four extra knives slotted through his dreadlocks. The narrow tips of these daggers are let through holes in his ears, around which sheaths of flesh are fastened a tiny slip of intricately studded leather. Coupled with the burn scarring his left cheek, the ear knives seem to mark him as Musa, reputed by some to be as skilled as Cyskuah, though his choice of riding partner is questionable — a slight fellow with a pallid face who scribbles in a heavy book.

Morel risks greeting the warrior by name and receives in token a handshake and the information that the stalk is heading to his own land to rendezvous with still more Unilion and undertake a scouting operation. With a glad heart, Morel turns Griggara back down the road to Tamziel, secretly proud that she has not got into a tizzy over the hundreds of dreadlocked warriors riding by, as other girls her age might have done.

"There must be more than three hundred Unilion," she breathes, awed, as the column still passes. Indeed, the golden shapes fanning through the grass are uncountable.

"Pity the kangaroos around here." Morel jokes.

"Pity the soldiers of Austral."

After spending the fourth night of their travel sensibly bunked down at a wayfarer station, Morel and Tamziel are recompensed for their tribulative journey on their final bivouac, finding a delightful and deserted waterhole to camp by a few kilometres from the capital. In the morning they bathe while the waterfall-fed pool is still crisp, breakfasting on a regal selection of fruits, but with the haughty and youthful agreement that the foraging in Ja Junction is nowhere near as good as at home. Then they hurry away toward the landmark hills and the preparing Nine Radiances, due to begin in a few hours.

Over those hills, Morel knows, will gather this day the armies of Curlewlion. His mind thinks back, as their perenties swagger along the forested trail that hugs an often forking waterway, to the resistance against gnosis for open war which had peaked in Omnipotent after some particularly gory depictions by shrewd playwrights. A long crack had opened in his homeland's philosophical harmony, one which the Gaian Screamers and empaths had been unable to prevent becoming personal.

He himself had always been unflinching in his belief of the need for a pre-emptive strike, and though he had listened to all the rhetoric and angst that had come his way from those who argued for the integrity of non-aggressive protection of their homeland, his answer had been the same to all of them: that people are spirits and that all is spirit. That in such event it was not a personal issue to attack Austral, merely an influx of pure spirit to preserve the destiny of the larger vehicles of the human race and the planet through which that spirit must flow — that it was egotism and cowardice to reduce a necessary balancing back to individual points of flesh.

Once over the fluted hills, the Omnipotentans find themselves in an ineluctable flow of humanity all moving toward a distant valley bowl dotted with great marquees and hover-props several hectares across, built for battle in the tireless pantechnicons of Omnibus. As they pass a huddle of gnarly grey heads idling beneath some trees while their horses graze, Morel catches threads of their conversation.

"…not that I'd have doubted a million."

"… done right. Get two million and it will be. And two's what we'll…"

The youth had never thought of what scale the war would take. He knows the population of his nation is over ninety million, but a million soldiers seems an impossible amount. Lower down the valley, pressed everywhere by strangers, he relents on his math.

Nervously, he observes to Tamziel, "It looks as if they've had a lot of goats here recently."

A nearby man speaks an answer to Morel: "A very great lot of goats, man. We shifted 'em out of here for the radiances, but usually they give us milk enough for all the Junction children to get their calcium. Wizard to meet you. Trobitt."

It is hard to place exactly where the man introducing himself — rich amber skin speckled black as though by a flicked brush, the trick perfected in the eyes — might have ancestry. But the short, stocky-built man with the cherubim cheeks and thin pate is undoubtedly of Unipean origin. He laconically steers them into a marquee and ladles three cups of shineark from an agitator brazier. They sip as they are squeezed slowly out by the relentless flow in. Out in the sun, the bells on the high-topped staves of Donkey Charmers gleam. Morel peers amid shoulders. He glimpses Wild Angels, their mirrored coats reversed in wait for the Moon, but their mocking, miming manner present. He can hear the twisting, sonically-cut cries of Gaian Screamer, though sees no sign of grass gown or birdskull circlet amid the press. A man walking strange, metered circles with horns of shell on his head piques Morel's intrigue.

"Mangrove Assurants," their self-possessed guide informs them. "Won't be battling due to their fondness for circles, but good souls. Let's catch the Khorustaming."

305

He leads them to a phenomenally large playing of the craft. A countless mill of people spinning over each other's heads and leaping, flopping, bluff-kicking, flat-hand punching, perhaps not as syncopatedly as Morel's home group, but in a huger writhe of chaos than he has ever dreamed of tackling. Tamziel and Trobitt slip into the maelstrom and as Morel edges to one side, he instinctively obeys a command to 'grab my hand' and is suddenly flipped through the air to be caught atop a human tower. Just as abruptly he falls as one of the bottom supports is knocked over, but they reform amid leaping attacks from other towers, and Morel loses himself in the game.

A voice founts simultaneously from a thousand solarmill speakers hooked to pavilions.

"My name is Furrow. I head external security for our nation. Well, I guess that we couldn't leave it all up to the Lion of Lion to just sweep aside our opposition when in less than two days they begin that grainy episode in our lives known as war. This is not an unprovoked attack by us, nor moralistic. As you know, a mutant nuclear program has been unearthed in South Austral with us as its intended guinea-piggery. This is a matter of survival.

"Those who can gauge such things tell me two millions are now here gathered at the second ever Nine Radiances. Among you are four hundred thousand who will attack Austral hedging bases across our border shortly after Unilion strike. Fifty thousand of you will follow on the heels of the Unilion, charged with communications sabotage operations as the Fist of our brave Mist. Roughly twenty-five thousand will be eligible as Vengers and be entrusted the levitant devices of war that Curlewlion possesses.

"Pending success of the border-base engagements, two forces of six hundred thousand will form each arm of a split coastal assault on ASA's Base Hamper and Base Constrain. Given that there comes backlash in Austral itself, and a world resistance response, the chance of success in this endeavour remains. In addition to these more active militant aspects, fifty thousand Indigo Mantles are volunteered to travel split among the forces; at present these same maintain a complete psychic blockade over the nation. If there is an Austral spy here, you had best start running to get your news through.

"Twenty-five thousand of you will also be selected for armed medi-vac detail. That leaves three hundred thousand — and that is exactly what we shall do. That number shall remain here — a well-armed and coordinated rear-guard dispersed across Curlewalion in case of snake bite. For all of you, some who will be leaving in a few hours, others who will train here for some days, may your gods protect. The process we now undertake is to determine the makeup of Curlewlion's companies, each of ten thousand people.

In order to find which Totem Company is yours and for whom you will fight, be you Venger, Medi-vac or ground force, we call upon the Nine Radiances. The ritual was used here one hundred and fifteen years ago to determine which founding refugees would settle where, although obviously we deal with greater numbers today. An accident of miraculous wonder happened during the radiances, for which they were named and which, judging by the earnestness of the children who have been preparing for days, you will observe again today. I ask you to cast aside pre-convictions of who you might fight beside, and open your hearts to the process. I give you Lucella Gendellwarry."

The strident tones of the self-styled faery godmother of Ja Junction are not unknown outside the capital. Morel is surprised it is not Tacleara that will have the final word, but happy to hear Lucella's legendarily bizarre voice for the first time. The New Guinean lady affects an immediate lightening of the mood.

"So's, people. What we's go'n' to do is have fun now. Ya! There's no winners, same's no losers. You's got to find the group you feel happy dyin'.... I means fightin' in. So. You's see those coupla hundred furry critures?"

At that instant, vast effigies of animals and birds and reptiles are raised on stilt scaffolding, a pelican towering above Morel to peer soulfully along its bill at him.

"You's got to walk roun' where you's feel you's should be. We is needin' ten thousand to get in roun' each critcher and give 'em a big hug. If we is countin' that number, the critcher's go'n' disappear show they's full. But…also, kids go'n' come along you know. 'La, la, la, I is borned already from my magic that makes me walk', sayin' allsortsa strange things an' this time, you's really can run away from them! They'll be carrying red banners. If one touches, you's gotta turn left, (they'll scream to anyhow). If you's try to dodge it, gotta turn right. That's the game. So you's decide which critcher feels right an' in fifteen seconds kids go'n' come. Noddle. Nooooodle — go!"

Morel heads toward the large dingo, but from out of the scales of a taipan come children in a line, laughing and singing. He rushes to the right to avoid the banner and observes the first of the radiances. Purple light forms around the children and settles in lumps upon the ground so that their incandescing trails will lead them back to where they came from.

Chapter 16

It's better to die on your feet
Than live on your knees.
Peter Garrett, musical artist and final prime-minister of Australia.

Nivat can barely conceive words for the smother of detritus and bizarre pulses of grainy light pushing against the hemp mask and his firmly closed eyelids, a fact that harries his artistic pride. He would so love to lyricise their five-kilometre crossing of the border storms on their third-last day of existence. None of the volunteers of the Totem Companies knew the storms would soon wink out, the knowledge considered too important to risk reaching Austral ears. Only the Homager and the Lion of Lion knew the storms would end because the Others — the Enyadding — did not have the strength for their own imminent retreat and Curlew's defences. Most Mist who had been trusted with the knowledge the storms would fail believed it was due to the Indigos who maintained them being sent to war.

After another eternity, Mako's voice announces heavily, "We're almost through." The crushing, lurching constriction is gone and Nivat removes his and Sanfel's dust masks, drinking in the dull panorama of night over desert South Austral. Musa unbinds his pride's masks and ensures the four Indigos and their perenties are hale before he moves the group forward at a trot behind the fanned out members of Pride Xanthus. The stealthy advance party of Curlew's army, eight hundred Unilion, each with a compliment of their pride and several Indigos, had individually entered the storms evenly dispersed across the border. Their charge was to destroy all South Austral scouting ground infrastructure and hover patrols, then rendezvous with the coastal attacks.

An hour later, lizard and lion steeds have traversed twenty-five kilometres of flat ground, and Nivat has scribbled a satisfactory account of their accomplishment, the colour of the stars and other bardic details.

Fiayrs, a gracile Indigo, holds her head and exclaims, "Hover patrol! Three pilots, twelve crew, one minute, eight o'clock."

"Okay, bring them down," instructs Musa. "If they're part of a bigger force, they'll be back to haunt us soon enough, and if not, they won't be missed for a good while."

In the distance appear three hovers. Simultaneously they crash and explode. The Korean, Mako, rubs his head and smiles grimly at Nivat as they continue. After another five kilometres it is clear there is no larger party. They come to an area more densely treed. Musa halts them and rides Marisk, his black Ra-king, eastward, all the cats following him except a lioness who stands beside Sanfel. Nivat watches Mako sip from his jacket straw and the dial on the cuff spin to show the remnant litreage.

Musa comes back, saying softly, "There's a bunker back there. Any of you able to get your mind underground?"

The aged Roland says he may, depending on zinc impregnations, and Musa does not object as Nivat nudges Sanfel after the men. The bard cannot tell where his brother's poised form is focused, only that it must be somewhere between the two crawl-stalking lion, as he asks Roland to "entice one out for a bit of air".

The greyhead's mirror-pool face glaciates with concentration as the two lion inch nearer the other. In minutes, peering around the tree he hides behind, Nivat sees a head and torso emerge from the ground. Musa silently charges the scanning figure, reaching the hatch as the cats drag their trophy from it, and disappears underground in a dive down the hole. After some minutes the Unilion emerges from a hatch further along the copse and wipes his knife on a tree.

As they ride back to the Indigos, Nivat asks, "How did you go?"

"I went growl," replies his brother. "If there were more than a dozen, then they were poorly trained."

Towards dawn the perenties, sluggish from cold, are halted and wrapped in thermal acu-point blankets. The Indigoes lie in the solar sheets from their ration pipes, charged for an hour during the previous day. Nivat guiltily reaches into his own pipe for the thin concession to technology. Only the day before, Musa had strenuously reiterated that any whiff of modern gadgetry would be likely to disturb the lion.

Shumbril, the African radiotelekinesist, leaps up. "Automnals. Fifty units. Four hover scans closing in five minutes."

Musa moves among his cats, fiddling with their jaws. "Well, you guys can't help," he observes to the Indigos. "Fit your TMJs over the head and back, tree your perenties, and lay low."

Nivat watches the Unilion's hand flash from a small pouch and into his Ra-king's mouth. The hollowed diamonds are an exact fit for Sanfel's four lead molars and good use for the gem cache entrusted to the Lion of Lion after personal possession of any mined substance was banned. The bard shrugs out his spear, and Sanfel looks a question at Musa.

"Oh, alright. But I shan't give any ode if you depart us."

They meet the first of the artificial life just before the hover scans spot them and make an eager beeline their way. The automns assume pairings, breaking toward the brothers at increasing speed. Musa kicks a rock up into his hand as Marisk hastens his pace in counterpoint, and flicks it casually to explode an automn's head. Nivat steers Sanfel wide, pursued by two hover scans.

Like bulky antique model planes with a span about three metres squared, the robotised hovers have a laser on each wing. Two automns crouch to target the pair, but three lionesses barrel into them, crunching through the stabiliser stow above the left hip before skipping back to cover, leaving the artificial intelligences with their chemical blood gushing out.

Nivat jumps from Sanfel, hand-springing into a high left twist to avoid the strafing lasers of the banking hover scans. Suraque, the third male of the pride, charges from the side, leaping at the slowly turning hovers. He pulls one down, and the other careers toward the trees. Nivat sprints after it; jumps antelope-like from a log and kicks it hurtling into the dirt. He rolls, warming intuitively and physically to the fight, as two laser rays intersect where his head might otherwise have been.

The bard props behind a tree, watching Musa and Marisk dance aside, under fire from two remaining scans. Musa spears one irritatedly, pulling out his skewer as Marisk rips a wing from the other. The Unilion charges at the automn pairs herded into a group of less than twenty by the side-striking lions. His spear pins a pair together, a knife takes a third, and Nivat is overjoyed to be able to trot from cover and plant his spear into the head of another. As Musa closes on the middle of the group, the bard sees Marisk's claws streak out, and the Unilion smash and kick the plastic heads from shoulders, so that the neck cabling comes pouring out. Soon there are only smoking automns and Musa's lamentations for a warped knife.

"Doesn't that hurt your feet?" Nivat asks, retrieving his spear. His brother, like all his cult, wore only pigskin moccasins.

"Yep. Like poetry hurts your brain. Everyone's fine except little Camsay…" the huge, sweating man stoops to apply some salve to the foot of a sleek, gangly-framed lioness,"...but the toe will mend. Let's get some shut-eye."

"I hope they've done their job and androids don't swarm up out of the ground from the direction we've come."

Tamziel addresses her lover vaguely, but he knows of what she speaks. "Man, you gammon Zeil? Those Unilion eat, like, charcoal breakfast and dream dine. Sixty thousand Mist and Fist crossed the storms as well. It's 'automnals', anyway!"

Morel and the girl have the bouncy, playful nature common to Omnipotentans, perhaps due the locale's affinity with the Gaian Aboriginal Merger, but today they will fight under the banner of the Eel Company. Their standard flaps close to them, and its glistening teeth and scales gleam in the noon sun. There is an eel fashioned onto the helmet of the Mist Commander standing by the two Unilion up near the props' pilots.

"It's weird," Morel says. "Everyone here's sort of eely. Like us, I guess." The two are indeed lithe and wiry.

Tamziel looks around. It is true. Their companions are sinewy and tall, displaying many darting eyes and strong necks of different design. The border storm rolls mutely into itself before them. Shudderingly, all three hover-props halt side by side and land. Muffled screams and explosions come from the foreground. Morel squeezes her shoulders firmly, then paces to claim a wattle tree to piss on. He looks across at the preparing lines of the Plover Company: tall, solid, already frenetic in laughing chatter like their namesake.

Beyond them, he can see the Curlew Company, marching with discipline up to join the Plover. He had been tempted, three nights ago, to stay in that group; just so he could fight amid the most beautiful women he had ever seen. As he had looked at the congregated inquisitive pastel faces with their huge eyes, an Indigo had served wise counsel upon him with a phlegmatic comment and he had moved on. Ironically, Curlew Company would attack the same base as him.

The hover-props of Eel and Rock Wallaby Company are stacking against each other in the form of a low, interlinked triangle. Plover Company's prop now locks to the fore of this hollow, creating two forward oblique openings where the heavy ballistics gather, the same augmentation achieved at rear by the Curlew prop. Many Vengers are checking over their machines as Morel ducks inside the defensive cave, just ahead of the Curlew and Plover Companies. Inside, luminates glow along the three-metre thick, core-diamondised roof, as do screens, showing the imminent battle landscape; the border storm.

Tamziel and Morel calmly check over their arsenal and supply. A short-range laser and its crystal clip. A sling shot. A detonby. A transposable material unit currently in the form of shoes that will absorb a blast from a mine. A first-aid kit, the mainstay of which is bandages: vege film for wrapping around laser burns to seal out oxygen. A ration pipe containing a solar sheet, a combat staff and the nine days' ration provided against need of retreat. Last are the water flask, water jacket, gas mask and aerosoled personal arsenic dispenser. Jamie, the Mist Commander, had told them that if they were captured, they would wish they had remembered to use it.

The youths exchange a long hug, sloshing in awkward silence. On the screens, the first of the Vengers — Curlew Company hover-bikers — disappear into the border storm. Those of the other companies follow, swallowed by the grey static.

Then, abruptly, they are visible, along with the glistening hovers, crustaceal missile towers and bioform domes of the Austral base. Explosions boom but fizzle on the algalate domes, though a missile tower topples dramatically before return fire smashes deafeningly onto the hover-props. Hundreds of Curlew and Plover ground troops charge the mile-distant base. The screens show a line of Vengers electrocuted and the plummeting ruin of them and their bikes. Any following riders suffer the same or shy away from the danger.

"Good," he hears Jamie affirm, and his puzzled look rewards him the aside from a Plover threading his way to battle.

"It means the Australs are expecting a sky-borne assault."

Morel studies the screens. Two Unilion are shown charging out, trailed by their stalks, their spears and the claws of their Ra-kings needling into a group of fleeing solders before they move on a distant automn mass. It will be some time before Jamie mobilises him; she has only just signalled for the first of the Eel Company to attack. Nevertheless, he fits his earplugs and recalls Tamziel to hers.

Many Curlewalion troops are cut down by sniping from the towers, but now four cumbersome bolt hovers — heavily armoured cones with a tiny cockpit and a massive missile shaft — patiently align two towers, stalling right at the edge of the hover netting. After several shots they bring the high ASA positions down. One of the bolt hovers escapes the vengeance of the other dozen still-standing towers to bob back to the props for rearming. The ground assault moves faster, though beset by automnals that seem to arise from the ground.

Morel's second glimpse reveals a briefly opening metal hatch spilling plastic. One screen shows a Curlew Company woman, well aware of the ploy, skim her detonby past an emerging automn to explode underground. The youth sees a Mist runner from Jamie heading over to his block of fifty. They are ordered out, and in a whipping scurry of lizards, he and Tamziel are thundering out with the others.

The fifty eel riders wheel their perenties as one toward a pack of automnal dogs. Morel, feeling light-headed, scoops up a rock to display improvisation to would-be watchers and slingshots an artificial beast. The strike makes no impact whatever. When a plate on its head spins in a roaring whir that would be deafening but for his earplugs, Morel scrabbles for his laser and drops his assailant in a little pile of flame. As his perentie spins to thrash into the pack with its tail, he draws his combat staff.

He slips from the saddle, standing his ground to puncture the plasmic stow nourishing two of the speeding four-legged automns, hit by the blood and dim cries of resistance from his companions. He glimpses a leaping abomination to his left, but the neck of his perentie smashes down onto the fake dog, and the youth smashes its pinned plastic spine. The cavalry is re-mounting — a medi-vac team waved away by the Eel-fighters — their ten fallen comrades far beyond repair, though five of the riderless lizards are hale enough to send skittering back to the props.

In a minute the group is within sight of the detritus of bikes and scorched bodies marking the hover netting. Suddenly, a cloud of hover-bikes streaks in two lines straight through the mesh, dropping from on high. The rigorous silked frames of their riders bespell Agents as surely as their knowledge of the computerised shifting openings in the netting marks them enemies. The lines thunder dementedly overhead, splitting as they turn, to better bombard the whole group. As Morel races toward the gap beneath the hover netting, which he keeps assuring himself is there, few of his companions are with him, and Tamziel is gone from sight.

There is a mounting drumming behind, a vibration that shakes the ground. He turns to be swept up in another wave of Eel riders, rushing along with them beneath the net. Morel's backward glimpse had also shown the lines of mounted Agents being decimated by Eel Vengers in hover-packs. From behind an earth-covered pantechnicon, a metallic black triangle rises, then wings silently toward them, blazing death from its lasers amid man and beast, scorching the sand beneath the youth.

As the Sacubus is forced to turn sharply to fell a prototype hover car kitted to support a Venger's laz-cannon, Morel sees two Curlew Company women in their grey and brown fatigues sail out of thin air, bump across each black wing, and slide off the Sacubus, arms back-swinging to balance the ten-metre fall. The youth prays they survive the debris raining down on them from the ship torn apart by their detonbys. The Eel block quickly regroups, and Morel skids in beside a still safe Tamziel as they weave under the largest remaining tower, ducking laser fire.

A black-maned lion soars straight over the pair and rolls in a pile of automns, Tamziel firing a clean shot into the melee back over her shoulder as they come before the main battle of the Eel Company. Several blocks of their comrades are entrenched on either embankment thrown up to make the tunnel cleaving between them. It is obviously an old work, excavation supporting stubborn mulga along the slopes of tailing. Before the tunnel opening, sealed with massive concrete doors arched to fifty feet-like jaws of some monstrous bi-valve creature, mill hundreds of Eel and Plover fighters, as well as a Unilion.

Morel flops onto an embankment, firing at soldiers dug into the lower ground and the periodic close approach of jeeps. Detonbys explode behind him, and he sees saboteurs rushing to lay more charges through the thick dust. A group of Agents cad by on bikes, high and swerving to avoid reprisal as they drop grenades of their own among the Curlewalions. Another group streaks in lower, lasering blocks of his kin on the other embankment, then gaining the cover of the decline behind the tunnel roof. Morel rolls onto his perentie and spurs it along the embankment ridge, galloping to the peak just as the four bikes come back around from behind the tunnel's roof.

The perentie rears smoothly to rake its claws along the carriage of the lead bike, Morel springing out from the saddle and up as the lizard tumbles down the slope. The Omnipotentan dangles his legs into the head of a surprised female Agent, and is slammed sideways with the impact, but manages to blast a few rays into another bike as he corkscrews through the air, landing almost atop his perentie.

Bruised but elated, Morel rides back onto the other embankment, his praise for his strained steed becoming a curse at the sight of a helicopter hurling toward a group of Eel-fighters and a few exhausted lion fending off an automn mass. He discerns that the detonbys have still not cracked the tunnel doors. Following the helicopter comes a Sacubus, and the Eel soldiers flee back toward their perenties, leaving the lion naked amid the surging automns. Morel and others on the embankments fire desperately at the chopper, but its strafing bullets tear into the fleeing Eel-fighters.

317

Suddenly, the chopper slams down amid the automns, two remaining lion wearying out from beneath it. The unexpected friendly fire of the Sacubus recalls to Morel the marvellous skill of the hidden Indigos, but then he observes that a standard for Curlew Company descends from the triangle's landing rail — so Curlew Company had captured one mid-air. Behind the cockpit silicon, an indistinct figure gestures severely for those in the tunnel foyer to disperse. They hasten to the sidelines.

Missiles from the shimmery black craft thud into the concrete, finally shattering it. As the dust begins to clear, the Unilion, gesturing back his Ra-king, runs into the crater. A minute later he vaults onto his loyal mount, his hands butterflying rapidly to either side, screaming, "Retreat!"

Morel turns his perentie, as a Behemoth tank lumbers out from the tunnel and absorbs two missiles from the Sacubus. As the pirated craft ascends, the youth stares spellbound, though most of the Eel-fighters race away toward the cover of a downed ballistics tower.

It is only after a white burst from the Behemoth's lower pneumatic gun obliterates the Sacubus, and the tank rolls forward over the helicopter wreckage pursued by automns clustered in hundreds around their massive avatar, that Morel reins his lizard back along the slope. Just as he is about to cut for cover, the Omnipotentan sees the Unilion ambush the automn rear-guard and become embroiled in a seethe of plastic.

The youth plunges his lizard straight back down the embankment, pulping his staff into the chest cavity of a plasticised soldier, cracking it like a nut. Old Giggara rams down two automns with his head, and Morel impales one of the fallen, coming to ground and blasting a way forward for his perentie to thrash through as he turns to kick and jab the other automn's afferential cord. With his staff swirling in one hand and his blaster fevered in the other, Morel runs, trips, struggles up to see Giggara slain, and is slammed by an automn hand. A dagger streaks by, and he crawls toward the grisly cover of his perentie to watch the balance of the automns jauntily pursue the disappearing tank. Before him lies the silent face of the Unilion, each hand around a throat of two stilled automns pulled into his dust.

Morel has failed. Exhausted, he mouths sorry to the black and gold lion that limps about the twisted pile of dozens of automns, its jaws silencing any electrical intelligence still struggling. Suddenly fire rips along its coat, and Morel pales as another group of two dozen automns emerge from the tunnel. He leaps over the lizard carcass, stuffs his shoes into the transposable material clip and fires a gooey web that ensnares half the automns with its sticky filaments. At the same moment his right arm disintegrates, and Morel falls, inert with shock, as the automns thud by.

Conscious, but paralysed by pain, he wills death to find him. Instead a medi-vac team pull him on board and race toward the hover prop shelter, forcing him to drink and remove his earplugs so they can mouth senseless words at him. Dreamily, Morel observes the last big ballistics tower as they speed under it. Numerous forms descend on little ropes, some lasered by Agents while others swing on their snagging grapples, continuously spiralling scores of metres down the metal scaffolding to finally freefall the last ten metres or so out away from the tower.

As they pull under the prop's protection, the dull roar of the toppling tower does not disturb the subdued mood within. Two hundred Fist ring a group of Mist, Mantles and Indigoes. The youth hears Jamie's voice from the heavily guarded huddle.

"If that's the last of the choppers, will you make an attempt on the bio-domes?"

A man with a Unipean accent replies. "There's no point. But some of the damaged Sacubus might be vulnerable."

"Okay. Well, their Behemoth is down, but you guys need to keep chipping away…"

The painkillers in Morel's blood take him far from Mist intrigues. He awakens to the beaming face of Tamziel.

"Hey. They've taken over the bio-forms! The ASA soldiers and officiary have surrendered, though the Affiliates fought to the end. It's over, Morel, we've won!"

We won, Morel thinks syrupishly. He reaches to hug his girl. Remembering, he changes to the left arm.

We've won.

Nivat is amazed at how well his brother hides his impatience. The four perenties are still too sluggish, despite their acu-point blankets, to travel. The Indigoes brushing their gear into shape, or sitting to the last of breakfast beside a tiny fire, seem of more vital carriage, their faces less pocked and scored by pressure. Dawn had been and gone for well over an hour until at last the lizards had begun to thaw.

"How are they going?" Musa asks the psychics.

Nivat knows full well he doesn't mean the reptiles: could not have cared if they sprouted extra heads.

"We haven't heard anything more, which I assume means the Mantles are engaged in combat, or..." Mako's answer hangs above the note of despair.

Half an hour ago, Musa had been ecstatic with the news from Shumbril, the radio telekinesist, that Curlew victory over seventeen border bases was complete, one battle was undecided and two Curlewalion forces in rout due to a huge Miomich presence at the bases concerned. Fifteen minutes prior, Roland had received an aid call from some of his psychic brethren who were accompanying a trapped Fist group under fierce duress from the enemy ten kilometres to their south-east.

320

The cats are stretching and rumbling in empathetic angst with Musa, diamonds showing in their gaping, restive jaws. The Unilion announces to Nivat, "I knew they were fooling themselves." The Mist's choice of scudder had been controversial among the Unilion. They argued the thick bi-wheeled bikes gave no accelerative option for retreats and no performance in steep country. The Mist were insistent. The silent bikes were the perfect workhorses for the gear needed to bring down the radar towers, and in drifts of tens were small enough to be untraceable by their prey. Their superior pace to perenties was obvious.

Finally, the Indigos arise on their steeds and Musa drives them and Pride Xanthus at a gallop south. Nivat feels Sanfel's muscles beneath him steeling for the battle he must have scented, rumoured by the distant cloud of fork-tailed kites. Even the bard wonders what the Mist had been thinking as they crest the last ridge before the siege. It is apparent from a wrecked radar tower on one high dune that its three undamaged lookalikes had also been intended Mist targets. They had left their scudders and a rear-guard of half to either side of a vege-fuel estate, claiming most of the flat plain amid the steep dune systems.

A litter of automns and Fist to the north shows where one rear-guard flank had been decimated, forcing the whole group to hide in dunes. They are now dragooned between the estate's perimeter fencing, along which cadets cram. Agents snipe from the high dunes. No doubt there are several heavily armed estate guards amid the dunes over which three estate choppers buzz. A platoon of desert soldiers, comprised equally of man and plastic, closes the trap around the sand hills in which the Curlewalions are being steadily massacred.

Nivat knows that Shumbril and the other three Indigoes, having delivered their close-range mind blows, would be hastily construing a TMJ shield. Austral soldiers posted to seal the battle perimeter had been felled by the psychics to allow Pride Xanthus in, and as Sanfel blares down the dune, the bard hopes there are still other Indigoes left alive that their four might concert with. Musa had ordered young Camsay, whose paw was still troubled, to guard them lest anything stumbled their way. The rest of the pride splays out before the bard, drawing the first unsteady fire from the Austral desert company. Nivat wants to shut his eyes. The stalk looks like raindrops about to hit a weir.

Pride Xanthus is dauntless. Possibly the most cohesive and disciplined in all of Curlew's justice cult, they fall first upon the desert-trained humans with lethal ingenuity. Each lead lioness bounds to strike, surging implacably on, maiming as many as three soldiers every two bounds. The beasts behind use their jaws economically to deal death to the fallen while extending their own knifed punches in a wider reach of despair.

Into the panicked confusion, Marisk barges, Musa's knife work keeping his Ra-king free to surge up the dune to where his spear sticks out of a high ranked target. The warrior wrenches his weapon from the corpse without pause, Marisk streaming toward the perimeter fence as the Unilion looks back over his shoulder at the combat swamping Saraque and the dozen lionesses. Musa whirls a knife into a bulky soldier steadying to target a visible cat, and satisfied, dips over the dune crest.

Inspired, Nivat lays tilted backward in the saddle as Sanfel rends his way toward Saraque. The bard hamstrings at least three pairs of running legs as a lioness leaps he and Sanfel. The animal and crunches into an automnal about to fire. Nivat's spear splices into a soldier targeting a lioness, and he leaves Sanfel to his werewolferies, joisting himself over the dune top to land spreadeagled on a laz-cannon mount that his suspicions had correctly targeted.

Nivat floors the operator, palm to nose, whirls in back-kicking a close assailant, then trains the weapon on a group of cadets attempting to intercept his brother and the three cats that flank him. The bard locks the cannon on charge and back-flips into a running group of soldiers, diving aside as the overworked weapon explodes.

Standing, he sees Musa lead a trine of cats over the fuel estate fence, and several lionesses pour down his side of the dune. Two estate guards, gleaming in coppery uniform, jog along the dune, and prop to target Nivat before seeing better quarry. They rivet a lioness with the intersecting rays of their sawn-off lasers. Nivat hurtles into them and stabs wildly, clobbered to earth but weaving up to stab again. Sanfel finds him staring bleakly at the dead guard's blood on his blade, and his Ra-king arrows him away, knife and claw gaining them the dune top below the fence.

The bard looks back down on the battle field, seeing the Fist retreating with determination toward the fence, covered by another pride just breaking on the platoon's western forces. The cadets are shuffling into a tight group along the enclosure, and Nivat cannot win past them to the hole in the wire mesh through which the Fist stream. Sanfel bears him to the side fence, leaping its three metres of razored steel onto a low roof immediately within. Nivat scans the fuel estate, gratefully registering that no earth wall has been raised around it; the encircling dunes obviously thought enough to abate smashloosers.

As he mentally urges his Ra-king in the direction he guesses the security building to be, he sees a helicopter plummet above the scrub and the barest glimpse of a spear protruding from its fuel tank. They cut through the scruffy windbreak, passing silos and processing sheds, and then spy a building below a small radar tower. Nivat plunges Sanfel straight through its green-glassed window and knifes the dismayed guard before he can pull the trigger of his raised sawn-off. The bard watches screens blink out as he lasers the circuitry interconnecting the estate's cameras and sensors.

Some of these show tantalising images of the Fist, rallying now that they hold flat ground. By the time the pair finish severing the security link, and skirt past the reservoir cisterns and through the hem of meagre scrub surrounding the celluripe crop to the new site of battle, the helicopters have been vanquished. The transposable material junctures have lived up to their press; a wreck near Nivat flaunts countless TMJ strands on its rotary blades.

Thwarted, the isolated ASA groups in the vicinity of the perimeter fence become incendiary for the Khorustaming forms of the Fist, which ignite upon the cramped battle sites like tinderwick. As lion resweep the hesitating, officerless cadet lines, they throw up hands, eyes glazing at the jarring roars. Unilion flicker through the hastily rent fence. The Austral retreat is a rout.

When all is accounted for, over three of the five hundred Fist and Mist are slain, the twelve Indigos among them. Resin of Pride Xanthus will no longer bear her diamonds into battle, and Pride Dios, in the dune rally, had lost two lionesses to the same laz-cannon. The Unilion and Mist meet in one of the guard rooms next to that interring the seventy cadet prisoners. No one seems to notice Nivat's frenzied writing.

Jiatara, Mist Commander, re-iterates her position. "You need only be here a day and a half, tops. Once the last Miomich held base is sorted out, there'll be hover forms bringing twenty thousand Curlew border reserve through here."

"Battle at Hamper will have begun by then," observes lanky Wudjina coolly, the last to arrive at the battle scene, himself a late arrival to Curlew from New Guinea.

"Which is why we have to keep bringing towers down. No one knows where automatically deployed missiles might be. We have to take down every radar to ensure Curlew even makes the coast."

"As soon as those soldiers relay news of us from their bivouac, Affiliates'll napalm this whole damn farm rather than leave it to us." Musa asserts.

"We don't think so, my friend," says eastern Unipean, Antorsi. "The vegi-fuel is too important for the choppers, not to mention the big ocean stows, for them to raze this place. We think they'll send whatever else is at the bivouac, four or five hundred. You guys will love it. Come on, someone's got to watch the forty wounded Fist and prisoners. Help us here."

Musa, Wudina and Kasbit confer and grudgingly give assent that the Mist depart. They leave behind many scudders, although twenty are filled by estate workers eager to support the cause. As the afternoon progresses, Nivat joins the other thirty workers, Indigos and wounded Fist in the storage basement. While he sits at his journal, he feels unnerved by the workers, mostly silent or uttering loud laughter about nothing. Roland had assured the bard that their statements of support for Curlew were genuine. *Why wouldn't they be?* Nivat thinks, putting down his pen. *Abrasioned skin and frayed nerves seems their only reward from years of service for South Austral.*

It is dark outside when screams and the thrum of laser fire come dimly through the earth. Around dusk, the platoons from the nearby desert base arrive. It seemed this quadrant of ASA defence had been exhausted of helicopters, for the re-punitive Austral force had come on foot, jogging to the accompaniment of hover-bikes.

Pride Quingan lion, hidden about the warehouses, slip from the shadows to disembody the unfortunate soldiers scouting within reach of discovering the basement hideout. Nivat presumes the same safeguard was in place around the cadet prisoners, though Musa had suggested he might just free them. Nivat would not wish to be soldier or Agent out there.

It takes the bard a while to determine where he is that morning as light falls through the loading trapdoor. He rolls from his solar sheet in time to see Wudina tramp bloody pools to the sink and emerge, after a long wash, still red tinged, owed to the bruises and welts all over him. Nivat shares porridge and a conversation of iron glances with him, before the Unilion disappears back to battle.

Musa follows the ritual shortly after. The bard has never known the man so tired.

"What's happening out there?"

"There's a group of plains wallaby already snuck through the fence to graze, crazy buggers."

"And?"

"And. People dying, knives getting blunt."

Musa takes a bamboo pipe, weed and matches from a satchel and puffs deeply, quickly emptying the pipe and returning all to bag as he steps to the trapdoor.

'Wish me forgetting,' he says, billowing smoke, his words burring in the thick blue stream that rushes through them.

Nivat spends the morning playing cards with two young worker lads. He loses badly through constant wondering whether to burst to the aid of the Unilion. About noon, the hatch stirs and a young Curlewalion soldier ushers them out to lunch. He tells Nivat they have evac'ed Wudina, his legs broken by a falling hover bike. Otherwise they have buried four hundred and seventy ASA personnel, the battle having finished before their arrival.

Nivat secretes himself in the abandoned celluripe field to record the epic deed. It is a grizzly poem and as he looks over it, he is glad for the distraction of Luvi, one of his card partners, offering to show him around.

Expecting a tour of the harvest machines or oil plant, Nivat is surprised when Luvi leads him some kilometres out the north gate.

"Well," he offers by way of explanation, "you know if the hover-props that transport the oil all fail, the government made a way to get it to the coast. Even if no haulers are able to get through, they can still get the oil out to the cities. Ah, this is it." Luvi stops by a strange algalate encrustation along the ground, rising a bit like a soufflé. After digging his arms into the sand in several places, he smiles. "They said the levers are always there somewhere."

The algalate folds back, dimly revealing stairs descending into darkness. Nivat follows Luvi down and hears him push something unyielding. Light springs from the ceiling.

"The sleds make the light," the youth explains, pushing a wide wheeled sled slowly along the tracks in which its wheels rest. Soon there is an obstruction of metal, with another lever, in the tracks. Just as well, for the drop in tunnel, revealed by what the light shows of it, is steep.

"One day I'll ride you," the youth says, slowly pulling the sled back up the tracks.

As they return to the estate, Luvi explains the tunnels descend some ten kilometres, relying on perfect design for inertia to carry the sleds back to the surface. At that stage a smaller tunnel accommodated a pedi-plane that was 'sledded' on its wheels to be vaulted high into the sky at the tunnel's end. Pedal power could carry the planes nearly a hundred kilometres, and they were equipped with a lode ore to trigger an indicator of where the next tunnel system lay. There were also mirror tunnels running the other direction to return the planes. All of the sled sections, geared to access natural high points of land for the plane launches, were spaced well within the descent arcs of the planes. Someone had certainly tested and planned the system, unused for decades.

In the common room Musa bitterly informs his brother he will turn for home, being unable to cover the thousand kilometres and more to the coast in the time necessary to have an impact at Hamper. He is grieving for this and for the death of Resin.

Nivat waits a while, considering the restrictions of the cult regarding the use of technology. Then he describes to Musa the tunnels, sleds and planes made from celluripe, powered by pedalling, and asks if such would constitute technology. In fifteen minutes, Musa has arranged for Pride Xanthus to journey back with Kasbit and in half an hour the two brothers are speeding, with the backswept muzzles of their Ra-kings illuminated by the kinetic lighting, deep through the earth beneath South Austral.

The emergency delivery system is failsafe. They make the coast range in two days, snagging excellent game for the cats, and as they camp the second evening by the last pedi-plane tunnel, the buzz of helicopters in the foothills reminds Nivat that tomorrow they face no unprepared desert force, but a vital muscle of the W.A.R. sneer. In the breaking dawn, as Musa pilots them in a slow spiral down from the great height of the range, they see a Sacubus some kilometres away, but if it notices them, it has more pressing victims.

"I was thinking," Musa says as they come through thick clouds, and the ocean and naval base appears below, along with the sprawl slightly inland of Hamper's martial might. "All those dispossessed faces at the fuel estate…like slaves. If we get through this, I want to press to Byron. All those revolutionaries dying along the coast have never even savoured freedom. It feels like a betrayal."

An incendiary explodes off their left wing, but Musa rights the pedi-plane as Nivat mentally prepares. He sees distant flashfire, the Curlewalion Navy's grim exchange. The amazed faces of a squad of hover bike Agents turn to them, along with yellow ripples of hastily directed rays — quick laser bursts as they screech past. Fire ignites in the vegetable panels comprising the plane. Nivat can see what has stalled the Curlew army on one side of the earthen wall and trench that marks the Hamper perimeter. Every time troops cross ditch and wall, they are swept aside by an intricate tunnel system of armoured tubing able to extend out of the ground at points of weakness amid the Curlew Force.

"I'm going to try and shut it down," Musa yells above the clamour of battle, squinting through the smoke. "If I don't see you at the hover-props, head south. Our Ra-kings will find each other."

With that, the warrior and Marisk leap from one side of the burning craft and Nivat and Sanfel from the other, the bard silently opining that there is no muse for miracles.

Chapter 17

The little group sits facing each other steeped in a muddied, acrimonious mood, the oppressive atmosphere mirrored by the tight canopy of macadamia leaves, monotone green above them. The whine of harvest robots carries from somewhere in the orchard, and except for the idle sparring of the marrankur lying in the leaf drifts, silence prevails. Between the twelve Enyadding, psychic counsel rages.

"I think knowledge of Enanyetam's double betrayal must lead us urgently to one question. Where now to proceed?" Lornahe supplies.

"Surely we must join the others at the venom-line. For a hundred or a thousand years we might hide in some northern fastness, but the armies of the Serpent would roll over us at the last."

"Jouflaeght thinks truly. Maybe the others are right and Aruan may yet hold some key. I remember you yourself, Lornahe, once ventured that it was prophecy flawed by interpretation," intercedes Rillarbar.

"We have seen of what perversity is the blood of the father made." This from Kumarren.

"There is also his mother's blood in him," Rillarbar counters. So through dusk and into the dark, whilst the marrankur restlessly gobble orchard rats, the counsel continues, before the dozen immortals move.

"We should help them," Rillarbar hisses imploringly. From atop Fadtown Private Hospital, the Enyadding look across to revolutionaries fighting and falling across the torn periphery of the Affiliate building. A smouldering tank mars the flowing lawns. Agents steadily slaughter the rebelling mass.

"We instigated this. For nothing. Nothing at all."

"Enanyetam's actions today would have provoked general uprising, regardless of our designs. Verily is this his battle," Lornahe hedges.

Low to the roof to avoid randomly strobing laser bursts, Rillarbar thrills to see the dissidents storm the Agency, but shortly he is aghast at the gruesome vengeance which sears through their retreat. He Mend maps the machinations of the Realliance for escape.

"Come. We must aid them. These are true spirits of this land. It cannot be coincidence that we are come in time and can cuspidate."

Lornahe rolls from the roof edge onto her back, murmuring, "It does not much matter now, but if we are to act, it can be only to alleviate the closeness of their pursuit. Our energy and time is needed if we are to make the rendezvous two weeks hence on the venom-line."

"Your point is valid. Then let us act as we may."

Rillarbar and Iskamorb crouch at the rooftop edge, high as they dare reveal themselves to stray laser fire, waiting for each of the others to make a body and mind link behind them. They are twin foci of the cuspidate and Rillarbar intensely watches the sky through which helicopters ferry the remnant Realliance away from the Affiliate building.

As he prepares to empty his mind for his strike, one thought keeps recurring to the Enyadding. Iskamorb had that day journeyed to see, with his own eyes, the sculptured cocoon that had precluded their interview with the fireseer.

"Is there no doubt that the material was condensed of antiquated star fibres?"

"None, my friend."

"Then he must have traded firefeather to receive such gifting. There is no telling what they will do with it, but I suspect they may fall against us."

Truly, all seems lost to Rillarbar, though his channel of the group's power is as precise as Iskamorb's, The two pursuing helicopters plummet, their pilots dead.

The tree canopies above the ridge bend in the wind, but no breeze reaches Sway where she sits near Alawry and Seffern, closely savouring a stash of edible berries from her wakening forage. It is a wonder of the age-fire, Rulsert had explained, that wind which travelled across its shared plane was transmuted simply into deeper purification of the water in the spring.

Sway considers the effort which had been extended for the maintenance of this refuge and hence the prolonging of her life. In particular she marvels at the picture Brawyndy had sketched in response to her morning's question. Sway had known that the Iridestine site could not truly be toxic. It seemed Aruan's father, on his self-imposed exile, had forged some contact among the mortal world.

Of course she had known at once the Piercing name, yet could embrace only tenuously three generations of the family having acted as the fireseer's worldly reach, labouring to screen this Iridestine from human trespass.

Brawyndy's second-hand tale passed on to her the rare meeting with Boabben in desert country, since the seer himself had relocated an age-fire here after prophesying it would be needed for the future defeat of the Serpent. A later vision stipulating Sway's role in the battle, and that she might be found first at the government planning tower and then at the gardens, had reconfirmed the critical necessity that the relocated age-fires remain intact as secure places of retreat. Initially, Piercing's ancestors had ensured the Iridestine's sanctity in the bounds of a farm run solely for that purpose. Franzus Piercing, buff-cheeked tycoon she knew from the papers, had inherited the land with all Piercing assets.

He had applied for the development of thirty Rightings on the land, minutes from the city with an ideal view as it was.

By ensuring compulsory soil testing for environmental hazards was conducted under his own wing, Franzus had tailored a court result to show massive poisoning of sub-strata. He had forced a backlash by protesting the building restriction in court, where it was ruled the site be excised from human usage for two centuries. Not even the Densitution in the valley fold could burst its seams up into the gully. For all his efforts to maintain the two Iridestines, it strikes Sway as perplexing that Boabben's sanctuaries have been little used by the Enyadding over the centuries. Brawyndy reported they had used this Iridestine twice, and three times the garden site. It was almost as if Boabben's efforts had been solely to secure her own safety.

Sway consciously immunises herself to thoughts of the monumental forces at play around her, mentally recharging with colour visualisation and intuitive bridging via memory retrieval. Afterwards, she naps in the spring sun, waking intermittently amid the subdued mood of the Enyadding, their farewell dirges mourning into her rest. She joins Brawyndy at the pool, both bathing unselfconsciously, feet settling into the stony sand of its shelf. The immortal, seeing her scrub the wild berry stains on her palms, advises Sway the spring will fulfil her bodily needs, no matter how long they remain here.

Sway fills her belly with the water and feels no hunger as sleep approaches again, but a mineral vitality, as though she were enwombed within the planet. Next morning the inky-haired warrior flows easily between her combat forms, feeling supremely flexible and enterprising a whole new ground sweep that gives her defending leg an extra kick. Fortified, she joins Luracet and Brawyndy on a slope upwards of the pool, where the immortal women sit amid a remnant patch of rainforest, the aubergine leaves and teal trunks of its trees unknown to Sway. Brawyndy nods repeatedly at her in calculating approval, and Luracet's smile is broad as they bask in the healing current of the day.

After a while, Luracet gently telepaths to Sway, 'It is not that I fear the ears of others, only that we hope you can get used to this mode of mind. Tomorrow, our hejir will take our feet toward Addlable. Twice this length more we must then go to reach our brethren, in convergence on the venom-line. Among them are many who will be ill-disposed to Aruan's efforts and your part therein, yet meet we must. This is the final battle. These things each you know, save the notion of 'venom-line'.

"This warped energy you are, however, aware of. It crosses the site of nuclear weaponry testing undertaken more than two-and-a-half centuries gone by. Tests we did not know the danger of until it was too late to warn the tribes, though our number has been few enough to offer them more than cosmetic aid these last long years. The modern association for this energy path is that it dissects the land and naval base known as Mjölni, each the vastest of their kind on this world. There is, in these happenstances, no coincidence. It is along this line, reaching far out to sea, that the Serpent sinks its venom. Long has he wrapped his malice along this great ley, the resultant bruising of the land undermining the nearby Iridestine balances to the point of collapse.

"The energy link of violence it taps is great, feeding on the electrolytic fluxes of the radars, prison screens, autoginisers, ground flares, as well as the massed combat hype of soldier drills. We estimate that using this link alone, the Serpent will be able to ingest the Aleris in less than a month. And yet the venom-line, greatest strength of the Serpent, is also its greatest weakness. It believes we cannot directly attack it along the line, where it bulks no pre-warning defence, knowing our spear would almost certainly be unmasked by the many monitors of war at Mjölnir and that then its instruments would obliterate us.

The looming Curlewalion-Austral war may give us this slim thread of hope — that the base's inner defences will be obscufated and that machinery and personnel will be drawn off, weakening the Serpent's core strength. If we can gain the line at its most direct point, we should need only some few hours to sunder its writhe forever. Tomorrow we shall leave, Sway. Enjoy the Iridesce spring, harbour your strength. The future's buds curl each around madness."

"It is not all doom and gloom. Though mostly," Brawyndy professes. "And even near the end of the world, a mortal still must eat. Be assured, true-heart, tomorrow when danger is gone, I shall take you hunting with the marrankur. It is un-sooth to be matching against monsters with only water in one's belly, no matter how good the liquid."

The thick blanket of forest around the reservoir looms at last toward them, their pursuing Affiliate hovers long since lost to the dark. As the choppers whir to stillness on the dam wall, Jania and the other Indigoes crowd cautiously at the hatchway. Keevan herds the able-limbed among the Realliance around each machine, exhorting a last effort from his troops for the night, as the composited steel is cast from the spillway on a final brief flight. The Affiliate pilots are steered, still witless, along the wall and out into the jungle by the silent command of Jania's group, taking over from the Curlew enthrallers.

Lou comes alongside Keevan, jiggles his rocket launcher back around his shoulder and presses his leader's hand firmly.

"A victorious defeat, me mate. You all done well."

"Maybe. Can you take first shift on the battery with the rear-guard?" Keevan looks over the sandbagged gun mount surrounding the hatch. "There may be a few hovers heading by shortly."

After thus ensuring an Affiliate deterrent, Keevan follows the other escapees down into the wall honeycombs.

It is not until morning that forces mount against them; ground troops on either flank of the wall and a floating armoured pontoon. The Affiliate, unable to risk damage to the reservoir wall, lose most of their soldiers and the pontoon before they hit on the idea, late at night, of using a mechanised floating arm to sweep the defence structure aside. The rebels in their seized crypt watch as, one by one, the outer wall, sluice and sub-surface cameras are disconnected by automns. Dawn yields a grim forecast for the Realliance. A ragged laser cut incises the hatch, and automns flow at the heavily defended entryway, repelled for nearly two hours by defenders in a haze of gas and smoke; the whining cyber-mechanoids seeming to bemoan the ban on their macroflex weaponry

Keevan pulls his contingency behind the second hatch, closing it with a determined slam on an automn's leg. Each minute of the next set of hours seems seconds, as the cutting crew pry away the next obstruction. Keevan knows they can hold them longer in the tortuous passages between the second and third hatches. As the carbonised plastic faces leer through the rent in the defence, the defenders share a likeness to trapped rabbits.

Sway feels the silk protective against her; insulation from the lick of frost below Alawry's paws, thanks to the alchemical repairs Aruan had performed beside the age-fire hours past. Silk is no protection against the soul-sapping ugliness of the execrations from mines, garbage ingestor ponds and Remnants dotting the land — and no shield at all against her heart, keenly aware that every inch northward brings Mendez closer.

Saraedjul, in limbed stride beside her, is a model of calm forbearance, only her loin covered, feather cloak now rolled tightly across her shoulders in readiness for battle. Sobering, Sway realises that there is little to allay the throbbing of the immortals' great hearts, unless it is she herself. In mid-afternoon they stop on the edge of a sprawling reserve of low mountains, a banner of the wild lucratively stocked with kangaroos for tourist cameras and pay trails for rich walkers.

The group separates to hunt, and Sway and Brawyndy soon find themselves amid plump game. Sway apologises to the kangaroo spirit as she kindles a fire, then cuts a haunch from each of the marrankurs' kills. The solid nourishment is good, but there is desert still to cross, and water reserves that should be plentiful in the river basin here are a dubious prospect already. Brawyndy creases her face in elemental commune; the theme of water shortage lies as silent between them as the river's voice in the desolate cascades.

"It is strange," Brawyndy murmurs at last. "A week ago the marrankur bathed and drank along this course."

Sway is mildly comforted by the glugging skin across her back, and turning from studying the scummed diggings of kangaroos in the river bed, she finishes her meat, thinking that at least there is no point her pining for a dash of salt.

"We lost them."

The words are shards of ice to Slitter, wrapped in the warm solicitude of the campaign trail and delicious scheming. He cracks his gloved fist into the face of the tech Agent and hurls him from the hover form, stalled at its maximum height of a kilometre, blasting laser fire into the screaming man as he falls. As the Poise One turns to the nearest tech, the woman qualifies, "We've temporarily recorded a misalignment between geographic data and precise placing of the terrorists."

Slitter is confident they will find them. Two nights prior, The Poise had demanded all Agents return to their precincts, broaching news of uprisings in Fadtown and Byron. He had robbed Slitter of a chance to catch the girl, but perhaps had also afforded the second Affiliate Command an opportunity. The aural sub-imagers had snagged the crafty terrorists on the move this morning. Perhaps those enigmas would lead him to a bigger prize.

Already he had the marsupial body, and the autopsy revelations of glandular anomaly had stirred a clamour for funding to build coercive automns from Slitter's bio-gene department. That reminds Emmanuel of The Poise again, only this morning carping about an invasion of Curlewalions and his desire that Slitter shore up the border-base defences. Activating his robo-secretary, he brings the face of the Resonance up on screen.

"I want you to focus the study of your idiocy on one thing today. Ensure all border bases are hover-netted. That's all."

The Poise One gazes out at the clear blue sky, willing the refugee army attack.

"Sir, we've found them again."

Slitter nods. He feels he can live another century and a half given this type of thrill. Somewhere out there his hover forms are tracking the strange terrorists' signals. He has spread the fleet thinly in case his quarry's ability to foil sensory pursuit extends to some aptitude for long-range psychic viewing. Even if it does, they will not be looking at the height of a thousand metres; grav-judge ruled out a hover's functioning above three hundred metres really, though his could squeeze another twenty-five centimetres from the drives. Slitter watches the tech crews move slowly out, distending across the screen, and brings up the Acadabourne squadron leader on his comlink. He is to be reserved in the very distant background for now, but Emmanuel will have need of a ground force soon.

"Bring your three thousand on, slow and steady. We don't want to spook the game."

The gathered group moves even quicker now, the marrankur surging into the dusk. Sway is glad night hides the scar waves tormenting the land. For a while they are plagued by sonorous bellowing of haulers blaring down their sand-blown haulways. By morning they have reached a silent desert, and all their eyes nervously regard the stark tracks of smashloosers; land torn to the quick by the hungry winds.

Before dusk next day, the group reach the Murray River, not far from Addlable. There is no need to brave a public bridge. The river is bare and its mud a hard enough pan to support the broad pads of the marrankur. As the Lellying gather on its far bank, agape at the river's parched carcass, Aruan announces, "We are pursued."

Rulsert speaks for them all, his words distracted. "We must anyway seek the rock-shelf waters. The land there is intricate and perhaps we may lose them."

"Perhaps. Perhaps I shall fill the river with fire to halt them," broods Fire's Whim.

The group is constrained after the strange spectre and grim jest. Brawyndy, twisting her hands and smiling blandly as she strides alongside Sway, says, "Our newest enemy is wily indeed."

Angelo stalks back toward the old freeway tunnel. Half of the survivors from the beach and twenty of their new allies await. Placern and Quorce are near-invisible, and silent as always in the laneway shadows beside him. A toothy grin betrays Napirya's deep shadow on the clothing seller's other flank. The aboriginal has full reason to be pleased. Their mission had been a success, a subtle rewiring enough to electrocute every person crossing the hover-stack roof — Quorce pulling the bodies out of sight, unseen by ground security, over an hour that had yielded a litter of corpses. These are times in which it pays not to feel compulsion to visit an Affiliate Social Club. They are times of blood, Angelo reasons, as are all those that affront guerrilla groups.

Beneath a massed tangle of orchard prunings, along the wall of some buried building, through dirt tunnels reinforced by metal, they come slithering and groping to the town home of the Welving. The old tunnel is dimly lit. A wash of voices shares in the success of the returned demolition groups, who have destroyed a factory and a veg-elec line. Angelo is heartened. The chaos of this night will provide ample distraction for the Welving guides, with their innate streamlined cunning, to find a way through the security cordons and bring the knot of a hundred rebels to the reservoir. If Keevan's group still lives, three nights after their retreat, dawn will bring them fresh hope.

A Welving woman moves about distributing soup with precise actions, and shortly the gathering is served. A young rebel is talking with one of the rare teenage Welving — only select among the mystic warriors, he knows, have left their forest home. Angelo listens in on their exchange, eyes steaming around his food.

"So you can just call up the trees to attack Fadtown?"

"Narry. Trees be movin' of their own hungers. We be seeing a pattern, feel what they're feeling, and it's like they take only food that's adrenal-charged and soul-decayed, like those dupes from the beach. Maybe they smash the automn to get at the silica in them."

"So they feed on chemicals released by the Riven?"

"Yes, something in people like that is nutrient they need to be able to move."

"How is it they can move, and how can they strike as one with you?"

"We are not sure, but trees have always moved. Their branches, their feelings, their dreams. We are allied to them, so maybe they gauge our need for aid. The strange thing is that the trees are moving but the dryads yet sleep. When I soothed, Dakini was certainly in the clouds, so…"

Angelo turns from their banter, considering their elstworldly new allies and the events of the past two days. After arranging for hovers to carry the wounded to the healing retreat of their mountain territories, each of forty of the Welving guerrillas had taken half-a-dozen rebels across the hinterland towards Fadtown. En route, the parties had surreptitiously laid booby traps, undermined small hover-stack foundations, or broken down fences in reformation camps, orchestrating the first guerrilla resistance to the W.A.R. government and its loyal Austral citizenry.

The picture Angelo had received from Quorce regarding the secretive Welving called to mind a group of white aboriginals. Their inception had begun with the prophecies of an immortal red-haired Irishman with a tall frame. The translations of these by Nancy Welving had stipulated self-memory as enabling Earth's destiny, as well as a coming time of suppression for which the group had long prepared. It had been begun by Nancy's three children as an art commune, but its members were able to live confluently with nature by dint of rigorous training over generations.

"Then we are brothers," Angelo had beamed, expounding his tale of rapturous meeting with the immortal. Quorce had listened in a wondering envy, but supplied that they were more like cousins. With a primitive sort of pride, he had qualified that the Welving could go without water and food for days, remaining completely still, halt all animal poisons within their cells and practice conscious dislocation of every ligament. They had followed the message of the convict — 'Boabben', Quorce had named him — for three centuries.

Looking around at those Welving here, Angelo sees they have reason to be proud. Never idle, they have cleared away dinner, replaced the cooking area with bedding and are treating the tired muscles of the rebels with precise stimulation of pressure points. Quorce comes to sit alongside the tailor-poet, an arm around his shoulder such as is their token for friendship. From a neck pouch he takes and blithely chews a little charcoal. Ingesting it is daily ritual, to show that the fire never goes out, merely within, but the sacred stuff is issued extensively, particularly for camouflage. Angelo embraces the image of dark being made light in some hidden alchemy — the shadows of the world's dream have come forward to fight at this transient point in time, and he can believe all who seek to shine are mere facets of some crystal from the deep.

She sniffs the air as some general of old, caught behind enemy lines might have done — long and calculating. Foremost of her kind for almost two thousand kilometres, she shakes from the cliff face and hears the stony dirt crash from her body — brachiated muscles of lichen wrapped in a fungoid skin harder than horn — into the valley below. As the dryagon spirals before the rock face which she has lain behind for many millennia, she recognises emotions: great rage that has compounded for three centuries against the humans, and a dawning worry. Something had caused the trees to stir, to risk themselves against the machines of man.

Her twenty-five metre long articulated wings unfurl with a sudden snap of purpose. There on the plain lies the city of man. *Let them not have hurt any of her trees.* Her gigantic square jaws grind, spurning the thought as she powers through the gash in the forest rent by the plummet of a river she can thrice recall changing its bed. The golden leaves of her eyes glint in unexpected welcome of pleasure. Detouring from her flight of wrath, the dryagon plunges to the floor of the valley and seizes two of the unnatural ones, mid-rut, in the fortress of each claw. The creature's dark skin begins to infuse with pink as the photosensitive organisms drink a charge of starlight.

As she swoops over the hills, the minor glare of suburbia stabs her eyes, and she drops her burden to shade them.

The Giditteas roll along the top of one of the strange caves as the dryagon passes on. Let them return to the lands which birthed them. Now to find the things that should not fly, should not roar in the air and disturb nature's kingdom…

Calliope's focus shifts between the beer in her hand and her husband on television. She does not even bring the drama of jealousy to her high-cheeked, classically beautiful American face as she watches Rick, in his role as Gibbon, wrap his hands beneath the waist of a bathing-costumed blonde — even though ostensibly, none of the characters in the serial, *Clearwater People*, are acting. The world's most successful television show is ad-libbed between its characters' real life profiles. Rick and she had been relocated here from the States on the strength of his flagging surf career and continuing performances of rock and roll at various clubs. These were the qualities he had injected into the show, aside from a natural attraction for blondes.

Calliope mainly keeps the show on for the too-loud background music of the torn, soulful, slighted lover type, sourced from the last millennium, that is its unvarying accompaniment. The noise drowns out the hinterland's suburbia. Though theirs is a large, open home, finished in cedar and boasting twenty-four hour holographic gardens, the area abutting it is for secondary production, mostly factories pandering to *Clearwater People*'s needs. Show business has literally carved a nook for itself: accommodation for stars nuzzling uneasily into the squalid, obdurate Remnants, home factories, knock shops and residences for soldiers. Outside is a constant ferment, but Calliope wonders if the guard on her door is to keep it out or her in.

She hears the clang of the automated garbage truck a second before a bill for their week's groceries and a receipt marked 'Valid Rubbish Tabulation' slides from the slot in the phonet. There is a little note on the bottom saying that Fadtown Security Office is closed and to use the one in Ballina. As she files the note in with the weekly security information, she reflects that things seem on the blink at the moment. There is no longer water in the taps and they have been dry showering for days. She wonders what people drink who have no Clearwater goons to bring them bottled supplies.

Her lifestyle is enviable, she knows, but somehow falsity seems to pervade its glamour and abundance. Days on the beach, when Rick deigns to take her to work with him, she is filmed as an extra on the most exclusive set in the world. Even the markets, with their colour and bustle, are a controlled representation of the idea of freedom. She accepts there are pockets of great beauty left in this land, more than in the States, but at least back home nobody pretended things weren't grimly moribund.

Calliope finds herself wondering about Curlewalion again, if things could be any better up there. From news reports it seems others have wondered the same thing; local insurgency causing minor damage and some human deaths over a couple of days. Anita Morass had been injured filming Blue Brigaders responding to a riot of skit-warped teenagers on the beach. It had looked serious to Calliope. The phonet was down all over the hinterland, and access to either Fadtown or Byron was prohibited. Various media conjectured the government had withdrawn stored water in preparation for war.

She switches off the television and stands before the wall-length window, pulling chestnut hair into a bun to discern the sounds of the night. There it comes again. A woman's agonised screaming. Now a man's. Dogs bark and houndings erupt as the distance pronounces screams and gun blasts. Something has engulfed the whole suburb in its frenzy. She hears Dan, the door security, curse, then laser fire flares, and something hits the decking.

Peering past the curtains, she sees a pool of blood roiling from the stump where Dan's neck should be. The shape of something massive, dog-like, but not quite, flits across the street. In her shock she has a moment of clarity, gauging that the Gidittea she has just seen could cause a social boiling pot to overspill. She begins her own chaos workshop, screaming and crying alternately, the illusion of a suburban housewife tearing away from her.

After a few minutes she takes a deep draught from her beer, reaches across the counter for her lipstick and applies it to the viscous skin of the television set, spelling out, "Dear Rick. Have an unreal life."

Clenching her fists in a final triumphing over doubt, she opens the door to a world of shambling forms, dim screams, and broken souls. Shunning the hover, she picks up Dan's laser and begins walking. If there is a revolution out there, she thinks, it is in the distant mountains, though truly revolution is within. She swings onto a greenway, her shadow following curiously in the streetlight pools

Chapter 18

Furrow receives the news of the last two border bases' capitulation as a spirit of merciful transport, his trepidation able to spill to other concerns as the messenger's perentie clacks from the Common Tryst. The vast open hall is barred to all but those pertinent to turning the wheels of the war, and with the retraction of the border storms, is heavily guarded. Triple the number of Indigo Mantles that usually attend Homagers are scattered in pairs, silent and watchful as the geckoes adhere to the roof battens.

The natty campaigner studies the computer imagery. Their clean sweep in commandeering the border bases will certainly slow most attacks rolling toward Curlew from the desert. Those last two bases had been wrestled at some cost from the grasp of the W.A.R. government.

The Miomichs — ASA-trained psychics defending them — had been stronger than imagined, and while he and thousands of other powerful Indigoes had forged a way to overthrow the Cabbals killing all unprotected Curlewalions within ten kilometres of the bases, their skills had been unable to protect Curlew. The two ASA base commanders, frustrated at the troops pouring through the breaches left by destruction of their thought soldiers, had fired a parting shot of ten self-guided missiles upon Curlewalion. Only one was stopped, reportedly by a young girl using radio-telekinesis in her dreams.

Without satellite guiding, none of the warheads found serious targets — the permanent energy cogitator and dense urban zones were unscathed — but their distance programs were accurate. Early yesterday two had exploded visibly on the edge of the Magician's Apprentice, a bluff with minaret-like features at the northern end of the lagoon. Five became craters of smashed trees somewhere. Of the remaining two, one had collapsed a hill onto a road bank, and one had brought a cliff wall down onto a Zen temple.

The security bulwark has only just returned, hovering hurriedly back from Solana, and he sweeps a jumble of missives together, noting his computer indicates the commandeered hover netting fully in place around Omnipotent, Omnivore and Omnibus urban centres. The only notes of interest come from Unilion — one reporting a rumour of massing vessels in the pirate peninsula, and one commenting that all seemed predictably chaotic in the banished lands.

Furrow didn't like to think of the Unilion riding through the banished lands, where every rock could hide a home-made gun, every bird whistle could be signal to a pack of lurking desperadoes. But then, Furrow didn't like to think of the Lion of Lion at all right now. Two days ago, Cyskuah, their leader in Lans' absence, had shambled into Solana on his huge, sable Ra-king, Forego, both bearing ghastly wounds. The Sectariat's sisters sewed, bandaged, splinted, and prayed to the stars. Forego did not survive, but the lacerated aboriginal did, perhaps due to the olivacea grafted to his laser-fried back. When Furrow arrived, the old sea-dog had been more laconic than usual, understanding that desire for retribution kept the colossal warrior alive and hoping, through brusqueness, to maintain the Unilion's resolute wrath without risk of distracting him with human affinities.

Cyskuah was having his bullets out, using only a marijuana anaesthetic, as was the Unilion way. His unsmashed eye engaging Furrow, brown iris in deep red retina, he had rumbled with memory and reported the culmination of his three-week chase.

"We found out they were using a tunnel system, you know, the renegade murderers. Suddenly looking like a guild of maniacs when a whole bunch of them rampaged through Wurpitta, and dragged people down to the library catacombs. Anyway, after watching a couple of days, Forego and Crane and I caught one of them coming out of a tunnel. The rat wouldn't squeak, even with Forego roaring

346

in his face, so we buried our first man and thought about that tunnel for a day. The librarians were hostage or something within, so we didn't know how the tunnels ran, but we decided to risk it.

"Four of us dropped in while the others waited with the cats on the porch. Eventually, we met the reception committee just as we came to the opening into the main basement. We struck back around a bend in the tunnel when the laser fire started and they sort of swaggered down after us and learned that a Unilion spear can curve around any bend — which not many survive to tell their families at dreamdine. There were another four behind the spear cushions, and I had to deflect some good shots with my knife as we charged, but we all gained the basement.

"Down there were a heap of neurology artefacts. Enough to fuddle the head-goo of ten thousand gimps. That explained the fast shooting in the tunnel, I thought. Sure enough we found electric adrenal units, nano party balloons, and fight-suit cell clip horrors; all the stuff that's banned in Austral. Anyway, we went up and cased the library, expecting a solid sort of stoush, but there was nothing: no hostages even.

"Takika and Bodra and Cholas brought their cats through the front door, and all of us poking around in the basement soon found six more tunnels. They were wide, heading deep from the look of the slope. We ate, then I gave the nod. We got one tunnel for each stalk. My cats started to get hackly after a few kilometres, so I blew some smoke rings. At ten we hit this sort of human robotoid zombie lair.

"I could see people passing casually in the far distance of the chambers, so I spotted that for bedrooms. Right in the middle a vast screen was broadcasting colours and number codes and a heap of zombies were entranced like it was old Spielberg or something. Others of them were trying on different lady zombies while watching this colour kit slowly modulate and I saw — to the right of the cavern — a lowered area with just the heads of cybernetic humans in combat practice. Anyway, no one was watching me, even the big guy who looked the most focused and was probably meant to be minding the tunnel.

"I suppose I should have pulled back, but I wanted a look behind the curtaining at the left, and I really didn't want any of these chumps free to sneak out of their tunnels while we reinforced. So I asked the big guy for directions, and when he turned around, I put a knife through his eye. He didn't fall quietly. He starts bellowing and striding around trying to pull my blade from his brain. Forego brought him down, and I wrenched my knife back as this guy just keeps groaning, and the zombies turn to find the cats in mid-leap among them.

"One of them sort of flashed copies of herself all around her real body but it didn't interrupt Pynge's focus. Another sproings out a barbed tail as she goes down, and I flash Corrie to get out of there but the tail went through her leg in trade for his jugular. That's the first time I've seen a cat hit in a brawl when it's not tired. Suddenly, I wondered how the pride would like the zombies, but had to keep moving toward the cybernecks because they were well aware of me by now.

"Five of them come up with metal scalps, all clacking these glitzy arm swords out through the muscle wall, so I hit one on the head with my spear, like a drum, and when they came running along, all miffed, I pushed them past with snorkel holes in their livers. A laser snuck down at me from a little alcove, so I lost my main knife, and then this clown came tumbling at me with big, doggy teeth, like that was supposed to upset my spear work.

"Next a guy starts spitting his teeth at me and one got in under my guard, just missing the wrist vein, but my spear didn't miss and I whirled into two fight-suited lasses who did some pretty improbable kicks, thanks to all the nerve-conduited sensor loops. They eluded my spear a minute, by which time the stalk was in trouble.

"Lunatics were running onto lion jaws and paws and just not letting go. The cats were getting stymied by a burden of grasping cyber-fingers. Young

Transom died with metal in his heart from this fellow like a praying mantis, with great, jumping barbs for legs and a sort of extra-swivelling, sharpened wrist bone. He hopped around with my spear, and I ran to the melee to kick aside the big guy from the tunnel who didn't know he was dead.

"Forego bore me up, and we harrowed their masses awhile as my ear knives came out. I slit the huge screen and struck a match to the fluid that spewed out, and I hope that was distraction enough for some of the stalk to escape. I ordered retreat, and Forego and I were already fleeing through the curtained area toward a likely tunnel behind. Before we were out, I saw their experimentation zone — and they didn't just cut up willing initiates. There were bound forms being milked, of who knows what, down there.

"Up top were a few supply birds, some mules, a little camp on rough ground, nothing that would be too obvious from the air. The goons there didn't even pause before laser beams came flying off them. They were half-robotic reflex for sure, and we both got hit, then we had to evade a chase from a couple of their sharp-shooters, who were luckily dull."

Furrow had asked Cyskuah what the total gathered numbers were likely to be, but the big man shook his head.

"Say a thousand at each cavern, that would make six, plus supplies, contacts. We would have thinned that, but maybe seven or eight thousand still."

"So, up to eight thousand cybernetically enhanced enemies beneath their very feet. Alright, palanquin, I'll deal with it."

"It's Unilion business. Ravella will handle it." The man's face twinged, from what Furrow suspected was some tearing wound, as he sat up to catch the security adviser's eye.

Furrow didn't like the risk — the young deputy, Ravella, had made two mistakes Furrow could recall — but he could not gainsay that eye of dry earth.

"He'll have to take a hundred Unilion and leave fast."

"He rode at the head of a hundred and fifty yesterday."

"So be it. We wait."

Cyskuah grunted a token of conclusion.

Furrow thermal-moulds the screen before him, trying to configure the new Curlew advance positions, but he is distracted. Neither Saliska or Tacleara had fronted for his arranged meeting two days ago. One part of him desperately wants Lans to return and pull the Unilion out. Another part considers his coastal rear-guard of twenty-five thousand and wants to deploy them for Solana. He need focus. He needs to provide a disciplined model in the atmosphere of uncertainty and strain suffocating the Homager, so it can manage the nation's utility.

Tacleara, who might have driven off the accusative and wounded mood blighting the seven, has inexplicably disappeared. Lans may be alive or dead, and with Saliska gone AWOL as well, he is the last adviser his people have. Turning from the tantalising reflection of his camp bed on the computer screen, Furrow moves about the night, discussing issues of workshop supplies, checking on the quality of perentie saddles and dried food bound for border bases, and pushing shineark beneath Doherty's nose where the woman is slumped in tabulating figures of war-wounded.

Saliska awakens again, vomits, and drifts back into self-recriminations about her choices. The radio-telekinest had monitored the lower Lullarelly green section for a day and a half, as Tacleara had asked, especially Merion Farmer's holding. There had been strange things in the airwaves, subtly frequenced, but definitely there. Conversations with automns over the sea, image compunction lever snares, with their invidious alpha rhythms wrapped around a single ego's overt suggestion — Merion's. There was Daguerette spore flashing all over the deep-psyche, their marketing serpenting a toehold into many of the innocents she had screened under cover of a farming zeitgeist. Strong hints of products that could sell themselves in the privacy of your head, for which you could trade mind space to own, or even, regarding some of the more elite modalities, be compelled to enact murder to enable full union with their neuro-seeding.

She had actually garnered the name of a merchant ship captain, and plans to unleash on Curlew a hold filled with giganticised automns. Enough evidence of treachery to have several dozens of lion shortly ripping at Merion's fit haunches. She had sent her evidence telepathically to Tacleara, unsure if she'd touched the woman's active or dormant energy field, for she received no definitive reply. Her own cloister of Indigoes had been otherwise focused, and on some cursed impulse she had decided to attend one of Merion's recombinative rituals.

She had known it all a ruse from the first but she had joined the few dozen people milling around with the triple helixes of niche biology painted on their naked bodies. The woman were offering around a flower to smell that had been scientifically impelled to bloom. All the other minor miracles of those biological systemising proponents, the painted-over, wooden features of Merion, were all fallacious. A decoy. She could feel the anxious thrumming of subterranean computers running cast-typing on the crowd, and clearly hear the conversations of Daguerette toys with people's as yet innocent subconscious. Her own powers she shielded — close as a candle on a night-walk over a chasm.

She had slipped around the interpolative fibrillators, and behind the solar electrolysis stills had found the stairway. Sure enough, air from a vast cavern chilled her exposed skin as she peered over the edge of a rock shelf, using just enough of her gift to pre-empt the threat of being surprised. A litany of instruments bulked down there; somnambulistic people staring at pulsing screens, or embraced with invisible deep-cell projections like insane ballerinas. There were power-drunk faces too, of those connected to chittering machines by wires plugged into newly-made cranial apertures.

And there was Merion, strutting in demented glee, impatiently wiping along sleek, khaki-clad legs with those large hands — hands larger than a farmer of minds should need. His blond curls bobbed over everything, adorning a plumper version of himself than that offered by the simulacrum on the lawn above.

Saliska had glanced along a thinly screened alcove, suddenly uplit by some whim of a computer panel, revealing Merion's experiments on human energy conduction. She had goggled at an old man, boxed neatly in a contraption that transparentised his skull; at people linked, cord by cord, to the terminal of an engrossed young programmer; at people spiked with metals through their still living organs — and had let out a little yelp.

So, they had caught her. Four of those women with their metal hands, though she had ensured at least two would require metal jaws to ever cohere again, and now, here she is, resurfacing to the horror once more. Saliska follows the cabling tracing around her spine, that she knows is let through her brain by long pins, and that descends into a tank of swirling, coloured water. Even if she could reach a mutual Indigo, she can no longer call for help.

They have wired her into their main attack frequencer, and shortly, Merion himself had enlightened her, she will be killing off 'fools and cretins and working for progress'. It is not this that makes her sick. Her sight plays again to the line of vials inexorably filling with liquid — antidote. She knows it to be against mind attack, but at what price it is produced!

She looks at the nearly hundred people being milked by the cords and nano-spheroids, looks again at where their…but they are missing, every one. Leaning forward in her bonds, Saliska vomits in racking agony.

Tacleara observes the gathering dusk. It will be a dark night, but the empath can see with other than eyes, even in these unfamiliar ASA lands. She douses the luxury of her fire with the remnants of the pannikin of shineark, and swallows a capsule of the ruby-leafed herb from her personal supply. It will enhance the fluidity of all her muscle synergies and slow her adrenal gland a little. She will need to be calm but precise, and she can always speed her glandular system up later on with some of the powder from those bizarre bulbs, labelled as such. Resisting a backward psychic glance at her homeland, committed to the one chance she is destined to provide against its ruin, she throttles off on the hover bike.

Mendez falls, nearly off the artificial cliff of the jetty this time, trying hard not to think about the barnacles along the tide mark of the massive freighter. It is fair enough. He certainly stands out amid these people with bones thrust through every raised surface of their faces and hair tied back in anything from sharkskins to nunchakus to lace stockings. He handsprings and parries his assailant, rocking low like a gorilla, then whirls a leg around his body to lash the stolid Chinese, carrying through a second whipping kick — Sway's teaching — which concusses the dazed man.

"Third time lucky," says a corpulent, hemp-suited man from the shade of a coconut palm, applauding soundlessly, then snorting with disinterest into the bird claw threaded through his septum. The Spaniard re-starts the long walk down the avenue. Its lining palms grow from the bellies of hundreds of old freighters filled with dirt. In the distance he sees ships, ineffable as would be expected for this port — largest in the world save Mjölnir – the pirate bay of Seazure.

It is early in the morning when Furrow, huffing over the brazier, finally gives up and wriggles in under the solar ewer to trigger its charge mechanism, having to wedge his head right into the bell of its zinc form base to do so. It is already emitting the faint heat that the zinc will transpose to the basalt hot plate purely by light agitation. He crawls out again with the beginnings of a migraine and retrieves his pot of shineark from the smaller brazier. Looking around, he sees every one of the Homager slumped dead. Twisted grunts come from the two dozen Mantles cordoning the inner Common Tryst, as they too wilt into coma or death.

Though shocked, Furrow is relatively clear-headed as he dodges to his computer console, types his personal code for imminent attack to the coastal rear-guard command, adds 'psychic,' then deletes the files. He reaches the public alarm system, geared into the solarmill speakers, just as the hover spots him — its crew no doubt as surprised as he that someone still lives. Rolling under some shelving, Furrow abandons caution, snagging a laz-cannon from new partitioning.

He quickly reduces four hovers to flaming wrecks, hoisting the sagging butt of the weapon back up, the warmly glowing charge crystal a golden fin above his shoulder. Two forms run heedless through the nearest conflagration, stumbling like fire-gusted branches toward him until he punches the flaming head of one, and slams the cannon muzzle into the fiery face of the second. Another few minutes and Unilion will fall upon the gathering attackers in roaring fury. Several youths on perenties race toward the thick press of body and soul-warped foe. Strictured into attacking from the lagoon end by the thick gardens on either side and the jumble of hovers and supplies at the Tryst's rear, about forty ungainly forms turn toward the feeble challenge while a few clomp in Furrow's direction.

The youths are lasered precisely into strips, but one of the saurians somehow survives the bombardment and inflicts a chaotic reprise before it is downed. Furrow re-loads the unwieldly cannon, his hurried shot gagging the approach of two monstrosities, arms lengthened to hang from tissues ensnared with holographic scenery. The septarian defender appropriates a smaller laser and drops behind some packing crates. It occurs to him as odd that no Unilion have yet responded to the alarm summons. He steps out to aim at a woman with an elongated metal jaw and top lip along which runs a little magnetic needle. Her eyes are askew, as though focusing on a will other than her own.

Too late, Furrow sees the flash of cyborg metal to one side and feels laser fire swell along an arm as he crumples. His heart contracts, and shudders on the verge of stopping, before finally it returns him to his smoking ruin amid the advancing, swaggering horde. Suddenly, the sybarites near him turn to the accompaniment of hoof falls. A pair flee promptly. Others fall, domino-like, from the psychic blows of a ringlet-haired rushlight of a girl redeeming Curlew's darkest hour from atop a camel.

She helps Furrow to sit, snatches a first-aid kit from a bench top, maniacally applies a wrap of vege-film to his arm, then gasps, "They must be after the lasers. Where?"

He pants in shock. "Bottom shelf...next the doubled-up tables...blue bags." Furrow recognises his saviour as one of the Dew. She loads the bags into large canvas panniers astride the camel and then helps him to mount the animal. With a horror-struck note in her soft voice, she says," These...things I have only separated from their brain sparks briefly, and soon their synaptic fires will return. Which way?"

"We must find Unilion help. Turn right along the lagoon."

They jog away, the girl leading the camel into the tea-tree thicket as the main body of sybarites arrive in a cloud of what Furrow deems to be kit-set hovers never seen in this land. He growls as the betrayal hits him.

The girl guides the injured man to sit against the cushiony bark of a waterside melaleuca trunk. She slaps billabong mud along his charred arm and then, her bushy brows drawing down as though to seek counsel from the calm line of her dark lips, places a palm in front of Furrow's mouth. He feels a breeze like ice sweep down his oesophagus, and the pain in his arm instantly ceases.

"How did you...How did you know what was happening?"

"I was going to get wattle bark when I heard the alarm. We were close enough to see an outline of what was occurring."

"Thanks. I'm Furrow, by the way."

"Senastim."

They follow the branching trail low and left, its upward fork rising steeply toward escarpment tableland. Between lagoons, amid palm and fig glades they thread. Soon, the camel digs in its heels and lets out a low murmur.

"What is it, Mairetraya?"

"She smells lion," Furrow states. "You must wait here."

"It's alright," she says to Mairetraya, tying her bridle to a tree. "I won't be long."

With Senastim helping by hefting vine loops out of Furrow's way, the track soon brings them to the Foalswon Swamp. Hundreds of lion mill anxiously around, and Senastim at once attunes with a few old females, causing the male angling low toward her to cut away. Many seem to know Furrow, brushing agitatedly past him with bare interest. While the adviser calls booming hellos, Senastim explores and finds every Unilion dead.

"They kill with their minds. I saw it at the Common Tryst," Furrow says, numbed.

They retrace their steps to the camel.

"I think," deliberates Senastim, "that we should send the lion to the Tryst. For their revenge."

"Yes. Can you orchestrate that, my dear?"

"It is done. Where now?"

"Within an hour the first of the rear-guard will be here. They'll stabilise things, but we should hand these lasers out amid the villagers, just in case the sybarites make design in that direction."

After Furrow stumbles into the first house they come to, Senastim realises there will be no need to travel about distributing the lasers. Dozens, then hundreds of people begin to stream beneath the wide turf-grown veranda, eager to receive and share news with the adviser. Furrow pronounces the Unilion delayed by tactical complications. He stresses, after cross-confirming the nature of their foe with Senastim, that only people knowledgeable in the rigours of psychic protection should risk approach to main areas of battle.

Furrow receives word that frenzied lion have won a blood bath to secure the Tryst area and the threatened nearby larder and hard-technic workshops. There is a mass of citizenry engaging the cybernetic humans along the desolate hill flank of Ja-Stung Creek.

"Where the old open cut is. They can't be thinking they'll take the cogitator — it's half a mile deep."

As Senastim helps the wounded security coordinator onto a medi-vac hover, he impresses his point, asserting, "No fear, child, none at all. It's always guarded by distant Mantles, like zealots in their vigilance. I put nearly a quarter of Chudich Company down there, fiercest troops in Curlew, and all the computer checks, locks on locks no — "

Very nearly, right as the medi-vac departs, there comes a shuddering bellow resounding through the air to land as though the precedent to a tempest, gorgon-sired. The solar locomoters whine along their influx. Lights flicker and die across the house, and a contagious cry of 'The cogitator!' surrounds Senastim.

Men and women race into the lane, crying the names of their children. One of the previously hospitable residents of the large house, a venerable Melanesian man with laughing jowls beneath his cheek tattoos, retrieves a sack and begins distractedly moving people aside to place items of kitchenware, clothing and food within it.

Senastim finds that Mairetraya has taken advantage of the fracas to consume the tops of fruiting shrubs verging her palm-tree tether. The brunette smiles at the beast's equanimity, stroking a dun flank and savouring its earthy bulwark against the mounting disorder.

Finally, a tall man, anomalously blond-haired with a Japanese-featured upper face but blunt jaw, begins concerting people to the effort of investigating the cogitator site. At the last minute those youths arranged to accompany him gabble of electromagnetic radiation and something about an uncle whose underground housing must be affected by the power surges. With a wry glance at Senastim, the tall one leaps atop a lizard and jolts off, his skirted gown fluttering behind like the cassock of some Charlemagneic knight.

More explosions come to the villagers' ears. Closer this time, as though from among the densely occupied village wynds just beyond sight. A strange hover, with snubbed ends and no evident windows, looms overhead. It casts an ominous shadow across the garden.

A Negroid woman stops pretending to practice Khorustaming moves and murmurs, "What in Zanzibar's trove is that?"

The next minute she is tossed across the lane, Senastim throwing up a hand and grabbing Mairetraya's rein tightly, as a wave of fire washes out from the detonating bomb.

A tamarind tree collapses almost atop the camel, but the pair are unscathed as the dust clears to show the building opposite, modelled on a lotus, with a rainbow of natural polished timbers, smashed into a flaming wreck. The mosaicked garden wall, its umbilical curves representing the fallen flower's stem, is also a slag of rocks and jumbled roots topped by a burning corpse. Another hover idles into view, this time shedding laser bursts from ground fire, and Senastim rushes the camel away through gardens and a communal scour, ducking under flapping clothes, to emerge in a wynd-way.

The blond-haired Japanese rides toward her, yelling for all to hear, "Automn attack! Land and air. Automnals! Rear-guard dis — "

One of the hugest automns Senastim has ever seen steps from beside a sculpture of ovoid boulders and obliterates the brave man with a blast that makes a hoop of the body as it sloughs from the escaping perentie.

The girl leads Mairetraya back under the washing and stuffs wet blankets into one of the camel's spacious panniers. Into the other she wrestles her legs and hips, whispers, "Go find the people", and curls the rest of herself within, making a quick slash with her knife in the canvas and giving the animal a little mental shove to get her moving.

The innate understanding and resilience of her beast is soon proved as it works its way steadily toward higher ground amid the razing of Curlewalion's capital. Scrunched inside the pannier, Senastim is not sure she should have made the eye slits she peers through. The massive automns stride the lanes of Ja Junction, torching every building not made of stone, lasering children hiding up in trees, women who stand shielding their families, as well as soldiers of the rear-guard who are massively outnumbered and, unable to recharge their lasers, having trusted to the energy cogitator conduits — outgunned. Numb and sweat-caked, Senastim notes a group of Dingo Company, three human towers propelling staff-wielding human missiles to sail down upon automns that everywhere advance toward the defenders' high position atop an orb.

The effect of the Khorustaming is devastating, en-heartening the tormented spy and reminding her of bizarre fruit bats descending to rob the sugars of electricity from the automn trees with surgical impalements of their staffs. It is short-lived. Simultaneous grenades land right upon the raised Dingo standard, levelling the towers as the plastic Vikings move relentlessly on.

Mairetraya clops around a matted group of automns that writhe in a transportable material ravel. She enters a wynd-way filled with screams and the sprawled detritus of buildings, their carved beams and intricate stained-glass windows smashed like a final tribute across the bodies of their builders.

They reach the grove-filled country of the hills. A flash of patchwork yellow and black leaps from a rooftop onto the automns that cross an intersection just ahead, the fierce defender raining an acrimony of blows onto the marauders. She winces as the laser fire slices by Mairetraya and terminally scorches the lion. Only one automn rights itself jerkily as they pass. At least it was a tooth for a circuit, Senastim thinks. She does not look at any more.

The camel passes from the curving lay of the wynd-ways and safely gains a wild fringe of rocky paddock, loping into thin forest of melaleuca adorning a boulder-dominated cant. Chancing the possibility of rogue scouts, the girl flips withy limbs to the ground from her pannier and throws the blankets from the other. Carefully, she winds an upward path, all her eyes vigilant.

Once they have trudged over the broken shoulder of the escarpment, Senastim mounts Mairetraya and they speed across the broad and grassy plateau. Their luck holds through two occasions on which automn hovers bloat into the mid-distance and then pass on. A little group of Vengers on hover-bikes extend a bare head-flick to the escapees as they whiz closely by. Far away, explosions erupt sporadically along the Gentin where larger farming villages hug its broad banks. The sight of the river is heartening, the same view the camp of the Dew, hopefully hidden now, had commanded. Scanning the ground beneath the camel's hooves, Senastim finally spots an old fire circle and dismounts, calling a greeting as loudly as she dares.

There is no response, but then a jubilant Ramalia rushes from behind some shrubs to embrace and lead the newly arrived fugitive to a nearby scouring from a washout. Here the girl kisses Mairetraya farewell, with a command that she return to the herd. Another figure comes from the gloom for her to kiss — Joachim. Her grandfather cuddles her over to a clearing amid the carts lined nose to tail along the creek bed, the whole painstakingly roofed with long saplings, grass and scrub. Senastim delivers news of the Homager and Unilion demise, and of the sacking of the capital by automns.

Jesella nods grimly as the girl speaks, then the matriarch says, "An ill day, child. This screen we built on seeing the distant evils along the Gentin. No cover will hide us from the infrared of automns or spare us from their endurance. It may be that safety will lie toward the Gaian Aboriginal Merger. Travelling in small groups we — "

A sudden blast of trumpet, barking low and clear, and then squalling in a hair-raising static, silences the counsel. As the startled Dew creep toward the edge of the hollow to trace the noise, the soloist's arousings are lapped by waves of dreaming fluting, then propelled on a following roll of congas, reverberating defiantly. Ten or so figures approach through the grasses, and when near enough to see the instrument each carries, a tall aboriginal man throws back his chest and sings operatically.

"We are the Peacebeats, come to meet the Dew. Larker sent us!" he yells into the silence as an afterthought.

As the Dew emerge, the man expounds that Larker, in conjunction with their group, has built an impregnable sanctuary against such disaster as invasion, and that they must hurry. Shortly, the strange guides lead the bewildered caravaneers off the plateau, following skilfully along creek-sides and rocky terrain so they remain hidden from infrequently passing hovers. After two hours they come to a plain before brooding, vertiginous cliffs.

"Heaven," declares an inky-eyed woman with generously broad Portuguese features and a violin strapped around her shoulders.

Esandril screams, "Automns!"

Two groups of gargantuan plastic, totalling at least a hundred, manoeuvre from around a hill bluff and pour over the lip of a hollow toward the unarmed group. The tall aboriginal flashes Senastim an indulged, gloating look.

"Now we can play for them, "he says crazily, beginning at once a plangent lilting interwoven with high sonarisms on his didgeridoo. Four of the Peacebeats position alongside him as the balance rush to face the other automn column. The Dew are soon enveloped in a frenzied tempo of sound which saws sharply off at its climax, only to blast in little snarls of speed and then cycle into its swarm-like cadences again. The fiddlers and drummers send a whistling harmonic singing to join with the woodwind hootings. Senastim sees that their guides are not completely mad after all; one by one, the automns collapse, a single grenade launching out in time to fall and spew a cloud of dirt on the defenders.

"Ah. They don't like it!" guffaws the didgeridooist, wiping grit happily from an eye as the Portuguese calls them on. To the echoing tune of the woman's strident bowing and an accompanying haunting song with a plunging chorus — 'those who have fallen in love' — which Senastim finds herself joining, the tired group threads the tunnels through the cliffs and arrives at the sun maze. Though night, the crescendo-shaped path across the lily swamp is on display, delineated by a golden emanation of light that fans out from somewhere on the far shore.

As they cross, the light recedes with them, until there is only a honeyed nimbus that Senastim watches descend amid the huge boulders of a hill. It is like some child of the black mountain rearing behind it. Fading completely as it nears the group, the light is replaced by Larker. The enigmatic youth is wrapped in smiles.

He begins hugging the Dew, but just as he gets to Senastim, the aboriginal calls out, "We brought about a thousand people in at dawn, herders and friends of the Peacebeats, who we could convince of the threat."

Larker nods, explaining to those of the Dew nearby, "I only had a day of warning before the attacks, and you were hard for Cory and the others to locate. More will be arriving all the time."

They thread around the boulder jumbles at the hill's foot and along the lush valley fold. About the river, people laze, singing or jamming softly, but it is at the mountain that the Dew stare. Carved flowingly into its flank is an amphitheatre of smooth stone a mile wide upon which four great pavilions hunker — walls of boulders roofed with slabs of rock. Surrounding the amphitheatre is a vast bastille of stone, hundreds of metres high and carved into the semblance of trees at its height.

Joachim shakes his head and starts up the mountain path alongside the other Dew. "The house of the hitchhiker!" Senastim hears him joke. She lingers as the Peacebeats disperse, talking in captivated tones, then walks toward the tawny-haired youth.

"You know, I always thought you were the doom of my people, because the vision I saw most recurrently after your coming was of the automns back there, and us unarmed. But all things extend in twin directions, and I was never quite sure." She taps a lump of gold around Larker's neck, probably exposed during the building, which looks a lot like a three-legged camel.

"I am sure of one thing, though," she says, her gaze boring into his blue, rockpool eyes.

"I love you," Larker finishes, the words smothered as they hug in a delirious rocking and squeezing. They fall on the ground together and then into sleep beneath the long striae of cloud-parted moonlight, pressed against each other as blithely and naturally as two grains of sand.

Avery Tule, styled Merion Farmer by his employers all those decades ago, smirks as he watches feedback readings that show a total destruction of the junction Unilion. A better result than he could have hoped for. It may be he owes that spying hussy an extension to her life. The hover nets and small town suspicions had foiled things across the Om triangle, and on a screen linked to the old man's lobes he can see the electro-psychic representations of the Unilion pets destroying his attempts to ransack the Tryst. He still had his reserve in Solaris, outside Sybilla Bong, presently ensuring his control of the Sectariat's revolutionary antigravitation data — a valuable kickstart.

Now the Poise One is as good as a sealed ally, he can sell his completed brain synthesis research piecemeal to his original employers and start work on a whole new automn, one based on side streams of his experiments. He reaches the mercenary commander of Slitter's Asiana automns on the telekinetically enhanced radio frequency.

"Stan. Avery here. It's a big green, mate! Yep. The Unilion and Homager are down as agreed...You can get here that quick? We'll only just have time to get the energy cogitator taken out before you arrive...No. That's true. A fucking million — I won't believe it until I see it. By the way, send a dozen units wired to my code down to my place. I've got some interesting programmes for them to deliver to Slitter. Sorry: excited. Mr Slitter. Okay, over." One million automns made in Slitter's private Asiana laboratories. He salivates. "That many will reduce this stinking freakdream back to the dirt it was built from," he growls to no one in particular.

Avery gathers his hover bodyguard around him, and as they speed to the battle at Sybila Bong, takes a last look at the pitiful city of Ja Junction. In a week he is certain Curlewalion will be no more, and he can use these lands to churn out more automns than ever Slitter did, yet his will have adapting neuro-circuitry. He will rebuild the north, he promises himself, and one day the daguerettes will fawn at his feet when he remakes the meaning of psychic space.

Chapter 19

Stories don't stop at the boundary gate...
They were here before any of that.
Indigenous Liaison Officer

Musa is running at full tilt through the soldiers, one knife deflecting laser fire whilst the other drops his prey. Marisk is a flash weaving low near his master, falling dominoes of troops the evidence of his quicksilver hamstringing. A blurred glimpse of a metal cone swooping toward his brother catches Nivat's eye, and he hurls a knife at the object's trajectory, turning to engage a duo of running W.A.R. personnel with first a spear throw, and then a bounding side spring that lands him atop the spearless one.

As Marisk retrieves his spear, Musa's own shrills past him into a laz-cannon operator who had been pointing the snap-fryer straight at the bard. The lion are closing together, and some of the troops issuing from the tunnels consequently fire undisciplinedly or even turn back on ranks at the sight. Suddenly, another tunnel noses to the surface not far from the lion, spilling four hover-bikes that whiz around behind the beasts. On the rear of each an Agent steadies a rifle. The craft flit immediately over the Ra-kings, bunched in a group at a height of six metres. Just then, as though guided by Ares, the pedi-plane that had spiralled in a minute's flaming indecision loses all glide capacity. It plummets onto their thickly helmeted heads — the Agency-issued headgear, unlike the soldier's morions, greatly muffling sound, even of a roaring fireball.

Ahead, Nivat glimpses Musa and the cats within a tunnel, its mouth closing. The black mermidon urges him forward. Flicking his spear inside, Nivat takes two steps, and with a diving roll at the clenching metal aperture, misses. He stands tightly hissing: "Arm". The skin above an elbow is wedged in the titanium door. He hacks off the inch of caught flesh, including the pigskin of the shirt, binding the arm with the shirt scrap, muttering, "That god-sent flame should have obscured their stowing away. What reception awaits down there."

They emerge, bloodstained, sometime later, amid a jumble of pressurisers, workshops, and stockpiles of scrap and sand. The tunnel entry itself is beneath the footings of a radar tower, a shed opposite creating a kind of cul-de-sac, past which troops surge, trying to staunch the new determined push from Curlew.

"So you took out the main power feeds," Nivat observes, knuckling at an eye. "I suppose that's where my spear is?"

Musa grins and nods, then yells. "Up!" leaping to grab the side of the scaffolding.

His brother copies as the Ra-kings spring onto the shed roof.

A stream of anthropeoms flood into the cul-de-sac, milling in hundreds over each other, yawning mechanical jaws and growling while thousands more of the robotic dogs course by below, toward the wall defences. Bard and Unilion scale to the tower's top as the artificed lifeforms mill confusedly, most cluttering away. Thankfully, neither their position nor that of the completely exposed cats is fired upon from any of the ballistics embrasures in the lofty concrete security plinths. These are capped by the tall rods of gleaming transmitter cones, the nearest only a hundred metres distant. The confusion must be hindering their efficacy. Agates, choppers and Sacubus cloud the sky, and maybe half a million humans and automns seethe below, battling either to hold or take the outer earth wall.

Some threads stand out from the tapestry of desperate mayhem: a blue-faced Omnipotentan, flung by Khorustaming adepts to purloin a passing hover bike; a wedge of focused Agents, lethal in their training and silk suiting, felled by no visible means; an Agate fighter, roaring low to strafe a lizard cavalried group successfully driving through massed automns, the vanquishing plane then skittled from the sky by a single shot from an old Venger held above a hover-pack.

"Take the dorm tiers!" Nivat bellows again. His bard-trained voice booms like a stentorian's, although he realises few will hear him over the inarticulate blare of the battle. Strangely, he notices many Curlewans have lifted their efforts, and several Charmers actually vie to bring down a chopper with their old rifles. All but one are felled by their combatant as they turn their backs, the survivor hewing a way through an anthropeom pack directly toward Nivat.

The bard suddenly has the unnerving sensation of feeling his call to arms reverberate up through the ground and into his mind, a sort of rumbling sonar of compulsions. Then he spots the orchestrator of such a wonder — a bibliotheque supreme. Propped against a burned-out hover, a small brown berry of a woman, clearly a Gaian Screamer by her shamanic accoutreage, holds her hands toward the ground, her lips moving wordlessly. Momentarily, she catches Nivat's gaze and nods, before the space between them is filled by the bold, stilt-walking figures of a dozen seal servers, naked but for focals to delineate the targets of their blowdarts, wielding extending bamboo staffs and kicking with their canegrallator props. So the Screamers could communicate with those not of their ilk if they had to.

Nearly at the juncture of the sheds, Nivat glimpses the spectacle of the foxers.

The most dynamic of all Curlewalions' warriors have gravitated to the head of the assault, their Khorustaming flows exploding into the fever-pitch mode of foxing. All of the warriors are slightly built. Several tiny Chinese women are among the leaping background forms, as is a wraithish Tibetanese-featured man. The defining similarity among the foxers is their high and agonizingly graceful formwork, often including spontaneous joint aerial kinetics. While foxers bound off each other, kicking passing leapers higher as they themselves descend, and even transmuting laser strikes into laser fire-breaths through some bizarre spino-neural adjustment, Nivat bullies forward.

He is near enough to Musa to see his brother swathed in a mist of spurting blood and flying plastic, drawing fire from several hover-bikes, as well as a Sacubus striking chaos about him with its short-wave laser pulses, unable to more than singe the rogue Unilion.

Inspired, Nivat roists off an automn's head, screaming as he leaps, so that his words shiver through the barrage of man and machine, carrying across the forty metres of space to where the Curlew press is thickening.

"To me, Curlewa!"

He lands, raking his fingers across the maniacally eager eyes of a gang of cadets, just stopping short of an automn's hard head which he side tackles, and in the process at last finds a weapon. Musa-like, he stomps the automn's head half off.

It is only a truthie, a stun laser to which the cadets are restricted, after an uprising they had been involved in fifty years prior — but with it he gains respite, dropping bodies with delicate blasts and back steps, clearing a wide circle that the foxers finally flood into.

Feeling as though his outer skin has been peeled off and he will, at any moment, mango-like, ooze out, Nivat gropes along the concrete wall of the shed and collapses beside his brother. In a short space of time, foxers and Fist secure the area, and the Companies of Curlew entrench within and around the dorm tiers. The brothers are aided toward a basement respite.

Nivat's attention wavers briefly toward continual explosions along the coast. "Hang in there," he whispers to Curlew's Navy, then descends.

Tabaveres spins the Interloper around as soon as the last torpedoes are loaded, threshing through the twenty minutes of water between him and battle. He watches on a vid link as the machine's arms load and prime the munitions bay and glances at Portia, the still-napping mechanic, and at Jeyndylier, the aboriginal signalman, still looking strained. Both are slightly built, a far cry from his time in the Curlew-led Free Ocean vigil, when his crews had been brawny monsters as often up top with guns, pirating Austral patrols or carrying mines to a sleepy cruiser, as working the gadgetry.

Tabaveres slides off the reef and noses aside a glut of near-invisible mines, active only in the absence of a complicated sonar code. Both the reef and the mines are for the protection of the fleet's supply and rescue mother. He thinks of that big ship's big captain, Segduerel, and ponders the guileful showmanship with which the Maori had greeted the Interloper and its hold of wounded. "Just like the old days, hey, Beaumont?" When they both knew that in the old days a hundred torpedoes would have lasted a sub this size a week, not an hour.

She is a sizeable craft, the largest submersible left in the attack; fifty metres long, twelve metres wide inside with three metres of reinforcing. So no matter how the grey-blonde man fiddles the gamma imagery and bluffs their readings, they are difficult to miss. This time a flock of Cormorants — tiny naut-bots with a thirty-centimetre long exploding spike for a beak — burst into the water above Monkeybottom and swish toward her from all sides. Tabaveres flicks out the two boarding arms and knocks a handful of little bots circuitless as Jeyndylier glowers off to a laser hatch. A number of Cormorants slip by his defence, and Beaumont Tabaveres grimaces at each explosion along the roof, though they can do no real harm.

He sends a cluster of magnetised steel out of the aft and throttles the turbines away from the prematurely detonating Cormorants, powering toward the ASA carrier pontoon. Thus far the problem has not been getting close enough to the kilometre-wide platform, but getting the torpedoes through. Beaumont brings up a slow motion recording, detailing the defensive systems of the pontoon, while distractedly punching off a couple of inertiac torpedoes at the shape of a Sacubus, not far above according to Monkeybottom's scans.

"I've never seen someone gloat over a picture of a thermos hitting a ship before." Jeyndelier hunkers over the recording beside his captain. Both the men had been markedly more distressed some half an hour previous when studying a close-up of the suspended particles comprising the pontoon's bio-shielding. That disturbing footage had shown some unknown type of bio-algalate absorbing the warheads sent at the platform, seeming to unfurl and join into a carbonaceous mass at the trigger of heat. To test the theory, Tabaveres had recorded his launching of a frozen flask of cellular stabilisers and he looks now at the definitive frame of the cooled object striking the platform.

Tabaveres releases the torpedoes that the mother ship had snap frozen for him, yelling "go code frigid" into his intercom even before he sees his missiles hit their target.

As Monkeybottom turns, two little subs rise out of the sand on her port and fire at the platform. Explosions hit the carrier from all sides.

An exultant nautileer's voice calls down the intercom, "Platform's sinking. Well done, Beaumont!"

Tabaveres knows there is still another platform to sink before Curlew land positions will be safe from the massed heavy artillery and guiding systems that such institutions boast.

Up ahead, forward scanners delineate Araluen, largest rammer and hover launch in Curlew's flotilla, surrounded by large, shark-like shapes. Visual contact shows her beleaguered by Shoal Saws. The two subs Beaumont had left on guard detail are gone, and instead the robots, relying on kinetic energy dispersed through the group, are intent on the hull. They ignore Monkeybottom, a saw each side of the one with its arms holding its whirring middle over the hull, pull with their detachable cablings to spin its saw in deeper.

Tabaveres lines up one on the hull's far side and pulverises it with a torpedo, prompting a Saw in the hull to be propelled by the closest robot at Monkeybottom. The razored body bites into the submarine's thick armour and remains there droning and stuck. Tabaveres glides under Araluen and catches one of the fleeing Shoal Saws with a crushing boarding arm, dealing the same to the protruding Saw in Monkeybottom's side.

"Tabaveres! All set for action one-zero-three?"

Djesayn Sumat, Mistress of the Araluen, receives Tabaveres' affirmative over the intercom, and Monkeybottom's close guard, as her ship builds speed for the attempt to sheer off the main automn loading rampway verging from a breakwall. The double nose of an Austral butterfly sub pushes toward Araluen, trading torpedoes with Monkeybottom as it manoeuvres to strike the rammer. One of its warheads explodes alarmingly close to his thinly armoured propellers, but Beaumont's nerves are steady as he slugs projectiles into the twin cones of the butterfly's exposed nose, shattering the smaller sub.

Djesayn's voice crackles. "Mission success."

As the nautileer glides back into open ocean, steering towards the reef in a polished turn, Portia claps her hands sharply once, saying happily, "That should ease the Mist's anxiety over their hill bases being outflanked by automns."

"True," muses the captain. "That is, at least automns won't harass the prop bases via river conduits. Where's my forward eyes? Jeyndeylier?"

Tabavere's depth-sounding read-outs have suddenly become a monotonous line and the aboriginal signalman ducks frantically from instrument to instrument.

"No way, man! Beaumont — long-range down, surface retronometers, even the bioscope — we've lost the lot."

"The closed circuits are still up. Doolriga, have you lost all external signals? Okay. I'm going to issue tactical viabilities across the fleet broadband. Let me know if you receive."

Tabaveres moves across to a little fold-out drawer and takes out the vocal nub, as Jeyndelier sequences the broadband.

"I hope this works; passing the word by intercom will be too slow." He takes a focused breath as the aboriginal indicates readiness. "All units, this is Tabaveres. Expect contact with a Romantine or Foamercion within minutes — the big girls are on us. It's not tele-psychically induced because my externals are down, despite Psi shielding. Suit up, folks. Don't get drawn into any shallows. Make trines, or at least buddy up; cover your flanks and save the torps for the robot craft or swimmers. Over."

An almost immediate "Message received" comes through from the rammer, Doolrigah, and Portia hands Tabaveres his suit, belting her aqua-lasers on and checking the workings on their mine launchers. The crew huddle around the peri-camera link, Monkeybottom cruising just high enough to maintain good visibility. A shadow darkens the monitor to the left, and Jendylier tracks the peri-camera. Less than a kilometre away glides the dire colossus of a ship. "Foamercion," grimaces Beaumont, as lesser shadows streak from the keel.

As the first of the streamlined, robotic submarines approaches, Portia and Jendylier, nervous, catch it with separate laser coils, Beaumont reflecting there is no real point in their conserving power. Anyway, he is too busy to chide them. He starts off a dozen torpedoes and still the automated Sharks approach, their barbed mines jettisoning into Monkeybottom's armour, there awaiting critical mass before they explode. He sweeps the boarding arms — without external monitoring, a blind exercise — along the submarine's body; hopefully dislodging some, then manages to torpedo a statically shielded laz bomb only metres off his stern.

The peri-camera imagery cuts out, and he punches torpedoes along his last line of sight, praying they strike the stubbornly thinning droids, while he waits for Jendylier to re-instate another camera. As vision returns, he wings a Manta Borer, a thin plane of saline algalate designed to disable turbines — and notoriously difficult to spot. Demonstrating his ocean war skills, he swiftly destroys three more of these. Portia and Jendylier's bodies buck with frenetic lasering. Catching movement from the corner of the screen, Tabaveres angles the draught and brings the cameras to bear on three W.A.R. submarines all as big as Monkeybottom. Instead of fleeing as the Mjölnir commanders would expect, he continues the turn, powering toward them.

He expels the boarding arms and lessens propulsion three-quarters. The arms whiz away to the fore of his craft, absorbing most of the first frontal torpedo assault. At that moment the barbed mines go off along the floor of the vessel, and the nautileer lands heavily with a curse as water seeps up beneath him.

"Portia! Fire up the evacuation platform. Jam front torpedo bays on continual fire, Jendy!"

Tabaveres locks his course, dashes to the rear of the Interloper and tethers oxygen pipes, bedded in the floor, to the restraining poles Portia has snapped into place. She locks both captain and signalman into the body harnesses, completely stricturing them, save for the arms. She lets Beaumont know the eject leverings are primed and straps herself to her pole. Tabaveres holds the rudimentary second tiller before him. He has only done this twice before, never on a vessel so large.

"Let them come," he mumbles as the craft shudders around them, ropes of sparks and water coursing past their knees. Then he hits the override and eject button, and the floor, to which they are attached, drops away, the evacuation platform roaring backward with just the open ocean and a metre or so of steel between them and the propeller.

Tabaveres guides the reversing rocket around to one side and eases the propeller through to forward. His crew's discipline enthuses him as they ignore the relatively harmless droid Sharks and fire on the Manta Borers for the brief moments of slower speed, as does the scuttling of the central W.A.R. submarine, that sinks slowly even as Monkeybottom's last torpedo scoots well beneath the enemy, his beloved craft nosediving, soon parodied by the foundering Mjölnir submarine.

Now upon the fastest vessel in the ocean, Tabaveres zings up toward the port out-flier of the original attack trio. Weaving easily around torpedoes, he pulls alongside in bare seconds, slowing to a glide and emptying, like his crew, his entire mine launcher into its propeller. A pack of Shoal Saws and Manta Borers begin to surround them, and Tabaveres streaks surface-ward. Dodging several laz-bombs fired by the Foamercion, he makes for her ponderous hull.

Before breaching the surface, Tabaveres ejects the propeller and tilts the speeding platform obliquely. They rocket out of the ocean beneath the looming side of the ship, travelling seemingly too fast to survive, but the dispersal mechanisms automatically drop them to the platforms' tail. Their weight squares its self-magnetising bottom into a rough parallel with the side of the Foamercion, into which it slams.

Beaumont is amazed that his teeth do not bite through the padding of the oxy-disperser he pulls from his mouth. His arms are painfully dislocated. Beside him, Jendylier fires staggeredly at the little cockroach droids come to investigate their imposition. He actually scuttles all of them, and no further curiousness is extended them. They are stuck firmly to the seaward side of the Foamercion, some twenty-five metres up, centrally marooned on her fifteen-hundred-metre long haunch.

In the distance prowl four more battle cruisers, massive like her.

"Shit," purrs Portia, gingerly rubbing her arms.

"What now?" asks Jendylier.

Directly above their horizontally jutting bodies, three hover-packed Agents storm towards them.

Tabaveres, bringing a laser up to his face, begins to laugh. "Thank Creator for that."

"For Agents?" queries Jendylier asininely.

"Look beyond them," supplies Portia, "at the sky beacon."

A huge, fluorescent Jolly Roger spreads its death's-head leer across the clouds.

"Pirates!" all three exclaim, then learn what it is to be prey.

The Agents' first pass reduces Jendylier to a frame of steaming bones, Portia just managing to clip one into an exploding plummet. They come around again from below, an Agent slurrying Portia and flying by Tabaveres with a smarmy wave while the captain sprays laser bursts blindly below, and marvels at the oceanscape while drinking in the attack formations of everything from cruise liners to octane-powered outriggers. With an armada of countless thousands of ships, and against all expectations, the pirates have indeed arrived.

Nivat wakens to groggily overhear Musa's conversation with a group of Mist.

"...think the Secretary of Operations is here then. If he coheres Affiliate strategies, taking the hub will be an exercise in blood."

"None of the Indigo groups believe so. It seems they were able to remove the Zone Command because his workload was stressing his shielding, a lucky break really."

"And all Squadron Leaders are dead."

"Some by kinesis, some in battle. Thirty-seven, which was the total our information had posited."

"Okay, well, let's not wait till dawn. You've got to bring all the companies in from the props. Bluff charge into the lee of the Cyc with a few thousand, and pull everything else from the courtyards into two wings, while strobing forward from the centre alternately in groups of a hundred every half minute. Darkness gives thin aid. The automns will be lethal but their air attack is annulled."

"Sounds fair, Musa. Alright," the Mist leader turns to an Indigo, "let's spread the word, seed to leaf."

"Brother, you waken in time for the last push. Let us join the Ra-kings."

Hundreds of attackers flow up the basement stairs. Just then cries erupt from a clustered communications group of Indigoes beside an enthralled group of Mantles; chill cries of despair.

"Curlewalion is taken!"

"O! The Homager is no more!"

"Automn's have sacked her green cities!"

"The Unilion are slain by —"

Suddenly, blood spurts from the noses of the Indigoes, the same from the Mantles. Whether the message from a desperate cabal in Curlew had shocked their defences, or some coincidence of increased attack from the government psychics had occurred, Nivat does not know. Musa yells in a flat voice, as hands poise at earplugs to heed him. "This news must not leave here! We have seen what a weight of grief might reap, even on the sharpest of minds. Let us mourn our home when first this fight is won. And let every fighter here exact a fury of revenge this night. Curlewalion!"

Taking up Musa's cry, the horde streams from the basement and mingles with the thousands of warriors threading around and dying in tank and particle destabiliser fire. Musa directs his brother up a ladder-way to the rooftop of the dorm tiers where a roof-mounted battery is the only protection for a miraculously still-concerting group of Mantles directed by several Indigoes. Five of Curlew's hectare-encompassing hover-props, having defended the tiers for the past hours with their bulk, are levering obliquely upward, three moving to cover the decoying central charge from air strike. The other pair float away to join with the props coming from the hills on the two wings of Curlew's main assault.

The grim orphans look out toward the dimly visible island of Hamper's main defensive institution, nicknamed 'the Cyc' among the companies. Its single eye of particle-destabilising wrath — a huge block of concrete, steel and algalate, is covered in thousands of W.A.R. troops and hovers. Approaching Vengers are plucked from the sky by swift beams flaming from the Cyc's eye, but the ground assault flows like a beaching wave in a wide ring around the outer layers of automns, trading detonby blasts for bolts from destablisers and laz-cannons, and beginning to erode the plastic resistance.

Musa shakes his head mordantly and paces to the other side of the rooftop, the sweet smell from his pipe enwreathing Nivat where he stands feeling, more than listening, to the sonorous rumble of the props gliding away. As he watches, inken forms blot into the missile-raining sky, shadow-shapes deeper than the black of night, like the denser tone of mud upon dark earth. The apparitions have a fierce angularity and momentous size, but their cursory habit etches them into a human resemblance. As the phenomenon continues, the bard witnesses haloes manifest atop each patch of sable stain; piercing globes of nacre into each luminous orb, greens and subtle pink flickering through the ivory crowns.

Nivat knows these fearsome phantas to be the workings of Wild Angels, having twice before seen Curlew's living conundrums reverse their dour cloaks of black, trapping and somehow transmuting the light of star and moon through the mechanism of finely wrought glass plates adhered to the inside of their garb. Yet these projections are of a far greater size. A large enclave of Angels must be gathered below, for hundreds of the disquieting, though entrancing, omenic figures people the sky.

The shapes begin to dart jerkily forward, in approximation of running, and the bard gasps as they clutch their halos in pointed fingers, holding them out like shields to mop up missile strikes from the base fortifications, he never having dreamed that the Angels' sky fetches could be so tactile. The figures of light and shadow actually overtake the props to assail hover-packs and choppers, swinging their lodes of light into the enemy, every second fetch torn apart in such engagements, but others advancing until lost to his sight in the distance.

His brother returns, still pensive. Sensing Musa's brooding mood, a mantle stirs, greets the Unilion dreamily and accepts a puff from the pipe which Nivat has just declined.

"What transpires?" the dark warrior asks flatly of the psychic.

"Their Miomichs were concerting with another group down the coast, previously beyond our notice, which we have just destroyed. We are holding our radio frequencies open and giving Hamper's a lot of static bursts. Their troop movements are too chaotic for us to more than stab at passing craft."

"Well, see if you can deal with at least one of the marksmen who are covering the central corridor, I think from behind that pile of iron next the shed. We've got to get through there. Is there anything else over the sand pile at the eastern foot of this building?"

"No, just sand."

Musa is already dropping off the roof as he implores Nivat to follow.

A nuggetty shape in the sky, far bigger than a Sacubus, diverts Nivat's attention from their preparative ambush of an Affiliate group. Suddenly, the shape lights up, exposing a massively armoured hover like a swollen antique helicopter. From under it, a search beam swathes across the Curlew attack, and a blinding laser cuts the near victorious companies to dust, incinerating thousands in a controlled burst, including fringes of Hamper troops, and causing a stampeding retreat that is cruelly followed by automns.

"What is it?" Nivat gasps as approaching Vengers on attack props are dropped from the sky, the only possible cause being magnetic disruption.

"It was built to destroy Herovers," answers Musa, sternly lighting a pipe and watching the disastrous retreat. Without warning, the ungainly hover turns and blasts the Cyc, steaming its edifice for a full minute of cacophony. Then it wings skyward and explodes with a searing flash that reveals the Companies of Curlew returning to the attack. Another explosion of noise roars out from somewhere, mounting to an earth-trembling crescendo.

"Lion" says Musa, as the first intelligible outline of dawn delineates the forms of thousands of lion bounding toward the dismayed, command-less ranks of South Austral.

The delegation sits atop the captured hover-pontoon watching the thrashing schools of sharks rend the bodies of the dead — friend and foe — bobbing on the outgoing tide. Away in the hills, Nivat knows, the surviving Curlewalions are sleeping, not celebrating. There is little to celebrate. Curlew is betrayed and taken. Over three hundred thousand of the ground forces, all of Curlewa's navy and countless pirates lie ruined.

If it had not been for the timely intercession of their wild allies, they would not have overcome Base Hamper.

"I no kapasa," says a monstrous Russian pirate, agate-studded chains pierced through either cheek. "You ipso the bon Indigo group got bumpa havings night, and the two Mantling soon later. How the fire angel being bumpa?"

To Nivat 'fire angel' seems a good name for the deadly apparition of the grotesque hover, and he watches the faces of those Mist present crease again at the mystery. Lans, sunken-eyed but astute as always, talks quietly and slowly so the man will understand.

379

"The answer lies not far from your own pirate home. We Unilion travelled over a hundred and fifty kilometres a day to reach the battle. Last night, soon after we had all met up, we found a strange group gathered around little fires. They must have left while still the border storm remained, for they travelled on foot. There was one among them who could speak Ionan, and he told that these magicians had some time ago received a vision that they must come to the ocean to destroy 'the flying death'.

"Three dozen aboriginal warriors were their bodyguard — seventy kurdaitchi from the Gaian Aboriginal Merger. These were real bone rattlers from the deep places beside your borders. Certainly the biggest gathering of medicine men that the world has ever seen. I have no doubt they brought the hover down."

"Let's hope that the Base Constrain attack has seen such luck as ours," says a wistful blond spokeswoman of the Mist. "We must now to Mjölnir with a quarter of our numbers against ten times the force. Curlew is fallen, and there is no home for us unless we can definitively purge our foe. I hope some of our brethren may make it through to join us from the west coast that at least Mjölnir shall not laugh."

"They shall not laugh," says Lans. "The fall of Hamper will rock the world, and the force that hits Mjölnir will be experienced and united. Though we Unilion must see what can be done for our homeland, our hearts are with you."

"Well," booms an energetic little Mexican woman, "we pirates getsy this base for our new lands. We shall see how pluckas around here savvy party, hey?"

A great laugh goes up among the gathered, and the delegation says its farewells. Musa approaches the hulking pirate, and after a brief conversation which Nivat does not hear, the Russian goes to the edge of the pontoon, screams thrice like a parrot and directs members of the flotilla with manic gesticulations. Lans and the brothers hug farewell after Musa explains his burning conscience to reach the Austral revolutionaries. Lans wishes him luck but asks how they hope to come to Byron. The cough of a dinghy motor interrupts, and tall masts glide alongside the pontoon. A hawser erupts from twin hollowed trunks of once massive trees, lands beside Musa's feet, and the dinghy clunks away.

"On a tri-masted outrigger," he says, "plenty of room for the cats." He signals the Ra-kings, who arise sleepily from the dock edge bristling, perturbed by the black fins below. "Look, there's fish for you in the boat," mollifies Nivat, coming alongside, and at once the lion flump into the canoe to gorge happily from a basket that the pirates stowed on board. With a shrug, Nivat joins them on deck, and unfurls the pink, orange and blue sails.

As the two Unilion suddenly become beheaded by a cloud of Lans' smoke, Nivat hears his brother tell the cult's leader that he expects the south-west trade winds to bring the outrigger upon the shores of Nascent Walls within a week. Stepping to the end of the boarding between the two logs, Nivat flips out the simple booms and locks them in place.

"Look after whoever you find alive back home," Musa implores Lans from where he lands lightly beside Nivat, the hawser coiled over one massive shoulder, "and greet the bright stars for me, my friend. Tell them I shall join them soon."

Chapter 20

Keevan and Lou fight side by side. The old man's helmet, cannibalised from one of the many fallen hub, is cracked. Outwaiting the current bluff of Agency fire, Keevan glimpses scorched stains — a jarringly evil omen — on the curlew and lion he crafted with his own hand, each wing topping the morion. The automns had been replaced by Agents half an hour prior. Only three have succeeded in slipping by the grim repellers ensconced in the little and last tenable chamber of the rebel base.

Back there are the dregs of exhausted and wounded, yet obstinate rebels. Forty. At last accounting. Keevan expects each of the Agents who broke through claimed a life at least, just as they will — in an hour, or a day — inexorably destroy every vestige of the Rainbow Realliance hub. Keevan is wounded, on top of the broken ear that still erodes his balance. Luckily his artist's dexterity enables him to fire with his left hand. His right is a mess fused to the armoured glove. A group of four Agents simultaneously storm the corner, having built numbers under cover-fire. Two roll low whilst a pair prop to target the defenders.

Keevan and the ex-foreman ignore the incoming fire and combine their blasts upon first one, then the other of the low streaking attackers. The synchronised laser strikes effectively stun the Agents. Lou presses back against stone, dodging the imprecise cover-fire, but Keevan receives a wad of laser strike in the chest, bursting the huge gel bag of retardants he had strapped there, unable to find any undamaged silks. The blast sends his shot wide, as another strike on the helmet knocks him agonisingly into the wall. As he falls, he gets off a shot at one of the recovering advance duo, and sees Lou rush out across the fifteen metres of space between their foes, staggering as four blasts hit him.

Impelled to the ground, Lou's next punch targets the leg of an Agent, and as the Affiliate falls, Lou's elbow lifts upward to authorise the transaction. Keevan's reprieving fire is too late; hitting the standing Agent only after her close-range shot to Lou's head has killed his friend.

Even as he glimpses rebels scurrying from cover to finish the prone ground attack, the spark of determination is sapped from the Realliance leader. Strangely, a press of strained, mordacious-looking citizens, interspersed by near-invisible pools of calm — men and women with faces smudged grey, attired in green-and-yellow-striped camouflage smocks — storm into the cavern. Within a second the last Agent is felled.

A big-boned, part-Italian woman comes up to the stupefied leader. "Keevan? Keevan Pufreig?" At his nod she imparts, "I am Camorra of the Byron Libertarians. Angelo Hardy told us where to find you. Everybody listen! We've overrun the Agents outside. We need to evacuate into the catchment reserve."

It takes them two days to safely reach the Welving mountain fastness. They travel slow, despite the medicating skills of the Welving and copious supplies of pilfered medicine being distributed among the Realliance. The strange, Zen-like warriors treat Keevan's macerated limb with a poultice of forest herbs and ash. By the time he follows the tired party in under a drapery of interknitted vines and ferns, and greets Angelo, his fused stump is hale enough to clasp the man's shoulder. Both friends tacitly avoid the ghosts of blood that flit behind their eyes.

That night, in the thick darkness of the Welving camp, with most of the two hundred rebels accommodated on woven slings dropped cunningly from folds among the trees, Keevan tunes in and out to the low but open voice of one of their hosts. He is fascinated by the eldritch skills of this bizarre people. Mosquitoes are repulsed from the camp by some ingenuity, and the warm, colloquial commentary of the Welving man penetrates the grimness of the velvet dark.

"So, if any are displeased,' offers Ensallidor, "or made ill at ease by the idea, let them vocal now."

From the encircling beds a rebel clears her throat. There is no need to talk loudly over the languid forest. Other than for protection, the dark lends anonymity.

"I am not sure of our ability to overthrow the Affiliate in Blissbrain, though I concede to your reasoning that the coastal stew of malcontent is ready to over-boil given our fire should catch and hold. The more so if this recession of water supplies is as widespread as you have gauged. But relying on trees to close your planned trap is calamitous naivety. I saw them at the beach, but it may have been some coincidence…the malfunctioning of a genetic experiment. Our…less than two hundred, even given three hundred Welving hidden in ambush will fall like flies if the trees do not uprise."

"Let me assure you," intones the speaker, "that I plan from an intricate knowledge base. My people have lived in this forest over three centuries. We know the hearts of the trees and this new tide in them. The honour of the Welving is pledged that the trees in the river slums of Blissbrain will rise to close the trap. Is that enough for you?"

"Yes, crazily. It is."

Following the spine of rainforest between the state borders, aware of the Welving stealthily multiplying their forces from the shadows, the rebel group make Blissbrain in two days. All along the journey, waterways lay barren, but the Welving had distributed waterskins among the rebels, and they were topped up from barrels at a hidden jungle camp before they came to Quaintsand's capital.

Pre-dawn, the Welving disperse into the swamp lands. The rebels reach the city by peak hour and travel in small groups, their target and bait an outer city police station. The mood overlying the grey of the streets is coloured, but only by a red rumour, like a photograph being exposed. Empowerment cadets everywhere distribute bottles of water to long queues.

Angelo observes graffiti reading 'Curlew Coast' splashed along buildings and even over a public hover shunt. One large group of automns stand rigidly prominent while helicopters prowl the skies. The tailor sees an Agent shoot dead a boy on a bicycle for failing to stop when summoned, but he continues his nonchalant plodding in trail of his companions, all dressed as cleaners.

A little later, with the police station at last in sight some way down river, trouble strikes. Disguised as slum couriers, Keevan's group, with their code and message-scrawled bare torsos, are penultimately placed to Angelo's rear-guard group. From a hundred metres away it is clear to Angelo that the automnals are more than routinely thorough. The helicopter buzzing uncompromisingly above renders his doubts immutable.

He glances at his comrades, primed in readiness and so, as Keevan's group conjure lasers from within their torn pants — two killed as the automns' macro irradiators erupt — Angelo is able to almost instantly clip the power drive to a laz-cannon assembled unerringly by three contributing rebels, and destroy the chopper. Like a cannonaded wasp nest, the peripheral riverside police station begins to disgorge automns and barely differentiated forms in their glitzy uniforms. Some of the rebel's advance parties are close enough to engage them; Angelo swinging the cannon for rear-guard and skittering two choppers off into the gloom of the city, no doubt to return with their big, triangular brothers.

His group hurriedly deconstruct the cannon and reach the police station after a flashfire exchange with four automns, by which time the building is a ruin, pockmarked with smoking craters from hundreds of detonbys, its surrounds littered with bodies, friend and foe. Their plan has successfully attracted a major response. It is all Angelo can do to thud up an embankment over stacked civil order signs and leap gracelessly beneath the fleshy appendages of a vast fig, as a Sacubus glides by the station dolloping out laser fire and strafing bullets.

Through back lanes his group retreats, glimpsing other fleeing rebels streaking across the dilapidated wharves that shoulder the river. Angelo educes, by the occasional inextricable explosion amid the automns which hunt them, that the Welving already cover their retreat. Before they can get well clear of the rotting slums, and hopefully cozen large numbers of ground and airborne Affiliates to follow into the mangrove wastes where most of the Welving await, there is a bottleneck of land to negotiate. The river's branching pushes up against a shaly spur, dotted with torn Remnants, and the only way past this juncture is through an old market site over which hover-stacks jut through clouds of partly trapped noisome gases roiling off the water.

The Agency response, despite, or maybe because of the manhunt in Acadabourne, and recent nearby uprisings and social instability, is unexpectedly acute and formidable. They hold the bottleneck with a mass of ground personnel whilst more snipe from the spur and hover-stacks, or lithely hover-pack down onto the milling rebels. Surviving automns from the station and slum patrols approach through the distant haze. It seems that before they could spring their own trap, the rebels have been caught in the Agency's snare.

To Angelo it appears the river offers the only way out, and as he contemplates its filth, the shocking sight of two lion leaping from a big log, bearing spear-wielding barbarians in their high-slung saddles, jars across his senses. There is only one thing they can be — Unilion from Curlew. Putting aside the questions as to the how and why of this miracle, Angelo charges the enemy in their bloody wake, his poor mind floundering to keep pace with the sudden mood swings of his spirit.

For three days Tacleara, without sleep or even rest, has plied her embrocations among wounded Curlewalions along the western coast and nearby desert country. The shower-scattering clouds had brought life back to old dust wherever she was led. Her healing skills were accomplished and deific. The slight, spirited woman privately mourned she could not be among the medi-centres where the thousands from the border campaign or from the conflict she had been told about in Curlew suffered and perished from wounds that her herbs, when coupled with her applicated lore, could heal.

The second part of this equation forbade salvation en masse. She formed the only able conduit to divulge the powers in the dozens of plants and their intendant hundreds of combinations. In an atmosphere of such massed suffering, her focus would be drawn too wide, the herbs rendered ineffective or even dangerous. Also, to the south-west, Larker's portal would open — the thin chance for which she had to be ready to release her storm. So Tacleara travelled, succouring other travellers as she went.

As did their counterparts on the continent's opposite shore; Mist and Unilion advance-scouted along the west coast toward the distant base, Constrain. She even found a group of aboriginals from the Gaian Merger lands, ambushed and left mostly ruined by an aerial patrol. They had been bringing their own private vendetta toward Constrain, because the base was constructed on their ancestral country.

Mainly she treated the Fist: a group on the coast whose retreat from a failed radar sabotage had gone badly wrong. One even worse inland, surrounded by the massed debris of a strong column of Automnry that Indigoes had failed to intercept. The Unilion in need were fewer, their gargantuan beasts she treated as often with the vibrant dried blue of selhasi for lymph stabilising, as the inner sap of desert pear to encourage cell amelioration.

Tacleara backtracks, ration pipe shaking in hollow complaint as her hover bike shows an age surpassing hers. That centenarian frame is a poise of focus. She has just learned from a Unilion that a block of the main Curlew regiments, eighty thousand strong with soldiery and Indigoes, Vengers and its own medi-vac, has been decimated by an Austral helicopter patrol that slipped

387

through the Unilion and Indigo teams designed to prevent such a catastrophe. He had advised that he did not know the precise location of the combat strike, but Tacleara had followed her own nose back north. Psychically double-checking with the Indigoes among the battle block that they are forewarned of her approach, and cresting a dune, she views the might of one of Curlew's fingers of war before her, remedially little reduced by the morning's helicopter strike.

As Tacleara and her scudder are helped aboard the moving hover prop — one of ten — she empathically seeks for the most preponderant Mist upon the floating raft. She fans the subdued emotions around her into a careful assimilating of the morning's valuable lesson, plying the empathic wave form as best she can. She has little time and has largely left her people's emotions to their own evolutions. She feels a lightening of the mood around her, probably sparked by the Indigoes disseminating news of her arrival.

The authoritative little Ethiopian woman whose name Tacleara plucks from memory's retainer as they hug, gives a quick précis of the battle.

"Fifty helicopters, my dear. Hopefully we jammed their radios in time, and certainly none will fly back now to warn the base. Some carried bombs, some missiles. We buried over five thousand, almost all ours. Seven thousand have been evacuated. Nine hundreds the medi-vac did not see fit to move. Internal damage. A small team is nursing their passing, which will not be long."

"Nooljaki, I am a herbalist as you know. A combinative treatment for grave wounds I have unearthed. I can save and evacuate all but the most acute. I need a hover."

"Tacleara. I can give you a hover, for many of the slain were Vengers. They alone pilot the aerial assault. We have docked a dragonfly aboard a tech prop as reserve should we need it. You can fly it. Though they are lethal in storm fronts, and I think you have stronger need for a shovel."

"How many can a dragonfly bear?"

"Three hundred. But I don't think you will fill her hold."

"I will take the craft, thank you, and may the stars protect."

Tacleara hovers the hundred-metre long craft from the prop, its wings for stabilising loads as yet furled, and follows the Venger guide several kilometres to a plain of the living dead. Now she focuses stringently. Yellow sand. Mix dose. Charge; apply. For thirteen hours she moves among the ravaged of Curlew's companies, reapplying every hour. Most often she uses the cataplexic combines, and it seems that she is far enough advanced in her practice to achieve the impossible. By dawn the dozen medi-vac have secured two hundred and eighty-nine in a stable coma state, half upright in unfolded canvas slings within the dragonfly.

Tacleara is grateful to see Jorgen pilot the craft upward, her heart as heavy as the dead they had slung into fires below. She has just enough energy to bring a slight coercion of reassurance to her three medi-vac crew as the wings unfurl, and she informs them they are not travelling northward to Curlew lands, but south.

Larker has been secreted in the flower cave for a day now. The large natural chamber at the back of the main bastillion is named for the huge rocky semblance of a selhasi flower at its entrance, crafted to open and close its petals at his word. They are shut behind him now, Senastim orchestrating the crescendo's psychic defences in his absence. The cave has proved necessary, shielding him from the turmoil of the half million survivors they have harboured in the crescendo vale and from the constant repartee of laser exchange with automns attempting to scale the cliff walls. Mercifully, the Peacebeats have been enjoying detonating incoming airborne incendiaries harmonically.

Larker feels the Hobbogyre tighten their focus. They are concerting from all over the land to tease a window onto the limbic dimensions where these meet the earth, most hobs gathering at the site of the initial rending, or on the ley-line usurped by the Serpent — the continent's strongest. In the eye of his mind, the rhabdomancer sees Tacleara unloading her cargo of Curlew soldiers, herbally enshrined in a suspended animation of body functions. She has found this precise spot based solely on her gut instinct. Surely, Larker broods, she will be able to make the change.

Delicately, methodically, Larker splits his mind into three. With one portion of himself he travels along the currents of the Hobbogyre's Blissbrain grid, travels back through time to a great pyramid by the banks of a river, aware of the distant approach of three immortal groups, come to bring annihilation. With another he immerses himself in the desert ley-line by the gathered of Tacleara's reclaimed air strike victims. With yet another he meets the tendrils of Tacleara's mind.

'We are ready. Are you prepared, Guchiehay?'

'I…yes. I have asked them, Larker, in their wide awake minds. Everyone had agreed to volunteer. Only I wonder…we have some two hundred and eighty of the thousands of Immortals. How shall we know who to exchange?'

'I do not know. It may be that more may come through — or less. Some effect shall prosper if you have merged truly with the herbs. It is all we can hope."

Tacleara's mental voice is thick with emotion and he steers her toward the high ground of her practical aptitude. *'They must stand the transition. The immortals are construed of great resilience."*

'I have given them a high dose of volpure, to elasticise the tissue integrities, and desert-blind, for emotional sovereignty. It has incorporated completely, perhaps due their willingness for this journey, and the adaptogens coursing through their blood. We are ready.'

'So you must be, for in ten minutes it is begun. Watch for the doorway. The signs will be prevalent. Bring as many through as possible.'

Retracting his thought-link with Tacleara, Larker's focus is tight enough that he sends the awakening firefeather power down through his feet and into the energy line controlled by the Dark-Ley Serpent. He stands in one of his selves, near to Tacleara's group, though unseen by them. The safety grid of the Hobbogyre channels his firefeather-enhanced questing along the wildest edge of that Earth ley, where its pulses are still clean, too powerful for the Serpent to sully.

In the cave, Larker breathes once every minute, in union with these pulses. His anchor back into the time-distant part of himself holds firm, strengthened perhaps by the rapturous vitality of the planet in that remove of its spin. From the vantage of this self, he watches as those Lellying able escape from the Serpent by dissolving into the leys. He has bare minutes. With an intricate plying of his will, he reaches across to the limbic void of that older dimension. Out-time, and white-hot nausea sweeps his being. His mind alternately schizophrening and stabilising under the pressure, the shaman flexes his aura against the complexity of hob safety channels for bounding his consciousness. Next, Larker plaits twin warps of power from the Earth and the planes of the astral, and stretches the cord between the two nodes his spirit activates: the one of distant time, the other of out-time. He trickles a little of his consciousness, like bubbles of air escaping the intensity of his sealed vacuum, to thread into the hobs' seeing, and fractures under a crushing weight, surrounded by dark unknown depths. He feels the earth shudder around him as though it will invert to a helix and slice right through his mind. Compelling his energies to a final exertion, he pushes out along the hobs' grid. Now his spirit locks in embrace with the Earth-mind, and he lights his wick.

Musa hurls his spear into an Agent on the edge of a hover-stack and rushes alongside Nivat's charge, the two brothers yelling 'Curlew' as they smash into the Agents pushing from the bottleneck. The black Spartan excels at his knife work, the first flinch in the lines allowing him deep into Affiliate ranks.

Nivat, directing the rebels to focus on the spur, turns to see his brother plying his steel in ceaseless arabesques, as the two Ra-kings harangue a wedge of Agents separated along the broader tract of river bank behind the Unilion. Musa's eyes blaze with an intention harder than steel. He allows an Agent's overt defence to impel across his own throat and into the Affiliate behind him. Suddenly Nivat knows that those eyes, maybe too hard, are the only place where Musa's dauntless embrace of the world could crack. Every other part of him is martial, empowered according to his will. The bard turns from the inevitable and retrieves Musa's spear from a cadaver at the spur's foot.

He walks over to a woman who mutters while pointing her gun at a charred hover-pack Agent. Placing his hand on her shoulder, he asks, "Your first kill?"

She nods.

"It's alright," he says. "It doesn't get easier."

She laughs faintly. As he sheathes the weapon and their eyes meet, Nivat feels his heart contract with her tall beauty and presence, intense for its combine of rawness and determination. Musa bundles over and washes his weapons through the water by his brother while most of the rebels still fire confusedly at the retreating hover Agents or regroup from a push against the automns.

Even before Musa notices her, Nivat observes the woman attend the big man's movements with a captivated air. There is a stench in the air, a foulness seeping through the slain Agent's uniform where the soil of his body tries to merge with the earth.

"So," the Unilion looks around at the quieting chaos. "What are you people doing?"

"Well, all this — " she begins in an American-tinged voice before Musa cuts her off.

"You never know where they might have recording circuits. Just whisper."

Though tall, the woman has to stand on tiptoe to press against Musa and lean her mouth to his ear. The thirty seconds it takes seems to Nivat to pass as an anguish, by which time rebels have gathered around, and his jealousy is rendered abruptly a fearful, naked thing that he conceals with his will.

"Okay," Musa booms. "We're from Curlew — to help. We just destroyed Base Hamper! But let's do this thing..." he stresses, over the cheering, "Let's move. The Lion are on your side, folks."

Angelo is beside the lion-mounted men as the party streams along the river bank and squelches across a reedy bog. He notes that whatever has been affecting rivers and reservoirs of fresh water has no influence on salt water. Leaping a tangly fence, they reach the higher ground of a rubbish-littered paperbark forest. The branching channels of the river's side stream are delineated by mangroves. They advance some three kilometres through these twisted trees before a thick squadron of hovers whir overhead, and the tailor hears troop movements yelled across the water in crisp Affiliate code.

The rebel leader yells, "Spread out and keep moving," but their Curlew allies are already a blur moving toward the enemy.

Nivat and Musa have already drawn back knives when they sight the river once more. A mass of Agents are unloading from shunts at the water edge. The brothers strike fast, felling what claws and steel can reach, then leap behind the buttresses of the mangroves. Again they attack the edge of the line of hundreds. As they predate once more, a huge bristling metal tentacle slashes down through Musa's spear. He and Marisk leap separate ways and the Unilion rockets off a knife at the new enemy. Five metres up, through the operating panel, the knife pierces an Agent's eye. As the machine tumbles, Marisk falls with it, dying, skewered through his midriff by a barbed leg.

"Go," Musa yells at his brother, flinging a knife at Marisk's neck to finish him, backing with awkward tumbles as barb and tentacle whip through the trees.

393

Two of the machines, with millipede legs and three whips of steel, pursue. The brothers are unlucky. The machines were developed to destroy the nests of smugglers in these swamps who had been eating into the government's drug profits before advent of the nimble insectoids. Musa hurdles logs, striving toward higher ground, and ducks into a thicket just as three whips close on empty air.

Sanfel and Nivat plough up a hillside a small way ahead, dotted with rocks and bigger trees. It is strange country, rising almost geometrically, but the Unilion knows the big trees mean safety. Glancing back, he sees a woman, the one with the American lilt, lying along a branch as high as the window of the machine. She steadies her weapon at the Unilion's nightmare pursuer, which she smashes with a laser blast. A writhing leg rips through the branch, and she falls, but is up and running as the machine alters its course toward her. Smoothly, Musa exploits the chance, aiming his last knife at the exposed operator. Through some sixth sense the man ducks. Agents, he knows, can be stern adversaries. This one actually turns to smirk at Musa, the hungering legs he controls waving toward the Unilion once again. The woman uses the reprieve to reach Nivat on a narrow ridge. The bard pointedly plants his spear butt in the ground before lion, woman and man duck from view of the desperate cameo. Musa plucks it and turns in one move — yet too slow. A whip slices through the butt, Musa falls, rolls from under the legs and flees, defenceless.

Over the ridge, the others await him. Like relay runners, they make a renewed burst of speed. The insectoid is slowed along this flank of the hill, angled almost exactly as the last they traversed, but covered with thick debris. The four escapees look back to see a tree grasp and crush the machine with leathery branches. All around them, wraith-like bipeds, with heavy-lidded, leaf-shaped eyes and blank faces, rise from the earth. As one the fugitives realise the ground beneath them is a pit over-capped loosely with vines. As they plummet, the world turns the darkest black and slowly fills with the flecks of a billion stars.

Having sent the four medi-vacs back north in the dragonfly, Tacleara watches as a dome of blackness a hundred metres high, and appearing to tunnel into the earth, swallows her reprieved patients. With her last body consciousness before the herbs comatose her, Tacleara opens her palm, thinking of the rainbowed light Larker had gifted her. A cone of radiance spreads from her hand where it lies still upon the desert floor, trailing like steam after her disembodied will — given astral wings by the herbs — into the limbic dimensions. As she projects herself deeper into the void, the Marrafar and Opsweyed burst as a powerful side stream of feeling, their energy looming, then receding like a mirage. It is a power dulled by anger, fear and hopelessness, and Tacleara realises it will be enough. The balled life-force of her country's people will apportion for that force, which the immortals must represent — a sort of moving, volatile nothing — so that when Larker bleeds the ley fluxes back onto the exact signature of feeling when first the immortals had been condemned here, there will be a chance to draw them out.

Finally, the two groups intersect and Cleara pushes the mortal onto the vortex-bound immortal energy. She is disoriented by the turbid emotions around her, the raw ache of feeling…of feeling…

Suddenly she brushes against a feeling of solidity, of love, of light. Tacleara wearily opens eyes on a milling and bizarre group. She tastes blood in her mouth and wonders as she collapses at the sight of a lion amid the strange ranks.

The hand, huge but gentle on her shoulder, is covered in orange hair — as is the face regarding hers. The immortal's eyes, though bemused, are venerable, wise.

"You are needed," she tells the Marrafar Enyadding, her empathy bridging the language barrier, "to the south-west, by the remnant Enyadding.

You have been sundered from time, three thousand..." Tacleara's oesophagus clogs with blood and she smiles as a great thunderhead dilutes to mauve and lets forth a deluge.

Chapter 21

While Boabben ponders, one finger slates around the leaf weal on his chest. Almost, there had been two more age-fire leaves seared through that broad rampart of his ribs, yet eventually the faeries had vacillated on attempts to sing or shadow-snare the leaves from him and accepted one each that peace would be assured. Boabben was slowly forgiving the hob's partly expected remission of his promised help. Nobody liked to be around two faery tribes at once, and hobs were by nature a sly and calculating bunch.

Yet it had been Fortusenay who — in consigning to him the understanding of Fae dynamics, of their weaknesses and strengths and, most crucially, of their naïve relationship to the Serpent or Needthrall as the Hobbogyyre named it — had first sparked in Boabben the idea to steal two more age-fires. For one already purloined, he had gained the knowledge from Fortusenay, along with sworn understanding that the hobs, long hidden allies of the Enyadding, planned to use the firefeather as catalyst in restoring the time-sundered Opsweyed and Marrafar back to true continuum, claiming they were already priming two human candidates to facilitate the bridging.

The immortal recalls the earthen creature — turning the gold leaf up to the sun and studying it whilst huge lips had swung aside on the hairy face to address him in its harsh Latin dialect.

"That's what it sunk the ships from Portugal, from France for. Needthrall wanted Englishers here, but not to harness their energy. It wanted the Facú here, the last two Fae mobs together; because of the war it knew was likeliest seed between them."

The hob had then imparted to Boabben a litany of the Serpent's preparative coercions, from wood types it had prompted shipbuilders to choose, to its compelling of the transfer of rabbits, sparrows, fruit-thorns and foxes by the conquerors, all designs to make passage and a toehold by the Facú in Wowbrae-held land possible.

"Facú couldn't have flown here unaided. They can only propel using their shadings, like Wowbrae use tonings; even Enyadding couldn't leap-frog the whole way to England! No! Faery got star filaments meshed through their blood, but there has to be specific ecological dynamics for that to become volatile."

Antiquated star filaments. Now there was a glorious thing, and Boabben supposes his present anti-gravitational home is like a warlock castle, as it is made from faery blood. When he had confirmed with the hob that neither Fae tribe knew of their role as pawns to the Serpent's three centuries of energy harvesting, and were therefore ignorant of his own need to stop them from warring, he had bargained hard. Each age-fire given had ensured peace between the Fae, their dynamic needs able to be sourced through the crystal. He had gained an equivalent weight of blood from each tribe for the leaves and so had his shield from which to launch the rescue.

In seven days the Lellying will all meet. It is ironic that Lornahe and the others had found him too late, after searching more than a year, since his first theft had been detected. Regardless of whether their intent had been punishment or re-conscription, their hand is now forced to yield to Aruan. Boabben would allow the attempt, but not the self-sacrifice of his son, that part of the plan being abhorrent to him. Mention had been made only of the girl's sacrifice in the garbled prophecy that Nancy Welving had recorded as he spasmed at her feet. Meantime, there is that composite, even now blending with the water tables — a little firefeather reserved from those traded, and a pinch of star filamentation. Hobs were fickle but knowledgeable beings and had proved impetus for Boabben's alchemical subterfuge.

The drying of Austral's rivers, as the water sucked into dryagon and dryadic awakening, would sign the truth of the times for any who could clearly see. Let the sleeping warriors of the planet be woken at this, the Earth's most crucial juncture.

Let tree and wing and dryad stir, at last. Surprised, Boabben feels the dawn-dreaming come upon him as it has not for the ten days he has been in his little castle, and his body sprawls against the roof as he journeys — back this time.

Images flash untranslatable before Boabben. A branch of gold and black flowers densely packed...two curved, newly risen loaves of taut rye bread. Then the dreaming begins to translate, and the bread becomes the elliptical cheeks of the Wowbrae, flower-carved war club out-swinging to emphasise statements...the words becoming coherent.

"The way across the world's brow is fraught for any on two legs. The coastal shoulder I would deem superior, where the waters from the Colour Blossom Fold will join your goings and form road to their source."

The faery's navigational advice seemed dubious to Boabben, perhaps because delivered in the most clipped of tones — as always when the Wowbrae spoke English — preceded by lisping whistles as the words hit the drilled holes in the being's few teeth. Nancy, teary that day for the parting that was to come, corroborated a slow trickle of pioneering reports describing fearsome rivers, impassable ravines and cloyed thickets beneath behemothic mountain eucalypts. So he and Tourmal had vacillated no longer after their months of lingering alongside the blazing gentleness of the artist, often among several Wowbrae. Nancy Welving — she had been there to record in stroked paint the seven prophecies that had so maimed the last days of their friendship. Boabben's future-seeings had taken on a feral strength that threw him into fits, leaving blindness in their wake for many hours.

Four prophecies delineated the future in an improbable brutality, three were hidden in oracle that would only coalesce into meaning in far distant times. Each had eroded to ash Nancy's empyreal features, the clear or shadowy foretellings of coming bleakness driving shafts through her rapture.

So Boabben had climbed the ridge chaperoning the settlement of the woman he had come to cherish but could not bear to touch for fear of the long days through which his amaranthine life would be empty after her mortal passing. He had turned his chin to the night and eternal solace of the wild, his heartbeat catching in folds of his throat and finally erupting in the four stag-topped gums upon the height. Below, fire burned in omen through two misty nights before the watching eyes of every Scottish and English settler but Nancy.

They had been right, his beloved friend and the strange hum and skirl of faeries — impish embellishment to her world, Boabben thought. Without doubt these coastal plains present a yielding tree cover and unhindered course. The forest through which they journeyed was a vast temple, opened by the studied burning of the tribes in age-old tradition. The immortal smiled to watch Tourmal bound toward him, tracking the shore of the distant billabong where the marrankur had been scouting.

Their pace over the plains country surged to counter the pressure of winter's grasp, though Boabben paused often in some patch of sun to watch the brightening of vine flowers, or the grass trees amid the uniform mauve of clumped wallaby grass. Before dusk he halted, ensorcelled by the beauty of the waterside. A wide billabong lapped rosy trunks of redgums. The waters, having secured the totemic shading of these giants, had advanced further to mooch among grasses that tilted seed tassels into the calm, seasonal wetness.

By the makeshift spillway of the pool — a woven cradle of two tree's industrious roots — the immortal sat listening as the bare murmur of the water's questing was joined by the measured 'block block' of a frog half hidden in the flaking bark of a butt the colour of bruised moon stuff. In the far distance, the long line of snow-dusted mountains became saddled in mustard from the last light, the foreground of scattered billabongs crystallising with a skim of toffee, as though cauls of bunyips he had heard one of the vacant-eyed shepherds ranting about.

As the stars arrived, the glow from many striking off the water, Boabben lingered, and while the heavenly congregation slipped away around Orion, Scorpio and the ever patient matriarch, Venus, he compared this cool, wild land to its northern counterpart. Crocodile lands, the Lellying had called the ragged, red country, brittle as newly fired spinifex. Boabben remembered its stone channelling strange resonances like a didgeridoo. A land carved by sun and flood with the gap-toothed smile of wisdom, yet renewing the spirit and body with deep comforts: the warmth of poolside basalt, the clear skin of gorge beaches washed to crystal, beguiling with green eyes of shade.

In contrast, this land of furry bodies within every nook, parrot and honeyeater clouds, endless waterways and imperious towering trees, reminded him of the three day long corroboree at the clan meeting he had attended with the Yallanded. Like the gathering, it seemed filled with shifting and inter-merging stories, its rains and currents of life as constant as the shuffling of ritual feet in dusty dance — a world between worlds, foreboding and impenetrable as the passing looks he had seen each of the tribe's kurdaitchi exchange. An endless, somnambulistic, spell chant of life. In its green thrall; its shadow and profusion of life patterns, Boabben found a comfort more to do with a limitless promise of fresh horizons than any yearning for his heritage.

As the dawn renewed him, the fireseer chortled at Tourmal's ponderous tree acrobatics, his leaving of Nancy already a scabbing wound. The marsupial was springing trunk to trunk, sliding many metres headlong down the vast boles or rampaging through the ivory and verdigris lattice of their crowns. In the end the chase was a failure. Tourmal had been trying through a second night to catch, on a matter of principle, a little grey-bodied hunter with a pot-brush tail, smaller than but as fierce as those other arboreal hunters, quolls. Boabben did not know what the tribes called it, but dog-mouse seemed appropriate for the fiery, tenacious face Tourmal had mentally provided to his curiosity.

"Flier more speed than a bird!" Tourmal coloured sulkily as he lapped from the pool.

"Why don't you trap it with your cheating hunting, and become seen-not?" Boabben queried of his bond.

"There marrankur here. I think they colour me, we big fight."

Boabben was surprised at first, but as they walked, he realised it was superb marrankur territory. Thick banksia clumps grew wherever a fallen giant granted light, and along stream margins and sandy hollows their stumpy limbs, like swollen insect appendages, were bullied into alliance with vines in shaggy tumbles, or usurped by trees thickly-leafed, scented and hued like fresh pepper — out-fliers from the vast coastal rainforest. Fern was more prevalent in the sandy country, and whippy splashes of yellowed wattle and an indigo-flowered shrub, both with fernlike leaves.

Afternoon brought them living sign of people. There was the monotonous thud of axe and smell of smoke, the haranguing of dogs.

"I will meet you on the brightness side of people nests..." Tourmal suddenly coloured, and Boabben thought his bond struck by some returned dog phobia. Then the marrankur added, "In the sun, beside two star trees." Tourmal sprang away, colouring a final, "Wait me."

Boabben gleaned around the colours the flash of a tawny marrankur, red like the north race, but smaller like Tourmal, and from the way the image moved with an extra articulation of hips, a female. Boabben stood smiling, then walked toward the settlement to see why the conduits of civilisation were connected to this place.

The link was tenuous enough that Boabben, standing before the railing fence encompassing three cabins of stacked logs and sheet bark, had to quest along the Mend Map to discover it. Not far distant was a vast river valley; the little track he stood on probably allowed wagons to meet ships that plied its lower waters, and this land was the closest flat space that would not be prone to the flooding of the river valley itself. Before nightfall Boabben had ascertained that the tiny settlement's economic grist was wattle bark, stacked in massive sheaves behind the huts, for sale to the coastal tanning industry, as well as the aside of one settler's fur interest, exclusively composed of platypus.

As darkness fell, protested by the scanty crescent moon, Boabben headed toward his distant rendezvous with Tourmaline, though yet a day and a half early. Light flickered uncertainly from a far corner of the settler yard, followed by a grudging crackling as the fire shed its earthly inanimacy to blaze into elemental configuration. Within its candescent rivulet swam several figures dressed so anomalously that Boabben's smile broadened with every step of his moth-like compulsion towards them. There were three young girls, one tottery, and an older boy, all dressed in finery of green, which emerald sentiment was heartily appropriated by the gowns of two women, the mothers he supposed, reaching a hand each to the tiny girl and older boy, and jauntily dancing around their partners to a canny beat of music.

The musicians employed tin whistle and bodhran, eliciting a distinctly high-stepping whirling of dress and agility of skipping from the dancers. Boabben was sluiced back to his native soil on the water race of memory, to like-firesides in Corkcounty fields and faces of childhood sweethearts and family, but only as a briefest journey, without the least of sentimentality. For him to evoke such a dance would be like to a jaguar carrying pollen — his body was not of such prosaic coarseness, but he studied the romping with an anthropological eye, discerning nuances of cultural expression he had missed as a youth. After many partner changes and rhythm variations, an obviously drunk man wore his way alongside the two barefooted and tattily suited musicians. The music gave way, only to be taken up once more by the bansheeing of the newcomer's bagpipes.

The two women danced a diplomatic reel, one snatching hands from her boy's ears, as the awful caterwauling rose amid off-key droning and scratchy pauses.

Then the party found the children's bedtimes suddenly pressing, but the Scottish outsider played on, unfazed. Boabben put a mile or so between himself and the woeful miscreance of noise. In the morning he found curiosity again drawing him to the huts, where a dancer from last night was flinging scraps among a devoted audience. Over a hundred large birds, their tails like shimmery white furbelows, milled about her feet — striding out of the flock with prizes of crusts or dragging porridge remnants toward them with huge feet. The terror of muses from the night before sauntered over and tapped his pipe barrel against the fence.

"Fatten 'em up, Ailleen. We'll soon have roasters and a bushel of feathers."

"We will not! They're the soul of music. You could do with studying their song more than that fire water you brew. Here…" the woman stooped and ripped a few small leathery leaves from a vine scrambling over a stump, "Broil some bush tea. Lord knows you need it. I can still smell the fumes."

"Whiskey puts yearning in a man's piping."

"It puts the devil — " With an exasperated little scream, Ailleen watches the asteroid of chaos that swept into the flock, bounding up and along the rail with a still-struggling bird in its jaws, then leaping away into dense bushes. Boabben saw two more of the hopeful hunters rushing along the forest floor to join it. Quolls. Spotted, cat-sized versions of a marrankur.

"You could peg a few of those blighters."

"Nary. They remind me of the wild cats of home. Did I ever tell you, Ailleen, of the wild…"

Boabben wandered off, approving of the little play, thoughts of marrankur recalling him to the need of finding a good route across the marshy valley before meeting Tourmal. The lowing of cattle greeted him as the track brought him over a rise, affording his first view of the valley. Avarice prevailing over common sense, two cattle farmers had etched holdings into the jungle each side of the river, whilst a crop of beans upstream probably represented another farmstead, its chattels hidden by a thrust of land.

Otherwise the wide, wet bowl was a disporting of pure wonder. Through gaps on its bank where huge trees had fallen, Boabben could glimpse the flush of the fast river and its mile after mile of floodplains covered in a shifting primordia of ducks, geese, herons, ibis and kangaroos. Towering, fleshy-topped palms spotted the banks and plains, and water sprawled in pools among a hundred complicities of green. The immortal became intoxicated, and issuing a wild yell, launched a madcap run down the hill.

Whipping through a grove of mighty tree-ferns, their trunks exotic mini-forests of jumbled smaller trees, ferns and vines, Boabben raced along the tight, pastel-barked limb of a sinuous river guardian hulked in dreams of strength and nourishment. It transported him up and out near the middle of the flow.

The river spanned no greater width than three hundred yards, running straight in both directions as far as he could see. Everywhere it was gloried by the petitioning of galaxies of hanging white star flowers, tree-trunk-sized slumps of lianas, out-leaning quadruple-crowned tree-ferns, purple-foliaged, columnar trees, uniformly geometric, and mahogany-trunked giants with filigreed leaves that excused their brutish gawping.

In the amber waters below, Boabben could see the mossy details on deeply submerged fallen limbs damming rough sand into pale drifts like river milk. He rolled his feather cloak in a ball and swung out over the flow from a knuckled vine that dangled from a titan's canopy. Boabben dropped, nonchalantly somersaulting into the surprisingly warm water. Around him a school of large black fish played, while a platypus, somehow surviving the Scotsman's nets, flipped away, trailing bubbles. As he floated along the aqueous road, two huge sea eagles flounced before him, squabbling half-heartedly over an algae-covered tortoise until it was lost to the water and the great ernes each flapped apart, reaching a claw into a convenient shoal of fish and swooping off in charmed penitence.

Boabben hooked his legs in a trailing vine loop and lay staring stuporifically at the colourful tassels of overhanging jungle while kingfishers, like animated slivers of the clearing sky, flitted past. With a sigh, he righted himself, and shimmying up the vine to the tree's crest, spread his cloak to dry and overlooked his new surround. Slightly upriver, in a clear chain of billabongs into which a side stream of the river overspilled, storks and brolgas hunted frogs or eels. It gave him a feeling of community to see these wanderers from northern lands lingering still in this cool paradise.

He noticed the valley was far warmer than its surrounds, sealed from cool winds in a horseshoe of hills and mountains but open to the coast and the warm air cycling off its massed waters. Soft voices below drew his heady ruminations to a group of aboriginals at a fire upon a bank of the billabong chain. With childlike euphoria he slid down the arching length of the slightly ridged branch and leaped into a catch of fern and vines below. He edged along the kangaroo-cropped billabong's shore to more closely study the tribespeople.

There seemed to be three families, all their members' faces bearing expressions of studied repose, their bodies a relaxed weariness. They reclined on thick possum-skin cloaks, children raking bulbs about the coal bed. Several tall, utilitarian spears lanced from the mud, while fish smoked in a bark contrivance for the continuance of their journey. Two huge canoes, chiselled from the trunks of mighty trees, were beached on the shore. Boabben thought the unwieldy vessels odd until he overheard some of the conversation.

An elegantly physiqued man, with little blooms of grey through his cut-back, curly hair, had sat up to speak, his spine lifting straight his neck with the fluidity of a brolga.

"Tonight shall we float to sea, praying for cloud to hide us from the white devils. We must bring the news that they now guard the river way from the mountains. Maybe we will be the last to journey from the solid water to the sea…"

A flock of ducks rose in unceremonious portent at the words, and Boabben stumped away, heart momentarily stung by cold vespers of harrowing fates. He intuited flashes of the stoic families buffeted by icy rapids, hurtled along the roar of water through deafening gorges as they migrated coastward. Of their stopping on smoother stretches, perhaps to improvise a lost paddle or poultice dislocated limbs. Especially, of their reaching becalmed waters at last, only to find their coastal plains had been conquered while they summered in the deep mountains.

Boabben tarried among ferns like scything tusks of mastodons and lawns of flowering herbs. The rhythmic gush of the river, plangent swan song, virulence of frog chorus and the affronted mistrust of snooping wombats gradually consoled his heart. Boabben walked across the river, its vibrancy seeming to tension his strides. He re-joined the cart path, following its weave amid the billabongs to a place downstream where the river widened, and most of the bank guardians had been painstakingly hacked away and burned. A small jetty ran out to the deep water, but its trestled legs looked to Boabben like the skeleton doll of some enemy kurdaitchi — it was an engineering hungering into the future, sounding the death knell of this place.

Immured in long grass in the cooling evening, Boabben sent forth along the Mend Map and found good passage north — kangaroo trails with tribal notches as guide where the swamps grew trees. Satisfied, he savoured the changing chorus of twilight, watched the shiftings of fruit bat and flying possums across the night and discerned the musings of fish along the bank margins.

Tourmal bolted up to him before the kookaburras had stopped their dawn exulting, his tail sweeping in lazy curves of excess energy.

"It is thick-fast here," coloured Tourmaline. "There are thick-fast places in the hills also. I think my cubs will grow safely there, though the marrankur are ant-bitten at the whites' axes and dogs."

They walked to the river, and Tourmal plunged in, Boabben hopping across the buoyant flow. "What colour will your cubs be then?" he queried of his bond. Tourmal paused, as though for thought, and the river sidled him away, then he struck out strongly for a branch, shook off his coat and pattered ashore. Boabben's head filled with images of two cubs with tawny bodies, jet tails and black spots on their legs. He chuckled, and Tourmal came alongside, smiling from one end of his muzzle to the other.

As they threaded through billabongs along mostly dry ground, the marrankur mock-complained about having to choose from so many types of bird. In the end he took a magpie goose, and the resultant cloud of exploding avians soon drifted back to their foraging, the valley's breast becalming again as it returned to the rhythm of life enshrined by countless millennia. Some kilometres across the great valley, Boabben knew the river intersecting their path was that which they sought, a living road to the mountain fold which had so haunted and called him.

A quarter width of the last river, bestrewn with glistening ochre and trailing continuous blossoms, white, yellow or red, it upheld the Wowbrae's sign of leading to the Colour Blossom Fold. As they ventured away from the plains, the river loped more circuitously around corners and narrowed until it was falling steeply, dropping from on high. Around them, breathing sighs of mist, endless hills jostled together. Through these the river cut rocky gorges, its bank thicketed in fragrant scrub, every tree stuck with flags and streamers of hanging growth.

The air was saturated with the honeyed scent of industrious wattle blooms, the slender trees clinging to the loose soil of the steep foothills. Where the land rose more broadly, conical trees with large blooms — a piercing pure red — proliferated, dazzling the valley. By nightfall the wayfarers had reached a continuously flat plateau and trekked along wombat paths beside the boulder-strewn flow. Persistent rain had set in, yet beneath a crowded canopy of dense rainforest trees, vines islanding the occasional marooned eucalypt, they remained dry.

Boabben trekked aslant of the river, following the Mend Map to the base of a small mountain, the only landform separating them from the tangible vibrancy of the Blossom Fold. Here he found a dry hollow at the butt of a gum and, with Tourmal's head asleep in his lap, breathed in the gentle vitality of his surrounds, constraining his excitement until daylight. When dawn's gold stained the curtaining mists, Tourmal and Boabben raced up the mountain. The plump birds with tails like lyres that Boabben had seen at the Irish settlement squawked aside, flap-hopping onto monolithic boulders through which the duo threaded.

The summit gave window on a sprawling plateau courted by clouds jostled together in pure white. The haughty heads of eucalypt monarchs, lightning scarred but dauntless, peered expressionlessly down upon these phantom falls. A few rocky promontories were the only other feature.

Boabben began to sing a traveller's song from his native shore, honing his mind as he applied heat to unbind the cumulus. In moments, the cover shredded into wisps of up-rushing shapes, like sprites, and was gone.

The unveiled dominion was a revelation of patterned and lush grandeur. Rainforest princesses were crowned purple, olive, yellow, white and emerald, while black cockatoos careened over their heads like butterflies in a sunroom. Drinking in the scene, Boabben's sharp eyes could make out three different species of the birds, black bodies individuated by stains of bold colour. Further, he could dimly see distant protecting mountains, and in the direction of the far coast, hills innumerable, sipping their morning mists. Flat, countless kilometres of shining lands, soft and hidden to the world below — the Colour Blossom Fold.

Boabben and Tourmal roamed the wide, stream-fed land, enjoying ever new wonders. Boabben sampled each spring with delightful result. Tourmaline was intrigued by the fluffily balled marsupials, like giant hares, that grazed on the mushrooms stippling the deep moss that spread in a continuous green carpet beneath the silver or gold-backed leaves of the canopy. Even the ravens here seemed softened — moving contrasts of tone highlighting the silver towers of the rainforest trunks, the deep drifts of wide, gold leaves, the minutiae of detail in tiny rock-nourished shrubs from which their sly beaks elicited red berries.

Marrankur and Mended loitered across the plateau in a blessed daze, together — or meeting after weeks in faint surprise, coming each around the trunk of an improbably wide gum. The fireseer witnessed snows daubing every plant white in a precise line along the plateau rim. Beyond this fussy requite of the snowflakes for solidifying, a sudden line of vegetation clear of niveous covering.

He witnessed the swelling of the waterfalls with snowmelt, pouring their thin bodies from the sharp back of the plateau, tumbling through space like millions of shooting stars. Then, in spring, the tribes arrived.

The forest filled with the singing calls of children darting naked through the painted trees, giddily screaming in the rushing brooks. At night Boabben sat enthralled near their fire, listening to the cadences of their voices rippling in the star-swooning air. There were discordantly few men, except for grainy elders, but the women seemed happy, sporting shell and possum tail jewellery, and one a dried hand which Boabben hoped was to honour a family member rather than to gloat at an enemy's fate. After a week, when he knew he had grasped their language thoroughly, he unbound the Veiling and walked into the streamside glade where the adults were relaxing.

There was no screaming or wily reaching for weapons. A few of the young women shrugged more tightly into their possum rugs, then the matriarch came up and placed a glad hand against his cheek, and everybody began talking at once. Boabben's story, that he had jumped from a whale boat, learned the language from a distant coastal group and followed his heart to this place was merely not the whole truth, but it was accepted gracefully. It was harder to explain Tourmal, whom Boabben introduced against the slim chance of errant spear. The creature's bizarreness seemed to increase Boabben's standing and lend him an authenticity of tribal, rather than white, persona.

Tourmal was such a delight among the children that many hardly noticed Boabben until the next morning. It turned out that this area actually functioned as nursery for two closely-knit coastal tribes' children. It explained the dollop of children and few adults. Most older women and some elderly men, along with adolescents, came in mid-spring to enjoy the plateau and manage the children who were here free to roam. There were no treacherous rivers here, or fierce fires, cutting thorns, burning sun or any precedents that another tribe might find the plateau. The many tiger snakes were food rather than fear to aboriginal children. With the children out of the main tribes' hair, those on the coast could see to weaponry, tool, and ritual maintenance — and wind-down after winter, before coming together on the plateau in autumn.

Boabben hunted the sleek, plump plateau wallabies with the young men. Tourmal often spent days with the children and returned wreathed in flowers or muddier than the little ones. Both chewed the leaves, delicately ridged golden spears of a beautiful rainforest tree that the tribe feted for their stimulant and mildly euphoric powers. There were long walks and tree climbs to peer at possum nests, excited catching of crayfish and the chicanery of calling owls to camp at dusk with mimicked calls.

Boabben did not leave to winter on the coast with the tribes. From his star-filament sanctuary, the dawn-dreaming memories present his time on the plateau as a contented passing of decades. Whilst the two tribes returned in their migrations, names and faces of the children were ever-changing as they became adults strictured to remain on the coast. If ever the tribes noticed his resilience of youth, no questions were levelled at him. He came to be a figure of magic in their seasonal forays to a magical land — and figures of magic came to him on the Colour Blossom Plateau. He sensed fetches of Wowbrae — lights and tiny winged figures — projections of their mind, through which he understood their elemental scoutings were conducted. He saw their actual selves rarely, crossing perhaps a dozen words with faeries per decade, with never Nancy's name among them.

The two hob goblins, who came, warped with power, trundling across the moss one day, claimed they had merely superseded the antecedent of his discovering them first.

"Surely, you will uncover us with that agile spying behind every tree and bush," averred the deep, rolling, European accented voice of the hob who introduced himself as Fortusenay. Boabben was never quite certain they did live on the plateau, suspecting them dwellers of the bower tangles in distant hills and that they had sought him out as a power ally, not as a neighbour who happened to share their sempiternality. Still, he was delirious with the peerage they represented. There were fringes of things like a Veiling wrapped around them, and Boabben studied their fluxing faces to try and determine if a force like the Mend Flows within them. Altogether, he felt more comfortable with the ancient, ocean-eyed creatures with their claws and contortions than he did with mortals.

"We see you are Mended," said the one known as Planghar on their second day's commune, apparitioning from behind a log.

"We have never actually spoken to any of the Mended. We are aware of each other and despite their mistrust of us, we like them, but sadly they have wrought great harm."

Then their shared interest in the Serpent had been raised, and over the next week, an alliance had been forged.

"We are studying the pattern. Maybe in a hundred, maybe in two hundred years, we will ask you for help," Fortusenay had suggested.

Boabben found the creatures fascinating, and Tourmal found them irresistible to hunt, many times overcoming their fleet aerial skills to be predictably rewarded with a dematerialisation upon his victorious paw swipe. Only two, Fortusenay and Planghar, ever counselled with him. Though, over the years he often saw others of the kaleidoscopic beings at their dealings with the nature kingdom, still unsure if they cyclically frequented the plateau or were there, hidden all along, perhaps even before warm-blooded creatures had called the Fold home.

The immortal would sometimes watch as one of the hob pair stood above a plant, seeming to talk to it all day in a sullen, grating dialect, quite distinct from the harsh Latin with which they addressed him. After cross-referencing many of those incomprehensible conversations with the Mend field, Boabben found a key for this other dialect from a gleaning that he had experienced it inside the Keeper tree. Abruptly, he could understand the language, and with that, realised the hobs were bartering with the plants, offering them waxier cells, increased rain or protection from marsupials.

Boabben came to think of the grizzled, pointy-eared beings as good-natured gangsters. He learned that they exploited patterns in nature for their own energetic accumulations, traded species' secrets on a whim, prompted droughts to pay a debt in blossoms to bees, rarely told the whole truth and were not incapable of standover tactics, like the hob he witnessed introduce bacteria with dire effect to a patch of intractable ferns. Once he overheard Fortusenay singing, and translated the Latin to:

"They will beat you black and blue,

The earth so violently covering up the hue."

His enquiry had yielded a straight answer for once. The song celebrated the way in which hobs had taught, for a price, some tree types to grow weak roots, to lightly cover hollows, and to then enjoy the resultant twists and spills of passing animals in a kind of vicarious transferral of warm-blooded sensations, with the prerequisite of a little blood fertiliser. Boabben made a note to watch his footing.

"But what exactly do you get from all these transactions, Fortusenay?"

"Well, because our origin is not with this planet, to retain our original essence we have to stay one step ahead of Earth forces. The patterns of the Earth are always shifting and we weave roads into them, little permanencies into the flux, by enlightened prediction. It is mainly the energy of the plants and their insights that we use to achieve this. The whole combination gives us our dissolvability via which we walk between dimensions."

Years later, seated on springy turf in a circle of boulders, and roundly pressed by red-leafed shrubs beneath a massive over-arching green-yellow gum trunk, Fortusenay had confessed that those restless stirrings in men's hearts, prompted by the Serpent, had once seemed a boon to the Hobbogyre. Vessels suddenly plied the world's oceans, reuniting much of the long sundered Hobbogyre race, who had then adopted man's Latin to be able to intercommunicate.

In the crush to gather plant collections in those empire-building centuries just gone, hobs had accumulated a mass of vegetative knowing. They had guided the fates of many explorers to success, disguised as light or an omen bird, acting as the whispering fuse of understanding between dark-browed mugwumps and skittery botanists.

For the service of moving whole plant families across the world and assuring them pampered propagation, hobs had been rewarded a boon of energy and new keys to pattern harmonics, but things had soured. By the start of the nineteenth century, when Boabben's interview took place, it was clear that too much land was being squandered, too much diversity and Earthen strength extinguished through man's driven greed and paranoia — albeit the Serpent was its cause.

"We will elicit an answer together, the Hobbogyre and the fireseer, for it was not only Lellying prophecy that featured you, but ours as well, too vague to tell what it all meant...still." The hob had disappeared, leaving Boabben in a whirl of revelations.

At one point, enticed by a spring day, Boabben and Tourmal sallied from the plateau into the low northern hills to explore that prolific land. They made slow going, nudging around thick mazes of saplings on the poorer, steep soils. The valley bottoms were bracken and raspberry if fire had passed at all recently. Still, by afternoon there were many hills between the duo and the plateau. Announcing the shift to a warmer climatic pocket were a consortium of eucalypt species combined with drifts of conical, purple-tipped trees not built to receive frost, and increased patches of large ground herbs.

There were thick sprawls of vine weighing down shrubs into obtrusions and snaking their minutely ridged tendrils through the forest. Boabben had discovered that these filaments could welt and abrade if catching on skin. A final barricade of this hillside's gnarly cloak indicated it enclosed the hidden sanctum suggested by the Mend Map — a wide substantial valley.

Just as Boabben hoisted his rolled possum cloak and they made ready to begin again, Fortusenay's voice hailed them. The hob sat in the fork of a young eucalypt pulling bark shreds away with idle claws and looked into the distance as he spoke, seeming to disregard them.

"You will need more than a cloak for protection in that valley, Boabben. Though, I would like to see Tourmal the hunted for once. To that impenetrable realm, beyond view of ocean or of mountains, are the outcasts of your friends, those banished from the coastal tribal groups. The criminals, the mad, lusus, totem breakers, all are exiled to the place; on pain of death should they leave its phantasmagorical shadows. You see, sometimes it is humans who will not tell the whole truth. I would not go within it. Especially toward the river's rise I would not dare. The interns are ever hungry. Sundering from the tribes has lent them desperate fierceness. Cursorial predators and human wolves stalk there. You are forewarned."

Boabben translated, colouring of the danger to Tourmal, but then in spite of, or because of it, he crept with the marrankur to the valley edge. It was weird country. Vines fell tens of metres through the sky from gum tops as high as those he had seen in the forest where he had sourced the cactus grotto age-fire.

The river flickered over long straps of water weeds and onward around islanded ferns like huge-bellied satyrs. Through the torn opening from a tree fall he could spy the water's twisting plunge through low hills beside the deeper green of riverine plants among the massed arbour of jungle. Where the river's catchment tapered back toward its rise, the hills along were covered in continuous drifts of vine, as though final locks on the vault of the valley. The sun fled behind the hills, and the explorers started back for the plateau, Boabben glad for the waterproof gift of the possum cloak before the misty night trek was over.

So came a year when both Boabben and Tourmaline, coat waxed grey now, caught a spirit of wanderlust in the breeze and followed the elders of the tribe — men and women who had roamed as youths with Boabben — down to the coastal camps. The immortal found a world obliterated and realised that he had been hiding from himself the fact that too few lately had come to the plateau, and the children laughed not as loudly in its glades. For a time they turned north and found all that strip of once-wide continual rainforest along the shore-side was now a hacked and weedy land, littered with broken cart springs and axe heads. Boabben came to a vast estuary and looked on horror-struck as four steaming ships passed, towing barges ten times his height, piled with bodies and bodies of great flat fish, some disc-shaped and some like anvils, indiscernibly old and every one huge, like the breeding pool of an ocean. As he sat on the lake shore, six more steamers towed barges of like plunder through the mouth out to sea. At one point he watched a bloodied whaleboat pull into the estuary touting the heads of two leviathans from the hooks above its deck. A barge chugged alongside it a while, its driver swapping pleasantries with the whale captain, for all the world as innocent as two Dublin ladies talking across a fence while pegging washing.

Tourmal wanted to check on his proud progeny down the coast, and after two days threading along beaches, they arrived at the great valley they had lolled in many years before. Not a tree was left on either river bank, not a fern in the quagmired mud of trampled hooves or neat fields of profuse crops. Only a few ducks ghosted on those lagoons deep enough to escape draining beside a murky river stuck with the carcasses of several cows.

But inland, away from the farms, eucalypt kings still held court over an undisturbed wilderness. For weeks they searched and together spied three marrankur, but none of a family likeness. At last Tourmal coloured urgently to Boabben, and there in a jungle creek was a tawny marrankur drinking, its black tail swishing. It lacked the imagined black leg spots, but greatly excited them both, though it hissed a retreat as soon as it smelled them. Their peregrinations took them as far down the coast as the broad inland lake system where first they had come ashore in these wilds.

A portage to the sea had been ploughed and scooped through the dunes, and Boabben sorrowed for the plight of the rare freshwater creatures as they followed the shore. Steamers chugged here too, their barges stocked with mightily girthed logs, and all of the forests on the hills around the lakes' headwaters had been cut to feed their trade. Docks that had been built around the original lakeside were now marooned in mud. The long, blind dilapidations of farmsteads stared out from defaced hillsides around motes of white and brown eagle wings pegged on ramshackle verandahs. Erosion was filling these once beautiful waters, claiming mile after mile of the lake system. Where high-shelled turtles had once swum, now grew hectares of weeds.

Boabben took to wandering openly in the crowded coastal towns, guised as a beggar, to more carefully know if his surmises of the wanton destructions of these people, no few once his own, were true. They always were. The glamour he had learned from Fortusenay turned Tourmaline into the semblance of a mangy dog, but they never tried to meet people, just wandered the coast until Tourmal sickened.

At last his bond had died, at nearly seventy, and Boabben buried him with a view to a stream under the plateau's silvery trees. The tribes had been lost to disease and abuse, and with them went something of Boabben's effusiveness. He leaped again onto the train of his destiny. He developed a plan which this time might well kill his old enemy, nemesis of life: the Serpent.

Boabben awakens from the dream, reorienting his whereabouts, and searches along the star-filament-enhanced Mend Mapping. The Enyadding coming from the north have just sidestepped the last obstacle prohibitive to their reaching the desert meet. Soon, thinks Boabben, knuckling disdainfully at moisture on his cheek, soon...all three groups would concert at the final assembly; the last of the Enyadding, whose Spear would source from a bare three score of immortals.

Thrusil, Maeddan, and the others numbering more than two dozen, watch in relief as the columns of soldiers pass the acclivity on which they hide. The Mend Mapping had warned them of this danger with ten minutes to avoid it. They had been right in the path of its approaching maw. The very thing dreaded ever since Aruan had sent a hazy message about a device feared to be a sub-aural scanner, two days ago. So they had run, immortal and beast, fleeting across the limey desert clay, dissolving their Veil as they hit the slopes. The marrankurs had stripped away soil enough for themselves and their bonds, and interred in the dirt, they had been safe from feared infrared sensors, from radar and sub-aural imagers. It had been a near thing; the closest hovers passing only a mile from their lair.

It was not a massive company, Maeddan reflects. Some six kilometres wide, but pragmatism had made it take the same path of exodus from Base Mjölnir as that which the immortals — desiring all speed — had sought for approach to the martial institution. There were some thousand assault hovers in its aerial ranks, double that in hover-bikes, a few chitinous Sacubus and one mammoth: missile-bristling thing, like the melding of three bloated Sacubus. There were maybe a hundred haulers carrying a double layer of automns on their roofs, with either supplies or live shooters within. Great flat-bed trucks on ten-metre wheels carried moles, digging equipment and crates of weaponry. It was perhaps one per cent of the combined Mjölnir land and air force.

Maeddan sighs, brushing dust off perfunctorily. "That lot can't be seeking to reinforce Hamper. It's too late, surely."

Endralion considers Dragon's Avatar, her grey hair hidden in dirt. "No. They go to plug another hole, I think. It would explain their central route."

Maeddan's head fills with memories of strange stirrings in the desert, unexpected events they had precursorsally glimpsed on their journey to the waymeet. "Then we were lucky. Doubly fortuitous that troops are drawn from the Serpent's ley, but luck is not always blind."

Lellying watch the fading dust, sipping from waterskins, then turn to the last hundred kilometres of their trek.

The soldier runs his hand through his regimented, shoulder-length hair again, looking out on red sand scuffed by low bushes, glad for the hauler that blocks the afternoon sun. He spoons the last of his too-hot meal into his mouth and then throws its tinfoil receptacle and spoon to the ground. Morris feels strange. Not just from being away from television twice in a row, or due to the interminable brooding of space out here, devoid of meaning. Something isn't right.

He has felt constricted, breathless, ever since the bizarre news articles. No rain had fallen in South Austral for over two weeks. Huge reservoirs, along with the waters of every river, had mysteriously vanished, and the rumours of the border bases experiencing terrorist attacks — maybe there was a connection. Maybe the scaremongers were right and Curlewalion had declared war, was right now propelling its cannibal hordes across the desert. To forestall his mental whirlpool, Morris seeks out Tinella. The butch blonde sitting in the sun is, despite her annoying habit, the only member of his platoon that he talks with. He swings his belt around so the knife lies across the zip, and interrupting her game of noughts and crosses in the sand with another woman, crouches beside her.

"Hey, Foury," says Tinella in the confidence-clad twang of an American accent, reaching for his crotch but fumbling a corpulent hand away at the distraction of the knife. They all called him 'Foury' because Morris did not peak perform in drills and so, lacking any bonus pay, could not afford other than glasses for his eye problems.

"Hey. You know, this might not be a standard enforcement drill. There's some big guns up there." He indicates the sky.

The women patently do not follow his gesture to the Sacubi that circle the camp, and Tinella says to him in slow condescension, "Foury. We are going to clear up this declaration of neutrality thingy in the border mining towns. Reopen the Regulative Enforcement Dome, sniff around for terrorists, and hunt that aluminium back to flow just like Captain told it."

"Yeah, well, what if there really is a war up there and we get sucked into it? I've been thinking I might hightail."

Laughter bursts, spittling into his face.

"What, you going to walk into the desert? What happens when your watch batteries run down? You won't know when to take protein regulators. Hell heck, you won't even have any. How will you integrate your brain every day without decrypter pills? I thought you were due to be superimposed on one of the old movie channels at the base; you said you finally gave them a voice sample you liked. You won't get laid if you don't promote yourself."

They had both stood, like bizarre jack-in-the-boxes, as Tinella ripped away his delusions.

"Look, soldier." She tugs his belt straight, "You can't even belt up right." She grabs his newly unguarded crotch. "You're a funny — "

A blast of inky red obscures Morris' glasses and he cleans them hurriedly as the other woman begins to scream. When he can see, his clunky eyewear reveals Tinella on her knees, eyes fluttering, with a razored spear of wood through her stomach. All around, dusky-hued creatures advance, more and more, though they explode into light where swooping assault hovers bring lasers against them. They are lissom, slender, but ropily muscled, with strangely leaf-shaped eyes, toothless mouths like interlocking horseshoes and skin which looks like knots of wood.

"Get down!" commands a bulky sergeant, shoving him to the dirt and blazing into the fray. A creature rises up from under him, hefting its streamlined sword of wood diametrically through the officer, ducking away from the man's eviscerated out-spilling and streaking by Morris, with the lightest, twig-like step across his thigh, to engage the automns defending from the cover of the hauler wheels. Lying where he is, Morris tells himself he knew something strange had been going on. He squirts a measure of Hygehyde into his mouth and fumbles around for a sensorial regulator pill — just to be sure.

Chapter 22

Mendez squints across the aluminium glare of the sea, the feat paining his blackened eye but revealing the sixteen other flagships of the armada stretched out fore and aft of their own. None quite aspire to the brash cavern of endless metal beneath him. The craft beneath the Spaniard was once a W.A.R. hover carrier. Two-and-a-half kilometres of streamlined, armoured plate that its new captain claimed he had captured using holograms and illicit computer codings to drive it onto a sandbar, stirred by a need to outsize his operations. Mendez is not sure he believes the further tale that he had done so with only three hundred followers to sack the crew of three thousand, but where Amphrymite Crealm was concerned, he knew doubting was best kept under one's hat.

Reluctantly, Mendez clambers from the old radar housing a recent trove had made redundant. He pushes his way past Zadia Palladium, a lavish-looking but abrupt African tech officer still muling over the innards of Crealm's fire catapult. She had earlier offered an impatient reasoning for her work, her lip curling at Mendez's obvious obtuseness.

"Suspich a boat jums our electrice, give 'im little bits this, kapice?"

The pirate's language was a mongrel of phraseologies stitched in a sort of pidgin of cool, and Mendez rarely knew if he was being praised or scorned. He therefore hurries through the babble of thousands of crew on this part of the deck and, skirting by the forbidding martial training arena, descends the interminable ladder hatches to his tasks.

First he feeds the eels. The big morays have adapted perfectly to life in one of the leaking holds, and Mendez throws them the rats gathered by other unfortunates, trying not to watch their gaping, half-metre wide jaws below.

Amphrymite purported to keep the eels as live food emergencies — truly he ensured back-ups for back-ups — but Mendez suspected it was to indulge his sense of humour by being able to gammon such as he had upon Mendez's plea to join his crew.

"You're scrawny, but you maybe alright to feed the eels." That half-minute interview with the two-and-a-half metre tall New Guinean, sporting sharpened bones contiguously through the skin folds of his arms, had been the tensest moment in his two torrid days on the main deck of Seazure.

Amphrymite was one of the few captains plying the longer passage west to war at Constrain instead of east to Hamper, and it was from the south-west that Sway called to the Spaniard's heart. Eventually the pirate had assented the passage, uttering an enthused "Pal-an-keen!" He had thrown out an arm, and for one awful moment Mendez had believed he would receive its embrace, before the buccaneer rapped the turtle shell somehow grafted to his skull and received a joint from his first mate, Inquist Flute, the two emitting a guttural orchestra of animal sounds and continuing excitedly with their war plans.

Those plans would soon be exercised upon reality, for the pirate flotilla makes good speed now it has cleared the jigsaw of islands and cays choking the oceans of the continent's north-west. By tomorrow the armada will engage the first out-fliers of Constrain's coastal defences, with perhaps not the same nobility of cause as Curlew's armies, but certainly with a matching fervour. As if stirring at battle's thought, Mendez climbs through two side hatches, retrieving a lubricating spray pack. He begins oiling the docking doors that provide egress to *Pairadice's* submarines. All around them, the Spaniard knows, are the bulk of the fleet's craft — submarines in their hundreds, now scouting and preparing their readiness through lilac waters, like fixated pods of orca.

Curled atop a fishing net, Mendez wakens with a start, throwing off his sheet as another of the sonic implosions barrages his senses. Dawn courts the skyline, and the flames from the rockets die to thick black smoke in the cleared hover launch area, drifting with a waif of wind to evoke a chorus of coughing and curse from dozing corsairs. The rockets, Mendez had managed to find out, after puzzling over his discovery of them in a hold, had a utilitarian function — the propelling of attack hovers fast to a pre-designated height. The Spaniard peers over the side of the old radar housing.

Zadia stares bemusedly, ever so sassily, back. A Raphaelite, Unopean-looking woman nuzzles her ear, whilst one fleshy eye swivels to also gaze at him. A bottle of something apricotty lies beside the impromptu bed. An arm reaches out from under the sheet, transferring it to the snorkelling mouth of a face blackly-haired, across which traceries of leaves fill in the remnant space.

"What's going on?" Mendez enquires.

"Orgy," informs the man with the bottle.

"No. The rockets."

"Oh." The man stands up, and Mendez is thankful for the extensive tattoos that somewhat console his nakedness. "Oh. Therst Capn's fine tall merd bringers. Some plucka musta savvy bad guys."

"Badder," corrects Zadia cinnamonly from the background.

"Up there," concludes the man, with the dioramic inclusion of a thumb jerked up. The black-haired forest wanders off, and most of the shipmates are grumbling awake.

And down there, thinks Mendez, spotting telltale billows of rising air out to sea. Dawn's skirmish ends without further disturbance to *Pairadice*, and the captain's voice soon distorts through speakers, while the crew eats a breakfast of coconut something.

"Ay. Pallankeen, my little chirogans. Three hours you all make ready bumpa the enemy. Any plucka needs savvy bumpa, get longside the arena. Ay. You catch bon stuff, put your stamp, put it my hold. Bon luck, mezzameats."

Figuring the reference 'bumpa' is to laser operating, Mendez heads to the arena. In his despair and subsequent exhaustion from trials in Seazure, he has given little thought to how his hitchhiking toward his love will actually translate as his safe gaining of landfall. Now battle lies between him and his goal, imminent and unavoidable. He presses the beads on his wrist to his lips, tasting only salt. In the centre of the roped arena, mostly clogged with racks of quarter staves, boar knives, swords and glossy caches of guns, a Japanese man halves the hollow balls of pre-milked coconuts with clean blows of a sword.

He turns a frizzy mane toward Mendez, who lingers against the ropes. A long moustache, studded almost elegantly with oyster shell, accentuates the elfin snub of nose.

"You kapasa bumpa plucka."

"What?" asks Mendez, distracted by the glistening steel and ferruginous black eyes.

"Have you requirement for armed combat briefing?"

"Ah. Yes, sir."

"Not sir. Chef. Or Anask. Anask Sliver."

"Mendez. Mendez Bathelar." The Spaniard slips under the rope and presses a hand more calloused than his own.

"Alright. Here," the mentor produces a belt from a tangle of gear and the gun to fit its holster," the safety is in the sensors on the handle in all of Crealm's stuff; so if you're touching it, it can fire. This thing like a throttle: up for wide or down; narrow blasts. To unclip the charger, three turns on that ring — gives a little — then slide it out." Anask holsters the weapon for Mendez. "But you're on a ship. Most of what you can shoot is a long way away. So you need a long-range laser. Okay, they're heavier, and they also kick more, so ease the flow out. Forget the scope, it's encumbering. Use these."

The oriental hands him a pair of focals. As they help to protect his eyes, Mendez leaves them on. Anask clips several indiscriminate lumps to his belt. He holds one by a string, then snaps it above his head, causing the released lump to fly upward.

"That's how a detonby works. That one's a trainer." He scoops a helmet up with his foot and snaps it on his head. "That's how a helmet works," he jokes, as the dud lands on it. "You'll find one somewhere if you search the deck. Now try those guns and practise with these couple of duds. "

Mendez checks the crystal lock, raises the laser's splayed weight, and fires at the holographic target. Holsters it and makes the practice draw. Over the repetition of motions and the mechanistic chatter, Sway's voice superimposes: "Let your arm be drawn up by the back foot's recession. It's a fluid counterbalancing, you cad, not swatting at a spider and stepping back as an afterthought."

One of their early training sessions in the cramped laundry of the share-flat, Bresleagh's florid overalls soaking in the sink, the dyspeptic and tone-deaf German woman long since asleep.

"Here, like this." Sway had brushed past him, room for only one to manoeuvre in the hideaway of that box. "Watch properly, Mendy!"

Even with her back turned, she had known that his eyes strayed to the long fall of her calves. "Okay, Giddy, okay. I'm a rock of concentration, truly now," but as she showed him the slash and lunge, her aroma had carried, wild and acidulous, had burned through his best intentions. Slayed, he fell to his knees, planting a kiss on her navel as she turned to look archly down at him.

"You are more handsome than any monger's wife in the Causican," he giggled, Sway exerting the barest pressure hold on his neck. "You are of strength magnificent, the set of your shoulders paling in comparison the widest of a tauro's horns."

"Hmmm," she growled threateningly, her fingers' pressure deepening painfully.

"Sway," he had said, springing up with the vitality and exuberance that had marked him then, landing knees astride the pile of Bresleagh's clothing atop the cleaning agitator, and barrelling her back over it. "You are a rose, and I grasp

426

in the hand of my love any of your thorns without let-go. To quote Walt Whitman, '… you have always been a rose'."

She had capitulated then, the blooms of his naming rising to her cheeks, and he had flicked his wrist to turn the agitator on. Coming back to the self he is now, a man he does not quite recognise, he sees his rays pierce the target centre. Satisfied, places the crystal on the nearby charge conduit, mouthing her name as he stares out to sea, while other novices are given the run through by Anask. After a minute he reboots the laser and finds the atmosphere on deck has changed. Many pirates have clad in focals and helmets, and the addition of weapon belts lends them a sort of uniform. Most are passing bottles between them ritually, and Mendez intercepts a tote from an absurdly flouncy, older, greyed woman gilded with gold on the skin of her bared breasts.

A huge water tank has been winched atop the radar housing from which issue thick hoses and nearby are laid out hundreds of rocket packs that stir the inkling of an idea in the Spaniard. The tethers and salt covers have come off the big assault hovers, and lights flash, marking yawning ramp-ways to lower levels of yet more hovers. Mendez sees Inquish Flute, the first mate, board a Sacubus adorned with the Jolly Roger and, as an afterthought, with the still-wet stencil of curlew and lion. Pirates begin to cluster around laser and artillery batteries as top deck hovers power up and ascend to an easy matching of the ship's eighty knots.

With an existential numbness, Mendez moves about the mounting displays of the crew's bravado and plucks the last fruits of his preparation for battle — a helmet, a gas mask and a knife. Eventually, he comes to the prow of the ship where pirates dance a formal hornpipe to the accompaniment of several drummers and whistlers. Other more ribald music is provided closer to hand by guitars, amid a group sitting on the vast, coiled hawser. Mendez catches the tail of the lusty sing-along:

"…If you leave a sweet girl from Curlewali

Sing Toorali Oorali Ay…"

The guitarists throw down their instruments and lurch off to trap a flagon in its passing. Mendez finds himself cradling one of the guitars and is soon approximating a reggae rhythm on its four remaining strings.

As Mendez stands, nodding at some cheering, the *Pairadice* pulls ahead of the other sixteen ships, most of them converted freighters with their lesser clouds of hovers. From atop her wheelhouse, the gargantuan holographic projector suddenly animates, and a Jolly Roger leers from a hill behind landfall a few kilometres away. Mendez registers the distant flashfire and steady booming of the battle for Base Constrain. Missiles dart on the edge of sight from deep bays within the prow, as laser repellents yowl, catching and incinerating incoming projectiles blindingly close to the *Pairadice*.

Inquish's hover wings along the ocean's becalmed surface, dropping elliptical mines as greetings to enemy nautileers, then shies skyward, wary of correspondence from the depths.

Mendez feels a strange dispassion as he realises battle is engaged, even as rollicking cheers resound among the crew. Through their focals, all can now discern the nearing spectacle of the conflict. A bevy of pirated assault hovers buzz the naval fringe, obliterating a supply craft, then levelling ranks of waiting automns on the base's big pontoon before powering back to the fleet. A ripping tear in the sky is slim warning for the trine of Agates that roar over the *Pairadice*, flooding the deck with laser fire, easily dodging both her automatic and manual repellents with their sleek speed. Luckily, only one of their missiles hits the ship's side, which she absorbs like a suppressed sneeze.

Pirates career about the mid-deck, dousing gear and comrades.

"Watchback port bulwarks!" cries Amphrymite's voice over the speakers. Mendez, gathering smashed glass and detritus, draws a blaster and peers over the bulwark in time to see a magnetic-legged thing, like a bloated scorpion of the sea, target him with a blaster. He dodges the hot spray, relying on his roundhouse once more, as the android clunks aboard and is promptly lasered.

In the brief glimpse afforded, there had not been many of the sea scorpions. Perhaps they were a distraction for something direr. Believing the wily pirates will not suffer from his desertion, he heads over to the hover-packs, and after a brief inspection, straps on the nearest. As though his one deed of clumsy valour has freed his debt to the *Pairadice*, Mendez takes flight with a clear conscience. Making for land, though everywhere beset by the stygian brawl and sharded lights of war, he is more inwardly composed than ever, merely gripping resignedly his long-range laser and fuzzing the harrowing near-death, mid-air encounters into a pattern of breathing and evading until he reaches shore.

As the Spaniard sees his shadow skip across the concrete of the base, a gun from a security plinth strafes him, puncturing a hole through his foot before turning to other targets. Mendez sees his blood ribbon away toward orderly groups of Agents running through a courtyard — betraying, with garden and low rise dwellings, an officer's residence.

Mendez draws a detonby, attaches it to his hover-pack and pulls its priming cord. He knows what the glinting thing angling toward him is, has seen targeter darts used to deal with non-compliant gangers on the high-rises. At the tenth count of a possible fifteen, he drops from under the pack and free-falls toward the hedge of bushes he hopes will be thick enough. Six metres above the ground, he relaxes, employing skills from his chrysalis-handling workshops, and remembering to drop his laser, hits the bushes. They hold him. They also pin him. A branch has pierced his cheek and the roof of his mouth.

The yearning in his heart refuses consent to the wish that the targeter or an officer's investigations will end his suffering. Slowly, he saws through the branch with his knife and pulls out the thirty-centimetre long splinter. Following three attempts, he grabs a solid lower branch and hauls himself as silently as he can through the thicket to the ground. After investigating for bitterness, he presses a wad of congealed, spongy sap from the bushes onto his mouth wounds to prevent his airways filling with too much blood. He removes his shoe, straining acrobatically in the dusty confines of his vegetable prison. The foot wound shows no bone, but an inch of flesh is sheared from the side of the arch. The Spaniard places leaves over the blight and applies a stripped portion of sock thrice round it, binding the whole with a boot lace. With the last of his strength, he removes his other boot and places the remaining sock over the bandaging. Then, head wedged in a branch fork, passes out.

Disoriented and weak, Mendez has to focus beyond a discordant symphony of layered pain to recall his whereabouts. Light pools outside the darkness of the cocooning bushes. On the hill is the hugely lit taunt of a Jolly Roger. Memory trickles in around his sensory functions, lubricating and uniting them to a single purpose — escape. He is lucky no automns have spotted him with their infrared through the hours of his faint. He smells cigar smoke along the hedge, and lacking a better prospect, snares his long-range laser from above him, tucks it in his belt and crawls painstakingly across the rotted leaf mould toward the malt and burned shellfish aromas.

Close enough to hear two men talking, Mendez pulls off his sock and approvingly feels only dried blood around the bandage. He interpolates from the smokers that the rift in the Curlew army he had earlier noted from air has now been advanced, with Austral forces surrounding five separate groups of what the two men call terrorists.

"We've halved their forces, sir. It won't be long now."

"Capital. Well, I suppose I can get back to Mjölnir then. It wouldn't do for the Compellance to be absent if anything gets through to us there. I'll distribute my final orders among the captains."

Mendez pricks up his ears, daring closer until he can see the lacto-silk-suited pair, adorned with badges of office, studying wine glasses and surrounded by a crescent of Agents with turned backs and raised guns.

"I doubt anything will, sir. The armoured corsair ship is stubborn and two more of their holed tubs survive by clinging to her skirts. The sharks will feed again soon."

"Good. The three Foamercion Reinforcers that I have placed as blockade half way between our bases will no doubt ensure that is so."

Maybe it is the thought of all those brazen, adaptive and anarchic souls being shredded by sharks that makes Mendez sacrifice his safety, however tenuous. Wriggling out of the hedge, he snaps a duet of detonbys toward the turned backs of the bodyguards, then fires his short-range with ghoulish effect at the Affiliate commanders on the bench. As the charges go off, Mendez crawls straight into his plumes of chaos. The clearing dust reveals the dozen bodyguard stunned or dead. Figures rush from the hundred-metre-distant officers' wing and a man peers out of an alien-looking, obviously armoured hover, training his laser on the aftermath.

The Spaniard spies him first and fires on the man's hand, disarming him. Turning to flee, his back now receives the crackling surge of Mendez's next shot, and he collapses in the doorway of the craft. Mendez struggles to a hobble, as Affiliate laser fire veers toward him, then he lumbers up into the hover and seals its entry. With a yell of self-loathing and viciousness, he stabs his knife through the slumped Agent's neck to make sure. Mendez had studied dynamic engineering for two years. There is little that the officers, staring dismayed at their two dead leaders, can do. Slowly the elite craft ascends.

The escapee props the little black spheroid over the centre of the base where laz-cannons blast it from every still-standing plinth. The turbo lever beckons appealingly, but the Spaniard instead investigates the control panel. He concedes that even if he can use the craft to somehow find and extricate Sway from danger, there will be no place left to flee if Curlew falls. Five missiles are primed via the screen display. The micro cameras still afford peripheral vision, so he scopes a security plinth. There are just enough missiles to methodically level each of Constrain's towers of defence. In the panic light of a hundred candling Austral flares, the battle is revealed to Mendez.

Vengers spring from thin air to harry the Austral forces following the confounding of the plinths. Mendez witnesses two Curlew wedges reuniting as he spooks in behind an Austral helicopter detail. The metallic pack had been homing in on a hillside that blooms in sudden flowering of ten thousand golden-black blossoms. Below, lion skip aside as Mendez smites the choppers down among them. A stalk has arrived — to his knowledge it would change the nature of this battle. Out of projectiles and low on charge, Mendez nudges his stolen orb out to sea.

There he waits, high above the *Pairadice*, until he spots his quarry. Three Agate jets, again beleaguering the boat, manifest from nowhere. As they strafe the pirate decks, Mendez drops, like some insane ladybird hunting grasshoppers, to instantly bob behind the fighters. With the last of his charge, the Spaniard lasers down two planes, then grinds to *Pairadice's* decks, piloting solely by magnetic differentiation. A wary group of buccaneers train their blasters on the doorway as Mendez steps out. Among their number is Anask Sliver who yells, "Friend Mendez!"

Crealm himself hover-packs over to the little group, and disbelievingly gawps at the craft, offering a whiskey flask aside to Mendez without taking his eyes from the bright toy.

"Yetso, how did pluka catcha this?"

"By killing the Affiliate Command."

"Ho! Ay. Well, true we make main yak bumpa their platoon to kapasa matchy what you be done. You don't mental I borrow her a bitsy?

"I don't think he'll be upright long enough to answer," observes Anask.

By the time he awakens, Mendez's foot and mouth wounds are sewn up. The morning light falls on clean bandages.

"Coconut something," Anask pushes a bowl onto the crate before him, and Mendez stands wincing as he eats, testing the foot and looking over the bulwark. The *Pairadice* is now moored alongside the quay, as is one other pirate ship. Anask smirks ear to ear as he explains that Mendez's purloined craft had made the difference in obliterating the naval defence.

"Four thousand pirates across there fighting. They're a bit stuck, but Austral's hemmed from two sides now. It's the last of us, except a skeleton sub crew in case they've any ocean reserve. What would you think," he asks, motioning to a cut-away, two-person attack hover, "if we go along there and help bust through? It would boost the pluckas' morale to see the assassin supreme among them."

Mendez consents and Anask helps him into the cockpit. As they skip over the shore of high cliffs, they see the pirate forces dispersed in a wide bow, mainly fighting automn and cadet units which have formed an emergency coastal rear-guard to sponge up the unanticipated attack. Though greatly outnumbered, their unpredictable and fierce battle presence seems to be winning them advance. They boast mobile shields of salvage plate, pushed on wheels. From behind these, an occasional fighter blasts up in a rocket pack. As Mendez, at Anask's suggestion, hums toward a group of cadets employing a mirroring tactic, they pass right over the stolen cylinder hover, broken and charred, but somehow landed safely by Crealm, who booms from alongside it through a megaphone:

"The assassin supreme and Chef go bumpa upabove!"

There issues a chorusing cry of approval, and then Mendez is among the cadet forces. He locks his cannon mount on, infuriating the enemy, and rises steeply to keep the pursuing hover-packers between them and ground reprisal. His cannon splutters and he flings a few detonbys down amid the automn ranks, as Anask sunders two lower hover-packers from the air with his long-range and throws a knife into a third cadet who plummets from their own high position. Laser fire shudders along the bottom of the pirate craft and Mendez pulls it higher. They rise straight into the path of a Sacubus's laser, the hot bolt melting the hover's rear and sending it corkscrewing toward the epicentre of Austral's amassed forces. By locking magnetism to one side, Mendez manages to induce a slower spin, more like the drunken descent of a paper plane.

"Plague spawn, right in the midst of them! When we land, throw your detonbys, Mendez Bathelor. If we don't hold long enough for the pirates to reach us, see you in the next world!"

The hover strikes a quickly evacuated patch on the drill lawn, skidding along one side, then flipping onto the cannon mount bars and rolling twice more, nearly pinning the Spaniard's arm beneath its bars before halting. Mendez tosses detonbys out as he wriggles from the harness confine. He puts his back to the hover, luckily landed on edge to form a shield, and watches Anask Sliver dance before him.

The Chef maintains a periphery of space around the hover; his greatest danger being slipping on the blood of his beheaded opponents. Infrequently, he uses his blaster on automns, as does Mendez, keeping the kitchen clear, while Chef chops. Mendez swings his arm over the wrecked hover, trailing a detonby to keep their blind spot unassailable, only to have his arm grabbed and forced back to his body.

A near-naked man ducks beside him with the advice, "Lion and Unilion pushing through now, my friend. Better stick to blasters." Then he disappears, a tunnelled hollow opening briefly in his wake. The full meaning of the man's presence sinks into the Spaniard's mind, as lion, one dripping blood from its smile, leap the hover. The Austral force is compromised without the cohesion lent by its senior officers. Curlew can crack it like one of Sliver's husked coconuts. As Mendez braves an exposed position, to target rearward across the hover, he sees the other leading edge of the rebel army's blade.

Dark is that razored menace — a loin-clad, black peril of skin. Before Mendez's eyes are warrioresses, sweeping aside the enemy in a chilling, maenad blood-letting. Women as young as twelve and as old as seventy. All reap an undifferentiated glut of death. At first he thinks them solely women, these scions of the wild, living caterwauls of the damned Earth and pennants of life's tenacity, but then he sees men among them, shunting the prey to and fro from spear to nulla, each coordinating packs of eight or nine dingoes.

The dingoes, golden or gold-black, pure as the original voyagers from the slow log-punt crossing of disintegrating Gondwanaland, feisty as if claiming a new continent following a decade of sea travel — pull Agents to ground, where warriors deftly spear the prone foe, shouting new directives to the pack all the while. The warrioresses, conjoined to the soul of some dreamtime ogress deity, too fell for all but the bravest camp fire whispers, outcast from rock gallery inclusions, splinter the straining South Austral defence, finally allowing the pirate horde to conjoin with contingents of Curlewalions.

Before a scab has time to form upon the lacerations dealt the Austral army, two strategic bio-algalate domes slump from volcanic inner explosions. Base Constrain's end is inevitable. Mendez, realising the Mist have destroyed the Austral psychics, witnesses a spat of Affiliate and troop leaders collapse as though struck by some suddenly freed hidden force — the Indigoes and Mantles.

Later, as he sits in his honorary role alongside battered Amphrymite, and Mist and Unilion captains, he pays little heed to the final plan of advance upon Mjölnir, other than to endorse the idea with his vote.

In a dreamy exhaustion, he recalls the warrioresses and how their boomerangs had swept arcing in behind enemy hover-packers or tilted beyond sight and reaped a falling kill of helicopters. He replays a scene of one who had clubbed three cadets aside while yet burning from a Sacubus's exploding hemistatic fuels. He imagines a clash of arms, or even of mere wills, between those molten Amazonians and the Unilion deadliness he feels certain would be their gender opposites and knows who would emerge victorious. There is no transpiring of such theoretical meeting. By the time the remnant force of some hundred thousand hale of the Curlew Alliance leaves the next day for its final confrontation, the matriarchy, along with their men, dogs and dead, have vanished as swiftly as they had come, back into the desert.

A small lizard patters away from the grim reprieve of some long calcified bone, which island in the sand waste had cooled its feet. It seems to Maeddan that the words of Lornahe's final admonition skitter away with the grains flung up by its tiny claws, caught in the wind that Mjölnir's kilometre high rampart of dirt and sprawling perimeters of smashlooser-deflating metal trees cannot tame. The lizard had gleaned no shade off the immortals standing amid the ungulate's bones. Only ten kilometres from the base's hub, they remain Veiled and the sun striking from their copper skin fractures into other dimensions.

"Look at her. Like some princess upon Seffern. She should run off and guard with the marrankur — no doubt from the cut of her she can fight — instead of daring on the peril of the Enyadding."

Maeddan feels her grasping like litmus for some impression, the full gravitas of their brethren staring past them, watching the others come, their trying counsel resolved to at least assess her strength. He crouches beside Gawn while the hind immortal group edge forward, as though they stand on a precipice instead of on this endless pewter plain. All the other marrankur ghost in the mid-distance, pitifully distressed by the poison that courses below the Lellying, thrumming through the venom-line.

Maeddan watches as the delayed delegation pass piecemeal through gaps in a thick column of scouting automns. The plastic intelligence ripples with a spasming reflex for guns, but the subtle infrared signals cannot overwhelm the neuro-programming that nothing is there, and the column continues jerkily along its rote course.

Quickly the baker's dozen of wayfarers cross the last kilometre, Maeddan noting that their pack of twenty-three marrankur is one shy. After a boisterous conference with his own Gawn, the marsupials lope eagerly away to prowl and guard with the rest. Dragon's Avatar reads exhaustion on the features of his dozen kin jettisoning themselves to ground, and the same etched on those of the mortal, though her face is undershot with implacable resolution.

After the group has watered from skins filled at the Lellying's nearest northern age-fire, conversation begins to flow, skirting patently around the matter of her presence. It is clear even to Sway that the verbosity is a thin veneer over silent mental exchanges deeper than her rudimentary keys can access: power play and testing, certainly of her. A hooked-nosed male with an aged face trapped forever in suspended animation, betraying him to Sway as one of the rare, original immortals, crouches lightly before Aruan, and with hand on heart, gives a long courtier's nod.

"It is meet to see you have all safely come, Fire Whim. Notable that our own deployment travelled further and has yet awaited you a full day. Our time here has not been listlessly spent. We have worn away the outer inveterate defences of the line. There is no doubt the Serpent is preoccupied. Many craft and soldiers have been drawn off by Curlewalion forces that have penetrated a W.A.R. cordon three hundred kilometres to the north, with a remnant surviving their victorious coastal attacks. Also a reserve of our enemy's power, perhaps more a psychological prop, but one we cannot pinpoint, is missing — visible only as a rent in its etheric energy."

"The news is sweetening to a heart near soured of hope, Kumarren. Our time has not been idle either, our journey reaping the fruit that can yield us victory. Our delay attributes to the guile of a lesser enemy, a cunning wretch of high perch among the Affiliate. With many vultures he followed us, and we were hard pressed to elude him. Yet such we have done."

The encircling crowd around the red-haired flame exchanges its consideration of this news, a second of shadow passing among the group, seemingly innocent of their sudden intensity of focus upon their youngest member.

"You are certain of this?"

"I am, Lakellewan."

"How so?"

"I far-cognised our enemies hidden high at the zenith of their hover's function. We led them to rocky lands and there dazed a mob of kangaroos, thirteen, near the age-fire. We passed a little of our field to them, through Iridestine power, enough to register on enemy tracking. Two marrankur drove the mob north-east as we came west. I monitored the enemy's full number pursuing the decoy."

"Well, enough of the past, except that portion of it represented by the Serpent." Many of the immortals gaze at Sway in forthright study. Maeddan continues. "We who are sempiternal are now ironically out of time. We must take our positions to vanquish our nemesis."

A squadron of Sacubus pass by low overhead, and in the din the Enyadding fall into silent counsel. When all can hear again, it is clear to Sway she is the subject of argument, defended by Brawyndy.

"… all that we do is risk, Lornahe. The Mending opened to variability before the birth of my son, and it is riskier to force an old pattern, than to flow with nature's change. Into the gap of our need has come a superlative specimen, just as Aruan prophesied."

"Yet also, Brawyndy, is now made manifest great rupture in the Serpent's guard. Sufficient that we sixty-one may, three centuries more learned than our prior attempt, destroy it. Now, while chance lasts. For such will not return if the girl fails."

"Enough. Enough, Skyather." Maeddan balls a hand emotively by his creasing face. "We will vote. Those who wish to accede that Sway be the Cuspidated barb of our lunging Spear, sit. All who object, stand."

Sway remains composed as several figures sit, about twenty altogether. It ends thirty-one to thirty in her favour.

Still standing, Maeddan pronounces, "I also would have sat, but I save my energy against such spuriousness. Let Aruan and Sway prepare themselves. Our Spear shall form behind them. We use, my friends, no shield of defence."

Aruan conducts Sway to an indistinct patch of ground, raising his eyebrows as they sit to face each other. Brawyndy stoops to hug her, then Sway and Aruan are alone as the other Lellying prepare, just beyond hearing. Sway dreads the words Fire's Whim is about to say. Her mask fractures a little, and she focuses on the philosophy of destruction for renewal to distract her heart.

The zealous immortal utters, "There is no going back from here. For either of us."

The rip to promote the healing.

If she survives to meet her love, she will, Sway affirms, as Mended, mourn Mendez's loss through every day of her amaranthine life. Best to let him go from her heart.

"Are you ready?"

When a tree is battered, the roots only search deeper. Goodbye, my dais. You cannot follow me where I travel.

"Yes."

"We will harmonise our breathing, Sway. I will link with you via your visualisation of the basic forms. You with me, via the fire; I will open the door to its source. The others will interact with us, but maintain focus always on the flame. Once your essence is enshrined in the astral, it will be prone to the same grievances of sustained harm that can kill an immortal in this bodily form — and if you lose your astral thread, so will you lose your body. I will let you first get close to the vileness; you shall need for courage a little of the feather — but only a little. By slowly leaking you my essence, you can get right atop it before it recognises the energy pattern. Goodbye," the Lellying concludes, closing his eyes, "and valiant victory."

Boabben watches as his son and the Sway entwine their cellular information, their minds, and their temerity. A streamer of pride blows across his heart to see Aruan's supreme aptitude, leading the woman's spirit out before the Lellying Spear and hunting down into the world of the grotesque one. He has primed the woman skillfully; her focus is rare indeed. Suddenly, Boabben apprehends a wrongness. He narrows his focus back to the desert plain, now mired from rainstorm, where sixty-two bodies sit in trance while Gawn stands alert, paws dug into the mud, tail threshing and broad head angled in suspicion — then abruptly flings his seeing out across the plain.

Astral, Sway travels at speed, diving behind Aruan's energy field. Billowing, white smothering bubbles churn around her. She concentrates on Aruan's searing fire, and the blinding press of water clears, her experience slowed to a dreamy world seen through a golden mantle.

You will soon be more adept and lethal in this form than in your body, Sway,' affirms Brawyndy's clear voice in her mind.

The intensity of gold increases, its texture tactile to Sway, feeling as though the wide seas are her wings, her children, her history.

Aruan, his essence superimposing across her every sense, as though inside her, his resigned, tight smile so close she can discern his pores, places a fiery hand on her navel. She feels her life-force mostly leave her, flow down into the earth, then return altered. Her soul is hinged on some slow tumescence of power, growing exponentially. In mastery, the part-immortal damps her emanations, attending to wariness, ignoring the ecstasy hanging over her.

Then Aruan cries, 'Behold!'

The golden light is superseded by a dim grey, her caution now framed with shock. Below them, as if the seabed, stirs coil upon coil of barnacle-encrusted malice. White eyes, if eyes they are, seem to be searching, and for an instant their connection passes over her. She apprehends it cannot see her yet, although she can already discern the supporting energy threads and intimate the thing's mood and weaknesses.

Take heart, Sway. Our power is yours to wield, informs a voice she pairs with Maeddan.

She glimpses the figures of the Spear in semicircle behind her. Every colour and form of glowing creature have the Lellying become, entities both beautiful and forbidding, their own battle memory and advice merging with the golden fire in her soul.

From Endralion — a tree with root legs that paw, bull-like, at the water — she receives warning: *...not to guard any prepared fighting form, but to spontaneously blend as many as —*

Incongruously keening, Brawyndy's presence rattles through her awareness, also touching the others, judging by their elemental simplification back to astral selves, which retain a cloudy hint of their universal souls.

Get back to the plain. Danger! Get back!

Aruan sweeps her up in a ball of fire, and Sway is bundled suddenly back into her body, instantly aware of three things as she slams back into her corporeal form. Firstly, water: torrents from the sky and pools about their bedraggled bodies. Secondly, her physicality is vitalised: the heart slowed, muscles tingling, but somehow faster and stronger. Lastly, she shares the Lellying's far-sensing, at least enough of it to appropriate an impending doom. Three kilometres away a ring of dust is drawing, as a noose, toward them.

"Everybody retain dispassion," barks Maeddan. "This may be a coincidental play and whatever it is, we can slip through or go over."

"I think it is the Affiliate tag," Aruan concedes. "I don't know how, but they have tracked us."

His words appear vindicated in the rain-smirched outline of hovers spiralling down above them. Sway sees the predatory shapes of troop carrier buggies blaring toward them from every side. A distant rhythm comes to her hearing — automn feet.

"What treacherous net is this?" gasps Rillarbar.

"We have yet hope, tenuous though it be. A smashlooser may intercede between us and destiny," says Maeddan.

It will take us too long to manufacture its likeness.

Sway can attune the immortals' every mental exchange now, invited or no.

We are too few to mind-still.

We can but wait and hope.

The first group of hovers lands, pouring out Agents alternately pointing camera-like boxes or lasers toward the immortals. Other hovers cast their malaise from a stalled position immediately above. A chair-like contraption, enthroning a helmeted man with a painfully grafted pate of black hair above sallow, leathery features, descends from one of them.

The leader. Can any fell him?

He is protected from my reach. Some discordant neural wave device bends my mind's flame, like water the sun.

"Greetings, my strange terrorists," the seated man says in a voice like cobwebs and migraine.

Sway sees thousands of Affiliates jostling to close ranks.

"Or should I say terrorist, supported by immortals?"

Beneath the transparent helmet, the man smirks. He sits just in front of some especially shiny troops, his eyes roaming triumphantly from them to the empty hundred metres of space inside the cordon.

"You know, I strive for a refined sort of immortality myself. Though, I would do more with it than contrive some effete plot in a desert on the edge of an unassailable base. But enough preamble!"

He stands surprisingly fluently, a sash of knives and guns prominent across his tall frame, armoured centimetres thick of various cloths.

"Why not show yourselves? We can see you with everything but our eyes — and I'm certain we can kill you. I offer you impunity. I would not malign the flower your span represents. Life you may long have — under supervision. You may be part of the world's greatest society."

Sway absorbs the exchange of thoughts: agreement that holding the Veil only draws off their energetic reservoir.

"Show yourselves!"

The Lellying suddenly appear, causing an agitated ruffling in the Affiliate ranks.

"Hmm. Black, are we? How very cosmopolitan. Except, of course, for Sway. Send her to me; her crimes are dire."

The Enyadding form a protecting circle around her. Sway, however, slips in front of their shielding.

"I do not get sent, Slitter. What doom you represent, I meet unflinching."

Sway steps towards the Poise One, hands upraised, gaze resolutely fixed upon him, upon the little pulse in his neck beneath the double layer of silks and underlying mineraline, thought-deflecting weave that her newly empowered energetics reveals to her through the rain like some wriggling snake beneath bark. At a fifteen metre distance, just as Slitter's elite bodyguard move to intercept her, Sway shakes from her sleeve the quartzite flint kept there since the Murray River, and in the same motion, flings it into Slitter's throat.

Before the Agents hit her, she sees the stone shear through the first silk, slow at the second, and scratch his jugular.

443

The bodyguards, under prior orders not to kill her, burst in a wall upon her. Sway deftly leaps the first to assail her, propelling his head with a hand into the helmet of another. She glances a centimetres off the top of one's head in landing, rocketing the boot into another's sternum. Sway comes up in a whirlwind of mirror roundhouses, cartwheels, grasping an assailant's laser and flipping onto his shoulder bone, igniting the fuel tank of a buggy with a quick shot over the ringing Affiliates. She lands, a leg curled each around an Agent's throat and dives onto her hands, whipping the bodies out and up behind her, cracking their spines and propelling them into the melee.

As an Agent plants a kick into one side of her face, she rolls her cheek aside and snatches his leg forward along its trajectory, punching diagonally into the groin and staving off a frontal assault with a flurry of finger blows. A man whose knee she dislocates is finally able to glance a baton across her head as he falls. The blow, even through her silk, disorients her, and within moments Sway is hidden beneath bodies pinching into her every muscle, restraining her with boots, elbows and palms. In seconds, her legs and arms are bound in confine belts. She is hauled upright before Slitter, idly rubbing his throat. A mass of Agents lies tangled in the mire, bones cast at grisly angles.

"That," the Poise One says, drawing a blaster, "was just eerie." He shoots her point blank in the stomach. Sway doubles over, sparks still flowing from her, and Slitter tugs off her balaclava.

"Positively eerie," he repeats, pulling her head back and rubbing her severed ear across her face. He casts her bleeding form to the ground and motions his bodyguard.

"Truss the terrorist to the Y-sonic; we'll kill her after I have a chat."

Lornahe screams an emphatic "No!" She rushes at Slitter, elegantly dodging a stream of interceptors, or punching them down, then leaps at the ghoulish leader. A dozen blasters ignite her flesh and she crumples at the Poise One's feet.

444

His attention is snagged by erupting chaos amid the Affiliate ranks, yelling and wantonly firing blasters and cannons.

"What the hell's that?" demands Slitter over an intercom.

"It appears to be more of them, sir," crackles back.

"Fuck!" Slitter instructs that Sway be loaded onto a hover. "And this immortal. The old thing is still alive. Mortalise the others."

But the others have disappeared. In their place, marrankur pull down Agents, breaking the circle in several places. With them is a huge lion whose smile glints like diamonds. Sway is thrown up onto a waiting hover, glimpsing Agents and automns on the plain felled like stooks of wheat by some invisible reaper. Lornahe is dumped next to her, and Slitter and his remnant bodyguard board the craft. As it ascends, a spear slams into the deranged Affiliate leader's throat, right through the tears left by Sway's shard, its butt passing halfway out the back of his neck. The bodyguard rush to circle their dead commander, so Sway does not see Musa spring over the hover's side, hurling a knife into the pilot even as two laser blasts catch him, one on the shoulder and one on the thigh.

Sway feels the craft plunge and strike the ground. As the Agents topple with the impact, she is accosted by the bizarre sight of her rescuer using an Agent's spurting jugular like a hose to douse the fire in his skin. The masterful, honed giant, unable to stand on his leg, side-rolls to hamstring an Agent, and streaks a dagger, produced from an ear lobe, into another protagonist. Sway cries out as an Agent delivers a careful blast from his laser into the back of the huge lion's head. Musa's neck jerks back so that his eyes blaze a last fire into Sway's own, turning pure gold, and then a still white.

A fraction later, a severely lacerated lion drags the offending Agent down, its jaws locking around the man's skull as it collapses in rigor mortis atop the warrior. Sway expels the rudimentary contents of her stomach and realises that the plain is calm, peopled by the standing figures of Lellying and marrankur, as well as hairy hominids of both squat and immense cast. The last thing she

445

hears before succumbing to the blackness is a woman sobbing profanities in an American accent.

Chapter 23

Boabben attends solely to the impending strike against the Dark-Ley Serpent. He does not wish to glimpse the battle between the combined Opsweyed and Marrafar, and the force of near half a million W.A.R. personnel he had noted hastening along the venom-line. No doubt the base's radar hints had been finally validated by some garbled communique about attacking immortals from one of Slitter's illicit Agents just before death. If the Lellying's brethren cannot halt the response of Mjölnir, then no warning to the Spear will succour them.

Boabben is elated by the Hobbogyre's keeping of their word and achieving the miraculous resurrection of the time-sundered immortals. These had fought well in the minutes prior, cleverly forming Spears of their own to kill remotely, while a roving, dynamic band had brought down the automns and several hovers. They consolidate their shrewdness by meeting the Mjölnir horde with only a small visible group as lure, ensuring many kilometres between the gathering violence and the Serpent's energetic feeding ground.

Which is well for the Lellying Spear, whose members need most not to have an energised Serpent, their ranks already severely depleted. The tiny Lellying tribe is still the only one that can bring Spear against the Serpent, for the hurried attempt by their brethren had failed in such long distance energy transfer.

Yet Sway had been saved by the Opsweyed, their regenerating as acute as ever, her wound staunched and organs rebalanced. A tiny figure in Boabben's seeing, she is backdropped by the momentous evil and glowing with the life-force poured into her by his son. The Spear is primed, Lellying matrixes rawly fused and abridged to Aruan, awaiting only final transfer of his power to explode into Sway's barb.

She has decided on a direct assault, rebalancing the breadth of her psychic and cosmic weaponry. Drifting closer and ever more brightly toward the fiend's white field, Boabben apprehends the moment she is suddenly made fully Mended, as does the Serpent, fluxing in consternation.

The full quota of her core of power she flings into the field of evil, breaking through its defences at the last moment by skewing the Lellying flows savaging along her thrust. Light fractures through the featureless monster, and great brown jets ink into the oceans. Boabben knows the world's nemesis, sorely aggrieved, is not dead. His son, however, soon will be. The ancient Irishman wraps the tendrils of his essence about Aruan's body as his son's astral form wanes, drifting in slow torpor through the stained water.

It had come as a wave of noise and incorruptible might across the skyline, the clustered egg of Mjölnir's first defensive unit.

The hatchlings of attack ooze from the mass, now they have found the flimsy prey of less than fifty Opsweyed. Choppers in hundreds. Light tanks, as well as the behemoths and hover-dooms. Countless automns, anthropeoms and soldiers on hover-bikes led by clouds of Sacubi all spill toward the decoy.

Nivat and the enigmatic American woman, Calliope, are Veiled by thirty fast-trotting Marrafar, with which their beasts thankfully keep pace. They comprise the second reprieving decoy, their task to burst into visibility when the current besieged group Veil, allowing them to re-energise. The bulk of the Enyadding are walking somewhere about in half-tranced groups, formed into mobile Spears, mind-stilling or coercing the Sacubus and helicopter pilots to override their own critical guidance systems and crash their craft.

The hidden warriors strike everywhere amid the hover-bikers, but for every hundred soldiers stilled, twice as many ride on. Shards from a forerunning Sacubus burst asunder as it is targeted by a mirroring triangular bi-wing. Nivat and Calliope veer, as do the Marrafar, in desperate avoidance of the possessed Sacubus whistling toward impact with the ground they cross.

The mortals' psychic channels had been opened that they might communicate with marrankur and Enyadding during battle. A handful of minutes and kilometres ago, they had unceremoniously torched the bond-animals of two of the slain Lellying immortals, whose own bodies were already dust with the departure of their spirits. Onto the pyre had also gone Sanfel, and Musa, afforded no backward glance. Battle shall comprise Nivat's mourning rites; such would have been in accord with Musa.

Away from the Marrafar, they are now visible. Nivat rises from his saddle and gauges the soldiers' approach, hurling a spear as training or bravado makes them swerve in a following pattern to target him. The spear impels the lead rider from his bike, swiping the bike behind. Hurriedly, Nivat and the marrankur re-join the Marrafar. Calliope is there, at the rear of the immortal group, gathering speed. A helicopter that had seen Nivat, circles bemusedly overhead, unloading an angry cough of bullets at the apparent mirage before swooping off to join its frenzied flock attacking the Opsweyed decoy.

Two of the big Marrafar in the line of blind fire stumble, and Nivat feels a blade of culpability razor his soul. Striking one more obliquely, the offending bullets seem to glance from her thickly matted hide. But the other roars as a bullet passes through his trapezium, spraying blood, and Nivat waits for the giant to topple. After a moment the being actually turns its head to him, winking and spitting out a bullet simultaneously.

The token lifts a shroud between he and Calliope, and he meets the brunette's dazzling eyes, leaning in the saddle to orate.

"My tongue speaks not, but tastes the word of him,

Like wind, he lifts us on now his smoke shall cover our fear."

She nods, defiance filling her athletic frame. Sun glints from the twist of hair at her neck: Musa's last lobe-dagger, exchanged for a too-late kiss.

449

Get ready, a Marrafar voice deliberates in Nivat's mind. We will try to draw them in on themselves, spiralling the troops back west.

"I'll be with you," Nivat calls to Calliope as the group crashes through an out-flier of the anthropeom mass homing in on the twenty of the decoy not yet shredded to dust.

"So…will he," Nivat thinks he hears an American voice say, and they hit the back of a mystified squad of soldiers as the decoy vanish — and they themselves become the target of Mjölnir's uncoiling menace.

Mendez, piloting one of the last remaining craft of *Pairadice's* proud hover fleet, is amazed that they are unchallenged right up to the huge warships. He grips the levers tightly, hair-triggered to pull away from danger, as Anask presses his well-adapted nose against the silicon.

"Those Foamercions," the Japanese says slowly, awed, "they're kaput." Mendez shrugs on a pair of focals, observing smoke rising from the W.A.R. crafts, one riding lopsided on the water.

The boats clustered around them transform at closer inspection into a hodgepodge of trimarans, canoes, antique battle cruisers, compeloid rafts: a fleet of thousands. Probably half of the original, to judge by the flotsam on the choppy sea.

"The Horn of Drums!" exclaims Anask excitedly, then radios the news to his captain.

"Your timing's on the nose, my people. We were just start gittin some tired there," beams the ebullient, zestful Horn of Drums elder, voice like a paddle-wheel.

The delegation consider each other in the aftermath of embrace and victory.

"They job growed muscle on him, but maytimes we busticle, truze chillie 'sonely you pluckas not bumpa so bon, ay," praises Amphrymite, thrilled that his crew had not even needed to join the land battle against the W.A.R. soldiers enforcing the blockade to inland. Also, Mendez reflects, the jaunty New Guinean had been invited to salvage the Foamercions, so *Pairadice* now bristles with bulky new toys.

"We might have been lucky, friends," adds a blond Mist Captain, his face young, but eyes flecked with capability, "that we did not here engage any of the Agency — only soldiers. Affiliates suckle at Mjölnir's breast."

Eyes twinkle within a round, yet sculpted face denoting the central African heritage of a woman who offers to the informal circle, "In the Horn, we have to garden alongside elephants. Twice is pardon granted a wanton herd, then we will protect our livelihood by stronger means."

"Mjölnir is not a battle we hope to win, even given your help." The statement of the Mist leader is as plain as the big-boned woman of apparent Chinese genesis who utters it. "We truly stand in awe of your quick response to the Indigo summoning. But we do not ask that any more of you should follow your hulls to a foreign seabed. We fight now to avenge the suffering of our land, not for any chance victory. Hope is high that you might entrench amid W.A.R.'s confusion, and be able to worry her western ocean fleets if you return home."

To this, the rangy, black elder, evidently the highest incumbent of the Drumidian force, bows his head, running a hand through hair that luminously betrays his senescence. Softly, he says, "This W.A.R. government's nuclear aggression cannot be let to go unchallenged by free nations. To distract our enemy, we have here met in one unity, met and had triumph. We knew that Curlew had fallen before we were a day from our coast. Thinks this man, now is for unity to stick with us. Now we put in a thorn to Mjölnir's paw and hear him roar. To have maybe triumph there, is meaning we can scratch them from this Earth. Anarchtica may already, our discovery finds, be fighting…we can win!" He looks to his six colleagues, and the set of their faces is stoic.

The Mist Captain claps his hands jubilantly, saying, "So be it! Let us not waste a minute. Mjölnir is near five hours for the fastest of ships — then we shall tremble the mighty."

The pirates and Horn of Drums warriors crammed shoulder to shoulder with Mendez are polar opposites in style. The *Pairadice* had taken aboard a thousand or so of the coy, smartly robed Africans who outnumbered available berths in their meagre battle-loved fleet. Curlew hover forms had accommodated ten times as many.

There is a bustle of crew on *Pairadices'* lower levels, these decks forlorn of most of their hovers, though boasting a compendium of gadgets stripped from the Foamercions. Among these is the field inducer, steadily flooding a W.A.R. operating signal that precludes the enemy's missiles from exploding during current skirmishes. Laser and strafe fire it cannot prevent, and top deck is no longer the place for the good-natured, yet lopsided sparring between pirate and Drumidian that had accompanied the voyage's initial hours.

Mendez, the rumbustious pirates and grave, humble Drumidians watch the screen's specks attenuating the first undersea wrangling with Mjölnir. It is a massacre. The be-dotted Mjölnir subs, one after another, are erased. Commanding directives from the captain distort across the ship's intercom, his gobbledygook advising crew of the dangers represented to hover and boarding parties by targeter darts while outside of ship defences. There is some qualification, possibly about how to neutralise them, then translated versions follow in various Horn dialects. Recognising the impending signs, Mendez bumps through the press to a hatchway accessing a lower level.

There, before a rampway, and among a few crew and hovers, he finds Anask Sliver.

"One last flight," the Chef says, flourishing long fingers toward a thing like a magnified wasp cocoon.

Just one more. Then I will be free to find her. Mendez can feel Sway is somewhere near. *It is not inconceivable she is held prisoner on this approaching base.* "What is this thing, Sliver?" he asks, clambering up to the console beside his friend.

"A bombardier."

"And they're the bombs?" Mendez flicks his head toward a dozen men and women from the Horn, settling into the contraption's centre while they matter-of-factly check over each other's hover-packs.

"We have a ballast of shock-mines to deliver, but Amphrymite also wants to get as much airborne as is possible through the hover netting."

"Hover netting?"

"Crealm's got maps." Anask's headset crackles and the eyes of the Japanese man twinkle. "Time to rise and to shine, comrade."

Mendez, at the head of three other cocoons and a motley flanking escort of stripped back assaults, ascends the rampway to purr above the vast deck while he gets the feel of the heavy craft's handling. There is a staccato throbbing and ominous double boom.

"Something's shot with the tracheo fulminisers, Chef."

"No, friend. Look down."

Mendez stares through the stained algalate porthole by his feet. On deck, Drumidians beat huge metal drums, or more-traditional one-players of skinned-over wood. The chorus begins to mount, and Mendez sees through the side window a mirroring scene upon the Drumidian frigates and the surviving pirate freighter — all gathered behind *Pairadice* for the final leg to Mjölnir. Mendez overhears the captain's muttering through Sliver's headset, and Anask signals absently.

"Head back north a few kilometres and build up speed. Crealm expects we may have to dodge subterranean greetings when we run the net."

Mendez lumbers the bombardier over the trailing Drumidian fleet, this first wave comprised of vessels towed or large enough to keep pace: methane yachts, solar catamarans, trawlers, outboard dinghies in their hundreds and squat merchanters. Among them he notices many boats torn to fragments and a shunned, sinking frigate.

"It's ironic," Sliver says, intuiting Mendez's brief diversion of focus. "The Drumidian nautileers are the most tenacious on the planet. The antiquity of their fleet is actually an advantage because W.A.R. subs can't profile their propeller signatures. But they couldn't save those of their folk who were hunted here by Agates. Or entirely prevent flak from underwater hitting those floating coffins."

Mendez thinks of the astonishing warriors who had sparred so convincingly and unpretentiously on the top deck. They were a race from a dry land, and many of the drowned had not even known how to swim. He throttles tempestuously as they approach *Pairadice* but the groan of the hover-drive is drowned by the roar of an Agate squadron bursting from all sides. As though Crealm had been lurking hopefully beside his new toys, it takes a split second for each of the assailing craft to become a tortured ball of flame, most of which crash onto the pirate deck.

Pairadice fires bolts from her laser cannons triumphantly across the sea, searing under the speeding bombardiers and their escort. The Jolly Roger leers once more in the cloudscape above their enemy's base, though compared to the sprawl of Mjölnir, it seems mere graffiti in the back lanes of a metropolis.

The World American Reform government's new hammer of Thor is a star of five points, its crown knifing inland along the venom-line, the two great feet flopping over the hundred-metre-high red cliffs of the coastline and plunging into the ocean. Its height claims a kilometre of the scribbly, clouded blue. In the calm bay between its sea feet are dozens of Foamercians and other warships. In evenly radiating rings around the W.A.R. base, extruding from both land and sea, are various clusters of towers indeterminably purposed, save for the two-kilometre-high radar stacks. Mendez wonders to himself why they even bother with hover netting.

Several Agency and automnal hovers glide languidly toward the bombardiers, now advanced close enough to the outer defences that human can be discerned from automn behind the scenes of the nearest towers.

"They're waiting for us to hit the net," Anask says. "So they can rifle our bones, I suppose." He concentrates on an imager before him. Different to Mendez's own, it shows an attenuated narrow scope over a downloaded navigation programme. "Veer thirteen degrees!" demands the Japanese. "Drop altitude to two hundred and twenty metres. Okay, hold. Straight now."

A laser blast scorches up behind them and Sliver yells, "We're through!"

"Never.... a truer word, Chef," laments Mendez, rolling the bombardier under a laser blast from a nearby tower, as he watches a Sacubus rise in a beeline straight for them.

"At least we have surprise on our side," flusters the co-pilot, turning to the Drumidians to yell, "Get ready!" In the brief opening of the middle bay, Africans hurriedly leap out.

"Do you think we can get to the closest arm of the base, where it forms the harbour cradle?" asks Anask; voice still cool, yet slightly anxious, clutching the machine gun and staring through his porthole.

Mendez takes a moment to answer, watching the Interceptor barrel along his imager. He is piloting ever higher, knowing the Sacubus will have to curb its speed near the dome of the hover netting. Finally, he kills the power drive, neutralising their electronic simulacrum of the Interceptor's imagers, and they drop sharply. His ploy works. The Sacubus wings by, responding confusedly, with only a feeble blast emerging from a manual laser hatch. Mendez powers away, building speed as he dips.

"Yes, if I can hold this line for a minute; but shock-mines won't damage the structural arm."

Mendez snatches a glimpse through the side window. The hover-packers have dispatched two automn hovers and three of the Sacubus. He pilots down level with the cliff tops as Anask leaps into the bombing bay and primes the shuckers.

"Okay, you are truly supreme. Just hold it steady."

Mendez sees Anask's rain of mines, stark against the white-flecked sea, fall toward the nautical ramp-ways and automn piers, as he comes over the base itself and twists around the cording straps of fire from the wall mounts, trying to gain altitude.

"Ah, I've got some for you guys, too," croons Sliver, then a bolt catches them squarely, roof panels explode outward, and the drive is terminated.

Mendez ducks toward the Chef, who is pulling down seedfalls of clear polythene soaked in algalate. He buckles Mendez's evacuation ball around him and triggers the bay doors, still equipping himself.

As the Spaniard falls, the massive wall of the Mjölnir sea arm comes into view. He spots three smashed cannon turrets and beyond: the clinically calm spread of the naval bay abuzz with movement. As the algalate threads begin to obscure his view, growing with the friction, he glimpses a writhe of troop movements and explosions to the east, deep inside the defensive perimeter. Surely not the Curlew Force so soon, he wonders. Mystified, he harnesses himself fully and fits his earplugs as the swelling algalate excludes all light, the fallseed sending a quivering jolt and lash through his muscles, its spongy mass absorbing the strike of land, rolling him dizzyingly until it begins to dissolve, as designed, upon contact with the sea.

Calliope swallows her gorge. With a short-range blaster, she realigns the face of one of her young countrywomen. Remorselessly, she picks off the staggering soldiers, having just witnessed this knot being targeted by their own grenade-hurling ranks. Things like that had been occurring profusely throughout the last ten minutes of carnage and she didn't seek to understand the phenomena, any more than those catatonic marionettes she shoots could show an understanding of why they fight upon foreign soil. They are cogs of endemic hate and power abuse, though not links valued enough to merit so much as face shields for their helmets.

The rebel drops to a knee, bottom lip held in her teeth as she strives to laser two hover-biker gunners — first. Her blaster flares, then sighs, enervated of charge. An Agent on the back of the leading bike targets her, and Calliope surrenders her fear, thinking instead of the ascetic Unilion whom she had become so drawn to through the five hours she had known him. The first beam slices the dirt about her twice. The second gunner also misses.

Suddenly, a massive hairy leg slams into the foremost driver's head as her marrankur descends, its kick flipping the hover, impelled by gravity into the dirt. The rear Affiliate is forced to bank sharply, then swerve around the column of a tower that serves a purpose unfathomable to Calliope, and skitter low past her in attempting to correct his steering. She dances sideways toward its slow turn and lashes a fist into the torso of the driver, dodging the machine's heavy collapse.

The two bruised Agents recover quickly, as does the American's sense of blessedness. Her marrankur protector, ghosting from thin air, delivers the only blows of death, dragging the driver's spine from his skin through his silk armour, even as it angles forward to crunch the gunner's neck, streamlining its deadly face, tufting up an ear and emitting a low whistle.

Calliope curses the inbuilt self-destruct mechanism that Nivat had warned her was a feature of Affiliate lasers. Mounting her marrankur, she clutches instead a purloined knife and glimpses Nivat running alongside his own apocalyptic beast, pulling one of two spears from its stow on his back and sending it twenty metres into the gunner leaning from a helicopter above him. The blonde bard draws a laser, and targeting automns with economic bursts of fire, slips onto the back of the marrankur, weaving toward the enemy. While he had fought alongside lion, modern weaponry or tools were forbidden him, believed by the Unilion to break the subtle links between man and beast. No such stricture now applies, and as he disappears amid a tangle of foe, Calliope notes that his laser use is as refined as his words had been. Thinking of his voice, she is suddenly frightened, perhaps to lose the link he still represented to her memory of Musa, and earplugs or no, she hears the loud beat of her heart.

The erupting streak of marsupial fur beneath her, disdainfully brushing through automn lines, bounds toward a group of soldiers, charges, pushes off the trapeziums of two personnel staunchest in targeting him, and sails into a curtain of billowing smoke, tilting his hips high at the last to avoid the curl of laser rays from targeting automns. Calliope has to throw out an arm for balance.

He lands in the midst of twenty Marrafar surviving from the decoy group. Calliope is aware her mind is divided. One-half ponders the miracle of the marrankur finding the immortals and their dimensional Veil, doubly hidden as they are amid the cover of the three smoking tanks. The other half is howling with agony.

Not even the safety of the Veil can prevent the laser burn which has already engulfed her arm, delivered by one of Slitter's carbonised children just before her mount had reached sanctuary. A Marrafar rushes to her, and Nivat watches a ball of flame shoot from its upraised hand as it lays the other to her shoulder. The deep ache in Calliope's bones is flushed away under the hairy palm, and the skin puckers and blisters, but is intact.

The being stands, level voice huffing, "Not as good as the Opsweyed, but if you tie these around it..." here it stoops and uproots a bush, rapidly working dirt and fibre away from the roots and producing a few strips of moist pulp, "...it should heal."

"Thank you, old one," says Nivat quietly. "Calliope. You look like a spectre. Maybe 'tis in compare with our hairy allies."

She smiles at him, his old-fashioned words and sensitivity. She is nauseous, shocked, but Nivat is safe! He is here adhering the poultices to her arm and her heart is a tired, glad thing. As Calliope had journeyed with the brothers and the thousands of shaggy immortals, Nivat had passed her his journal of barding lays to read, to distract the overwhelmed woman from the alarming freak of fate that saw them both lumped along on the backs of the huge Marrafar, the speed of the bizarre beings curtailed only enough to allow Musa keep pace upon Sanfel.

The bard's polite manner had been a balm for her sanity. He had an aptitude for lightness, his smoky charms not going unnoticed, but his poetry had enflamed her soul. She remembers a title: 'The articulation of longing is belonging'.

As she masters the pain in her stinging arm, she takes his thick, stained book from her belt pocket to read the lay, amazed anew at the brothers' sail along a coastline in the fever pitch of uprising, and the ragged dissenting Austral populace, starving and forced to dig for water in the sands due to the strange recession in natural water bodies, occurring also to the north.

'Dolphins led our little ship, like pardon

That sped full sailed past the coastal garden

That everywhere was bloomed with war

Or with its spent fruit and neither roar

Of Ra-king nor cry of we two brothers

Come to the fields of slain, where foes entwined like lovers

Held freedom's march in every resurging rebellion

From fallen Hamper, until they met the Gladstone battalion

Of Two-score thousand troops of W.A.R.'s

And, in course, their robotised killers on the bloodstained shores.'

Calliope pauses as the blare of tanks sound from the distance to replace her earplugs once more. The immortals seem undisturbed, several talking with Nivat close at hand, as they wait for the battle to pass them by. She studies the Icelandic man covertly. He must have trusted her to give the journal into her keeping, even though he claimed to have sworn off barding after the double shock of losing Musa and finding out the immortals, who he had suspected of manipulating the world, had lost so much through their efforts to defend it. Nivat is filled with pain only matched by his devotion to record the truth, she divines — and by his sense of honour. She feels a sense of kinship with him as she turns to the lay once more.

Nivat comes to stand behind the American, taking courage in hand and smiling to himself. This hiatus may not last and he wishes to tell her of his feelings.

"Call...iope," he begins, suddenly flustered. "My heart seems to rest so easily on your shore. If, that is, if we — "

Abruptly, the shuddering of tank guns redoubles, some rogue hover-dooms headed their way, and the immortals rush past signalling a follow. As Calliope mounts, she gives him a studied, blank look, Nivat unsettled that his words had not had any effect at all.

The fielding of tanks by the W.A.R. command against their unknown foe is a blunder. The inner shell of those brutish hover-dooms is a suspended solution of constantly electrocuted alkali. Into the outer armour had been blended, while the plating was still setting, magnetised gold and lead, so the tanks are impervious to the minds of even the strongest Indigo cabal.

The Enyadding Spears, however, slip silkily through the psychic barriers of some of the hover-dooms, coercing both their drivers and gunners. A few are all that is needed.

Nivat and Calliope pass, with their band, into the wake of the battle, roiling off in dust and chaos, chasing its own tail. Missiles from the marionetted tanks devastate the artificial intelligence ranks. True to their name, the coerced hover-dooms drop Sacubi from the sky like good old boys in a duck pond.

Removed and hidden by Veils from the tumult, the invisible Spears steadily direct the floundering of the Mjölnir forces. Mayhem saturates a field that is all but bereft of tangible opponents, except a few reserved from each Spear, who flit alluringly before the foe to tease Mjölnir's brigades toward its furthest north-eastern perimeter. The landscape across which Nivat's band journey is a jigsaw of charred automns and tanks, broken fragments of hovers, and drifts made of the bloodless corpses of soldiers, felled without firing a single shot. They will, none of them, reach Walhalla, Nivat ponders, or whatever heaven their glamorous sense of heroism had promised them as reward of a noble death.

The sweeping Enyadding mind attacks have left a moraine of devastation behind, as though a glacier had formed here and receded in a course of minutes. Their hairy comrades lead Nivat and Calliope through the awful detritus to others of their kind, along with the shorter Opsweyed who are grouped in formations of unmoving bodies that gradually fan out behind one immortal, the only ones who show the slightest signs of consciousness, with little muscle twinges or jerks. With them are the Lellying's marrankur, over a hundred.

Some untranced Marrafar reverently share waterskins plucked from the muddy ground, and the two sips the tired humans imbibe revitalise their deepest cells. Nivat studies the fore and background of the Mjölnir defences, the abatement of the deluge affording clarity for the first time

On the plain, but further north than the shadow of the main base's walls, a reduced cluster of maybe fifty thousand plastic, and even less human personnel,

461

is supported by a bare scattering of choppers and by those isolated hover-bikers canny or lucky enough to have been detailed away from their mass-stilled fellows.

It is notable to him that a vast force of ground assault waits fully marshalled within the hollow trine, some five kilometres distant, formed by the towering faces of Mjölnir's south-east and north-east wall. They watch the fate of the decimated W.A.R. forces on the plain, but will not be lured out. He can also discern telltale glinting from the burnished alloys of hovers, as the late morning sun strikes into gaping embrasures in both walls.

The Mjölnir command, watching curiously from safely within its walls, is sacrificing the last of its unexpectedly repelled first response, learning what it can, conservatively shoring up its defences behind a believed impregnable psychic screen.

Calliope exhales a sigh pitched between exhaustion and yearning hope. The bard looks down at her chiselled face regarding him with a look in which he reads wonder, sadness and relief. Nothing of the token he wishes for. She flexes her arm.

"You did a good job with the —"

The look of horror on Nivat's features guillotines her whisper. The Icelander runs toward the Enyadding Spears. The American stands, bracing against more desperation, and sees one line of Marrafar all leak blood briefly from their noses, before disappearing. The rest of the Marrafar are sagging, clutching their heads in woe or beginning to groan inarticulately. Nivat screams at the nearest surviving immortals.

"It's the Miomichs! They're mind soldiers. You have to warn your kind!"

The attack from W.A.R.'s psychic forces sees one of the seven remaining Enyadding Spears slain, as well as two of the Opsweyed, before they can negate the threat. Calliope and Nivat sit tensely amid the sorrowing, hairy Marrafar, watching while remnant hover-bikes and ground forces regroup upon the battlefield. The immortals take shifts to guard vigilantly against their hidden enemy, their attack turned to an arduous defending of their minds. As Nivat stares in dumb shock, he hears a female Marrafar say to Calliope, "We now are the hunted."

Suddenly, he clutches Calliope's arm, stating simply, "Look!"

Inland, from the north-west, streak hovercraft — a few at first, then more. Some target the regrouping forces on the plain, reprieving the vulnerable Lellying Spear at the venom-line once more. Others head toward the packed host of ground forces, yet unmoving from their assemblage before the walls of the main base.

"It's Vengers," Nivat informs her. "Curlew's actually broken through all the way to Mjölnir."

Most of the intrepid pilots who assail the W.A.R. fortress are promptly dispatched. Laser positions erupt like fireworks from high on the concrete bastions that egress droves of Sacubi. Some of the attackers strike at the enigmatic glints coming from the wall apertures and some even pass within.

A brace of Agates roar over the south-eastern wall, and this time Calliope grabs Nivat's arm, pointing to the northern horizon. There is a blot that slowly swells there. Nivat petitions the ironic Marrafar woman to tell them what she makes of it.

"It is an army. Two armies — at odds. The Mjölnir forces outnumber whoever these our allies are, yet still they advance."

Nivat notices a ripple in the amassed brigades before the wall. He strokes his mount's ruff and watches the battle close at hand between the Vengers surviving the Agate flypass and the Affiliate hover-bikers. The regrouping Curlew Force on the plain again becomes a rout, as scattered groups of Mjölnir forces rally in the near distance. The approaching force from the north has advanced close enough that Nivat can dimly see the standards of the companies from Curlew, as well as the clouds of Sacubi that beleaguer them. A number of Marrafar also watch the approach, their faces set with guarded optimism.

"They seek to win the inland door to the base, crowded though it is with W.A.R. thralls," one says.

"They are too small a force to succeed, surely," observes another.

"Yes. Their hundred-something-thousands will be a third of that before they can engage the walls."

"Are the marrankur still actively coercing, old ones?" Nivat asks, keeping his voice level.

"They may not here do so, for within the Veil they could draw the Miomichs to us, though they themselves could hardly be mind-stilled," answers an Opsweyed, his size matching the warrior-poet's own.

"They could fight. Why have they remained here?"

"They could fight if they wished, claw or coercion, though their reticence is twicely reasoned. Outside the Veil their Sending cannot protect them from all eyes, especially those of automns. Their priority is to protect the Lellying, and they pace themselves now, that their bond's safety may be continually assuaged."

"May I ask their aid to help my country people?"

"Their decisions are their own."

Nivat easily encourages his mount to bear him, then uses the emphatic wave he had refined throughout his time with the Ra-king to add leeway to plea to the other marsupials. A few marrankur begin to restlessly mill about him, but the bulk of the pack remain at rest.

"Did you reach them?" asks Calliope.

"I don't know; the pack mind is deeper, but I have pictured my request and an image of the plain free of ground forces all the way to Curlew's position."

They wait. Most of the milling marrankur re-join the pack, while the Curlew advance becomes mired.

"I don't think they're coming?" suggests the American.

"Well, perhaps they are not such fools as I...what do you mean, coming? You cannot join us, my sunlit friend. You have avenged Musa's honour, your...feelings for him should demand no more of you."

"Nivat," the woman says, turning with a shy smile to pat her mount. "It is not by love for your brother that I am driven."

In a flash, she folds her legs along her marsupial's spine, tucks her feet into the paired, knotted dreadlocks by its shoulders, and they spring onto the plain. Whipping her long hair from her face as she passes him, she says, "It's you."

If he lived, Nivat vows, it would be as a bard, and each of the next seconds he would make verses of a ballad. Streaming after Calliope, the marrankur pack needle by him, and his mount gives an eager happy cough as they pursue.

Sway consciously relaxes, realising her summations about the drain to her power core from that initial whomping attack were right. Not her core exactly, but the geometry of shifting flame which Aruan had passed to her. It was that mighty seed of Earth-fire she had propelled at the putridity.

Although she had received the critical components of the keys of immortality and the ciphers to Aruan's compendium of Mend-flow idiosyncrasies — deepening her psyche like a galaxy birthing — the unique fire he had given her was unstable. She had sensed it would not graft to her soul and so had thrown it, while yet vital, at the Serpent, daring to hope she could sunder its connection to the venom-line.

She had knocked it severely from its power axis but had spent her major weaponry. As the ocean clarifies before Sway and the facets of the Spear each realign, she intuits, with a lurching fear, that the Serpent is not at home. If she had broken its hold on the venom-line, it would be forced to appear before her, as only a pillaging of power from the Aleris could then have saved it.

Sway reaches to the memory of Aruan's burnished essence and the courage to face what is before her. Wrapped around the Aleris is an effigy of the Serpent — a flagella composed of tiny residual energy forms, a poisoned mandala to guard its treasure, competently linked to its creator. Much is to be learned from even these deadly and tiny ersatz guardians. In the interlocking of their pattern, Sway reads where her blow had forced her enemy's design on the Aleris to panic forward — searing the crux of its being on the inner defences of the Stone.

She investigates deeper and finds something she may be able to use, a fraction before the Serpent manifests, metres from her, surging at a thousand kilometres an hour. She saturates her whole aura with the one angst the thing had recently held, more a questioning of its own judgement than a genuine source of fear. For the briefest instant Sway blends that paranoid dream with her own self. Hesitating before this mirroring verification of its own fear, momentarily confused as to what had actually struck it, the fiend splits its focus.

It hits Sway only with its distracted force, instead of both body and mind. She drifts blind in a shrieking snowstorm of pain, every cold flake a fracturing of her being, a knotting of her bone and muscle memory. Through the tumulting pain, Sway sees a flickering in the distance. Screaming, she claws toward it.

As they race toward the imperilled Curlew Force, looking for a weakness in the encirclement, Nivat yells to Calliope, "There's no automnal presence. Thank the star of child's dreams!"

The marrankur can now hunt amid the enemy without fear of their sensory trickery falling on the non-receptive plastic brains of the automns, wherein illusory Sending is transparent. They do not know the automns have been diverted by the Mjölnir command for their efficient deployment on naval destroyers needed to neutralise a severe threat to the sea docks.

The marsupials hit like a tsunami, opening a breach for the Curlewalion force to break from the stranglehold, then recede back over the shore-strand of their victims. Nivat and Calliope fight side by side. The sheer terror of their cumulative apparition and the marrankur Sending, coupled with the reinvigoration of Curlew's ranks at the stirring sight, wins a wide circle of respect around the pair.

But they face massive opposition, and the Curlewalion fighters are already exhausted. The fresh-faced troops outnumber them three to one.

A well-intentioned Curlewan leaps at a hover-biker a second before Nivat's mount. Instead of adapting to the chaos, the woman panics. She twists her torso around quickly and pulls in her legs, which trip the marrankur, and the woman, targeted by the gunner, falls onto marrankur and bard in a messy outcome. Nivat sends a knife after the bike to discourage its return. Suddenly, a storm of well-aimed strafing from a Sacubus forces them into the path of a Mjölnir attack redoubled in fury.

Nivat slips from the marsupial lion and leaps one laser's hunger, bringing his knife up as he lands to try and, Musa-style, deflect the next volley. He is partially successful, dropping his knife as a little of the ray burns up his arm, smouldering beneath the thick shirt. The marrankur rips down a dozen Agents, an embodied plague of swarming, russet death. As laser fire glances from her face and she rolls to put it out, a chopper, homing on the mayhem like a carrion creature, buzzes over, leaving a legacy of bullets in the marrunkur's stomach.

Nivat watches two Agents push each other exuberantly, drawing Bowie knives as they rush toward the kill, but they fall before the beast, each other's knives buried in their necks. She, blinded and confused, hobbles forward and swats a paw into the corpse before her, then slumps, her jaw dropping open.

Nivat, where he lies clutching his arm, senses a soldier's fast-approaching boot, his last glimpse of the battle.

The Mjölnir taste of victory is short-lived, as the marrankur get the rhythm of their coercing. Around Calliope, soldiers turn on soldiers, allowing Curlew to pick off the enemy command and return cohesion to their own force. The American ploughs through the madness, searching out Nivat, but her mount wilfully disregards her clear wish to penetrate the battle, and instead rushes back through thickets of conflict and out across the plain, to re-join the marsupial pack grouped beyond the dust.

Two fast hovers descend rapidly over the triumphant Curlewalions. "You have to ruin those," Calliope shouts in a cracked voice to the marsupials, knowing they cannot comprehend her, and stares, transfixed by premonition.

A dozen or so ground-cannon beams announce Curlew's defiance, but only strike and bounce from the hovers. An impossibly thick bolt of laser fire halos down from each of the craft, wide as a large tree trunk. Methodically, the new marauders clear the plain of even their own remaining force, just as if the weapons were erasers. A group of raggedly athletic refugees break toward Calliope.

Fifty metres away, a beam flits over them, and where it only grazes some of the escapees, they might fall headless, or as a paired remnant of limbs. Where the beam is enveloping, it leaves only a puff of smoke. The craft tracks back to the epicentre of massacre, its ray passing along the ground only metres from the marrankurs' reclining meditation. They do not stir.

Calliope weeps dry tears of despair, her waters fled from her, thinking of Nivat and such ignoble end after all that he had been. As if in a dream, she observes one of the beams change its angle, pointing into the sky as though some creature or machine would be deranged enough to fly there. The hover's vapourising ray actually increases in width, before it burns into the side of its fellow monster. The besieged hover bursts in a booming eruption, incandescing purple and green as it plummets, the explosion spinning its traitorous attacker a thirty metres into the air, where the devil-craft sticks, upside-down in the sky.

Her mount nudges repeatedly at her, and Calliope climbs onto his back, trusting the creature to lead her over the plain, realising that it was the marsupials that had somehow overridden the nightmare-craft.

She assumes the other death-hover is disabled, and the marrankur come after her in a proud, deeply disturbed following. After some moments, she turns from her blighted shock to glimpse, one last time, Nivat's place of final defilement. Staring on nightmare, her eyes distend as though her soul tries to climb out through them.

The marrankur pack does not follow, and the other craft has not been disabled. The explosion, resulting from its possessed captain's destruction of its sister ship, had caused disorientation to the marrankur's secondary attempts to further coerce him into initiating self-destruct. Anyway, he had been almost instantly slain by the petty deck officer.

The craft's elite Agents had restored her and begun to look for anomalous explanations, beginning with an examination of the scorched plain. It took less than a minute to locate a heat signature, just beyond the recent site of battle.

The marrankur grimly maintain their Sending, obscuring themselves from the crew's naked eye as the shadow falls over them. Bemused to see nothing visible, the in situ captain lasers the heat signature.

"You FUCKERS!" Calliope screams, the anguish ripping her throat; then the tears come.

Mendez takes a deep breath and kicks through the disintegrating wall of the fallseed. The ocean is cold and relatively clear, though walls of water from manoeuvring Mjölnir ships slough around him as he surfaces. Grasping a knife, he allows himself a smile at his lone figure of menace, surrounded by the most powerful assemblage of martial might in the world. Still, there is a challenge to it. Overhead, another bombardier has won through, and its pirate or Drumidian crew dump a load of hundreds of small items that marble into the water about him.

Flinching, Mendez dives to avoid them and ascertains two things on resurfacing. One is the crew of the now flame-engulfed bombardier cannot have had chance to evacuate. The other is that a hover-pontoon of automnals has spotted him. With the feel of his final smile on his face, he dives toward a preferred demise of drowning.

Two balls of blue light fluoresce below him. He kicks deeper and sees mini W.A.R. submarines with scorching along their bodies. They sink slowly to the nearby seabed, as he had known they would. Mendez follows, reasoning those dropped balls had been electrical transferral mines capable of passing a charge through a small enough vessel into anything conductive inside.

His lungs rebel as he reaches and gropes around one of the mini-subs for its external oxygen regulator. It must be there, to facilitate emergency repair work. Vindicated, he clutches at his prize, casting around for signs of unfriendly regard. It takes him five anxious minutes to extradite his recollections of the operating notes. Another five allow him into the hatch without flooding the craft.

Inside he is greeted by the rictus of three crew and insistent blarings on the intercom. He grabs one of the two men's identity cards — luckily both have black hair — and checks the log to learn the ship's name. He picks up the receiver, then at the last minute stymies at pronouncing the consonant laden name of the officer on the card and snatches a tag from the other corpse.

"Systems private McMahon reporting from N.D.O.4.11. Over."

"McMahon, what's happened?"

"Crew hit by electric-transferral mine. I was ou...hydroside," he corrects, remembering the manual, "removing some freak algalate snag from the propeller. I was blinded," he continues, voice breaking. "There's bodies in here with me!"

"Now hold on, sailor. We'll get you out."

No doubt they wanted the sub retrieved intact.

"Can you state last known position?"

Mendez reads aloud it from the log, pretending to source his memory.

"Two minutes to medi-vac. Well done. Over."

"Over." Mendez grabs a drysuit from a storage panel, into which he dumps the body of his assumed identity and his own wet clothes. He ensnares a first-aid kit, a rubbish bin and the log, igniting the latter in the bin. Hunkering over the flame, he tosses a little methylated spirits on the smoulder and sears his face and hair in the luff of flame. He treats his hands to a brief blistering as the hatch begins to turn. He upends the bin over the burning book and smashes a bottle of iodine to disguise the erstwhile smells of smoke. Scattering the bin mess with the ill-fitting shoes of the dead man, he wraps a bandage tightly around his face, save for his mouth, and affixes it with safety pins.

The inner hatch grinds open and a male American voice calls out.

"McMahon! Chris, I need the ID tags; salvage is all up to you guys. Private McMahon, hello. I'm going to place this oxygen helmet over your head. Now, you can still hear me? Okay. When we swim through the hatchway, y'all hear trolley propellers start. After count of three, there'll come a lurch. Keep your arms fast around my waist 'til we reach the medi-vac dock — there's more terrorists out there, son, than flies on shit."

"I ain't scared of terrorists." Mendez drawls.

"Navy boys," says his rescuer to Chris, who closes the hatch behind the evacuating pair as they shuffle into the wet-dock.

Although the sand shows no trace of tracks, Calliope recognises the place her mount has brought her, to where last had been the decoy Marrafar band. The animal does not seem avid to locate their retraced allies. Instead, it paws at the ground, turns thrice in a circle, and curling its legs beneath it, slumps to earth, brown eyes regarding Calliope plaintively.

She visualises the Marrafar, beams the image at her companion in the method the immortals had taught her and Nivat to use, and is shocked at the image she receives in return — a patchwork of colour that conveys the face of Sycanthrean — the dying Lellying, and then an image of dust.

The best healers among the Opsweyed had been unable to reverse the fire burning through that immortal's glands due the laser wounds inflicted by Slitter's Agents. Now it seems he is fled and thus...

"I'm so sorry," the American breathes. She visualises the marrankur and his Lellying bond running together through a far space filled with shining stars and mobs of translucent kangaroos, beams this image to the dying marsupial. It flicks its tail weakly and lowers its ears.

Calliope crouches beside her companion and lays a hand to its head, feeling the slow breaths of its fading. Then a pressure behind her throat opens out like a whirlpool, all of her senses flowing together into an ecstatic flowering. Her mind fills with colours she had never imagined, and her body courses with a tingling as though tiny birds erupt into flight within her veins.

Beneath her, a marrankur's life stills, and the last of a ten-thousand-year line of the subspecies, their physiologies adapted and refined by life alongside the immortals, is ended, but their unique skill and rarefied essence endures — through Calliope. By some unknown spontaneous dispersion, the abilities of precise Sending, of a connection to the immortal world connoting prolonged mortal years, continues its legacy through Calliope.

Bleary-eyed, she buries the miraculous creature, but even as she toils, she feels a great reaching of her being and a mobility of her mind. She spills her consciousness out across the landscape like rays of the sun, then practices the stilling of her emanations into stony union with the ground. Experimenting, she touches on the collated mental field of a great army: Curlewan minds. Gradually the intaglio of colours she receives develops into a picture of more than half a million breaking through the northern perimeter. A touch like frosted metal claws at her mind as she pulls, shuddering, back to her body, the caress of the Miomich an abhorrent awakening to the reality of her new mutation.

Centring herself, she makes for the place the Marrafar have moved to, some two kilometres back eastward. Halfway there, she sees one of the hideous, death-ray hovers, perhaps the survivor from the marrankur's attack, now given quick repair, slip from an opening in the base's wall and speed north — towards the Curlewalion army.

Calliope runs, not daring risk a Sending, to reach the immortals and beg their intercession. A squadron of helicopters clutter low nearby, and she makes her mind one with the sand and scant grasses.

She comes to the Marrafar group, Veiled now in concerted meditation with nearly sixty other Spears who have gathered at this place. She sends them warning of the peril evinced by the deadly hover, but it is as though she meets empty air. Their minds are elsewhere. Desperate, Calliope flings her senses toward the Curlew advance, wondering if she might somehow penetrate the craft and fell it, but she cannot even find it. She intuits its burning shell, smouldering behind the advancing lines, and she retraces the energy threads to see how the massed Indigoes and Mantles amid the army had striven to overpower its crew, many left dead from the strain of breaching the hover's psychic defences.

They had taken no casualties from the Miomichs. As the Spears slowly return from their hidden endeavours, Calliope discerns that they had been tackling the Miomichs, mounting the offensive to secure their own safety. They had held and weakened the W.A.R. government's mind hunters, inadvertently allowing the Indigoes free rein to coerce the hover crew. Calliope beams at the first Opsweyed to focus a gaze upon her.

"Well, you are something now of the marrankur, child," the being says sadly in her mind. "A precious thing, that their colourings should still live. We could not break the Miomichs, but we have weakened them. We are safe for a time."

Turning, on instinct, to look back at the base, Calliope watches as another of the death hovers speeds along a direct line towards them.

Leaving the medi-vac centre had been relatively easy for Mendez. After his bandages had been removed, he had stumbled from bed, played blind for the cameras he had patiently studied, and pretended to grope for the bathroom. Knocking into beds and patient manifests en route, he had found what he needed: the identity card of a Squadron Leader — sixth highest Affiliate rank — similarly enough featured to himself. He had tripped, coming out of the bathroom, and now was lower than the security imagery circuits could follow. He knew security would consider him fallen and be unconcerned, as it was the medi-vac's responsibility, not theirs. The Spaniard had scuttle-crawled to hide under a table in a side wing. The new nurse had not missed him, and after a few minutes of allowing his face to fade from security personnel's memory, he had quickly stalked down the main corridor, head down.

The second group he had met were cadets, and Mendez pushed into their camera-screening midst before accosting them.

"Boys, I can tell you," he said in an American accent, "I'm disoriented. Damn fools had me in that ward too long. We still have a chance. I'm the only one who knows where the terrorists were digging in from — vermin killed my unit. Now, direct me to…the Secretary of Operations. I'm dizzy from the explosions, but my hell, we'll take it to them. And give me one of those stuns, quick, and a jacket and a hat."

It had almost been too easy. Ensconced alone with the extremely jittery, tall and allergic Secretary of Operations, the other officers clustering to petition the Secretary fled when he shooed at them. Mendez had carried his bluff, bulked out his chest to which was affixed the badge of Squadron Leader, and said:

"No, sir, this is too urgent information to wait." He had maintained his air of disobedience-for-the-sake-of-patriotic duty as the Secretary scowled formidably, then ignored him to take the call.

"Hello, my Poise. Sir…well, we agreed that you wanted the troops exerci — no, sir. There's one left, my Poise. Certainly. Automns, sir, but those programmed to crew a Wrathray were unfortunately collateralised in the unexpected attacks upon the cliff pantechnicons. Ah…" Mendez watches the pallid man consult a monitor.

"Yes, reprogramming is complete in seventeen automnal units deployed to the launch bays. We can — Yes, Poise, Sir. But without the Resonance, procedural intricacies have been tested. Yes, my Poise, it is certainly a better option. Thank you. I look forward to your bodyguard practising their laser skills on me … Automns as crew would certainly solve the problems of psychic attack. Yes, I most certainly can ensure the flight-programmed units will crew the other Wrathray. Yes, sir."

As the Secretary carried the phone toward its wall mount, Mendez saw him shrink and heard the voice from the other end screaming, "Get it airborne. Get those mind-terrorists killed and stop that army, or I assure you, you'll be dead before the gene-labs get you."

Mendez is not sure if his request registers through the man's stunned, nauseated trance.

"Ah. Yes. A pass-in," he says at last, reaching in a drawer. He tosses a blue square of plastic across the table and picks up the phone. "Good luck with your interrogation, Squad Leader." The Secretary swivels in his chair to pick up the phone. "Samson, fit the Wrathray with automnals, get it airborne in three — What is it?" he screams, turning to find Mendez still there.

"Sir, I've been concussed. I don't recall the holding cell's location."

"Level F. Block C4. Out!"

The cell block is quite near the subterranean Mjölnir command bunker. Mendez's initial search for Sway is a harrowing trial. The warder tells him they indeed house a female terrorist apprehended in Acadabourne, but qualifies that he is unlikely to get more information from her because she has been three days in a hanging room. As the cell's double doors whiz open, Mendez fights down his bile at sight of the figure strung from her feet by the roof — but she is black.

The Spaniard investigates other cells, searching even those whose occupants date back two months. The facility does not boast the survival of its prisoners beyond two months. Increasingly frantic, aware that his ruse will eventually be traced, Mendez finally looks upon the prisoners from the morning's battle.

Sixteen restrained figures are cramped together on the floor, three of them clearly dead. Of the survivors, all are as destroyed as those recipients of constant torture he has just seen, except one. A young Icelandic man, garbed as a Unilion, stares with a thinly hidden defiance. Mendez realises he will need an ally to get out of this place, need one fast.

"This one might know something. I recognise him from the files. Get me keys to the clamps, a neck restrainer, and an interview room."

"I'm a friend," Mendez whispers as he propels Nivat into the room by the choking metal device around his neck that belies his statement, and sends the guard outside.

Chapter 24

Sway begins to bridge the diminutive spark of flickering life within her to the defunct energy signals of her astral body. She initiates one of Aruan's shortcut routes into a major cycling flow of the Mend and immures herself within the tiny remnant of his flame, feeling its freshness — both calm and insuperable. Risking explosion of her ventricles, she pulls the flame toward her heart, sourcing from her inheritance of his adroit siphoning of the Mend to quickly isolate what she needs.

Spluttering, alert within her astral form, she propels that self through the deeps toward the Serpent. Sway has not drifted far and quickly finds the scene of raging battle. The frayed Spear has disintegrated into separate skirmishings. There is no trace of those that are perished. Brawyndy streaks toward the foe, her burnished wings swept back and great eagle talons outstretched.

As she comes toward it, Sway sees the Lellying's energetic strike, the fusing of one of the Serpent's feeding conduits, and its release erupting like a burst blood clot into its power maze. The abomination collapses in on itself, and Brawyndy punches a wing into it as she passes, twisting to rake her talons across what might pass for an eye. The vastness regains composure, catches up the immortal and spits her distraught astral form, still clinging to a thread of life, away from it.

Sway senses doubt in the monster. Brawyndy has shown it the might of attacking Lellying strength. It is flustered and disoriented, and Sway impels her astral self at it, realising suddenly that her arms are become translucent dragonfly wings.

Speeding with abrupt swerves, she props before one manifest nightmare, goading it with kicks and scooting backward as it lunges, all the time prodding at its energy links. Teasing and harrowing, Sway begins to split the many chambers of her vision into particular roles. She is fighting reflexively with the Serpent in one seeing, in another watching the Spear hurriedly reform, and in others studying the Serpent energy matrix. It all gradually becomes naked to her understanding.

There is a great pyramid in its power configurations — the place which every iota of its studied hatred enters and leaves. A magnifier of essence, an exultant omnipotence exudes through its slick geometry, a mirror for the fiend of its deep felt pride. That pride and sense of dominance, Sway sees, has unwittingly become a snag in its creation, ossifying the fiend's flexibility so that its circuitry is mazed and snarled through having to navigate its self-glorying temple.

Bracing herself, Sway flips under the Dark-Ley Serpent's next lunge and deliberately grasps and pulls it, then smugly turns in circles before it. Never had one dared turn its back on the Serpent's indomitable strength! It flicks at the snivelling fly before she has completed a third turn — as Sway had known it would.

This time, as her resistance shatters and shockwaves propel her through the ocean, tearing out her life-force, she dwells solely in her unconscious — in her heart flame. From there she surges back, right in the midst of the Spear. She imports to them all to be ready, looping with blinding speed to streak at her surprised enemy.

Form a spiralling tumult, overlap your attack, rather than knife forward cleanly!

The pyramid's rigid perfection has already imbalanced as she speeds toward the answering charge of the serpentine form, the energy within it stagnating as the earlier wounding to the Serpent's pride radiates out through its whole enmeshed grid. Invoking her precise vision, and using a simple expulsion of Ki, rather than a Mend-guided blow, Sway isolates the place where the main flow runs to the pyramid energy temple and delivers her strike.

The imbalanced feeding line actually sucks the little bomb into it, along with the fatly, mal-proportioned energy cluster of the Spear's device. At the pyramid, power punctures the pride-jammed blockage. The Serpent explodes into a corona of grey light and Sway hazily re-joins her aching body on the plain.

Amilluk wonders when the dryads will show themselves. *Not before do Mjölnir's armies take field*, the Earthelic being thinks. *Theirs never been way of haste or forthrightness.* The hob is anxious to meet the beings before they fight and are killed or disappear back into the ground, taking with them the knowledge he wishes to trade for.

A little trade will bring to this frightening ugly a redemption. The dryads have the keys to considerable deep strata essence-ways, and the hob has been pondering what to exchange for them. His assignment is to conduct the trade, while also reporting on whether the hobs' redemption of the Marrafar and Opsweyed will tip the scales in destroying the Serpent and its human minions, as their prophecy had seemed to suggest.

At his last brief encounter with the gaiagenous elementals, some forty thousand years ago, his offer of a sonic equation, derived from the dynamics of cicadas, which would have allowed the dryads protective shields of sound, had been spurned. *They trust too much those wooden swords, but who wouldn't like little turquoise through skin. We could offer yellow blush for eyes; phosphor binding the min-min radicalised suits here.*

He spies a hover speeding above the plain, though not just any hover. Its massive power allures and captivates him. His face flushes rapidly in waterfalls of excitement as he considers his time window. *I can investigate and still make consultation with dryadery.* In the blink of an eye, Amiliuk transposes himself to the

Wrathray. Fast machines always fascinated Hobbogyre. In the old days, many was the hob that rode invisibly and ecstatic amid the motorcycle gangs, tinkering with the machines in the night to ensure the most fluid of speed on their stowaway joyrides.

On board the Wrathray, the automns have located the heat signature of the immortals and move to deal with them ahead of Curlew's approaching army. Amilluk is overjoyed to find no humans, with their irksome high-ratio electromagnetism, but only machines piloting the hover. With the barest thought, he collapses their robotic circuitry and attunes his energy to the craft, weaving its control functions around his mind. He is now giddily linked to it, but after a little fun he can resume his autonomy of mind by reviving the automns into aviating roles.

The hob spins the craft in a joyful spiral, the speed exhilarating him as he cavorts in loop-the-loops over Mjölnir. His speed is dizzying, but as he straightens out he flips mischievously the button that his prior pirating had taught him was to initiate the after-burner on other crafts. A woeful shrieking resounds through the hover, and Amilluk tries furiously to deactivate whatever he has initiated. It is beyond him, and the sound continues to tear agonizingly at him so that he cannot even revive the automns and escape his locked energy broach.

The craft descends slowly and the hob fatefully watches the scans to see the centre of the base beneath him disappear into a smoking nothing. A strange sound escapes from him as the craft plummets — the irony of it all is superb. If he could feel emotion, he would realise the staccato grunts flooding from him are tokens of hysterical amusement.

Calliope looks on at the continuing avalanche of Mjölnir's walls, tottering into the hole left by the death-ray hover. After a final catastrophic shudder, the collapse halts. More than half of the base still stands. Across the plain surges Curlewalion's army, and from the dust come forward the inexorable companies of Mjölnir, millions after millions. No doubt many had been lost in the crush of the walls, though this is not the most grievous loss of Mjölnir's.

The Miomichs are destroyed, one of the Enyadding declares in a triumphant psychic announcement. Tentatively, Calliope feels out the statement's truth. Then she begins a Sending, a ripping reach of vengeance against her foe.

Nivat and Mendez had held the cell corridors for two minutes before they realised the folly of their attempt, a mass of soldiers gaining steady advance on either side of their flimsily fortified position behind overturned cabinets. Then the roof had fallen upon the nearest of their menacers, fallen through the floor with a pounding quake. The pair had ducked into a side passage and down some stairs as the lights cut out, and all around them stone had tumbled.

Now the thundering calamity subsides. Nivat strikes a flintlight to descry the raggedly blockaded remnant of the stairwell.

"We are now safe. We cannot get up and no one can come down," he says.

Mendez refuses to concede defeat, Sway's face now haunting him. "We don't go up — we go down!"

"Boabben," says Brawyndy weakly, as Boabben holds her, flooding his life-force into her. "I thought your warning was a dream. An omen. But you are real."

"The vileness is beaten, love," the fireseer tells her.

Brawyndy nods, gradually recovering as Boabben trickles his flame into her astral form.

"No!" she says, suddenly emphatic, sensible with partial recovery to what is transpiring. "You must not give me your life. It was only valid for Aruan because of the threat. I do not wish to live."

"Even now, with victory?"

"Even now. I have seen too much of death. But you and our son will survive."

"He lives?"

"Go to him. Save our son. Leave me."

"Brawyndy."

"Leave me!"

"I shall come back for you." Boabben insulates her in a little protecting cocoon that will nurture her for a quarter of an hour, then wraps his essence around Aruan. Minute after minute, the fireseer guides his life-force into the distillation of his son's soul. As Aruan's face begins to focus, he stares suspiciously through the water, then says aghast, "No. She has failed."

Boabben concentrates to smooth the fever of his son's rebirth and lift Aruan from death's grasp. Finally, Aruan's astrality flexes.

But father, look! he insists in Boabben's mind, directing with eyes cold in conviction. *The Serpent lives. She has failed.*

Turning weakly, Boabben sees the energy thread. A tiny sickly thing that Aruan studies. There is a minute left to save Brawyndy, but he must be certain. He plunges along the energy trail and finds the Serpent alive. He had been a fool. Around the Aleris his enemy had left only blinds, a realistic simulacrum, grafting to this ersatz self the majesty of its whole energetic network, and removed itself to Mjölnir, scouting for emanations of despair and power to feed back into its matrix, and thus more quickly overcome the stone. Now it sped toward the base to suck from battle and despair the energy to rebuild itself.

Yet even that would not avail it. Sway's blow was lethal after all. His enemy lived only by grasping at its old sundered link to the Fae — through the firefeather foci that Boabben had granted, and which was now enmeshed to the faeries' psyche. The Serpent had reinsinuated itself, but too rawly to be impregnable.

The Fae fight valiantly for the dignity of destroying the Serpent along with themselves. Boabben understands his final prophecy, as he intuits the scale of the current battle. Neither party can survive; quite possibly the Earth will not either.

"Aruan. Destroy the Aleris. We cannot risk our enemy reclaiming that prize. The Heart-finger is weak. Command it against the Mjölnir navy — that should drain its last. Also, son, you and the Enyadding must get into the ocean if you are to survive and send warning — somehow — to the Curlewans. Get to sea."

Out of time, he rushes to embrace the astral blueprint of the only woman who had ever held him.

Zolaman's voice rings desperate in Nysha's mind. The Wowbrae and Facu leaders have not often communed, even since the peace accord.

"Is this some evil of the immortal's' betrayal?" the naturalised Facu asks.

"No. He was guileless. This is a fierce evil, one bloated on power dreams."

"It has overrun our hidden spheres. Even now it commands access to our antiquated fibres."

"As ours. We must unite to fight it."

"We will not win. Already our people are stretched to breaking; we can barely shield our encrypted Earth Leads."

"No. We cannot win. But we can hope to leave a trace of our beings — a seed of vigour and wonder in place of its hungering destruction."

"You think to enmesh the Earth Leads and the starfibres?"

"To drag time into the core of this planet's adoptive stratum, yes. If we concuss it, then briefly sunder all energy from this monster's grasp, it will be torn apart."

"It may make a mortuary of this haven. Jayanna's memory is already frayed. Yet the humans may calm the transition, if any remain devout to the truth purposing."

"They may. Anyway, we have no choice else. Prepare to draw out the static governances. Blend neutrality through totemic upwellings that, other than rock, might remain."

"May the eternal memory be your playground."

"And yours, at this end, my kin."

Calliope feels a deep respect for the gathered Curlewalions. With her new psychic penetration, she knows they had abandoned hope of saving their homeland, leaving behind untenable positions as well as secure bases to the ravaging hordes of mutant automns. They had turned from that horror to place themselves before one greater, advancing on their hover-props to within safe distance of Mjölnir's actinomorphic walls, then on their fierce monitor lizards to enact their defiance. Their pride keeps them focused, despite the unsettling spectacle of their allies.

As the two forces rally together, Calliope thinks of the initial aversion the Curlewans had shown to the chittering stick figures she knows to be dryads, but the fearless, wraith-like warriors had denuded the Mjölnir defences, and ineluctably the Curlewans had drawn up with their allies to expunge the outnumbering foe. The lines of soldiery, more than four million thick, had been punctured by the Indigoes. Bereft of leaders, the human resistance had fractured, scattering before the supernatural vengeance of the dryadery, snagging amid the ferocity of the Curlewans, and all the while subjected to the sudden buffeting of some invisible force that threw soldiers into the air or snapped them upon the ground.

Now, only the rote resistance of half a million automns stands against the united force. Calliope pushes her Sending toward the Sacubus, ready to fell it like the hundred she had already steered into the remains of the base. She notices the sky glow strangely and fill with flowing words; their emblazoned letters two kilometres high in three different scripts. One of these is like intertwining leaves, and she dismisses the Sacubus as she reads the sigils framed in the Curlewalion alphabet.

"Curlewalions, flee to the ocean. Get within the water. Now!"

She looks to a few gathered Marrafar and Opsweyed near her.

Tis Lellying sig, she hears in her cortexes. Fly to the sea.

Calliope streams behind the immortals, working toward the main group of Enyadding forming at a distance. The hairy beings clobber aside the automnals, smashing senseless the plastic foil, but other automns gun down Curlewans as they break toward the sea. Calliope wonders what new horror they face that must drive them into the ocean. She notices the dryads have vanished.

Nysha watches the twin fractal cords balloon up around the Dark-Ley Serpent and concuss it. The best bellflockists had hurriedly found new sounds to render into fuel for the hidden spheres, and it seemed the Facu had likewise found light sources pleasing to the spheres. The resulting subtly frequenced bombs the faeries had harvested from the core of the planet were usually employed against each other but never at the same time. Their combined effect was dynamic upon the Serpent.

Every sonic nuance upon which his people rafted, steadying their essence against the energy waves of the planet on which they had for so long been marooned, Nysha now sees pour into the river of firefeather that had just

begun to meander through all their minds. Hence down into the Earth Leads —
the magnificent energy portals geared to the planet's memory, flows the full
power of the Wowbrae, as undoubtedly does that of the Facu. Compelled by the
sudden influxing vital charge to vent some of their accrued force, the Earth Leads
flicker to the surface and wash a subtle hum of contentment across the world,
except in a dozen places where the faeries have angled antiquated star filaments
across their overflow.

The Earth-memory suddenly finds a condensed, otherworldly,
crystalline substance spreading across its receptors. Referencing its origin, the
Earth prepares for survival. In a split second, pulses from the Earth Leads trigger
a reaction of the massed single cell energy of the original planetary intelligence,
turning rock to jelly and mineral energy to fire, softening its shell as buffer to
frictional impact, while at the same time spinning tiny seed prints of life that
might endure beyond the imminent explosion.

Nysha feels the Serpent clutching, trying to burrow into the governance
crystals of the Earth. Then it is perished. The faeries' own anchoring encryptions,
built up over billions of years, are torn out by the fraying of the star filaments.
Momentarily, the faeries, being sucked body and soul back into the stars, become
the only mutable influence upon the self-destructing planet. Nysha begins to see
Jayanna the Blue from a great height, though in intricate detail, the fraying parts
of himself harmonically calling to his Earth encryptions.

And so the mapped interstices of space feed back into the planet's
receptors as the yanking of faerie Earthen particles pulls the leads outward,
receiving deep space, rather than core information. The planet begins to be
tricked in some places into believing it has moved forward into time, binding the
glorying song and colour of the Fae's fleeing encryptions as mutations that have
saved it.

But still the process of dissolution is compelled by the birth memory of
the planet, flashfire the osmotic upwelling in her bones. As Nysha begins to pull

apart, he sees the continents of Jayanna simply melt. North America and Unope first — already corroded by a soulless human stewardship — then Asia.

South America is more resilient, but evaporates into particles of forgotten essence, fraying out into the cold embrace of space. Anarchtica, Australia and Africa tremble, the latters' cities burning or plummeting into holes beneath them. Then the faerie finds the humans' memetic function has finally stabilised the desperation of their mother's death throes, the three continents enduring. Something will remain.

Nivat and Mendez had worked their way through a vent the engineer had uncovered, wriggling out into an abandoned storage tunnel just as the quaking had started again. Now the Bard watches Mendez slide over the sharp panelling of a deteriorated algalate door. Slabbed sections of the rock tunnel yield as Nivat, struggling with the reopened wound on his foot, chases his quicker companion toward the sound of the sea, as lights in the cliff base's submarine workshop fail, and automns fire chaotically at them.

The roof sags and thunders to ground as the pair race onto the intermeshed rocks of a breakwater and out past fractured remnants of docks and ramp-ways. It is as though a crowd of thousands has gathered to watch them outrun the crumbling cliffs. People cram the water, and the strange, rounded ships with razor prows churn what looks like pulped ice in a constant stream from beneath them. The rock beneath their feet catches fire, and the exhausted men flail their limbs into the sea, praying it is deep enough.

For both, it is as though they fall suddenly through a cottony rainbow mist, as the song of an edenic choir strung on the subtlest notes of nature pierces their cells, shifting their bodies and minds to a still equipoise. The most powerful Earthen ley-line fluxes, finally free, at its most mutable point directly under them.

As Nivat surfaces, he marvels to the blond man, "Did you feel that? It seems the whole schemata of my being has stilled. I feel — as if I've been made to live forever."

"So do I. Fantasticated," supplies Mendez.

"Just so, and because I know you're a sensible lad, I'll only tell you once now. Then, say, once every thousand years. Keep your handsome blue eyes away from my woman!"

Those blue eyes have just lit upon Calliope's distant figure, and he paws a wave of water toward the grinning bard, who slips seamlessly beneath the surface, somehow knowing he can breathe under water, his startling new clarity showing him where Sway stands on deck, tranced but alive, half a kilometre away.

Around Sway, the surviving Lellying huddle, exhaustion scribed into their faces alongside an elation that only clouds when eyes stray to where Brawyndy's prone body lies. The shuddering of the ship beneath them sounds a cradle song of reassuring mundanity to Sway, after the pantomime of unrelenting peril in which she has just starred.

The vessel is one of many amid the latterly arrived Anarchtic fleet that cycle a constant stream of water through hull-girdling pipes. They alchemise the inflowing ocean into crushed ice at the outflow using machinery developed to stabilise ice-shelves on the southern-most continent. In this manner the thousands of Curlewans in the water are protected from a sea grown so hot that beyond the bay great banks of steam rise up.

Sway knows, through insights from the Mend field, the Serpent had survived her attack, and whatever forces had finally destroyed it had caused the sea to boil and whole continents to disintegrate. She knows, too, that out toward the sea's centre, away from the superheated, stabilising coastlines, much marine life will endure. Yet the future will demand great work of restoration and restocking.

The immortal supresses a shiver as she glimpses the ice crusting the gunwale of the boat, remembering the frozen daggers that had burrowed into her spine when she had first met her enemy. She chides herself. That fire of unfettered violence is now extinguished. Looking upon the Curlewans around her, she feels they have heart enough for the task of rebuilding the world.

Curlewalion! What dream had she been smoozing in?

Cursing, she allows several level breaths before willing herself into astral form, appearing momentarily in the sky near Ja Junction, where she had let the bio-signature of her parents draw her. Below her are Prelisya and Duncan, slipping furtively along a dry wash about fifty kilometres from the capital. They are at the head of a ragged group of citizens.

Mum! Duncan! She beams her mental voice at them, stalled in the guise of a tiny dragonfly high above.

The pair tense in turmoil and confusion, gesturing fiercely at the group behind to lay low.

It's okay. It's not a trick. It's really me, I've learnt how to fight in astral form, and I can see you down in the creekbed. Just think in your minds.

Sway! Prelisya mind-cries. *Mendez was here. And the others.*

You're alright, my girl? When can we see you? beams Duncan.

Soon. I'm fine. Everything will be okay. Curlew has destroyed Mjölnir.

Praise the bonny Scots! enthuses her father. *We heard rumour via an Indigo, we didn't —*

Where's Mendez now?

Her mother's mental voice is hesitating. *No one knows, Sway. He disappeared, that first night.*

Mh-huh, well — shit, coming up the creekbed. Automns. They're huge. And over both hills to the side of you — you're surrounded.

Having seen the automns, all the static she had watched leaping at the backs of her parents' minds becomes clear. The muck of zinc and clay these guerrillas wear is a hastily construed protection against psychic treachery. The uprising had begun at dawn. Those like her parents who had gone underground were able at last to concert with Unilion — who had returned from the coast at a time when much of the invading force had withdrawn inland to reclaim the border bases.

Sway. Her father is emotional. It's not safe here, even for psychics, any more. You must withdraw.

It's alright, Duncan. Honestly. You guys deal with the few dozen coming up the creek. I'll get the flanks.

Not pausing to watch the imminent showdown, Sway speeds toward the humungous plastic forces pouring in a column down one hillside, increasing her own size as she flies. With her twenty-five metres of wing almost transparent, the automns only register her presence as she explodes amid them, each of her six hooked claws searching and kicking, slicing through a score of giants. Her tail bunches in under her and forward to bludgeon a cluster of the foe before they can steady hefty lasers. Then, she is rising, an automn in each of her front claws and another clasped in the pincer of her tail.

Three lumps of plastic fall from the vertical path of her ascension, although the heads she retains, hurling them like bombs into the seething mass of homunculi. The automns group together, backs abutting one another, as per their protocol. Sway dives, weaving around their steady file, until each set of claws ploughs into one such bundled group, riveting them into the ground. A sideswipe of her tail dismisses the last of their menace.

With a satisfied chitter, Sway ascends, narrowing her vision on the other hillside. She does not need the precise feedback from every lens to tell her what she is looking at. A mighty, astrally-enshrined form is in flight there, unlike any immortal she has seen before. Swooping upon the plastic, the knock of its bill echoing across the plain, is a kookaburra. Soon the bird speeds toward her, flicking a last piece of plastic from the sword of its beak. It hovers to fix her with a gleaming eye.

Greetings, sister. I am Larker. Welcome to Curlewalion.

Briefly, Larker outlines his own stewardship of firefeather, and Sway hears of the redemption of the Opsweyed and Marrafar, and of the existence of the Hobbogyre.

I have fought a few brawls today, Sway, but it is not to my style. The Curlewan Mantles from Mjölnir have conjoined with me. With their aid we shall evince a more subtle attack: one of sound. If they could feel, these creations would come soon to fear my laughter.

Sway notices, on the plain below, hundreds of figures clad in suits stuck with grass, camouflage that had fooled even her. When she sees the musical instruments hidden alongside many of them, she smiles at his plan.

Yes. We shall prevail here, but your speed is in demand elsewhere, at another battle that begins to the west.

Larker sends her an energetic destination for the astral folding, then streaks away — a flash of blue on nutty, velvet wings.

We will meet again soon, sister.

Morel wonders if the Unilion just fallen had been Lans — though even had the warrior not worn the same lumpy face paint of zinc that the youth himself sported, the ungenerous view across the rocky eave made recognition impossible. Changed in a bare three weeks, the Unilion Lans sported heavy bandaging across his skull and had spoken through a mouth distorted by a laddering of stitches, staring grimly through the eye not burned away.

"Tomorrow we make the last stand of our nation, not hoping to win, but to distract the enemy from our children and elderly as we lead them to more permanent sanctuary. In this way more may survive to join the hundred thousands in a secret stronghold east of the capital. Every one of you that can walk, I urge you to fight tomorrow with the grace of one who can sprint..."

Morel recalls his shock on seeing the Unilion leader's face as the man had stood to address his group of injured, and a few resisters, in a hole slightly less fetid than this, in which they had hidden a fortnight from ravening horrors outside.

As Lans outlined the plan for an ambush against the automns, he watched those around him flush with pride and enthusiasm. It was an effect the cult leader generated without effort or emotive tactics, his candour and honour transposing courage into the hearts of the troglodyte survivors as ineluctably as air might rush to fill a vacuum.

"Nearly a thousand Unilion, and many other elements of resistance like yourselves, will be secreted around Ariadne's Jump Up, and in every direction overlooking the merge-point of Vilasie and Gawatha Orange. Here a remnant of Vengers and rear-guard will lure the enemy. Your positions will be unable to be discovered psychically because, fortified beneath blessed unguate of zinc, Unilion veterans from campaigns against the cyberite lairs in Solaris are joining with those returning from coastal battles to prosecute their case against the traitors in a number of many hundreds."

Lans had finished quickly, having yet to visit many other bands, with the words, "No hope, no self, and no tomorrow!"

But the youth, Morel, does not look to these harsh inspirations as the signals flare on the plains, and he is the first to stream forward from hiding, dozens of hands throwing back the trapdoor. Instead, he remembers, as he raises his remaining arm to fire on a goliathan automn, the news of Tamziel's death, reaching him at last through a convoluted chain of messages. She'd been mind-slain on returning to Curlew, when she should have arrived to glory and celebration. That was before the temporary antidote to the cyberites had been discovered: clay and zinc admixed, proven enough to impede their tentacles. Her face in his mind, Morel aims a blast at the fire of a seemingly impregnable craft descending toward him. Slapping out flames, Morel drops behind a bulbous termite mound, heaping zinc paste onto the smoulder of his flesh in lieu of any vege-film to treat it. He tilts back his head in a moment's rest and sees that, truly, there is no hope. At every level of the sky, automn craft move, the nearest firing upon him, fractionally off-target due to a laser attack from a leaden-faced resister.

Rolling onto his back, the youth tracks the irrefragable hover, searching for a weak spot.

With his jaw open, he stares after the creature that — using a log seemingly affixed to its tail — roars over his head to instantly smash the craft. It whirls above the plain — some type of genetic bird it must be — dealing such swift blows of destruction amid the automn fleet that Curlewan attackers flee, willy-nilly, from the rain of detritus. Winging back toward him and dancing aside from pursuing laser rays, the aerial fury hurtles one hover into another so that they both tumble, off-kilter, to earth on either side of Morel. This time, as it zips above him, he sees its battering weapon is clenched in a pincer at the end of a tail rippling with powerful sinew, the log flailing in a wild following, as its wielder swarms sideways, completely altering direction, before lashing its tail to club twin hovers into shards. Astonished yet, he surmises the avenger is undoubtedly a dragonfly of incomprehensible size.

As he takes up his weapon once more, firing on automn groupings broken into disarray, he sees other creatures, huge also, and stranger by far than the dragonfly, join the assault on the automn fleet. In a short space of time there are no more able hovers and no sign of the preposterous creatures, only Curlewans standing about in awe while hundreds of surviving lion predate on remnant automns, coughing and roaring out their battle lust. Morel's caked visage cracks a smile, the world grown filled with wonder. For the first time he dares believe that his family may still live, and he shakes a fist of triumph toward where their redemption had sprung.

Stalled more than a mile above the battlefield, Sway looks down on a little one-armed figure, her vision acute enough to note the crooked smile he wears. Thuriskaen's voice sinks in, and she turns her insect head to where the immortal spins languidly in astral form. Suddenly she realises that no other of the Lellying remain.

Casting one more rote glance about the plain for sight of his face, Sway pulls herself from a fog of exhaustion and battle fever, resolving back into her body aboard the freighter, the sudden cold a knife of reality. A new world stretches before her. Aeons in which to grieve. She lets the polyps of tears swell, but admonishes herself that it is better like this anyway. Leaning over the gunwale, her vision follows her tears down into the balm of the profound expanse.

My mind must be overwrought to cast such a cruel deception!

Still, she dares not breathe as she ponders the watery mirage, all its features growing clearer. When she sees his Spanish smile, she knows she looks on truth, and seal-like, with a cry of wonder, she plummets overboard.

Her mind meets his in an ecstatic shout, tasting the wonder of immortality upon him, just before her lips meet his grin in an embrace fiercer than his hug, the two gyring slowly down through the sea, their union marked by a trail of effervescence.

Epilogue

Boabben and Brawyndy spin hand-in-hand above the planet, pure energy, the antiquated nourishing filament in which Boabben stores the power slowly disintegrating. They look on as Aruan and the others plunge into the sea. Watch as the faeries bind wonders of colour and sound into the dying Earth, partially tricking its receptor system into accepting that such is the future. They see four great continents with their tired slag of human cities dissolve as though they had never been and watch the awakening of millions of people to their true souls in the quiet realisation before death suddenly stills the planet's destruction, and their own.

Boabben observes the air, a-shimmer with countless fractals of rainbows and gold and silver halos. The skies, he knows, would now perpetually leak flurries of a heart-stopping, beautiful song. Not yet, but in generations soon to come, the fabric of Earth will be a dream that people will walk without their bodies.

In time the passage will pass from form.

The two immortals rush their consciousness through a deep, green forest, just before they slip toward the Icefields, the realm beyond eternity. Amid the trees, Boabben points out to Brawyndy a young marrankur lithely springing from a stream to ambush little figures flying on gossamer wings above the waterside boulders. Indeed, the faeries have left a plethora of tiny, self-sustaining energy threads originally created to bring them knowledge of many life stratas, especially human. As an ode to their remembrance, there were now spread over the forests and lakes and mountains and other such untrammelled places of Earth that had been immune to the cataclysm, creatures of spritely grace — trailing light and laughter and capturing in microcosm the universe's dream of freedom and beauty aligned.

The Beginning

Acknowledgements

With indebted gratitude to Rex Gilroy, for his intuitive explorations of Australian crypto-zoology and archaeology, Rebekah Hayden, my other brain, for her superhuman diaskeuasis endeavour and Benjamin Opie, for his shrewdly lexiconic support. Jonah and Farnaz have been friends in the face of my hermitage, Margaret Clifford, a valuable cog. Justin Dixon provided the aid of a valuable peerage, which, though lairy, was skumbled into the final polish.

With final thanks to my Sire, Bill, who fed, clothed and housed me for the duration of the project and who believed in the dream of the land.

Bryn Ellis

The skills of Tom Flood — winner of the 1998 Vogel Prize and the 1990 Miles Franklin Award for his novel Oceana Fine — have been invaluable in the passage of Bryn's manuscript to the edited form for publication. Bryn would have recognised Tom as a kindred spirit.

Our thanks to Ion Newcombe of Acrux Publishing in successfully bringing this work to print.

Thanks also to Artist Adrian Lockhart for his inspired cover art.

We are grateful to you all.

Shaaron & Bill Ellis

About The Author

Bryn Ellis was a writer, poet, a passionate environmentalist, an amateur naturalist and an intrepid traveller.

He was born in Melbourne, a brilliant creative student at Melbourne High, and in his teens Bryn discovered the natural world while living in the Dandenongs and exploring Sherbrooke Forest.

Bryn's commitment to a more sustainable world led him to a long active involvement in the fight to save the Goolengook Forest in the Errinundra Plateau in East Gippsland, Victoria.

His last adventurous journeys seeking material for his prequel to *Half Trace* were to Cape York and to Madagascar.

Bryn died in a single vehicle accident while trying to avoid wildlife. Bryn was thirty-four.

Bryn Ellis
1973–2007

www.ingramcontent.com/pod-product-compliance
Lightning Source LLC
Chambersburg PA
CBHW061030030726
47504CB00002B/314